Paul Charles
was born and raised in the ~~...~~
side. He now lives and works in Camden Town, north
London, where he divides his time between writing
and working in the music industry. The next Paul
Charles novel will be the sixth Christy Kennedy
mystery, *I've Heard The Banshees Sing*.

The other Christy Kennedy mysteries are:
I Love the Sound of Breaking Glass
Last Boat to Camden Town
Fountain of Sorrow
The Ballad of Sean & Wilko
The Hissing of the Silent Lonely Room

First Published in Great Britain in 2002 by
The Do-Not Press Limited
16 The Woodlands
London SE13 6TY

Casebound edition: ISBN 1 899344 79 9
C-format paperback: ISBN 1 899344 78 0

British Library Cataloguing in Publication Data. A catalogue
record for this book is available from the British Library.

1   3   5   7   9   10   8   6   4   2

Printed and bound in Great Britain by
The Guernsey Press Co Ltd.

FIRST OF THE TRUE BELIEVERS

The Autobiography of Theodore Hennessy

A novel concerning The Beatles by
PAUL CHARLES

THE DO-NOT PRESS

I'd like to thank Jake Riveria and Pete Frame for the inspiration. Big thanks also to Jim Driver for wanting to share this and to Andy and Cora for turning on the radio in the first place. Not forgetting Daria, for help with the words.

Gynormous thanks to George, Ringo, John, Paul, Brian, Mr Martin, Neil and Mal for the pure magic they brought into our lives.

And then I saw Catherine's face and I'm a believer…

Chapter One

Roll up,
Step right up
For the
Magical Mystery Tour.

In a way, I suppose, meeting Marianne – Marianne Burgess, that is – was as important to me as the legendary meeting that took place when John Lennon's friend, Ivan Vaughan, introduced him to Paul McCartney. You may very well laugh at the grandness of this comparison but see if you still think so by the end of my story.

John and Paul's first meeting took place at a concert The Quarry Men (John's then group) were giving at a picnic in the field of St Peter's Church in Woolton, a suburb of Liverpool. Why I call it a concert, I don't really know. By today's standard, concert is probably too pompous a word. It was more of a quick set of six songs delivered at four-fifteen pm, before the main attraction – a team of police dogs – did their thing. This was followed by another quick set on the back of a lorry at five forty-five. The Quarry Men did get to play a third set later that same evening, in the village hall. It was in fact around the time of the third set when John and Paul met up for the first time. The Quarry Men were nothing more, or nothing less, than a skiffle group, at a time when the skiffle craze was sweeping Great Britain from Land's End to John O' Groats.

My first group was a skiffle group as well. We were called Rocket 88. To be honest, we weren't really much cop. But that wasn't the point of skiffle groups; anyone could be in one. All you needed was a beaten up old guitar, a tea-chest bass or even a washboard, for heaven's sake. Anything at all that you could find to make a racket with. The only thing that was really important was to be able to get up on stage; that's how you drew the attention of the girls. That's all any of us were after you know; scoring the judies. And it was so easy if you were in a group. Girls would actually come up and introduce themselves to you after the show. Sometimes, one of them would be so anxious to get in before the others that she would find her way back to the dressing room between sets. Hey, that's the big secret out. Me and my mates in Rocket 88, and John, Paul, Stu, George, Pete and Ringo; we all wanted a reason not to have a proper job. More importantly, we wanted the girls and none of us were good enough to be in proper bands like Dead Loss and Pops Orchestra, but we *could* turn the girls' heads by making a racket in our skiffle groups.

And that night, at Woolton, make a racket is exactly what The Quarry Men did. I mean, you wouldn't say they were great or anything but they demonstrated that they had a natural raw energy. It was the overall noise that worked for them, more than the sound of the individual instruments or the strained sounds of John's singing. You could barely make out the words he was trying to sing. That was probably just as well though, because he'd learnt all the lyrics from a scratchy old record and, well, you know, these American singers didn't exactly attract the girls because of their diction.

Paul taught John the proper chords to Gene Vincent's *Be Bop a Lu La* (which The Quarry Men had just performed) and taught him the proper words. That was enough for John. A few days later, Paul was out for a ride on his bicycle and met up with Pete Shotton. It was Pete who told Paul that John wanted him to join the group. All this happened in July 1957 and The Quarry Men became a seven-piece band. Paul and John were on guitars and vocals; Colin Hanton on drums – he was okay, just okay though, as I thought he used to speed things up too much – Eric Griffiths on guitar; Len Garry on tea-chest bass; Rod Davies on banjo; and, finally, Pete Shotton on washboard.

John and Paul shouldn't really have hooked up, you know? I mean, really. John was a rebel: a rebel without applause I always used to say. He was about eighteen months older than Paul, which is a lot at that stage in your life; you know, when you're trying hard to assert you manhood. Here was this teddy boy, Lennon, with his TV haircut and then, right beside him, you had the baby-faced McCartney, more prim and proper and, at least on paper, better brought up – maybe even a bit of a daddy's boy. But he knew more chords than John and he liked Eddie Cochran, an American musician John absolutely worshipped. Both John Lennon and Paul McCartney were to lose their mothers. Paul's had already died of cancer and John's mum was to be killed, eight months later, in a hit-and-run accident. Apparently an off-duty peeler knocked her down just outside John's Aunt Mimi's house in Menlove Avenue. So I suppose the combination of all these elements was their big bond in the early days.

Funny when you look back at it all now and realise that those two teenagers probably sought each other out. They'd both played with plenty of other musicians, musicians with varying degrees of talent. Getting together, musically speaking, couldn't have been easy for either of them. Paul knew more chords than John but he was left-handed; therefore, he knew all the chords in reverse so John had to pick them up backwards and then imagine what the same chords would look like for a right-handed guitarist. It was a very difficult process but infinitely preferable to the two banjo chords John's mother, Julia, had taught him. So, when they met, it was like someone was working some kind of magic for them. By giving them each other and igniting their creative sparks, it was some sort of compensation after losing their mums. Do you know what I mean? Hey, I'm always accused of being a bit of a romantic but, with my hand on my heart, I genuinely believe that they met at a time when they really needed each other.

Chapter Two

Now, the location of our first meeting – that is, the meeting between Marianne Burgess and me – well that was... yes, that was grander altogether.

I think Marianne – Marianne Elizabeth Burgess, to give her her full name – used to hang around with a friend of a girl called Julie Arthur, and my sister, Kathleen, either knew Marianne or she knew Julie; I'm not sure which, but I seem to remember they all used to hang around together.

It's Kathleen's fault that I'm called Theodore, you know. I'd better explain the reason for that, I suppose. Kathleen was born fifteen months before me and three years before our sister, Colette. When she was born, my mum and dad had a big disagreement over what she was to be called. My mum wanted to call her Tressa; no real reason, supposedly she just really liked the name. My father, on the other hand, was adamant that the name Kathleen should be used for their first-born, assuming, of course, their first-born was a girl. I personally would have had a lot of trouble growing up with the name Kathleen, I'm sure! Anyway, my dad's mum, my grandma, was called Kathleen and so he insisted our Kathleen had to be named after her. The deal they finally settled on was that my father would have absolutely no say, no say whatsoever, in the choice of name for the second born.

Now you might think that my mother had some connection with Greece (and perhaps that's what she wanted my dad to think; you know, that she was pining for a long-lost Greek boyfriend). She told me herself, though, when I was growing up, that she just called me Theo to get her own back after losing out when choosing the name for my sister. The closest she ever got to Greece, or Greek men for that matter, was a Greek restaurant near the Royal Court Theatre. She went there on her hen night with a pile of her mates. Apparently, it was a very quick visit; she nearly threw up when she saw, and smelled, a mousaka and so they all headed off instead to a cafe beside Lime Street Station.

My mum and dad are Irish, you know. Well, in all probability, you wouldn't have known that if I hadn't told you. My dad is from Blackrock in Dublin and my mum is from Desertmartin in County Derry. She met him one summer when he was up visiting his relations in Desertmartin. They kept in touch by letter and married the following year, having met only three times. I find that quite amazing because they are still together and tight, very tight, after twenty-one years and three children. And, to this day, they are still arguing over Kathleen's name. The only real problem they had, when they fell in love that is, was that they had to leave Ireland. They came from opposite sides of the fence, if you know what I mean. They probably could have stayed and kept their heads down, but my Uncle Harry had already moved to Southport and he advised my mum and dad to do the same.

I hadn't really planned to tell you all of this stuff, you know. When I'm reading a biography myself, I always flick past all the early, formative stuff and get to the part where the story really kicks in. But it just kinda came out and I suppose it is important. I'll promise you one thing, though; I'll only bring stuff like this up when I feel it's absolutely necessary.

So anyway, back to how Marianne and I met. Our Kathleen was going to a big school do at the (once elegant) Adelphi Hotel in Lime Street, Liverpool and she was all dolled up, looking pretty as a picture. My dad didn't want her catching the bus and train by herself, so he sent me along as her escort. You should be aware how parents back then kept such a keen eye on their daughters, trying to ensure scandals were avoided at all costs; a wronged woman was destined to spend the rest of her life sitting on that dusty old shelf. Then my dad would give me that old lecture: 'You make sure no-one takes any liberties with our Kathleen or I'll skin you to within an inch of your life. We don't want her ending up on the shelf, do we?'

I tried to explain to him on one memorable occasion that there was little chance of her remaining on the particular shelf he was referring to (the one above our kitchen table), as it would surely collapse under her weight. My father wasn't very impressed with my observation and I received a stinging red ear as confirmation of that fact. Anyway, you can imagine that Kathleen didn't dare tell him that she had a boyfriend waiting for her at Lime Street Station that evening; she just went along with the plan and swore me to secrecy. She would have been a little over eighteen and I had just celebrated my seventeenth birthday.

I was in my Sunday best and had brought along one of my outlawed, teddy-boy string ties to slip on, while on the train. With the help of my sister, I had also tried to make my hair look cool by losing the parting and back-combing it, using water. My sister made a few costume and cosmetic adjustments, too. Personally, I always thought she looked great without any of that stuff, but there you go. To put you fully in the picture, this would have been late August 1957. Paul and John would probably have been playing somewhere around Liverpool that evening with The Quarry Men; though sadly not at the Adelphi Hotel.

Anyway, Kathleen, Bob (her boyfriend) and I all arrived at the hotel and, true to form, Kathleen immediately made a dive for a group of her schoolmates and started nattering and gossiping. That's when I saw Marianne Elizabeth Burgess. I fell for her right there and then. She was so beautiful. She was dressed in an ill-fitting black dress, wore no make-up and her straight, long, thick, black hair was parted in the middle of her head and fell down her back, nearly reaching her waist. To me she looked like a movie star. She had such a cute face, with sharp, brown eyebrows that contrasted completely with her jet-black hair.

She caught me staring at her several times and eventually broke into a shy, nervous smile. There was something oriental about her face, although I couldn't pinpoint exactly what. The other thing I remember about her that first night was that she was wearing the worst colour nylons I'd ever seen. They had kind of a yellow tint – maybe the colour had run in the wash or something like that – but it was just such a repulsive colour that I had to force myself to look beyond the uckiness of the stockings and see how shapely the legs were underneath. They were fine; believe you me, they were surely fine.

My sister Kathleen, Marianne and two of Kathleen's other mates made their way over to Bob and me. Bob had spent the entire time I was ogling Marianne going on and on about whether or not I thought Kathleen liked him. I didn't really listen to him and, to this day, I don't really know what I said: I was too busy eyeing up Marianne and pretending to be cool by pulling on a Coke bottle and listening to Lonnie Donegan. Actually, Bob and Kathleen never did go out on another date. I hope I didn't put him off. Really. But the truth is, it was all for the best. He was only after a knee-trembler, if he could get that far. Get that far with my sister indeed! I'd have given him a bloody nose if I'd known he had tried.

So, eventually, Kathleen introduces us all and at last I got to shake Marianne's hand. Kathleen had to remind me that the ritual of shaking someone's hand is but a brief affair and not meant to last the two or so minutes I held on to Marianne's hand. Marianne's voice was a little above a whisper. She had green eyes and didn't appear to like to smile. I knew I was on a sticky wicket because she was the same age as my sister. This meant, in Kathleen's eyes, that Marianne was too old for me. But being too old for me wasn't an issue with Marianne because, about five minutes later, this other geezer arrives, slings his arm around Marianne's shoulder and is introduced by Marianne as Ken, her boyfriend. Now, the slob looked to me like he was married. You know the look married people have; they've had starters so often that they prefer to get straight to the main course.

So, off go Ken and Marianne, leaving yours truly gutted; totally gutted, I can tell you.

'So, how come you've never introduced me to your mate, Marianne, before?' I asked, trying unsuccessfully to appear matter-of-fact. It was two-and-a-half hours later and we had barely caught the last train back to Southport.

'Come on, Theo, you're not seriously saying you fancy Marianne, are you?' Kathleen taunted.

'Well, you know, she's quite a looker. And… ' I hesitated, trying to work out what to say next; I was talking to my sister, after all.

'Don't even dream about it, Theo. She's much too old for you. It would be like me going with someone your age. Just wouldn't happen,' she replied, starting to laugh jeeringly.

'Hey, Bob's not exactly Richard Burton,' I replied, trying to get my dig in. But it fell well short of the target. Obviously, Bob was already history and her mind was elsewhere. He did eventually make something of his life though; he became a roadie for some of the hard-rock groups in later years.

'Not an issue, sunshine,' Kathleen cut in, seriously. She looked stunning when she was cross or serious. Just like my mum, in fact. The anger curved all the lines on her face to perfection. Kathleen, like my dad, had ginger hair. Unlike my dad, she was forever getting it permed in different styles, trying to find one that suited her face or, more importantly, would captivate her man of the moment. 'Marianne would have you for breakfast. She's a bit of a man eater.'

'*Really?*' I was hooked.

'Yes, Theo.'

'But she looks so innocent.'

'That's the giveaway, darling baby brother,' she said, smugly. She was always calling me that – 'Darling baby brother' – and I did wish she wouldn't, especially in company. 'They say it's always the quiet ones.'

'That's good news for mum and dad then, isn't it, 'cause you're as noisy as a skiffle group falling off their tea chest.'

'Ha, ha, ha,' she mocked.

'So, is he a married man, that Ken fellow?'

'Swear you won't tell anyone?'

'Which swear word would you like me to use?' I replied.

'Well, Theo, I'm still shocked she allowed him come to the Adelphi to pick her up,' Kathleen began, sidling up close to me. It was as though she wanted to make sure that no-one else would hear what she was saying. She needn't have bothered; we were alone in a compartment and no-one was going to bother us, at least not until the next stop. 'Yes, Ken is married. How did you guess?'

'Well, he was all over her like a cheap suit, wasn't he.'

'Yes, well, apparently he has left his wife and he wants Marianne to leave home and move in with him.'

'Move in with him! What? You mean sleep with him and all that?'

'And all that, Theo. As well.'

'God,' I said. I was devastated, flabbergasted. I felt a huge hole forming in the pit of my stomach.

Now I can imagine you're all out there, thinking: Yes, but he wouldn't be telling us all this story about Marianne if she'd run away with this Ken fellow, would he?

And yes, you are all perfectly correct. However, I wasn't to know that on my late-night train journey back home, was I? And in those days, I have to admit that such sadness and the space it brought was, in its own way, quite a pleasant space to be. I wasn't quite feeling sorry for myself, but I was totally preoccupied by the mature experience of having a broken heart.

Kathleen allowed me to wallow in my misery for a few miles before saying, 'Geez, I hope I have that effect on a bloke one day. You've only met her once and you're totally smitten.'

Well, I was going to be, wasn't I? I mean, here was a girl, Marianne Burgess, *just* out of my reach and very close at the same time, hovering there, or thereabouts, and she was worldly-wise already. You don't think so? Come on now, you don't mean to tell me she was going out with a married man and he wasn't riding her? And she was a sensation to boot. I mean, it's just every boy's dream, isn't it?

At this stage, I've got another confession to make. Sorry. Come a bit closer though; I don't want everybody to hear it. I was still a virgin the night I met Marianne in the Adelphi Hotel. Swear you won't tell anyone? Yes, like everyone else, when I was hanging out with my mates – you know, practising songs at rehearsals, hanging around Laine's Cafe with the boys – well, of course, we'd all claim to have done the wild thing. But you know what? If all the cafe stories were true, we'd not only deflowered all the able Manchester girls, but we'd been through most of Liverpool's as well. Come on… it's a known fact that the Manchester girls were easier.

So, was that what made Marianne more attractive to me? I don't know. You tell me. But she was beautiful; she was young yet mature; she was intelligent; she was local; she was unique (hip-length hair); and she was experienced. In fact, she was everything. Everything but available.

Chapter Three

John and Paul, on the other hand, were getting on much better with their budding relationship. They had both written songs individually by this point, and now they were starting to write together.

Did you know that they had already written 'Love Me Do' by the time John met George Harrison? George was already an acquaintance of Paul's. They attended the same school and travelled on the same bus each day. George was younger, much younger, about 14 in fact in 1957. But his guitar was his life. You see, that's the thing about these chaps – John, Paul and George – music. It was everything in their lives. Yes, sure, they wanted to avoid college, turn their backs on ordinary boring jobs and get the girls; but equally, they wouldn't think twice about taking a long bus ride across town just so they could learn a new chord on their guitars. You see, that's commitment. The rest of us would just have said, 'Ah, let's wait 'till the next time we run into him (the guitarist who knew the third chord) at a gig. That'll be soon enough.'

As I've already said, my first group was called Rocket 88 and we were a skiffle group after the likes of Lonnie Donegan. Lonnie's drummer, Pete Appleby: now he was something else. He was a total inspiration to me and the only reason I hadn't packed up drumming on more than one occasion. Rocket 88 played around, quite a bit as it happens, but there was no real commitment from anyone in the group. It was like a group where every member was on their own way to something greater (they hoped). So it never really had a chance. There was no soul there. If one of us couldn't get it together for a gig, the rest of us wouldn't worry; we'd just go out and have a bevy instead.

Then I heard the likes of John Lee Hooker, Sonny Boy Williamson and Big Bill Bronsey. There was some great music floating around Liverpool in those days, thanks to the sailors who'd continuously return to shore from America, laden down with vinyl. That's how we managed to hear such great American music. So, with the guitarist from Rocket 88, a good mate of mine, Vincent

McKee (who could also sing a bit), and Brian Kerr, who played piano (when we could find one), bass guitar and sang a bit, we formed the Blues by Three. Three people playing blues? Get it? Sadly, not many people did, and we practised more than we gigged. But that was okay; it was an excuse to listen to some great records and we were also able to chat up the girls by claiming we were in a group. But the promoters didn't want a wee group playing the blues. 'You'll scare our punters,' they'd say. We'd say, 'With a face like yours you don't need us to do that for you,' and we'd be on our way with red ears and bruised egos.

Come Christmas that year (1957), I decided to leave the group so that I would be able to buy a Christmas present for my then girlfriend, Rosemary Player. I was right miserable, I can tell you. I'd packed in my mates in order to buy her a present. I was on a kind of a promise, if you know what I mean, although I still wasn't sure what I'd do with *the promise* when presented with *it*. Well, unfortunately (actually I probably mean fortunately there, as I'm sure I would have broken out in a cold sweat if she'd said it was on), the promise never really materialised. The cow packed me in on Boxing Day! Can you imagine how I felt? Our Kathleen was well pleased, I can tell you. She never really liked Rosemary – something about a girl should only have what God gave her in her bra. I couldn't really work it out then and she wouldn't tell me. To add insult to injury, she did tell me that she thought Marianne Burgess was about to move in with Ken, 'the Married Man'.

Well, it wasn't as definite as that; it came more from a throwaway comment that Kathleen made when I was trying to get her to fix me up with Marianne. 'I wouldn't bother if I were you, darling baby brother,' she said, apologetically. 'She's just about to move in with Ken.' What a way to spend Christmas.

On the parallel front, George had now met up with John. Paul had told John about George and the three arranged to meet on the top of a double-decker bus; just the three of them on the top deck, and George with his guitar. Encouraged by Paul, he played for John and then... and then there were three.

Well, seven, if you include the rest of The Quarry Men. Around the time George joined the group, Rod Davies and Pete Shotton left, and John Lowe joined to play piano. But the nucleus had been formed. George also played for a time with the Les Stewart Quartet, which is where, if the timing had been different, he might have met up with Paddy Shore, who joined Blues by Three after I left.

Remember? I had to leave to buy *that* girl a Christmas present. Paddy Shore auditioned for the Les Stewart Quartet and my road to fame and fortune could have been sealed. It really is all down to timing in this life. All joking aside, I was literally that close – and here you have to imagine me putting the tips of my thumb and fore-finger about half an inch apart – to being a Beatle. Mind you, if everyone was off being famous, who'd be left to watch and listen to all the fabulous artists?

I must say, I was surprised at how supportive my dad was. I mean, everybody else's parents were giving them the: 'When are you going to get a proper job?' routine, but I think that, deep down, my dad was pleased I was having a go at trying to make something of myself. You know, using the opportunities he never had. He was very good like that, my father. He was a quiet man who always thought a lot about things. Then, when a subject came up or a prob-lem evolved in the family, my father would, from zero, spout off a quick, succinct sentence or two, which would have a ready-made solution contained therein. When the well-thought-out version didn't work, he wasn't beyond threatening the belt. Mind you, it was rarely anything beyond a threat. He'd always say to my two sisters and me, 'If you can't win an argument with words, walk away from it. There is no argument worth winning that you can only win with brute force and ignorance.'

My mother would look on proudly and say, without missing a beat in her dusting (she was always dusting something), 'Listen to what your father is saying. He knows what he's talking about.' Then she'd proceed to dust my father as well and he'd have to go off down the pub with his mates to get a bit of peace and quiet. When I talk about this now I realise that my mother and my father have never, ever disappointed me – as people, that is. They are good people; very much so, in fact.

After Rosemary dumped me, I threw myself back into a band again. This one was much more into R 'n' B classics and there were four of us. Vincent McKee again on guitar, Todd (just a singular name) on bass, Paul Peters on lead vocals and me on the skins. We called ourselves the Nighttime Passengers and we were pretty darned good, even if I do say so myself. That's when I got to see Marianne again. Kathleen brought her to see us play a gig in New Brighton. It would have been May 1958. We'd had a bad winter and this was the first beautiful day of spring. Kathleen and Marianne decided to go for a walk along the sea front and so I kinda invited myself along. Kathleen, God bless her, got the hint and made an excuse to return to see Vincent over something or other, saying she'd see us back at the gig – she and Vincent were always chatting away about something or other. It was a good day for me. The band was getting paid thirty bob and here I was, walking along the sea front with the lady of my dreams.

I have to be honest here, though, and admit I really didn't feel I was up to it. You know, chatting up Marianne Burgess. I felt way out of her league but, at the same time, I felt compelled to have a go. I just knew that I would kick myself later for not at least trying. I didn't care about being shot down. It was like I had to absolutely try and make a connection with this woman. I hope you know the feeling. It's like a panic attack. I had known she was going to be there with our Kathleen and, I swear to you, I was awake all the previous night trying to work out how and what to say.

The night before, I felt completely inarticulate. I eventually had to promise myself that if I should have a chance to talk to her, I would pass on it. I didn't want her to see and hear me as a babbling buffoon. And I had the chance, you know, to let the pair of them – our Kathleen and Marianne – head off by themselves. But when it came down to it, this wee voice inside me wouldn't hear of letting them go so I jumped right in, feet first, and off we went.

The thing that hit me most about Marianne was how sad she seemed to be. I mean, if I felt as bad as I thought she felt, I would just have given up there and then. There'd be no need to carry on. There was a song out a few years later; I don't know what it was called but it had a mournful tune and the lyric went something like, 'Why does the sun keep on shining? Why does the earth keep on turning? Don't they know it's the end of the world?' And that was the happy part of the song! Do you know the one I mean? Well, I always thought that melancholy melody created a mood just perfect to describe Marianne.

It's like she was out of time. You'd think that she was at least forty and had lost her lover or husband in the war, or he'd run off with another woman, or even another man! She looked like she was carrying the worries of the world on her shoulders. And what beautiful shoulders they were too. That day, on New Brighton front, she took off her cardigan to reveal a nape that was slim and slender, sculptured as elegantly as any swan's. If God created woman, and we believe she did, then Marianne was her finest moment. Perhaps God spent so much time and energy creating Marianne's body, she didn't have any time left to fill her happiness cells.

It's funny, you know, the way that sometimes happens. Marilyn Monroe, for instance. Now can you imagine anyone better to fill your dreams? I can – Marianne Burgess. But you don't know her, do you? So you can't imagine her, can you? But Marilyn Monroe: you can imagine her, can't you? I thought so. God's gift and all that. But could the poor girl find happiness? No way. Did she enjoy sex? Apparently not. Can you believe that? I can't. If ever there was a woman created more for sex – I mean from my viewpoint – she was well hidden. So my point is this: the camera *does* lie. The camera believes what it sees. It doesn't have the ability to look any further than the second dimension.

So, Marianne and I are walking along the beach. Her long, black hair is blowing all around her perfect features. She's wearing no make-up and she's still drop-dead gorgeous. Yet – and here's the important bit – she's as miserable as a New Year's Day hangover.

Lesser mortals would have given up, you know. Yes, she looked like an angel. Or maybe not, for that matter. If all the angels looked like Marianne Burgess, then God was going to have to do a lot of forgiving, if you know what I mean.

So, I decide to work my way up to a conversation. I've thought about this girl so much that I'm not going to give up on her just because she's being miserable.

'So, Premier have a new, top-class kit coming out in September,' I said. My brain immediately screamed: Hennessy, what the feck are you on about? Premier have a new, top-class kit coming out in September. Please! What are you trying to do here? Go home and get a knife, son. You won't feel the pain as much.

'That's interesting, Theo,' she replied, matter-of-fact and probably thinking: It's a shame he's Kathleen's brother, otherwise I'd be four hundred yards from here by now.

'Geez, I'm sorry, Marianne. What an utterly stupid thing to say,' I replied, hoping that honesty was the best policy.

'Well, I mean, it wasn't really. A stupid thing to say, that is. The only problem is I haven't a clue what you're on about. Who are Premier? Do they make army outfits? But why would you be interested in army outfits anyway? Unless, of course, you're being called up.'

'Sorry? No. I mean, what?' I answered, confused, amused and refused.

'You've got great eyelashes,' Marianne replied.

Marianne Burgess, the lady of my dreams, had just told me I had

great eyelashes. Do girls find eyelashes interesting, sensual or exciting? I'd never been led to believe that they did, but I could be wrong.
I mean, Vincent could be wrong. Yes, he was a great guitar player,
but what the feck did he know about girls? What did any of us
know about girls? I certainly knew nothing about the fairer sex,
even though I had two sisters: Kathleen, who I could talk to, I
thought, and Colette, who I couldn't string a sentence together for.

'Really?'

'Yes, they're *sooo* long, you know,' Marianne replied, smiling
what was to become her trademark awkward smile – a smile that
revealed a crooked upper front tooth (known in the trade as a distal
occlusion).

Shit! There, I've just given it away. I've let you know, at this early
stage, that I got to know her better. To be honest, it was never as
well as I wanted to know her. There, I've thrown in a bit more
intrigue (I hope).

This tooth abnormality created the illusion that Marianne had a
twisted smile; the end result being that even when she was genuinely
smiling, she always appeared to be sending you up with a false
smile. Like an 'Oh, really!' type of smile, when you've told her in the
middle of a heatwave that it's snowing in Whitechapel.

'Really?' I liked this phrase. It was keeping me out of trouble so
I was sticking to it.

'Yes. It's unusual in a boy,' she offered, elaborating on her original statement.

Aaagh! Oh shit! It's over before it has even begun. How could
she be so cruel to me? I am her best friend's brother. There is a little
decorum called for in these circumstances. You know? In this game
of life and love, you're allowed to be cruel to some people but you
are not allowed to be cruel to your best friend's brother. I mean,
how could she?

Yes, she had actually said, 'it's unusual in a *boy.*'

Me? A boy? Didn't she realise the danger I could be to her? I
could impregnate her with my male (very un-boy-like) seed and get
her pregnant. Is that what I'd have to do to show her that I wasn't a
boy?

Down in Liverpool, boys told girls, 'Stick this Smartie between
your knees and nothing will happen to you. Honestly! You'll be
okay. Believe me. Would I lie to you at a time like this?' But up here
in New Brighton, you know, we've got a different tactic. No, not
something like: 'You can't get pregnant the first time.' Believe it or

not, that's what the aforementioned Marilyn Monroe was told.
More like:'Ahm, just give me a minute to fix this thing on.' And
we'd practised it a few times. Well, we'd practised it lots really, if the
truth be known. We were encouraged in this exercise because
apparently, in the heat of the moment, it could be quite awkward.
So, in order to have a test run, as it were, you needed to be like in the
army. You know? Standing to attention. And when you've gone to
all that trouble, it would be a shame to waste it. Anyway, that's
another story or three hundred.

'Really?'

'Yes, Theo. As a matter of a fact, yes. And your eyebrows too. I
like them. They're full but not bushy. I can't abide bushy eyebrows.'

'Well, your eyebrows are quite cute too. How come they're a
different colour to your hair?'

Wrong question, Theo. Oh God, Sweet Jesus, dig me a hole big
enough to hide in.

'Well, Theo,' she replied, swinging around to look me straight in
the eyes. The wind, which had just blown a few breakers upon the
beach beneath us, blew her long, black hair in my face. 'It's usually
a sign that the girl has dyed her hair. Only in my case it's not, and my
mother's the same. You can come over to check if you don't believe
me.'

Was that an invitation and, if I accepted it, did I concede that I
didn't in fact believe her?

'No, no. I mean, it looks perfectly natural to me. I mean, not all
of a man's body hair is the same colour either, you know,' I said,
putting two prize size nines in my gob.

Marianne Burgess started to laugh. She tried to stop, but the
more she tried, the more the giggles took her over.

'Theodore Hennessy. I'm not sure I want to know that, thank
you very much indeed. And I'm sure that if I did want to know, I
wouldn't want the brother of my best friend to be the one to tell me,'
she spluttered, through her giggles.

Chapter Four

Well, I can tell you, I belted the life out of my drum kit that particular night in New Brighton, and I can also tell you that the beating of those skins was the only relief I experienced that night. But not too long thereafter, things were to change and to change for the better.

Again, it was our Kathleen I had to thank for my... well, you'll see.

Kathleen had been invited to a party the following Saturday week. The party was in Liverpool and, once again, my dad refused to let her go unescorted. I don't want you to think badly about my dad over this. That would be unfair. Every boy, but *every* boy, in Liverpool was continuously trying to get his leg over. At the same time, we all wanted to marry a girl as pure as the driven snow. It doesn't equate, does it? All kidding aside, the single biggest sin – the biggest disgrace that could be brought upon a family – was for a daughter to become pregnant out of wedlock. We're not exactly talking medieval times here, in the early sixties, but such a disgrace could mean, socially speaking, the end of that entire family. So, my father was simply doing what all other fathers did; ensuring their single daughters had a chaperone. Her official escort for the night? You've guessed. One Theodore Hennessy. That was until we reached the party and her unofficial escort, whose name I forget and am happy to forget, took over. I wasn't at all concerned because, and you've guessed correctly for the second time, Marianne Burgess was there.

And no sign of the Married Man either.

As George, Paul, John and their changing bunch of Quarry Men were gigging around, learning their new fave raves – and as John and Paul were writing together as John & Paul, and individually as John and as Paul – I was setting my sights on Marianne. At the party Marianne, for some reason, had chosen not to dress in her traditional black but was instead wearing a simple, figure-hugging, blue number. Long, black hair down to her waist contrasted with the short back and sides of my curly, copper-coloured hair. I had, if truth be known, especially groomed my eyelashes, and eyebrows, just in case the same Miss Burgess happened along my path.

And, along my path she did happen. But it wasn't as simple as that.

When Kathleen and I first arrived at the party, we made a beeline for Marianne and some of her and Kathleen's mates. The party was in a ground-floor flat, just off Tithebarn Street. I seem to remember the apartment consisted of a large studio room (living-cum-sleeping area), with double doors into a large back room (kitchen-cum-dining area) and a shared bathroom on the first floor. Its saving grace was that the back room had double doors that led out to a small, but well-kept, garden.

The music blared out from a gramophone player that was positioned just beside the back door, allowing the sound to spill out to the garden. Mostly, I remember the music of Elvis Presley. It had been just over four years since RCA had bought out 'The Pelvis' from his Sun Records contract. Supposedly, the Sun period was his best. I'm not so sure, but I can tell you that, in those days, he was one beautiful-looking man. Because of the mess he turned into, it became very easy to dismiss Elvis. But he was wild, really wild; probably the best-looking man I had ever seen and boy, could he sing. He had it all. He had the gift and the looks. But, as with the darkness surrounding Marilyn Monroe, Elvis was another seriously unhappy person. I often thought about the pair of them – Elvis and Marilyn – and their unhappiness, and wondered, with her virginal looks, if they could have found happiness together. I mean, if God has personally had a hand in your creation, you're hardly going to find peace and happiness with a mere mortal, are you?

Back to the party. So there we were – me, Kathleen and Marianne and three or four of their friends. Eventually, the friends moved off to mingle, then Kathleen spied her man and she was off, leaving me alone with Marianne. She was drinking Babycham and I was on my dad's drink, Guinness, which I'd grown to love. I will admit to having had to force myself onto it in the early days. But perseverance pays and that was certainly true with me and the Guinness.

'So, where's Rosemary?' was Marianne's first question to me, when she found us alone. I couldn't believe it. Kathleen had obviously told her about Rosemary. But hang on a minute; did that mean that if she'd told Marianne about Rosemary – which wasn't really a relationship – were the bits I'd been told about the Married Man equally exaggerated?

'Oh, that. Rosemary Player and I finished sh... we finished just after Christmas,' I stuttered, giving a selective version of the truth.

'What? You mean, once you bought her a Christmas present – one she no doubt encouraged you to buy – she dumped you at an acceptable time thereafter?' Marianne asked quietly, as she stared elsewhere.

'Forget the "acceptable time thereafter" and you've got it,' I conceded.

'It works every time. Didn't you ever wonder why seemingly unavailable women always seem to acquire boyfriends around Christmas and birthdays?'

'Does that mean I'm going to have to wait until late November with you?'

'What? Oh, yes. I mean, no. Very funny,' Marianne replied, appearing more concerned about my shoulder than me.

Hey, remember me? The boy with the great eyelashes? I'm here. Perhaps there's dandruff on my shoulder. Oh shit, that's it. That's exactly what she's looking at. How embarrassing. Why could our Kathleen not have told me? Then I realised it wasn't dandruff on my shoulder that Marianne was looking at. It wasn't even my shoulder she was looking at. She was looking over it. Over my shoulder. Then I twigged. She had positioned herself where she could easily view, over my shoulder as it so happens, the door to the flat. Marianne Burgess was waiting for her man – her Married Man – to arrive.

Feck this for a game of *shoulders*, I thought, I'm young, single – very single – and free and I'm not going to be used as a prop at a party.

'Look, Marianne, enjoy the party, hey? I'm going for a wander,' I grand-standed and was off before she'd a chance to reply. Get someone else to lean your door-glaring stare upon, young lady. There are plenty more fish in the sea. The problem was there weren't too many, if any, Marianne Burgesses. But a man has his pride, particularly if he's a *boy*.

I was always okay with the drink, you know. I mean, I realised at that point that I was meant to go and get absolutely rat-faced and redesign the patterns on the carpet as I left the flat. But luckily enough, I have always taken my solace in music, never in alcohol. However, as the evening progressed, I found myself sneaking a glance back at Marianne, if only to see this great Married Man of hers. I have to admit she looked very vulnerable. For me, a woman with naked arms always looks vulnerable. It's always been that way for me. Marianne's bare arms looked very inviting, but a man has his pride. So does a boy.

I was faking a conversation with a couple of people over the virtues of Buddy Holly when I felt someone squeeze my arm.

'Where did you run off to?' the voice said, barely audible above the racket.

I turned to find Marianne Burgess making a brave attempt at a smile.

'Oh, you looked like you were expecting company. I didn't want to cramp your style,' I replied, still somewhat foolishly upset.

'How considerate. However, my 'company' obviously isn't and I feel like a drink and some *good* company,' Marianne struggled. I could tell she was struggling. It was a choice of either striking up a conversation with me or going home alone and listening to Leonard Cohen. Hey, no competition; Leonard Cohen was nine years away from his first album.

No more encouragement necessary, I went off and found her a bottle of Babycham. Actually, I got her two. Supplies in the kitchen were running low. Talking about low, the hosts had kindly placed cushions and mattresses around the outside of both rooms to allow people to relax. With the amount of steaming up I witnessed on a few pairs of glasses, I doubted much relaxing was going on.

'Let's get some air,' she suggested, when I returned with my prizes.

'Sounds good to me,' I replied, and off we went into the garden.

There is a moment when you know clearly what you want from life and, for me, that moment came when we went into the garden. It was a bit nippy at that point so I took my jacket off and placed it around her shoulders, covering her vulnerable bare arms. She turned to look at me and head-butted me, right smack between the eyes. No, just kidding. Seriously though, I assumed Marianne was going to offer thanks, but the look in her eyes was more one of surprise, as though no-one had ever done something like that for her before. She took my hand and said something about how Kathleen had been right when she told her how considerate I was and she kissed me lightly on the lips.

I was so surprised at her confidence and style, not to mention good taste, that I just stood there in shock, like a dummy. But, from that moment on, I knew in my heart that I wanted to spend the rest of my life with this troubled soul. I tried to kiss her again, later, but it was awkward; the moment had passed and when the moment has gone, it's gone forever. But her kiss, brief though it was, had been magic. It hadn't been so brief that I didn't feel the softness of her lips. It wasn't so brief that I didn't have time to long with all my being to do it again, this time for longer and with more exploration. Her kiss came from nowhere. No hovering around for a few seconds while you go through the 'will I, won't I?' routine as your faces move closer together. All the time hoping, *praying*, that you're not misreading the situation and that you're not going to get a smack in your face or a kick in the goolies for your troubles.

That was it that night. She left half an hour later and, as she left, we touched hands. A gentle, unsure kind of thing. Not really shaking hands; more intimate and personal than that, if you know what I mean.

Chapter Five

I didn't see Marianne Burgess again that year.

I often thought about trying to contact her, particularly coming up to Christmas, when I planned to say, 'What are the chances of a short-term relationship?' But Kathleen kept me informed about her movements and an up-to-date progress report on all her waiting around for the Married Man.

In October of that year, 1959, The Quarry Men lost their guitarist and vocalist, Ken Brown, the man they'd nicked from the Les Stewart Quartet in August. They were now down to a three-piece group – the magic George, Paul and John – and had changed their name to Johnny and the Moondogs. Then John's best mate from art college, Stuart Sutcliffe, sold a painting for about sixty-five pounds and, rather than spend the money on paints and canvas, John and Paul persuaded him to buy a bass guitar and join the group.

We would now have moved on to January 1960, the beginning of a new decade. The beginning of *the* decade. One of the first things Stuart did was to persuade them to change the band's name and, following the example of Buddy Holly's group, the Crickets, they chose – or I imagine John chose – another insect, a beetle in fact. They changed it around a bit to Beatals (to imply beat music), then eventually, via The Silver Beetles and the Silver Beatles, they became 'The Beatles', which they will remain for all eternity.

We're now up to August 1960 and, in the meantime, they've had a few drummers. Left to their own devices, they probably would have been happy not to have one at all. However, promoters – and particularly a manager in the shape of Welshman, Allan Williams – persuaded them they needed a drummer to do things like tour Scotland as Johnny Gentle's backing group. So, Tommy Moore was recruited for that particular trip but, by the time of their first visit to Germany, Pete Best warmed the drummer's stool. By now, they were The Beatles and on their way, only we in Liverpool didn't really know it yet.

I can hear you say: Where's Marianne Burgess? Just hang on a moment. Be patient – I had to be. I spoke to her twice that year; both times she was with my sister, who refused to leave us alone – she had her own reasons – and so the exchanges were brief.

Meanwhile, down at the Reaperbaun in Hamburg, the boys were working up quite a set, playing anything up to twelve hours a day and occasionally meeting up with fellow scouser, Ringo Starr. Ringo – real name, Richard Starkey – was in Hamburg with another Liverpool band, Rory Storm and the Hurricanes; a rocking good band, with the emphasis on rock.

At this juncture, numerous things were falling into to place. Things that would be crucial to The Beatles' development, musically and visually.

The Beatles met Astrid Kitcherr, a photographer, and she was to prove to be very important – *vitally* important – to their image. They immediately copied, with encouragement and snips from Astrid, her hairstyle. She also turned them on to black leather gear. She was to prove to be even more important to Stuart, romantically speaking. Can you believe this? Astrid and Stuart met, fell in love, moved in together and got engaged, all in the space of a few months, and here I was, eighteen months after having met Marianne Burgess, and still no more than the briefest of kisses to show for my troubles.

Mind you, the Nighttime Passengers were doing very well, very well indeed. Vincent had started to write some songs and we were performing them in the set. We would have been great in Germany, absolutely great. There were so many Liverpool bands doing well over there that it should have been easy. Our manager claimed to know someone who knew someone who knew Allan Williams, 'from the old days back in Wales, like', and he was going to see if this friend would ask the friend to ask his friend, Allan Williams, if he could get us over to Germany. It never happened. What can I tell you? I was beginning to learn the hard way that it wasn't what you knew, it was *who knew* what you knew. But then I always thought that who you knew was part of what you knew. Anyway, we'd built up our own little circuit and were getting two quid a night at weekends and thirty bob midweek.

Romantically, I was filling in my time with Colette (not my sister, I hasten to add, but her namesake). She led me down the magical road of sexual experience again and again. I moved out of my parents' house and into her flat in the city. She was a really decent sort, but there was never any real love there, on either side.

We didn't need love, Colette and I. Good old lust was enough and the first time with her – my first time with anyone, as you know – was very natural. No cold sweats, no doing whatever she needed to do just to keep me happy. She was as eager for the experience as I was. When I think about it now, I was very lucky to have met her when I did. She was a great person to have my first sexual experience with. We did it in the heat and comfort of her flat and if I might have been a wee bit too quick for her the first time, as in after ten seconds, she was very patient and waited until I was ready to try again. We tried quite a bit that night, from what I remember. They say you'll never forget the first person you make love to. Well, I hope that's true; I know I'll never forget Colette. Most of my memories are of her in various stages of undress, encouraging me to 'get to know her better'.

It was all experience though, and crashing in her flat saved me having to get out to Southport late at night after gigs. On top of all of that, I had our Kathleen swear that she wouldn't breathe a word of it – you know, my relationship with the skinny, blonde-haired Colette – to Marianne Burgess. I didn't bother to hint at giving my father some important, not to mention juicy, bits of information. I didn't need to. Kathleen knew full well it would only take a single piece of my information to have her grounded for the rest of her life.

Actually, Kathleen and I had a great relationship. We were more like mates than brother and sister. She always played her boyfriends close to her chest – not too close, you understand. But she'd always keep me guessing about whom she was interested in. I always tried to persuade her away from dating musicians; well you would, wouldn't you? They're not really human, you know. This explains a lot, I hear you say. But we – our Kathleen and I – always had good chats, especially when she stayed over with me at Colette's flat. Notice the way I always say Colette's flat. I mean, I was paying half the rent, so technically it was Theo and Colette's flat. But that would have implied something, wouldn't it? It would have given out some kind of message, wouldn't it? Maybe a message that might have reached the ears of the stunning Marianne Burgess.

Once our Kathleen discovered my real feelings for Marianne, she was good about it. She stopped trying to dissuade me from furthering that cause. I also think she became more than a bit selective with her information on Marianne. You know, not really keeping me in the picture as far as the Married Man was concerned. But I felt that Marianne and I would be together some day, just because

I wanted it so badly. So badly? God, I thought about little else in those days. It was good for the band, though, because I would practise for hours and hours by myself. The noisy solitude gave me ample opportunity to dream up some interesting 'just suppose' situations concerning Marianne Burgess and me.

But I had fun. My life was fun. That was the good thing about my state of mind. It wasn't like I had lost Marianne and was moping around. No, not at all; I was hopeful about our future and saw life as a celebration. I've always been that way, though. I put it down to my parents' Irishness. The Irish have this great ability and capacity for fun. And I'll drink to that.

Obviously, I wasn't making enough money from the gigs, so I supplemented it by doing a bit of painting. No, not on canvas; window frames and doors to be exact. It was good because it was cash-in-hand and I could work my own hours, just as long as the job was done and I didn't leave painted fingerprints on the lady of the house's bottom. Aye, and don't think I'm kidding either.

The Beatles, on the other hand, were supplementing their income with another trip to Hamburg. This would have been August 1960. They were getting tighter and tighter as a band. Stuart stayed behind in Hamburg with Astrid and, pretty soon, Paul moved to bass. They returned to Liverpool as the bee's knees, and soon their reputation was second to none. Their shows at the Cavern Club made it *the* place to be. Everyone was simply amazed by this band. The remnants of a ragtag and bobtail skiffle group were now absolutely flooring audiences and the word spread around Liverpool quicker than one of George Harrison's famous guitar runs.

I mean, they were even packing out the Cavern Club at lunch time. I must admit, there were a few occasion when I skived off from a painting job to see their lunch-time set. The thing that always hit me about the band was that they were always having so much fun on stage. It was totally infectious. I mean, if they were enjoying themselves so much, what was there not to like? They could make the hairs on the back on your neck stand to attention. John was so raw and raunchy, and George's guitar work had to be heard to be believed. For one so young, he was well on his way to mastering his instrument. Paul was now on bass since Stuart's departure and, vocally, he was a bit of a belter. He played the bass melodically, more like the way he sang than the way you should play bass guitar. And then, to cap it all, the three of them would sing together.

Absolute bliss; harmonies perfected from the hour upon hour of stage work in Germany. And the blend of voices, agh. It was perfect, yet soulful, like they were creating a fourth voice. The Beatles don't really get enough credit for their harmonies. People always talk about The Beach Boys and their harmonies, but the boys from Liverpool did it for me, every time. Much more soul. I'll tell you, if you could have bottled what was happening on stage at the Cavern, you'd have put Arthur Guinness out of business. I kid you not.

Chapter Six

In the middle of all this madness you have a guy, a regular guy, walk into a shop, an ordinary shop, and ask the shop assistant in the record department if they have a copy of The Beatles' *My Bonnie*. The shopper's name? Raymond Jones. The shop's name? NEMS (North End Music Stores). The shop assistant's name? Brian Epstein. *Mr* Brian Epstein to us, if you please.

Was Raymond Jones the first record collector? Was he the first in a long line of vinyl junkies, or an 'anorak'? Who knows, and who cares? Enough that he was responsible for triggering Brian Epstein's curiosity. Yes? Another major part of the puzzle was in place. Still one more change to come, and a painful change at that.

Raymond Jones was the first person credited with asking for The Beatles' record, but that in itself meant that the buzz had already started on the street, as anyone at the Cavern shows would have attested. Within a few days, two girls visited the same store and asked the same shop assistant the same question. So, Brian visited the Cavern Club, lunchtime on 9th November 1962 and, like the rest of us, was totally bowled over by what he saw.

Now, the thing you have to remember here is that this wasn't an isolated incident. At that time, there were just over three hundred groups playing around Liverpool, including The Beatles and the Nighttime Passengers. The Beatles were by far the best – not to mention the most exciting and the most accomplished – but they were, nonetheless, part of a movement that was to become known as The Mersey Sound. A new sound for a new generation.

The first post-war generation, in fact. The first generation with an independence, and a want and need for their own music, their own fashions, their own style and their own voice. The rich, with their many privileges, had enjoyed this independence since twenty chickens would buy you a cow. But this was different. This was the first time that taste and style were being led from the streets. Teenagers, by their own devices, had money in their pockets. Money that was burning holes of liberty in their pockets: liberty

from their parents and their parents' ways and their parents' pleasures. Well, of course, we must remember there are some pleasures
– the ones that keep the world turning – that we all share and always
will. But we're talking about a youth movement here. Also interesting to note that the timing was right, if not perfect.

Equally, the timing was right for the other two hundred and
ninety-nine groups playing around Liverpool. But there was only
going to be one that would have that magic. I'm not suggesting that
any one out of the three hundred could have done it. No, if there
were no Beatles, none of the others could have stepped up to take
their place. At the same time though, this *had* to happen in, and
around, Liverpool. Liverpool had soul, you see. You could feel it as
you walked around the streets. There was a city pride thing going
on as well; we were proud to be Liverpudlians. Very similar, in fact,
to an Irish kind of thing; you know, a national pride. No matter
where in the world an Irish person goes, they are always Irish and
proud of it. With us, though, it was more of a city pride than a
national pride thing. Like the Irish, no matter where in the world
Liverpudlians go, they are always Scousers and proud of it.

So, basically, you had an audience, a large ready-made audience,
waiting to be fed. We were the first generation in decades that were
not living under the threat of war. We were going to let our hair
down (literally) and party. Make that PARTY! And, as I have
already mentioned a few times, The Beatles had a great time on
stage. They enjoyed themselves so much, the end result was that
band and audience together had an absolute hoot.

Mr Brian Epstein came along with his mixture of rebellion (he'd
been expelled from school aged 10 in 1944), theatrical experience
(RADA) and the organisational skills he picked up from his father
while working in the family business (NEMS). He instinctively
knew what needed to be done to move The Beatles, or 'the boys' as
he always referred to them, onwards and upwards.

He had them tidy up their act; no smoking or swearing on stage.
His tailor, Beno Dorn, made their famous matching mohair suits.
His hairdressers, Horne Brothers, did their hair after the style of
Astrid. And you know that synchronised deep bow the four of them
took at the end of their performances? That was a typical Brian
Epstein theatrical presentation. There's been talk over the years
about some of the Beatles, particularly John, not liking all this; you
know, tidying up their appearance and their act. Rubbish! They
were all happy to be in a group, happy to look like they were in a

group and happy to behave like they were in a group. They were ecstatic to belong. At last, they had that feeling of belonging. We need to remember John and Paul had been in a group together and playing for nearly five years – George had been with them for nearly three. They started to feel that at last they were on the move. They'd seen how little other managers had done for them but now they were seeing an immediate effect from the enthusiastic Mr Brian Epstein's style of management.

While all of this was going on, The Beatles were also putting the all-important road crew in place; a vital part of the organisation and they had the sense to recognise that. Neil Aspinall – always called 'Nell' by the group – had been road manager-cum-humper for six months before The Beatles appointed their new manager. He'd been an accountant lodging at Pete Best's house and, with a little persuasion from Pete, he bought a van to drive them around in. He charged them twenty-five bob a gig. When I heard that, I nearly dropped dead. Neil Aspinall, The Beatles' road manager, was getting nearly as much as my group were, per gig. And, let me tell you, The Beatles were doing a lot more gigs than the Nighttime Passengers were doing. I chalked that one down as another missed opportunity.

Neil was getting too busy looking after the boys by himself so Brian hired a doorman from the Cavern, Mal Evans (a former telecommunications officer at the Post Office), as his assistant. The Post Office was just across the road from the Cavern Club, so all Mal's former colleagues could look across and see him and Neil sweating their socks off each and every time The Beatles played the Cavern. Still, Neil and Mal took good care of The Beatles and that's a fact.

Chapter Seven

You could virtually touch the excitement surrounding The Beatles as they moved into top gear. It was electrifying. They were our band. We were proud of them. Word of their comings and goings, and Mr Epstein's trips to London to secure a record deal, was around the 'Pool quicker than a docker could run to the boozer on a Friday night. Yes, there were some frustrating times too, not just for the band, but for all of us. Every time someone like the 'Richard-head' from Decca turned the band down, he was rejecting all of us. It was not just The Beatles who were failing the audition, it was all of us; all of Liverpool. And we all felt equally bad about it. However, there were so many positive things going on – what with the gigs and John's writings in the local rag – that generally we were on an up.

Colette had a friend who worked at NEMS and the friend kept us up to date. Colette and I were getting on fine at this point. But that was the problem in the politics of the heart; doing fine usually means it's boring, it's a disaster. I have to admit, though, if it were not for bumping (physically) into Marianne Burgess again, we (Colette and I) would probably have been okay for another few months, or years; maybe even a lifetime.

I was visiting my sister. She shared a flat with a pile (three) of her mates in Whitechapel; not too far from NEMS, actually. I'd just turned into our Kathleen's pathway when a vision in black, gliding in the opposite direction, ran straight into me. It was quite a rude awakening from my daydream and I was about to shout something equally rude when I noticed the telltale waist-length, black hair. There she was – Marianne Burgess – large as life and twice as beautiful. And she was back in my life.

'Oh hello, Theo.'

'Hello. Long time no see.'

'Yes. Your Kathleen's not in.'

'Oh.'

And I thought for one desperate moment that that was going to be the sum total of our laboured conversation. I was expecting her to say something like, 'Okay, I'm off. See you in another eighteen months. Bye,' but she didn't. She hung around. In fact, she leaned against the garden gate. When I say garden, I mean a five-foot strip of concrete that ran the width of the house, separating it from a hedge (which, at seven foot, had grown out of control) and the gate. It was also the resting place for two dustbins, which tended to pong a bit when the sun was shining. You get the picture? Very romantic and all that, I *don't* think.

'So, was Kathleen meant to be in or were you just dropping around on the off chance, like me?'

'Nagh. I said I'd come around some time over the weekend. We're doing a gig tomorrow in York, sleeping in the van – those of us who can't find someone to crash with, that is – and driving on up to Carlisle the day after. So it was now or never,' I replied, still slightly hesitant.

You have to realise that here I was, for the first time in over a year, talking to the woman of my dreams – and not all of the dreams pure, I can tell you. And, in fact, I won't. Well... maybe later. Let's see how it goes, shall we? But for now, let's get back to the lady of my dreams. I was feeling so awkward; I mean, here I was with a chance to chat to Marianne Burgess. Now if I had known that I was going to meet her today, I'd have worked out what to say in advance. I'd have spent some time grooming myself and dressing up. You know, a bit of water sprinkled on my copper hair – which, like the hedge, was growing out of control – and run my fingers through it a few times. I was wearing a black leather jacket, a white T-shirt (at least it was clean), a pair of Levis and a pair of off-white gutties.

Marianne Burgess, on the other body (well, she'd nothing on her hand, not even the slightest bit of colour), was dressed in black: all in black. A black polo-neck jumper and a long black skirt – which just about reached her calf – and black suede boots. She also had a lightweight long (black) coat. This chasuble look enhanced her apparently translucent, snow-white skin. All this black tended to focus one's attention onto her perfectly sculptured face. Marianne did most of her talking with her sharp brown eyebrows.

It's a funny thing, attractiveness. Think about it. The remainder of Marianne's face consisted of a small, very cute, stub nose; a pair of ears (you had to assume they were in there somewhere, hidden forever beneath her long, straight hair); and the most inviting and kissable lips I had ever – and I do mean ever – set eyes on. But why was I attracted to her? I mean, what was it about her sad, green eyes that melted my heart? Why did I desire to kiss those lips so much? We all have our ideal woman, whose body we know completely, but she never has the same face. Our mind's eye always puts someone's face on our ideal woman. I have to admit that Marianne's features graced my Miss Perfect on more than one lonely night. But now that she was here, in front of me, I didn't have to imagine any more. I could see the shapes clearly from the way her clothes rose and fell about the contours of her body. But all of this took second place to her face, because of that face and the effect it had on my heart. Did that mean that, if she were to undress and reveal a less than perfect figure, I'd still be attracted to her?

Do you know what I mean? Does the body really matter? I suppose, in a very roundabout way, that's what I'm trying to say. 'Cause you know what? When you get down to it, down to the big moment, and your backside is doing a neat impression of a fiddler's elbow, do looks or beauty matter? Personally speaking, I usually have my eyes closed just as I'm about to shout 'Geronimo'. I'm too close to study the nose, the eyes, the mouth, the breasts, the bum, the legs, or anything else for that matter. So does all this verbal about the perfect body really matter?

Well, I suppose it must because Marianne had one (a perfect body) and, as we both did a bit of shoe shuffling outside Kathleen's flat, I was desperately trying to work out the shape of her breasts underneath her layers of clothing. The more she leaned back against the garden gate, the more her breasts strained against her polo-neck jumper. Every time she moved her legs, I tried to imagine how her thighs would run into the rest of her body. I tried to imagine the texture, shape and colour of her underwear. I do that a lot, you know. I see someone and I try to imagine what's going on; how their body is put together under the clothes. I like the mystery.

Marianne Burgess must have spied me stealing a glance at her breasts because she smiled. It was only a bit. She didn't expose her twisted front tooth and lopsided smile. She was offering merely a hint of a grin. She chose that very moment to catch the bottom of her jumper and pull it down. She pulled it down so firmly that the wool was straining to damn-near bursting point against her rising breasts. All of this was happening while she was simply leaning against the gatepost.

I'm sure it was an unconscious gesture and not intended to give me the trouser problem it just had. I rose my leg, as you do, pretending to position it on the first rung of the gate. The only problem was that the manoeuvre didn't provide the relief intended. Quite the opposite, in fact, due mainly to a very unco-operative pair of Y-fronts, with the 'Y' not quite at the front.

All the questions flying through my head refused to articulate themselves. They wanted me to do it for them. Some questions are so unreasonable, you know? But how could I possibly ask the main question that was screaming around my brain: 'Are you still seeing the Married Man?' I saw a way through the woods, though.

'So, this new man of Kathleen's seems okay. Have you met him yet?'

'No, not yet, but she's been telling me all about him. She seems to really like him. Have you met him?'

'No, not yet,' I replied, struggling to find a bridge over to the other island, the island that housed the question: 'So, what's the story with the Married Man then?' Maybe I should have waited for a while and got my feet wet, but before I had a chance, she gave me the opportunity on a plate for my awkward question.

'So, how's your love life? Still seeing Colette?'

Damn and blast our Kathleen, I thought. Damn and blast her! Mind you, if I was condemning her to hell (with the damn) there surely wouldn't be much need to blast her as well. But damn and blast her nonetheless; she'd gone and told Marianne Burgess that I was living with someone. *'Ahhh Kathleen, I'll take you home again,'* as the song went, 'I'll take you home again and drown you in the bleeding bath tub!'

Time for damage limitation, I thought.

Who was I kidding? Certainly not Marianne Burgess.

'Well, we're not really living together.'

'Oh yeah?' she smiled, this time showing her bent front tooth. Had she brought that out now as her ace to mock me?

'Well, it's her place, it's Colette's place, and she's letting me stay there until I find a place of my own,' I lied, reaching glorious dry land.

'Oh, I see. You're renting a room from her? I didn't realise the flat was that big.'

And I hadn't realised how big a mouth my sister had.

'Well, not exactly.'

'Oh? How not exactly?' Marianne Burgess continued, obviously enjoying herself. But I'd have my turn, don't you worry. And when the opposite side raised their objections, I'd do a *Perry Mason*, and tell the judge, 'They opened the door, your honour,' and have him overrule the objection and ask (and have answered) my burning question, 'How big... the Married Man, how big is his... his flat then?' But in the meantime, I had to concentrate on my defence.

'No, Marianne. You see, it's like this.... I mean... yes, I'm living there; no, I don't have my own room, and neither do we have a commitment. If you know what I mean.'

'I know what you mean, Theo. But surely the important question is, does Colette know what you mean?'

'Yes, she does actually. We are mates, apart from anything else, and the only condition she makes is that I don't see anyone else while we're... we're... ' I struggled like a drowning man and the missing words were my buoys.

'Well, for all your fancy footwork, Theo, you *are* living together. Spit it out, for heaven's sake. People know. I've known for ages. It's okay,' Marianne pulled me from the stormy seas, 'I'm in a similar situation myself, you know?'

Bombshell. Right out of the blue and I hadn't even had to ask the question. The way she'd stated it, I wasn't sure I wanted the conversation to continue in that direction. I had the impression I wasn't particularly going to like what I was about to hear.

'Oh?' I said, ducking my head involuntarily and squirming on the spot, waiting for the grenade to hit.

Chapter Eight

'**What are youse two** doing standing out on the street?'

It was our Kathleen, saving my poor heart once again.

'We both called to see you, separately of course, and got chatting,' Marianne replied, appearing disappointed.

'Well, it looks to me like you've been doing a lot of chatting. You'll both fancy a cup of tea then, and I've got some delicious cakes too,' Kathleen offered.

So, in we piled to Kathleen's flat. I was filled with mixed emotions. Part of me was happy to be spending time with Marianne Burgess, who seemed very keen to hear all about the Nighttime Passengers and what exactly I had meant by 'those of us not lucky enough to find someone to crash with'. Part of me just wanted to strangle our Kathleen for telling Marianne all about Colette and my domestic arrangements.

'So,' our Kathleen began (we had progressed from tea and cakes to wine, two bottles to be exact, and tongues were loosening up a bit), 'Marianne, when are you going to put this young man out of his misery and bonk his brains out?'

What? I couldn't believe what my sister has just said. In front of me. And to Marianne Burgess. I prayed for the floor to open and swallow me up. How could Kathleen do that?

Marianne seemed less fazed by the remark than I was, to be honest. She merely took another sip of wine and said, 'I'm not his type.'

'What? Are you kidding? Do you know how much he goes on about you? Ever since you two met at the Adelphi,' our Kathleen continued, relentlessly.

'Kath-leen, ple-ase,' I said, 'leave me some shred of dignity. God, I thought men were meant to be bad when they got together but this… this is just too wild for me.' Nor was it over yet.

'So why has he never asked me out then?'

Why had I never asked her out then? What about the Married Man? I'm not a fool, or a glutton for punishment.

'Obviously he needs his sister to help,' Kathleen laughed. 'It's obvious to everyone, except for the pair of you, that you're made for each other.'

Our Kathleen stood up and suddenly a lot of things made sense. Not so much to her, because she was wobbling all over the place. She'd obviously drunk a lot more wine than I'd imagined. That's one thing about my family, all of us; the more we drink, the looser our tongues become. Kathleen was making her way across to me. She succeeded, but only just. The last few steps became one as she lost her balance completely and dived towards me. She regained a bit of her composure and sat on my knee, her arm around my neck, squeezing it so tightly that I felt she was going to break a few bones: maybe her own, maybe mine, probably even both.

'Look, youse two,' she began, in a slur, 'you're my two favourite people in all of Liverpool – in all of the world actually – and I know you're going to get it together. Just fecking hurry up will you, the pair of you, or I'll be an old maid.' With that she slipped off my knee into my chair and pushed me out of it, as she made herself comfortable behind me and passed out. Even in her drunkenness, she appeared to be pushing me towards Marianne Burgess.

There's not much you can say after a display like that, is there?

Actually, Marianne Burgess did have something to say and she said it quietly. There was no need though; if The Beatles had been playing full blast in the room, I doubt they'd have woken our Kathleen.

'So, Theo. How come you've never asked me out?'

Honesty was the best policy, I decided. 'Well, I always thought there was a man in the background.'

'A man in the background?'

'Yes, the Married Man.'

'A married man?'

'Yes, a married man.'

Marianne Burgess took another sip of wine, more like a gulp actually, and her lonely, sad eyes fixed me a stare, which was mixed with sadness and vulnerability, yet challenging at the same time.

'Well, there was actually, and I suppose there kind of is, actually,' she admitted.

'But… ' I realised what I was about to say, thought better of it and shut myself up by pressing a wineglass to my mouth.

'Go on?'

'No. It's none of my business.'

'No, it's fine, I'd like you to be honest with me. I know people think things about us but they never have the nerve to say them to my face.'

Well, I have to tell you, I was mad at this point. Mad because, for the first time in two years, I was aware that my worst fears were true. Marianne Burgess had a man friend, which was bad enough, but the fact that he was married made it even worse. I mean, if a girl has a thing for a man that she's dating and you also fancy the girl, it's okay; it's a bit of a challenge. But when the other guy is a married man, it's another thing altogether. Everyone knows that when a girl goes out with a married man, he's only going to go with her if he's 'getting his leg over', as the boys in the band so romantically put it. So, it's like everyone knows she's soiled goods, as it were. Although I've never been able to figure out how, with all the men around getting their leg over as much as they claim, it was ever going to be possible to find a girl who was still pure. But that's another point and for another day; perhaps the same day when I would consider why I was living with Colette and what was going to happen when she met her potential husband. For now, though, I had only my madness and anger to deal with.

'Well look, firstly you know for a fact that he's a cheat. Why would you want to go out with someone who was such an obvious cheat?'

'But you don't even know him, Theo. How can you sit there and call him a cheat?'

'Okay, Marianne. Maybe I'm missing something here, but this chap is married, right?

'Well, yes.'

'Now to me, that implies he has a wife, correct?'

'Yes, Theo,' she replied, with an undercurrent of 'this is ridiculous'.

'Does he by any chance also have children?'

'Yes, as it happens he does. A girl of eleven and a boy of seven.'

'Okay then, that's a wife, a daughter and a son, yes?'

'Yes, Theodore. With your powers of reasoning, I'm surprised you left college.'

'There you go. That's three people, just there, that he's cheating on and in the worst possible way.'

'You don't know what you're talking about.' She fired her words at me like bullets.

'By any chance, would you mean that he doesn't love her any

more, she doesn't understand him and he's only staying for the children's sake?' I knew I was probably blowing any chance I had with Marianne Burgess, so I was just turning my sense of loss into spite and throwing it all at this beautiful girl – a girl who was fast becoming a woman.

'Well, no. I mean, yes. No, actually, he doesn't love her any more.'

'So, because he doesn't love her any more, that means he's not cheating on her and his children,' I replied. I could sense she was close to tears but I relented not even a little. 'Come on, Marianne, I would have expected more from you.'

'Thanks,' she said. A funny thing to say at that point, I know, but that's what she said.

'Does his wife know?'

'No, of course not,' Marianne snapped.

'And how, then, is he not cheating? How is he not being deceitful to his wife, the mother of his children? The woman he took oaths to love, honour and cherish, "till death do them part?' He's a fecking cheat, Marianne. And if you ask me, he's a worse one for cheating with you. Sure, you're not much older than his daughter.'

My anger stunned the room into silence, a silence broken only by our Kathleen's snores.

'So, you're planning to take on the daughter and the son as well? What happens when he gets as tired of you as he did with his wife? You know, once a cheat, always a cheat. How will you feel then? How will you feel when he's cheating on you, Marianne? Will you be so understanding when he's saying to other young girls, half his age, "It's sad but Marianne just doesn't understand me," and you'll be stuck with a family and a half, probably? You just be careful, Marianne Burgess.'

And then her tears came, through her gentle sobbing.

I rose from my chair. I'd been sitting on the arm of it since Kathleen pushed me out of it. Now I walked towards Marianne, then, for some unknown reason, I put my hands in my pocket and walked away from her, over to the fireplace. I turned to look at her, rising up and down alternatively on my heels and toes. Hands still in my pockets, rocking back and forth. Then I realised that this was exactly what I'd seen my father do in a family crisis. He would stand on the hearth, warming his bum, hands in pockets, and rocking from heel to toe as he lectured us about something. I was becoming my father! I didn't mind this, though. It was not that I wanted to become my father; it was just that he's a good man in a world of few good men and I could do a lot worse.

Marianne Burgess just kept sobbing gently. Well, I was partially to blame for that, I must admit. She seemed to be content there, gently sobbing away until I went over, bent down and awkwardly put my arm around her. 'Please stop crying.'

My protective comforting actions were all it took to start the full waterworks. I kept my arm around her in a 'there, there now' posture, but it looked and felt clumsy, as I was half bent over yet still trying to stand. So, I sat down there beside her and put my arm fully around her. She seemed to take refuge in my comforting sounds, i.e. 'There, there, please stop crying', because she turned around to me, put her head on my shoulder and her arms around me and clung to me. Marianne Burgess was clinging to me as if her life depended on it.

'God, youse two are quick workers after all,' Kathleen grumbled, as she stirred to life. She smiled at us and then, thankfully, turned over and went back to sleep.

Chapter Nine

From that day on, things moved, on all fronts, like a cat through a pigeon loft. I mean, maybe not as violent or as destructive as a cat in a pigeon loft, but there certainly were feathers flying everywhere.

Decca Records turned down The Beatles, saying that 'guitar groups are on the way out', yet simultaneously signing Brian Poole and The Tremoloes. You figure that one out. I must admit, I've never been able to figure out record company folk; Vincent McKee, the guitarist from the Nighttime Passengers, says that they are androids. This makes sense to me and explains a lot. It is, however, slightly unkind to androids.

Anyway, Mr Epstein (no doubt well groomed and dressed in his perfect suit) next took The Beatles' audition tapes to the HMV record shop in Oxford Street, London, to have some records manufactured so that he could distribute The Beatles' work to other record companies. I'll bet the chap in the record shop was from Liverpool. This chap in HMV liked the music so much he contacts Syd Coleman, boss of Beechwood Music, and tells him about the group. Mr Epstein visits Syd – a good, solid, honest name, Syd, isn't it? Syd, as it happens, know this other chap. This other chap turns out to be Gentleman George Martin. George Martin wasn't as impressed by the songs on the demo(nstration) acetate as he was with the overall sound. He did, however, invite The Beatles down to London for an audition on June 6th 1962: a red-letter day for Beatles fans.

Because George Martin was drawn to more offbeat records, he must initially have seen something in The Beatles that Decca and others had missed. He'd produced the Peter Sellers classic 'Goodness Gracious Me', and he had also worked with the Goons. The Beatles passed the audition. George Martin invited them to sign with the Parlophone Label, part of EMI, thus encouraging the Liverpudlian cynics – and there were a few of them – to shout, 'Ah, so much for The Beatles. They're now signing to a comedy label.'

Not to worry. The Beatles had their recording deal. EMI had

contracted to pay them a penny for each and every double-sided single they sold. It was a one-year deal, with a commitment for four singles. As with all recording contracts, there was an option that EMI could choose whether to renew at the end of each year. The royalty rate was due to rise by one farthing per year so that, if each of the four options mentioned in the contract was to be taken up by EMI, Mr Epstein's group would receive the princely sum of two pence per single. Mr Epstein, under his contract with The Beatles, would take 25% of this. The remaining one-and-a-half pence was for the Fab Four.

Whatever the terms they had agreed, they had what they most wanted: a deal with a record company, which would allow them to record their songs. It was time to take advantage of their contract and start making records. The recording career of the most success-ful group in the world was about to begin. However, there were more troubled waters to sail through before that. The trouble brew-ing in the background could have wrecked The Beatles' career in one fell swoop!

A question had arisen concerning the abilities of Pete Best. Being a fellow drummer, I'm in a bit of an awkward situation here. There is nothing as soul-destroying as putting in the time with a group: you know, doing the slog; the late nights; the bad food; the cramped, uncomfortable vans; cheesy, urine-smelling dressing rooms; promoters who rip you off; double bookings; internal fights; and, especially if you are the drummer, the lead singer stealing your girlfriend. As I say, you go through all of this in the name of music and *your* band: one for all and all for one. And you do persevere with all of that, then your group secures a recording contract and it looks like you are all set. Then you're dumped.

I'd have to say that Pete wasn't all that bad, you know; not really. He could keep the beat, and though he wasn't particularly flowery, he was solid. George Martin was probably the final Vox AC30 that broke the Comer van's back axle. He told Brian Epstein after the audition that he didn't think Pete Best was up to it and so he, as record producer, would be using a professional drummer for the first record session.

Pete was summoned to Brian's office – accompanied by his friend, lodger and road manager, Neil Aspinall – where Pete was duly informed that he was no longer part of the group. Ringo Starr had replaced him. Ringo was currently performing with Rory Storm and the Hurricanes at Butlin's holiday camp, up in Skegness.

Being the brick that he was, Ringo couldn't join The Beatles immediately as he couldn't leave his mates Rory and the boys in the
smelly stuff and just jump ship, so he gave them a few days' notice
to find someone else. Brian Epstein asked Pete if he would do the
next gig, which was in Chester. I'd like to have been a fly on the wall
when Pete gave his reply.

That was my lost opportunity. That's where my big chance could
have presented itself, you see. If only I'd opted for a new set of drum
skins and not a girlie Christmas present for Rosemary who, as I
mentioned, duly dumped me on Boxing Day. If I had made the other
choice and stayed with the Blues by Three, I would have met Paddy
Shore, who joined after I left. Perhaps I would have been around
and known him quite well by the time he, in turn, auditioned with
the Les Stewart Quartet. That would have been my chance to meet
George Harrison – remember when he deputed with the Quartet?
Next thing you know, The Beatles might have been passing their
EMI audition and, having decided to replace Pete, maybe, just
maybe, George would have remembered me. There you go; whatever will be, is. But you can't dwell on what could have been, and
you know what? No disrespect to Pete Best, but Ringo is a *master* of
the skins. He's musical. He plays the kit the way Paul McCartney
plays the bass. Not as a backing instrument, but as an instrument of
music. Few drummers, if any, are as musical and as soulful as Ringo.
Then, to add insult to injury to all us pretenders, he does it with such
apparent ease. A lovely drummer and a lovely man: Ringo Starr.

But, in June 1962, not many people knew how lovely he was
and, quite frankly, they didn't care. The fans were enraged. There
were protests and orchestrated shouting and chanting at the Cavern
gigs: 'Pete Best for ever, Ringo Starr never.' Poor George Harrison
even suffered a black eye at the fist of an irate fan. Was the whole
thing handled badly? I don't know. I mean, there is no correct way
to handle someone's firing. Pete Best had been the newest member
of the group, and he was described by the local rag as 'mean, moody
and magnificent'. He had a large following, didn't smile a lot, was
dark and, on the negative side, had missed a few gigs through
illness.

There was a lot of surmising going on around the 'Pool as to the
real reason for the dismissal. You know, things like John, Paul and
George thought Pete was too popular with the fans; that he was too
good looking; that they were worried his mother, Mona, was wanting to be too involved in running the band, and so on. Before Mr

Epstein took over management of The Beatles, Pete Best had looked after the bookings, collected the money and handled all the organisational stuff.

Maybe his face just didn't fit. I've been in groups where you just need to replace one of the musicians, not because of their inability but because they are a right royal pain in the arse. Anyway, encouraged by the excellent managerial skills of Brian Epstein and his operation, they – The Beatles – just got their heads down, pulled up their collective collar and got on with it. Hey, I've just thought; it may have been during this period that they developed their famous jackets. You know, they were pulling the collars up so much, to avoid the Pete Best fans, that they eventually pulled the collars off altogether, developing the world-famous look – not to mention saving future tailors hundreds of yards of material. Okay, maybe not. Anyway, they got on with it, even sending Pete Best a telegram wishing him a happy 21st birthday. He was on stage with his new band, Lee Curtis and the All Stars, and the telegram was read out at the gig. This little gesture would have helped to promote Brian Epstein's stance on the matter, which was, 'No hard feelings.' Mr Epstein wanted the world to feel that it was all perfectly amicable. Besides which, his current priority was The Beatles' debut single.

They'd already made their radio debut for the BBC, with a 'Beatles in Concert' on June 11th. You wouldn't believe the buzz of hearing them on the wireless for the first time. It gave us, to some degree, a taster for the coming months.

September 4th, they all piled into Neil's Comer van once again and headed down to London to make the first record. A special day. A *magic* day in the world of music.

Chapter Ten

The remaining flying feathers we were talking about, well, they were mine of course. They would be, wouldn't they?

But listen, in case you were wondering, nothing else happened that afternoon. I mean at our Kathleen's, between Marianne and me. We hugged for a time and she kept whispering 'It's not what you think', but I figured that if she wanted to tell me any more, she would in her own good time.

We sat like that for some time, gently rocking back and forth. I mean, I'm not a pervert or anything but it was great for me. I was close to Marianne, so close I could smell her perfume. It was sensational. Why do men get such a great hit out of a woman's scents? And while we're on the subject, why are we so attracted to the female form? The quick and easy answer is the procreation of mankind. But there must be more to it than that. I mean, that would account for us wanting to do the wild thing but it doesn't account for why women look even more beautiful after you've made love to them. And if this boy-girl thing is only to continue mankind, how come a broken heart (a) feels so bad and (b) can't be fixed in the hospital? I mean, it hurts me more than anything else I've experienced, but there is no doctor, nor dentist, nor surgeon who could help me with my ailment.

My unrequited love for Marianne Burgess. Marianne Burgess, with her lonely, sad eyes.

When I returned to Colette's that evening, I must have looked distracted or something because she immediately homed in on me.

'What's up with you, chuck?'

'What? Oh, nothing.'

'You look all sad, that's all.' She came over to me and took me in her arms. 'Where have you been?'

'I've just been around at our Kathleen's.'

'Oh, yeah?' she whispered, as she leaned closer into the nape of my neck, behaving like a puppy dog licking up to you. But, like a puppy dog, she was also using her nose to do a bit of investigating.

'This is not Kathleen I smell. I know her perfume. I tried it on myself. Who is this you've come home wearing, Theodore Hennessy?'

'I swear to you, I've just been around to our Kathleen's.'

'Theo, don't lie to me. Please don't lie. We have an agreement.'

'I swear to you, Colette, I haven't been with anyone else in that way. Honestly.'

'My father always says beware of people who use the word "honestly" when they talk to you.'

'What do you want me to do? Tell you a lie? Tell you I've been with someone?' I tried to smile, to lighten the conversation. Then I pleaded. You can see my problem, can't you? I mean, I had been with someone; Marianne to be exact. But I hadn't been *with* her in the way Colette would be assuming. It was a tricky one: come clean and not be believed, or lie and look like I was lying. My sister always told me never to play poker; she claimed that I have too honest a face. She didn't mean it as a compliment.

'Oh Theo, how has it come to this?' she said.

'Come to what?' I said.

'Come to us arguing about women,' she replied.

'But we're not,' I said.

'Then what are we doing?' she asked.

'We are dealing with you making a mountain out of a molehill,' I replied

'So, there is someone else?'

'Please, Colette,' I said.

'Well, if you believe I'm making a mountain out of a molehill then you are admitting that there is something there, admittedly something small, but something with someone else,' she said.

'Come on. How did you work that one out?' I said.

'Well, if there had been no-one else, you would have said "You're making something out of nothing," but you didn't. You said I was "making a mountain out of a molehill." Now, I'm no brain surgeon, but that implies there is something, or someone, no matter how small or unimportant you figure them to be.'

'Colette, please let's not do this,' I said.

'Do what?'

'Argue about other girls.'

'So I was right. There is someone else,' she said.

'Look, it's simple. The perfume thing; I was round at our Kathleen's and I bumped into Marianne,' I said.

'Oh God, not Marianne Burgess, the mystery woman, the love of your life. So she's the molehill,' she said.

'No, she's not,' I said.

'I know she's not,' Colette replied, 'that's what I'm worried about.'

'It's not what you think,' I said.

'Oh, God. How long has this been going on?' she asked.

'There's nothing going on,' I said, the snappy rat-a-tat conversation draining me, partly because I knew where it was going and partly because I knew there was nothing I could do to stop it from ending where it had to end. Colette was close to tears, and all over nothing. This whole conversation had spiralled from nothing and was now recklessly out of control, heading for the cliffs.

'Theo, how could you?' she whispered. I breathed a sigh of relief for the change in pace and tone. Perhaps a detour away from the cliffs was possible.

'Colette, honestly.' I realised what I'd said the second the words left my lips. I knew, with that one word, 'honestly', she would know a red flag had been shown.

'Look, apart from what I've told you about my feelings for Marianne over the years, she's a good friend of my sister's. That's never going to change. Right? Equally, no matter what I once thought about Marianne Burgess, nothing is ever going to happen between us. It was a dream I once had, but it's like we're on different planets. She barely knows I exist. She passes the time of day with me and is polite to me because I am her best friend's brother. It's that simple. Really.'

'So, how come you're smelling of her perfume?' Colette replied, still talking very quietly and barely holding, but never breaking, eye contact with me.

'Well,' I cleared my throat and decided that now things had settled down a bit I would take my sister's advice and quit the game of poker. I threw my cards on the table. Not a great hand, to be honest. 'There's this man, you see, who Marianne's been having a scene with. I think they're going through a hard time. We were talking about it and she started to cry. She looked so sad, crying about this man, that I really felt for her, so I went and put my arms around her and hugged her. She hugged me back and rocked gently in my arms until she stopped crying.'

'Theo, how could you?' she said, the floodgates finally opened.

'But Colette, I just told you, nothing happened.'

'That's what you tell me,' she sobbed.

'But our Kathleen was there all the time,' I pleaded.

'Yeah, and what was she doing when all of this was going on?' Colette asked, showing me a bit of light at the end of the tunnel.

'Sleeping.'

'Sleeping?'

'Sleeping,' I repeated.

'So how would she know whether you kissed or not?' she asked, fighting back her tears and wiping her tear-stained face with a handkerchief (my handkerchief, actually). Colette liked the man's size and my Aunty Lila had bought me a boxed set of four white handkerchiefs with TH embroidered in the corner, in green. Colette loved them and always had one with her. Now the proud TH was smeared with runny make-up and the handkerchief looked like a Christmas cake that had been left out in the rain.

'But the fact is, we didn't kiss, Colette,' I replied, a touch of impatience creeping into my voice. When you know each other as well as Colette and I do, and you have a conversation in which you address each other continuously by your Christian names, then something is wrong – badly wrong. And the day had been so great. Absolutely brilliant, in fact, until our conversation.

'Okay. So answer me this, Theodore Hennessy,' she began. I thought this was it, this was the big one, and she was using Christian *and* family names. I was in for the full monty. 'If she had tried to kiss you, would you have kissed her back?'

Ah, please, now that's not fair, is it folks? Come on. It's like saying, so if Marilyn Monroe wanted to kiss you, would you have kissed her back? It was like asking John Lennon and George Harrison, 'If Brigitte Bardot wanted to kiss you, would you kiss her back?' That would have been an equally unfair question to them because I'd just read in the local rag that they were both rather attracted to the French beauty. But I'd never been in a position to find out the answer to my question.

'Okay, I'll answer you that, but firstly you answer me this. If Tony Curtis wanted to kiss you, would you kiss him back?'

'Oh yeah, big chance, Theo. I wasn't sitting with him in my arms in my sister's living room, was I?'

'It doesn't matter. It's still a valid question,' I pushed, sensing a little bit of an advantage.

'Oh, don't be so bleeding stupid, Theo. Tony Curtis is a movie star.'

'Yes, but we're dealing with fantasies here, aren't we? You know, the land of imagination. Non-reality.'

'We're dealing with you sitting in your sister's living room with, by your own admission, Marianne Burgess in your arms. Marianne Burgess, who you have told me on numerous occasions was your big teenage crush. And you are sitting there together, and she's vulnerable and crying and your sister's asleep, and I want to know would you have kissed her if she'd let you. And you're refusing to answer my question. That's what we're dealing with,' Colette snapped, squashing my badly stained handkerchief aggressively in her hand.

'Yes.'

'What? Yes, we are dealing with whether you would have kissed her, or yes, you did kiss her?' Colette snapped again, in her best Lassie mode. She had the bone between her teeth and wasn't going to part with it until all the meat had been devoured. So be it. Let her have the bone and whatever other scraps she could find on it.

'Yes, I *would* have kissed her.'

That was it. Colette burst into an almighty fit of crying and through her sobbing, advised me that yes, although we'd agreed to have a loose relationship – i.e. we didn't love each other – she did, in fact, love me and had been hoping that I would eventually come around and return her love. Now, however, she realised, she said, that because of Marianne Burgess this could never happen. She also advised me that I had broken our original agreement – you know, the one about not going with anyone else when we were living with each other – so would I please get out of *her flat*. There and then. Immediately and for good!

Now, she had me on a technicality. I had admitted that if I'd had the opportunity, then yes, I would have kissed Marianne. But it was a dream. I was being found guilty for the thoughts in my dreams. Mind you, my father always used to say to our Kathleen that thoughts can be as sinful as deeds. My mother had another one that was something like 'You'll be hung for killing whether it's a pig or a human.' I'm not sure she'd fully grasped the concept but no matter. Either way, it was curtains for Colette and me. Finito. The end. Over.

But more importantly, and with immediate effect, I was home-less.

Chapter Eleven

I went round to see my sister immediately. Our Kathleen let me sleep on her sofa that night but suggested I move back in with our parents the next day. I was on the verge of doing so and was discussing the very subject with my mate in our band, Vincent McKee, when he suggested I move in with him. He had a spare bedroom in his flat and, as it was a great space in a great location – Sir Thomas Street – the rent was killing him. What he was suggesting was that the rent could half kill both of us.

So, I moved in with him the following Monday morning. At about the same time, The Beatles were in the famous Abbey Road Studios, recording their first single and B-side. This would have been early Sept 1962 (Sept 4th and 11th, according to those who know). They apparently re-recorded 'Love Me Do' on 11th, using Andy White (whom George Martin had already booked as the studio replacement for Pete Best) on drums and Ringo on tambourine. That's how you can tell the difference between the two versions today. If you hear a tambourine rattling away in the background, then it's the version featuring Alan White on drums. If there is no tambourine, then it's Liverpool's master of the skins in the drum seat. I've listened to both versions on numerous occasions and I can tell you that, as far as I'm concerned, Ringo's is the better version by far. But there you go; it's all down to personal taste, isn't it? Poor Ringo, though, he must have wondered if they were planning to do a Pete Best on him, too.

On October 5th 1962, Parlophone records released the first Beatles record to an unsuspecting world. A world where the iron curtain *wasn't* your neighbour's curtains, leaden with coal dust and dirt from the street. A world where the family car in Liverpool belonged to Mr and Mrs Lucky up on Dale Street. A world where a girl wore her hair up in a beehive and boys wore theirs down in a DA (duck's arse). A world free from a war that had all but mentally and physically destroyed our parents' generation. A world where two up and two down meant how many families fitted into a house and not how many rooms the terraced accommodation boasted. A world where divorce, bankruptcy, out of wedlock and infidelity were words not so much spoken in hushed tones as spelt out every time they were used. Having said that, I'm sure there were some very interesting variations on the spelling of the word 'infidelity'.

'Love Me Do' was the A-side, the main side, and the song disc jockeys were directed towards. It was backed with another John Lennon and Paul McCartney song, 'PS I Love You', on the flip side. At one point, 'PS I Love You' was even discussed as being the main track, but someone at EMI pointed out that this had already been the title of another successful song. On 'Love Me Do', Paul sang lead vocals and played bass guitar; John played acoustic guitar, harmonica and sang back-up vocals; and George played lead guitar. Originally, he played the melody of the harmonica introduction to the song but the quirkiness of John's wild harp blowing was elected instead. We've already discussed the drumming. Was it Ringo or was it Andy White? Hey, you decide. But one thing I can tell you for a fact: it certainly, not to mention sadly, wasn't Theodore Hennessy. Very sadly.

The single was numbered R 4949 and was released in the now famous Parlophone sleeve-cum-dust jacket. It entered the charts at number 22. We couldn't believe it. A group from Liverpool in the national pop charts. Not only were they local but they were also ordinary chaps like the rest of us. They'd stand their round in the pub, you know. Pop stars weren't meant to do that.

So, the following week, I bought the *New Musical Express*, the music paper that printed the pop charts (the week's bestselling records). To show you how confident I was, I read the charts from the top down – the first week, being unsure, I had read it from the bottom up. Top of the charts was Elvis Presley with 'Return to Sender'; then Cliff Richard with 'Next Time'; then Britain's current number one group, the Shadows, with 'Dance On'; then 'Dance With The Guitar Man' by Duane Eddy; followed by Frank Ifield; Brenda Lee; Rolf Harris; The Tornadoes with Telstar; Susan Maughan; and, at number ten, Chris Montez. Still no sign of The Beatles.

At eleven, we had Stan Getz and Charlie Byrd; then Del Shannon at twelve, followed by Ray Charles' incredible 'Your Cheating Heart'. Next was Marty Robbins; then Joe Brown and Pat Boone; and then... YES! YES! YES! There it was, at number seventeen in the national pop charts and sticking out like a sore thumb, dear old

R4949. I sent the paper flying up towards the ceiling. I couldn't believe it. I was so happy. I couldn't believe how happy I was. Vincent thought I'd gone crazy but when I told him what had happened he was equally jubilant. A Scouser group was in the top twenty. And there were over 300 more Scouser groups, including the Nighttime Passengers, ready, willing and able to follow. If I'd been fretting about Colette dumping me up to that point, I certainly wasn't afterwards.

The Beatles were in the fecking charts.

I mean, apart from Elvis and Ray Charles, and I suppose even Cliff (who was a wee bit wild in those days), you had to realise the kind of music that was ruling the charts at that time. The old wave was very evident. But now… well, this was the beginning, hopefully, of a new shift. The first new wave and, unlike the gentle lapping of the one that came before, this wave was going to smash and thrash upon the rocks before it.

There it peaked, R 4949 that is, at number 17. It stayed in the charts for a long time, about three months, and they say the majority of the sales were from Liverpool. And why not? I personally bought four copies. One for Colette – I kinda felt it was right to do that as the group had meant so much to both of us; one for myself (obviously); one for our Kathleen and one for Marianne Burgess, which I kept good as new and prayed I would have the opportunity to give to her. Talk around town was that Brian Epstein bought 10,000 copies for his NEMS stores, and wasn't he entitled to? Whether they were to satisfy the demand or *create* a demand didn't matter one little bit. And if the demand didn't live up to his expectations, he could think of the purchase as an investment. I mean, mint copies of R4949 are now worth about a hundred quid, each! So, his original investment would now be worth about a million quid. So you know what? The man wasn't a fool. I think that figure of 10,000 was probably correct because our friend at NEMS had told us that she thought The Beatles' single was going to do very well. 'Very well indeed,' she reported, 'if the size of our stock is any sort of gauge!'

Mr Brian Epstein advised us all, via the local rag, that The Beatles' first single had topped the 100,000 mark and that their new single, yet another fabulous song from John and Paul called 'Please Please Me', would be released in the new year.

In the meantime, all of Liverpool was abuzz with Beatles news. There were even rumours floating around that John Lennon had secretly married his girlfriend, Cynthia. As we all know, this proved to be true but at the time, no-one believed it. How could someone like John Lennon, a man with desires on Brigitte Bardot, marry a local girl? Could he? I mean, what chance did the rest of us have? Surely there must have been queues of girls throwing themselves at him, every night.

They certainly worked their socks off at that point. They did everything they were asked to do. All reasonable requests were considered, be they radio, TV, press or gigs. They were playing lots of gigs and then they'd play some more gigs. Mr Brian Epstein directed this part of the operation with the precision usually credited to Montgomery for his World War Two strategy.

A look at their date sheet found them doing, from the 28th September to 31st October, 29 gigs, 3 radio recordings and 2 TV shows. Included in this was the incredibly busy day of Oct 17 when they did a lunchtime session at the Cavern Club, then they drove over to Manchester to the Granada TV studios, rehearsed two songs ('Love Me Do' and 'Some Other Guy') between 3 and 4pm (for sound), and then again from 4.15 to 6pm (for the cameras). The Beatles performed the two songs as their debut TV appearance (People and Places) between 6.35 and 7pm. Then they hightailed it out of the studio, with the trusted Neil Aspinall and Mal Evans speeding them back to Liverpool for an evening show at the Cavern.

At the beginning of November, The Beatles sailed to Hamburg for a thirteen-night run at the Star Club. They returned to Liverpool on the 15th November and drove to London on Friday 16th for a radio broadcast with Radio Luxembourg. Saturday, they played (by their own admission) a disastrous gig in Coventry, at the Matrix Hall. Sunday night it was back to the Cavern for another of the 292 times they would play there, and then on Monday – boy, was Monday a busy day for them – they started off with a lunchtime session at the Cavern Club and then, in the evening, played Smethwick Baths Ballroom *and* The Adelphi Ballroom in West Bromwich. On top of all that, there were all the press interviews and photo sessions. They, quite literally, wouldn't have had a moment to themselves.

I'm telling you all this only because it serves to show you that The Beatles didn't happen by accident: they worked. But they were Northerners and hard work didn't scare them. They were talented – of that fact there is no doubt – but right then, when it mattered most, they were doing everything that was expected of them. And, on top of all that, they were professional in the old sense of the word. Yes, they liked to poke fun and they were irreverent, but they were also polite, well-turned out, punctual and charming. They had also developed into a great bunch of friends. Ringo was not only a great drummer, he also brought some social cement to the group. There were no factions in the band; it was very much a case of one for all and all for one.

People liked to work with them. Neil and Mal did their job efficiently and effectively, without the slightest hint of fuss. They took care of business; they took care of the boys. And the team – Paul, John, Ringo, George, Brian, Neil and Mal – took care, great care, of the fans. And you never had the impression it was anything other than genuine consideration because that's exactly what it was. John and Paul had been working at it too long, and too hard, to let band politics get in the way of the success that was now seizing The Beatles.

John would frequently call out to the others, 'Where are we going?', to be greeted with a reply of, 'To the top.' 'To the top of what?' John would continue, and all four would join in on their war cry, 'To the toppermost of the poppermost.'

And they weren't kidding.

Chapter Twelve

Christmas comes but once a year and, in 1962, it came in December. When I was young I was convinced that there were some years when Christmas might come twice or maybe even three times a year. I don't know how I figured that out; maybe something to do with the months passing faster in some particular years. But I'll always remember that particular Christmas for its bittersweet circumstances.

Now I bet you're thinking: He started to date Marianne Burgess, bought her a Christmas present and she dumped him on Boxing Day. Well, you're wrong, she didn't dump me on Boxing Day. The reason why? Simple, we still weren't dating.

True, we had become closer. I felt I knew her a bit better.

Vincent and I were getting on great. People tend to think that only couples need to get on well when they're living together. Wrong! When two flatmates are not mates, life can be pretty unbearable. You know when your girlfriend does the kind of things that annoy you, like leaving the top off the toothpaste; never washing out the tea pot; putting ciggy ends in the toilet; and leaving messy bedrooms with underwear thrown all over the place? Incidentally, a girl's underwear always tends to look less sensual to me when I've seen the same garments lying around the bedroom floor for the last few weeks. Where was I? Well, let me see, other annoying things like always tidying up in the living room; eating tomatoes with every meal; rushing to the toilet when you are shaving or washing your hair or cleaning your teeth, with a 'Don't mind me' as she sits down on the bog to do her business (the answer to your obvious question: there wasn't one, a lock that is); asking your opinion about what dress to wear, then *always* ending up wearing a different one; saying sorry for one of the above offences when you know she doesn't really mean it (*sorry,* that is); and the fact that the list she has of the things she hates about you is longer than the one you have about her.

But all of the above really don't matter because, at the end of each day (well, at least three times a week or, at the very least, during a Sunday morning lie-in) you know you're both going to do the wild thing. That's not going to happen with a male flatmate is it? Actually, now I come to think about it, with the rumours that were floating around Liverpool about Mr Brian Epstein, I'm not sure that that last statement is exactly correct; but I'm sure you'll know what I'm getting at.

Anyway, Vincent was the perfect flatmate. He kept his space clean, he kept out of my space and he helped to keep our space clean. He had no annoying habits and was a really decent chap to boot. We both thought we were on to a bit of a winner with the flat. Two boys in a group (we'd now become a great group by the way, and having a permanent line-up and lots of gigs helped), neither of us exactly God's gift to women, but we both figured the group would compensate for that with lots of groupies – a different one back at the flat each night after a hot, sweaty gig. The business, in fact.

No, not exactly. Not even close. In fact, none, zero, zilch. As November turned into December and Colette became a distant memory, I hadn't even christened my new bed. To add insult to injury, Colette was on her second boyfriend since my hurried departure. The first one, if you really want to know the truth, came three days after she dumped me, brazen hussy! That lasted a couple of weeks and then she met her new steady boyfriend, Josh. To add further insult to a growing injury, didn't she only go and meet him at one of our, the Nighttime Passengers', gigs?

Before I moved in with Vincent, he'd been pulling a girl every now and then; nothing spectacular, but steady. Now, with Hennessy in residence, his success level had dropped – to the same as mine: zero. It was different for him, though; he just went successfully from girl to girl, not really working at it or getting himself concerned about it. He didn't seem to miss them or need them. On the other hand, I'd just finished with a steady girlfriend. The girl of my dreams was still the girl of my dreams: Marianne was never going to transverse the astral plane. The mind does funny things to you, you know, when you're in that position; it makes you think that you're never going to go out with another girl again. The morning after Colette dumped me, I felt different. Maybe it was all bravado, but I thought, Great, I'll show her. I'm going to have some fun being single again.

Think again, Theo.

Maybe I was getting desperate and trying too hard, but one generally accommodating wee girl, Valerie (who I know for a fact had done the wild thing with at least two other members of the band) just laughed at me when I asked her out. I mean, she wasn't being malicious or anything, she just plain and simply laughed her socks off when I asked her. Laughing off another part of her clothing and I'd have been okay, but socks weren't much use... unless, of course, you believed the rumours floating around Liverpool about... no, seriously, just kidding. When Valerie stopped laughing, she moved closer to me and said, 'But you're Theo Hennessy, Kathleen Hennessy's little brother. Run away with you and find a nice wee girl to settle down with,' and she disappeared into the crowd, laughing.

God, was that my reputation? I was twenty-two years, three-and–a-half months old and I was respectable already. People had me pegged for someone who wanted to settle down at twenty-two bleedin' years old. I was young, I was in a pop group and I was meant to be sowing my wild oats. If I didn't hurry up there were going to be a few barren fields around Hatton Garden. So I did what anyone else in my situation would do; I went to my sister, our Kathleen, for advice.

I was completely honest and told her what the wee girl had said.

'And I should think so too. That skitter Valerie Jones knew she would have had the back of my hand around her ears if she'd tried,' Kathleen reproached me.

'What? You mean to say all the girls are scared of what my big sister will do to them if they go out with me? I'm twenty-two, Kathleen,' I said, in disbelief.

Our Kathleen was turning into a beautiful-looking woman. She had inherited my father's sense of mischief and my mum's classic looks, but now she was also developing her own individuality. I'd say she'd a lot more class than the competition. She was a no-nonsense girl, and I suppose it's easier to be a no-nonsense girl if you look as stunning as our Kathleen did. As I sat there with her in her living room that day, I realised for the first time that she'd blossomed into a stunning woman. It's funny, you know, this thing about looking at things from both sides; being on the inside, as it were. Let me explain. Here was Marianne Burgess, beautiful but apparently unavailable, at least to me. So unavailable, in fact, that you convince yourself she could never be interested in you, not even in the slightest. At the same time, you see another beautiful girl, my sister Kathleen, with all the boys drooling over her. All of them fantasising over her perfect body – and what a body, with her classic colleen purity – but never dreaming, for one moment, that they would get anywhere near her. But I knew, at the same time, she was as desperate to meet a member of the opposite sex. Yes, she was going to be more fussy and not run off with the first one who came along. But, at the same time, when she was sure that he was the right one and prepared to protect them both, I have to tell you that our Kathleen was just as desperate to get it on with the right boy as I was to get it on with Marianne Burgess. I tried to imagine Marianne Burgess sharing similar feelings but I never, for the life of me, could imagine myself in her arms.

I suppose what I'm trying to say – and one of the secrets I have learned in life – is that women are just as desperate to meet a man as we are to meet a woman. The main difference with them is that their desperation is to meet the *right* man. We, the male species, generally don't mind having a few false starts along the way. The gentler sex's main flaw, as I was finding out with Marianne, was that the right man always appeared to be someone other than the one who was asking them out.

As I considered Kathleen there before me, every inch my superior, I couldn't help wondering if she'd done the wild thing yet and if so, with whom. I know you're not meant to have those kinds of thoughts about your sister but, in a way, I was thinking then more out of envy. I concluded that she hadn't. I had her down as one who wouldn't need to wait to marry before she did the wild thing, but equally she was going to be as sure as possible that the first man she lay down with (as they have a habit of saying in the bible) was going to be the man she lay with all her life. Yes, she was as desperate as I was, but not so desperate that she was going to belittle herself, and shame our mum and dad, by having people talk about her. In her book, it would be all the more delicious when she knew for sure that he would be the right man. And what a lucky man he would be.

Anyway, we were talking about my sister's looks, weren't we? Add to her looks a head for figures, her organisational skills, her natural authority with her co-workers, and she would be running The Royal Court Theatre (where she was currently working in the box office) before she was thirty – in four years' time.

'So, what do I do, Kathleen? Since Colette dumped me I've not been able to get off with anyone.'

'Get off with? Get off with!' she repeated, in disgust. 'What a horrible turn of phrase, Theo. Please say you've not been able to *date* anyone else. For starters, you might find it easier in female company if you adapt your language slightly.'

'Okay, okay, I've not been able to *date* anyone else. The end result is the same. What do I do about it? Are there any of your friends who would go out with me? No, sorry, make that date me?'

'It's not like the market, Theo. You don't just go down, pick the ripest one that you can afford and take her home with you. A girl likes to feel wanted for herself and not for what a boy thinks he can do to her. Think of the girl first, Theo. All that other stuff will come later, but only if you get the first part right,' Kathleen lectured her captive audience. 'I really don't know why men always feel that they have to have a girl, any girl, by their side anyway. Can't you see all of that just gets in the way of meeting the right girl?'

'But, Kathleen,' I began, then hesitated, considering whether or not it was best to be totally honest. I decided to go for it. 'I have met the right girl.'

'You have? I mean, you have?' she spluttered

'Yes. Marianne Burgess. She's my perfect woman, Kathleen, but I'm never going to be able to get it together with her. Sorry, sorry. I meant, of course, that I'm never going to be able to date her.'

There, I'd said it. At last, I had shared my true feelings with someone. At last, I'd shared with someone what I'd felt since the very first time I saw her at the Adelphi. If she'd been a laughing and joking kind of girl, I'd probably have forgotten about her after a few months but, because she had that lost-child look in those lonely, sad eyes, she had haunted my mind every day since. I wanted to take her in my arms and protect her, shield her from what was bothering her; but, at the same time, I wanted to ravish her because I'd never seen a woman who looked so naturally, and classically, beautiful. She wasn't physically fragile, where you thought you might hurt her if you touched her. No. She looked perfectly capable of physical activity – the picture-perfect kind of figure. But she appeared mentally and spiritually fragile, and that was, I figured, where I'd have to be careful.

Well, I wouldn't really have to be careful, 'cause I'd never be in that position, would I?

Chapter Thirteen

Kathleen wouldn't be drawn on that. She didn't play those kinds of games where, when I'd say, 'I'd never be in that position, would I?' she'd respond with, 'Of course you will, darling baby brother.' Agh, no. No false hope from our Kathleen. Instead, she took the conversation in a more general direction.

We talked on about what I wanted from a woman. I didn't really know. I just felt I wanted to be with one. In my wildest dreams, I wanted to be with Marianne Burgess because I thought I could happily spend the rest of my life with her. But after that, why I wanted to bother with women I hadn't the slightest idea. I mean, it's all great from a distance, the whole package. When you don't know them, you imagine them to be this mysterious person but when you meet them, and after they've undressed very non-sensually, you find they have the same faults and flaws that you have. Then you find that making love is not exactly making love. It's hot and sweaty and messy and you find that those sexy bits you wanted, so desperately, to grab and touch are just bits of skin filled with fat. So it's quite easy to come to the conclusion that, mostly, it's not really worth the trouble.

I loved to feel as warmly towards a girl after the wild thing as I did just before. But that wasn't something I could articulate to my sister. We didn't resolve anything; you never do, do you? But it's always good to unburden yourself. And our Kathleen had a way of making me feel that I wasn't an alien.

Three days later, the Nighttime Passengers were playing one of our twenty-six gigs at the Cavern. It was an evening session, and who should turn up but our Kathleen and Marianne Burgess. You could have knocked me off my drum stool with a paradiddle, so to speak. Luckily for us, the Cavern was packed to the rafters. Well, it wasn't really 'cause we were in the basement (of course) and there are no rafters in the basement, but you know what I mean. It was packed to the top of the sweat-coated bricks in each and every one of the alcoves. And, even though I say so myself, we were brilliant.

It was one of those occasions when the gig was the sum total of the audience and the band together.

The band is good. The audience enjoys the music and shows the band that they are enjoying the show. The band feels excited by this so they become great. The audience reacts to the greatness and spurs the band on to even greater heights. I felt ten feet tall when I walked off the stage; mind you, I would have had to duck my head by one foot if I had been ten feet tall, to avoid bumping my head on the cellar roof. Mick the Bouncer showed Marianne Burgess and our Kathleen into the dressing room. Mick drank with my dad, so he'd obviously been keeping an eye on Kathleen, as his mate's daughter, like that generation had the (good) habit of doing.

There was a spot of head turning going on, and I was extremely chuffed that quite a bit of the head turning was for my sister. Mind you, if any of them had tried anything with her I'd have seen them off, I can tell you. I knew where they'd been!

Our Kathleen brought Marianne over to where I sat. She seemed happy, very happy. She told me she'd really enjoyed the show but, to be honest, dressing-room conversations are a bit unreal, aren't they? I mean, she'd hardly come into the dressing room and tell us that we were crap, would she? At the same time, from the buzz about someone, you can tell if they'd really enjoyed themselves or not.

Personally speaking, I've been to gigs like The Beatles or Ray Charles, and just stood, transfixed in the space, immersed in the music coming from the stage; it is the best feeling in the whole wide world. It's true. But you try and describe that feeling the following morning to your mates and it's impossible. I've tried many times and it's absolutely impossible.

I must have been gawking at Marianne Burgess or something equally unsociable because our Kathleen suggested we all go for a coffee in a late-night cafe down on Lime Street, near the station. That's probably why it stays open so late, for the railway station staff and passengers. Sounded like a good idea to me, so we said our goodbyes and disappeared. Vincent winked at me as I turned for one final glance into the dressing room. Did I say dressing room? I meant a hole in the wall that you had to reverse out of before you could turn around. I think our Kathleen spotted his gesture but she kept stum about it. Maybe he was even winking at her and I'd spotted it. Whatever.

On the walk to the cafe, I suddenly realised what our Kathleen had done. She had brought Marianne Burgess down to the Cavern to see me, doing what I was good at. She had wanted Marianne Burgess to experience me in my natural environment. At the Cavern I wasn't a little puppy dog, chasing around after Marianne Burgess' coat tails. I was my own man. I was in a great musical group and we were playing to our audience, and a full house at that.

It certainly seemed to have worked because there was a different air to Marianne Burgess that night. She was still dressed in black from head to toe but I swear there was a hint of a smile in her eyes.

'I hadn't realised,' she began, 'that what you do was so exciting. I thought that when Kathleen said you played in a group…' she paused to laugh out loud, showing her crooked front tooth. Tonight though, because of her smiling eyes, the tooth didn't look ill-placed. In fact, it added to her character. The one flaw on an otherwise perfect body made her real and approachable for the first time. The fact that she wasn't self-conscious – as I felt she usually was about hiding her twisted tooth – made her appear more human, more down on my level. I'm not belittling myself but it's just, sometimes, you meet a girl and you think; I'm not in her league, I haven't a chance. Forget it. So you listen to yourself and you do, you forget it.

Wrong.

Well at least our Kathleen says it's wrong. She says you should always go after what you want. Equally, she says to be prepared for disappointments. I think she probably got that one from our dad.

She's always asking me why so many beautiful women end up with ugly men. Simple: good-looking guys are too scared to ask them out. Who would ever have thought that Joe DiMaggio would have been able to talk to Marilyn Monroe, let alone marry her? Our Kathleen claims it's all down to chemistry. Mind you, I've noticed she's quite fussy about how her own boyfriends look.

'I thought when she said that you played in a group, that it was…' Marianne began for the second time, now trying ever so hard to pick her words carefully, 'well… you know, a bit like a school band.'

'You mean crap, Marianne, don't you?' Kathleen laughed across the table. She and Marianne Burgess were on one side of the table, yours truly on the other. Three coffees sat before us.

'Well, yes, in a way,' and she burst out laughing. Then she took a sip of her coffee and, as she did so, she had this thing that she did. She stuck the tip of her tongue out slightly before she put the coffee cup to her lip; as if to catch any potential drops that might spill. It was a very sensual thing to do and I'm afraid to admit I could feel myself about to change back from the successful and impressive pop drummer into that little puppy dog. She ran her tongue around her lips, and I swear I nearly fell to the floor. 'And the songs are excellent. Who writes them?' she continued.

Okay, this was safe territory. I was back on my own turf again. 'Well, the songs are mostly covers. The Beatles do some of the same songs, and then the songs at the end: "Be Glad", Vincent the guitarist and I wrote that one and "The Steam Machine", Vincent wrote by himself.'

'I'm impressed, Theo. I didn't know that,' my sister cut in proudly.

'There are a few others, originals, that we haven't put in the set yet. It's just that people like to hear songs they know.'

'Yes, but when your own songs are as good as "Be Glad" and "The Steam Machine", I'm sure people will want to hear them just as much,' Marianne Burgess, fast becoming the Nighttime Passengers' biggest fan, gushed.

We chatted there for about an hour and then our Kathleen said she needed to get home and was going to get a taxi. At this point, my drum kit would probably still have been sitting on the stage at the Cavern, unpacked, so I'd probably have to go around there tomorrow morning by myself, break it down and pack it away. As long as I got it out of there before the lunchtime band arrived, I'd be okay. Unless, of course, my good mate, Vincent McKee, had packed it up for me and put it in the van. Yeah, and pigs might fly.

I figured I'd walk the girls over to the station where they'd get a taxi. I'd say goodnight to them and then I'd call back at the Cavern, just in case. As we reached the station, Marianne Burgess must have still been buzzing because she said, 'I don't feel like I want to go just yet. I feel like a walk. Do you feel like walking home, Kathleen?'

'Away with ye,' Kathleen replied, quoting our dad's oft-used phrase, 'but I'm sure our Theo would be happy to walk you home.'

Does a bear shit in the woods? Allegedly! But in this case, *definitely*!

And so, that is how I got to be walking Marianne Burgess home. I wouldn't go so far as to say it was our first date, but you had to be thankful for small mercies, didn't you? Well, I don't know about you, but I did.

We saw our Kathleen off and Marianne Burgess and I walked down St John's Lane, arm in arm. Her move not mine, but I didn't

complain. I intentionally didn't walk too fast; I wanted this journey
to last forever and if not forever then as close to forever as possible
– at least an hour. It was a cold December night, a very cold
December night, but it was fresh and our way was lit by a full moon
from a midnight-blue, cloudless sky.

We walked in silence for quite a time, the moonlight showing off
the magnificent Liverpool skyline. It's funny, when you're growing
up you take all of that – the buildings, the countryside and whatnot
– for granted, but at that point, for the first time, I started to appreciate how spectacular some of the buildings were and how breathtakingly brilliant the Mersey looked at night, with the moonlight
sparkling along its stillness like magic dust. The same magic dust
that had me walking Marianne Burgess home. And the same magic
dust that had brought The Beatles back from Hamburg and the
birth of the 'Merseybeat' along with them. And, in my own small
way, I was proud to be part of that Merseybeat, a small part, but a
part nonetheless. Still a big enough part, though, for Marianne
Burgess to look at me with different eyes.

'So, you and Colette have spilt up, I hear,' Marianne started.
There were other drums working the Merseybeat patch now: the
famous Scouser bush telegraph. Maybe it was our Kathleen again,
only this time she'd dropped the right word in the correct ear. Sisters
are great and every boy should have one, but few are ever going to
have one as great as my sister.

'Yes, actually. Shortly after the last time I saw you. Remember?
Round at our Kathleen's flat?'

'Yes, Theo. I remember,' Marianne Burgess said, in a very soft,
childlike voice.

We walked on in silence so I figured she was thinking: 'That's
okay, then' about Colette, but for all I knew she could have been
thinking about her Married Man. That's a funny way to refer to a
human, isn't it? Yes, he was married but he was also a lot of other
things. Like he could have been a father, a son, a policeman, a taxi
driver, a school teacher or a carpenter, an Irishman or a Frenchman.
That could be it, you know? He could be a Frenchman, which could
be part of the attraction. Don't you think? But anyway, he could
have been any of these people but he was definitely still an individual, yet I'd been referring to him for over a year now as 'the Married
Man'.

Mind you, in a way that was a safety factor. That was all he was
to me and the less I knew the better. I didn't want to be able to paint

the features to this man who was with Marianne Burgess, so there-fore the thought of *them* couldn't hurt me. If I knew, for instance, that he was Irish and a good chap, I would think of my dad who was a great man and say, okay, I can't think badly of him. He could be an okay guy, you know. People my age were getting married too, so he could be someone like me. He might play in a group. You know, it's not outside the realms of possibility that the Married Man was John Lennon, if the rumours around the 'Pool were true. I mean the rumour about John getting married; there were no rumours about John and Marianne Burgess. Thank God. That would be the end. Marianne Burgess *and* John Lennon: where would my loyalties lie?

But back to the Married Man. Marianne Burgess liked him, for heaven's sake, so how bad could he be? It just suited my purpose to think of him as a cheat. It made me feel better to think that he wasn't worthy of her. But he'd been around a long time now. You don't think she loved him, do you? I felt that would be the worst.

All these thoughts were floating around my head like the stars flying about the galaxy above us, way above us, when Marianne Burgess dropped her bombshell. She just came right out and said it.

'I've finished with the married man.'

I refrained from jumping and shouting with joy on the street there and then. It would be a bit like dancing on his grave

'Oh,' was all I could utter. And it came out more as a grunt.

'Yes, I hated you for what you said to me at Kathleen's that day,' she began.

'But…' I protested, but she cut me off.

'I hated you because you were right. I thought about it a lot and talked to Kathleen about it a lot, and I realised that if he loved me the way he said he did, he would have left his wife by now. It's not that I wanted him to leave her, it's just that I was in love with him, Theo, and I wanted us to be together. But I realised we'd both have incredible pain to go through to be together: him with his wife and family and me having to deal with that, and deal with the torture of being the other woman. I feel sympathy for them now, you know. The "other women". I can tell you, you don't walk out of your house at night thinking, I'm going to find me someone else's husband. You don't go out thinking, Whose home can I wreck tonight?' Marianne Burgess said, pulling me closer to her with her entwined arm.

After a time, the distance to Whitechapel in fact, she continued, 'No. You go out and it's a great adventure and you don't know who you're going to meet. You just hope he's a decent guy and he'll treat you well. Once that happens, you breathe a sigh of relief. You like them. They are caring, gentle, romantic, handsome, clean, raggedy hair, deep brown voice... '

'Okay, okay, no need to rub it in, you know,' I interrupted, turning to look at her.

Marianne Burgess laughed, a generous laugh. Like in the cafe earlier tonight, she was happy to laugh and it was good for her. Good for her soul.

'So, you fall for him – for Ken – and you fall hook, line and sinker because he's everything you ever dreamed you wanted in a man. He's perfect. Too perfect in fact, so there must be a catch. There *is* a catch and when he thinks the moment is right, he hits you with it. He drops his bombshell: "You know I'm married." Of course, he confides in you that, "She doesn't understand me", "We've been growing apart for years", "We live separate lives", "We only stay together for the children", "We haven't had sex in ages", "I was going to leave her before you came along. It's nothing to do with you. You're not to blame. What we have is special," and on and on and on. But it's all too late because you're hooked, you're in love with him. Maybe you love him less than you did before he told you he was married, but you still love him. Your love was so bountiful that, should you take a bit away, there's still more than enough left to consume you,' she suddenly stopped talking, stopped walking and looked at me.

'I'm sorry to dump all this on you,' she said, looking me in the eye.

'It's okay. Honestly,' I replied, and she took my arm again and we continued walking.

'It's just, well... Theo, I find it so easy to talk to you and I've just suddenly realised that this is the first time I've ever discussed this with anyone. Kathleen knows that he's married but that's it. And it's funny but it feels good to talk about it. I don't know if I still feel great from the gig or great from talking to you, or just great because I'm relieved to be finished with him. All the lies, Theo. You wouldn't believe them. You knew they were lies the minute the words left his lips. You knew he'd just told you a barefaced lie but, because you loved him and you wanted to believe him, you tried to believe him and then you'd be let down again. You're waiting at home for him to come and pick you up and he doesn't show, no notice, no warning; you're just sitting in your poxy flat waiting for him to take you

out somewhere special, just like he'd promised. "Don't worry love,
I'll make it up to you." If I had a penny for every time he uttered
those words, I'd be as rich as the owner of that shop,' she said, as we
passed NEMS.

'Then you find yourself doing things you hate yourself for. Like
following him home to find out where he lives and then spying on
him; you know, waiting for him outside his house to see if he's going
to come out. And one night he does and it's with her, his wife. It's
this woman you've been brainwashed into hating, and she's fine,
you know? She's not a monster. She's quite a looker, in fact. But do
you know what's the worst thing of all? They look good together.
They are warm and loving to each other and it doesn't look like
there is a chance in a million years of them splitting up. But still you
listen to his stories and accept them. You were right, you know. You
hit the nail right on the head. "How can you go out with a cheat?"
you said. "If he's cheating on his wife, he'll cheat on you next."
That's what you said and that's what Kathleen said.' Marianne was
nearly spitting her words out, her anger getting the better of her.

'Then the word goes around that you are seeing a married man
and your mates sympathise with you but generally, most people
treat you as a socially unacceptable stealer of married men. I felt all
this negativity around me. It was so hard to shoulder. Then I
realised I must be looking miserable and sad all the time, because
that's how I'd been feeling. I remember when I was young and
growing up, I'd feel sad all the time. I didn't know why, I just felt
blue. I couldn't wait to grow up because I thought when I grew up,
I would lose the blues. I felt I'd be wise enough to work it all out and
get on with having a happy life. Then I grew up and my first... my
first real boyfriend is Ken; it's turned out to be a disaster and I feel
even bluer. I don't want to feel this way any more, Theo.' Marianne
Burgess uttered the last few words with so much desperation, I
really felt for her.

'And it wasn't my fault, Theo,' she continued, 'I didn't know. I
didn't know that he was married. Honestly, I didn't know. If I'd
known, I'd have sent him on his way with a kick in the whatsits.'

'Testicles, I believe,' I offered, trying to find some way, any way,
of lightening the mood.

'What?' she said, in disbelief.

'Testicles,' I repeated. 'You would have kicked him in them if
you'd known he was married.'

Whether it was the ridiculousness of my remark, the humour or just a release valve for her to finally get her confession over, she just laughed and laughed until she caught a fit of the giggles. That got me started and then we both had the giggles. Eventually, we couldn't remember what we'd started laughing about in the first place and by the time we did, we were outside her house.

We stood there for a time, neither of us knowing what to do. I thought she was just being polite, standing with me until I left, but it was bitterly cold and, with all the walking and laughing, I hadn't realised just how cold it was. So, there I was, about to bid her good night; truth be told, I was trying to work out if I should kiss her on the cheek, kiss her on the mouth or just shake her hand. These decisions are very difficult at the best of times but with Marianne Burgess, the girl of your dreams, standing in front of you, you just can't afford to feck up so you end up not wanting to make any decision.

Marianne Burgess made my decision for me.

'Will you come in, Theo,' she said, 'and have a cup of coffee?'

Is the Pope a Catholic?

Chapter Fourteen

Marianne Burgess' ground-floor flat was small. It wasn't really a flat; more of a bedsit. She had one big (ish) room, which was her living room-cum-bedroom. To the side of that was a very small kitchen, and to the rear of that was her bathroom. Beyond her bathroom wall, I imagined there was another similar flat. Two flats on each of the three floors, in fact. Her flat was very clean and equally tidy. Not particularly girlie – apart from the bathroom with all her make-up and clothes strewn around everywhere – but not exactly untidy; more a case of lived-in. I had reason to use the bathroom shortly after we arrived, and it was weird to be able to view Marianne Burgess's smalls so closely. As I have already admitted to you, I had considered her underclothes and how she filled them quite a bit over the past eighteen months. Now I could see the shape (brief) and colour (black and white). Not black and white on the one garment, you understand. Perhaps this new information would be enough to fill my dreams for the next eighteen months. It's sad really, isn't it, the morsels we are prepared to accept when the unobtainable is so unobtainable?

By the time I returned to the living room, Marianne Burgess had two steaming cups of coffee ready for us. She gave me a warm smile as I walked across the room. I pretended to look around the room, just in case my face was a telltale red from the embarrassment of having spied upon this person's undergarments. The room had, in the front-window alcove, a stripped pine table with three matching chairs. I mean, the chairs matched each other as well as the table. The table seemed to be her living centre as well as her dining area. This area was filled to overflowing. Along the window end of the table, she had a valve radio and a large letter rack, absolutely stuffed with opened letters, bills, flyers and whatnot. The other end had a eight-inch high stack of magazines and, to the right of that, a couple of foolscap notebooks, beside which was a Robertson's Jam jar, washed out and stuffed with pens and pencils. That corner of the table was obviously her corner. I imagined her sitting there in the daytime, writing down her thoughts – thoughts mainly about the Married Man, I guessed – sheltered from the sunlight by a light blue, flowered curtain that fell, full length, to the floor.

In the centre of the table were the tomato sauce, salt and pepper, which looked like they'd recently been joined by a sugar bowl and milk jug (in matching blue-and-white stripes). The little drop of freshly spilt milk by the milk jug was the giveaway. Looking back into the room from a seat at the table, you had, on your left, an alcove, a fireplace and then another alcove. Both alcoves accommodated the chimney. In the first alcove (the one nearest the window) was a cupboard, white-painted doors closed, about two feet high. Then, above that, were shelves and shelves of books. I didn't have time to examine them properly but there was a copy of Edna O'Brien's *Country Girls* lying open, cover up (ruining the spine, no doubt) on the sofa.

Above the fireplace was a print of an obscure painting. One of those disjointed affairs where the eyes were feet and the hands were plates. Works of art, which receive praise when created in kindergartens but, when attempted by adults, end up being exhibited in art galleries and costing thousands of pounds. Sorry, it's just one of my pet hates. I like paintings to depict scenes and people that are recognisable. The more I recognise an artist's success in detail, the more I like their work, which sadly means I didn't get Stu Sutcliffe's work at all. However, there are enough people out there whose opinion I respect, like John Lennon for instance, to lead me to believe it's probably my fault and that *I'm* missing something. It's just that, to me, a bowl of fruit should look like a bowl of fruit and not a carbuncle on a dog's street deposits.

Equally, I didn't have the confidence in my criticism of modern art to tell Marianne Burgess that I thought her print was crap! She apparently liked it; it was the only distraction to the unblemished whiteness of all her walls. On the other side of the fireplace, in the alcove, there was a Phillips Gramophone Player and a few records lying on top. The minute I walked into the room, I had noticed the telltale green Parlophone dust jacket of R4949, lying haphazardly beside Elvis Presley's *Blue Hawaii*, *West Side Story* and Ray Charles' *Modern Sounds in Country and Western*. The remainder I couldn't make out, but there were quite a few. Against the back wall – the wall that separated this flat from the one at the rear – there was an incredibly comfortable-looking sofa, which was covered in dark blue material and matched the two easy chairs comforting the fireplace.

Completing the circumference of the room was a door leading to a small kitchen, then on to the bathroom. It would appear that space was stolen from the back of the garden flat. Continuing around, you had the entrance door and then, on the final wall, a bed – too large to be a single and too small to be a double – covered entirely with an eiderdown, similar in colour to the sofa and easy chairs. The floor was covered with a well-polished, blue-and-white patterned oilcloth.

'God, I'm still buzzing from your show. I've had a great night,' Marianne Burgess said, suggesting an end to the evening, even though we were both still wide awake.

'Would you like me to go?' I asked.

'No, not at all. I'd play you some music but I don't want to wake up the neighbours,' she replied.

'It's fine. I'm happy to talk.'

'Yes, it's just that I've a great Buddy Holly album I'd like to play you. Maybe some other time?'

Encouraged, I replied, 'That would be fab.' 'Fab' and 'gear' were new 'Beatle' words to describe something great and *young*. I was trying it out on a stranger for the very first time and felt a bit self-conscious using it. But Marianne Burgess didn't seem to be bothered about it one way or the other, so it must have worked. We talked about everything, on and on for ages, into the deep of the night. The Beatles, our Kathleen, Manchester United, Ken (the Married Man), Colette (not my sister) and plans for the future. Mine was to try and get the Nighttime Passengers into the recording studios. I explained we needed to have a record out in order to move up to the next level. Marianne was very encouraging and supportive. Her ambition was to successfully complete her course at the teacher training college, pass her exams and then secure a job somewhere – probably away from Liverpool – teaching English.

Before we knew it, it was three-fifty and the gentleman in me stood up and said I should go; it was late and I was obviously keeping her from her bed.

Marianne Burgess stood up too and crossed the room to stand so close to me that I could smell her perfume, a heather affair.

'I've enjoyed myself tonight, Theo. You don't know what it means for me to be able to say that. I can't remember the last time I enjoyed myself. I like you,' she stopped and smiled at me. It was a wonderful smile; it was as though her twisted tooth had miraculously straightened during our long conversation. 'I'm thinking that I like you a lot.'

We both stood there awkwardly for a time. It could have been a few seconds, it could have been ten minutes, but I was happy just to be there, drinking in all of her and her words. For heaven's sake, don't you realise what Marianne Burgess had said to me? She, with her very own beautiful, sensuous full lips, had told me that not only did she like me but she liked me a lot. I suppose I should have tried to take her in my arms and kiss her. But I didn't want the embarrassment of misreading the situation and ruining the current magic. She took my hand; not like you take someone's hand to shake it when you greet them or bid them adieu, but she took my hand *in* her hand.

I could feel myself shaking. I wasn't ready for this. For what? She was just holding my hand, after all. I told myself to stop having these thoughts immediately. Marianne Burgess was being friendly to her good friend's brother. Simple as that. Yes, she was beautiful and yes, I'd been in love with her from the very moment I met her. On top of that, she was so incredibly, brilliantly beautiful and sexy, I wanted to ravish her as well. That's another funny thing about me. In my book, there are three kinds of girls. Those you fall in love with and you want to be decent with; those whom you are not in love with but they just turn you on so much that you want to do everything naughty you can imagine with them; and then the third kind is Marianne Burgess. For me, she was the only one in existence in this rare group, where you love them to death but you also want to bonk their (not to mention your own) brains out.

Here I was, so close to her that I felt I could smell the type of soap she used (Cussons Imperial Leather, I was sure), but all I was able to do was to permit her to take my hand in hers. Hey, I've got to stop being a wimpo with this girl, I thought, or the little or no chance I currently had with her would become a less than no chance. I slowly moved closer to her. She didn't back away. Encouraging, I thought. I took her free hand in mine. I was looking into her green eyes and wondering if my eyes betrayed the fact that I was scared. Perhaps not, because she was still smiling at me. I moved my head closer to hers, so that I was leaning in towards her. There was about a foot between us. I wanted to leave that space for her, just in case she was going to avoid me at the last moment. I leaned in further and tilted my head slightly to the right so that our noses would not prevent lip contact.

I was shaking. I was scared. Scared because now there was no way back. In a way, I was like a pilot committing his plane to a landing. He had committed to a course for the runway and at that point, he was either going to have a successful landing on the runway or end up with an almighty splat in the marshes beyond. It was one or the other. I was now so close I could feel her breath on my face. This was her last chance to turn her head away politely with a, 'Goodness gracious me, is that the time? I've got to be up at seven-thirty in the morning.'

Her eyes were still smiling at me, encouraging me onwards. I hadn't taken her in my arms; we were still just holding hands. Our bodies were still apart but now I was leaning towards her. That was the exact moment I knew I was going to have a safe landing. I realised she was leaning towards me and tilting her head slightly to my left. Noses were going to avoid a collision. Then I closed my eyes as I felt her lips on mine. Her delicious, soft, tender, inviting lips.

All the times I had dreamed and wished and prayed about kissing Marianne Burgess could not have prepared me for this. There had never been a kiss like this in my life. And it was nothing but a kiss. Our bodies were still not touching; we were still hand in hand and leaning towards each other, but the only other parts of our bodies touching were our lips. I know I go on quite a bit about Marianne Burgess but I have to tell you, her lips are just so kissable and I love to kiss. And sometimes, I just love to kiss without it being a prelude to something further. In a way, it's the best kind of kiss. It's pure. It's what you should do when you finish making love, instead of using it as a way to start.

And I'm sure lots of people do, though perhaps not up against the band van outside a ballroom. But try it some time. Pick a time when you know you can't possibly make love and just kiss for the sake of kissing.

I honestly have no idea how long we kissed for. I really couldn't tell you because it wasn't an issue. But when we completed our wonderful journey and pulled back from each other, I found that we were still holding hands and I was thankful we were standing a foot away from each other. I'm not saying that a foot was *entirely* necessary but I think you'll probably get the picture.

I hadn't spoken for quite some time and I still had no words to say. Marianne looked like she wanted to say something. It was like she had a question for me but she was running it past herself before giving it to her lips to offer up. Eventually the words came.

'Look, Theo, do you think, um… is it possible… would you be able… ' she was struggling and I couldn't help her. 'Um… what I'm trying to say is, do you think it would be possible for us to lie in bed together, without... without you know... us having to make love? I don't want you to go but I'm not ready for us to make love yet, so I'd like you to just hold me. I need you to hold me.'

My heart was threatening to destroy the inside of my chest. The girl of my dreams had just said to me, 'I'm not ready to make love yet.' Don't you see the significance? She was implying that *at some point* she *would be ready* to make love to me!

So we ended up that night, fully clothed, lying under the covers of her bed in each other's arms, slightly uncomfortable for obvious reasons, but in heaven nonetheless.

Chapter Fifteen

The '60s go mad.

They say that every year of the '60s was like a decade from the past. I think they meant that everything, and I do mean everything, was changing so fast. Cars, fashion, cinema, art, literature and music were all exploding in front of our eyes, into a multi-coloured rearrangement of the past. The Beatles were part of this movement; in fact, they may even have been the catalyst for the explosion.

Now from what I can gather, movements are successful if they are heavily subscribed to. The more parts to it, the greater the momentum. This was particularly true with the Merseybeat. At the point that The Beatles were about to explode onto the world stage, there were another three hundred groups in and around the 'Pool – continuously fuelled by the non-stop dole queues – ready to bring up the rear.

You could feel it spreading throughout the length and breadth of Britain. We, the Nighttime Passengers, were certainly aware of this passion and hunger for all things Liverpudlian, with our ever-increasing requests for gigs up and down the country. Every city, and most of the larger towns, now had a club given over to the 'beat boom'.

I mean, if you think about it, the music scene before The Beatles was one we inherited from our parents. I'm talking about Cliff Richard; Joe Brown; Matt Monroe; the George Mitchell Minstrels; Lonnie Donegan; and on and on. This is not to be dismissive of these artists, as we've already discussed that even Cliff was quite wild in the early days, and Lonnie Donegan had spearheaded the skiffle craze, which had been the first musical coat John's Quarry Men wore. But, my point would have to be that all of them, and I have to include Elvis here, would have been, and were, favoured by our parents.

However, the Merseybeat and the beat boom were distinctively ours and most of the members of this new ragtag and bobtail scene were abhorred by the older generation. As you might guess, this gave us a greater passion for our music. Once people with an open mind, like my mum and dad, got beyond the long hair and the attitude and all that, they *listened* to the songs they were okay with, and quite enjoyed groups like The Beatles. I think at the very beginning, though, parents were all a bit threatened by the new sound and the new fashion of a generation they no longer recognised as their children.

But that didn't affect the sales of Beatles' records; if anything, it added to them. Christmas came and went and Jan 11th 1963 saw the release of their second single, 'Please Please Me' (backed with 'Ask Me Why'). This song, the A-side, was not George Martin's ideal choice for the second single. When The Beatles originally played the song to him, he felt it was more of a Roy Orbison-type ballad, which wasn't a direction George Martin felt The Beatles should take. He preferred a Mitch Murray composition called 'How Do You Do It'. He even went as far as having The Beatles record a version of the Murray song but John and Paul were adamant that the next single, and all subsequent singles, had to be Lennon and McCartney songs. I imagine the other George (Harrison) had different ideas but he was keeping quiet until something came along.

Anyway, as it happened, they all had their way. The producer suggested a few changes to the arrangement of 'Please Please Me'. You know, speed it up a bit, give it a bit of life and, on completion of the recording of the new version, Mr Martin announced over the studio intercom to The Beatles, 'You've just recorded your first number one.' And with the infectious introduction (again John on the harmonica), who could blame him for making such a rash statement? The record was sold to you in the first fifteen seconds. You were hooked. The song pulled you in deeper and deeper the further it went along. It was quite a simple, if risqué, song but that came to be The Beatles' secret. Never try and be clever, Trevor; just get started (listen to the uniqueness of all their song introductions), get in, say (or sing) what you have to say and get out of there. No time for hanging around.

George Martin kept the Mitch Murray song up his sleeve and recorded it shortly thereafter with another Liverpool group who were also managed by Brian Epstein, Gerry and The Pacemakers. 'How Do You Do It' earned Gerry and his mates their first number one single when it enjoyed a four-week run at the top of the charts.

Chartwise, 'Please Please Me', is where some of the historians, also known as train spotters or anoraks, disagree. Was it the first number one single or did it peak at number two? This was February 1963. The answer to this mystery is simple. The single reached number one in the charts compiled by the *New Musical Express*. This was also the chart used by Top of the Pops and the radio, and also printed in a few of the tabloids. However, the 'official' chart, or the one used by the industry, was the one printed in the Record Retailer. In this chart, 'Please Please Me' peaked at number two. Number one or number two, it mattered not a lot. The Beatles had a smash hit single that stayed in the charts for the following eighteen weeks, and Liverpool went absolutely berserk!

The Beatles and the music of Liverpool were heard everywhere. They appeared on Thank Your Lucky Stars, and they toured the United Kingdom with Helen 'Walking Back to Happiness' Shapiro on their first package tour. The tabloids suggested a liaison between George Harrison and the sixteen-year-old popular singer. John and Paul wrote a song for her called 'Misery', but her producer thought it wasn't suitable so she never got around to recording it.

John and Paul were writing everywhere and anywhere they could at that time but mostly, it would seem, on the tour bus. They wrote 'I'll Be On My Way' for another Brian Epstein artist, Billy J Kramer. Meanwhile, Kenny Lynch, who was also on the Helen Shapiro package tour, recorded the aforementioned 'Misery'.

However, it must be reported that all was not as calm as the Mersey on a summer's day in the middle of the nation's, possibly even the world's, most exciting new songwriting discovery. Around this time, John and Paul were causing a few ripples in the camp by arguing (perhaps *discussing*, would be a better way to put it),or rather discussing, whether it should be Lennon and McCartney, as on the 'Love Me Do' record label, or McCartney and Lennon, as on the 'Please Please Me' record label. As we all know, John won that battle and, egos aside, because of the 'Mc' position in the chosen form, aesthetically he was correct. Such disagreements, if there were many or even any more, passed quickly as The Beatles lit up the faces of the youth of the country. Within days of completing the Helen Shapiro tour they were back out on another package tour, this time with Chris Montez and Tommy Roe.

The Beatles' first album, produced by George Martin, was recorded in sixteen hours. That was just incredible. The original idea had been to make the first album a live one and record it at the Cavern, so perhaps they wanted to try and keep that live energy by recording the album quickly. Or, perhaps it could have been that EMI, Parlophone's owners, were still not sure of the viability of their new group and simply wanted to keep costs down. Either way, the album was called *Please Please Me* (the working title had been *Off The Beatle Track*) and the sleeve told us that it also contained 'Love Me Do' and 12 other songs. The Beatles were photographed for the cover at the EMI building in Manchester Square by Angus McBean, and it showed the four fresh-faced Scousers smiling down at you. Not surprisingly, Ringo, the last to join, had still not adopted the Beatle haircut.

Tony Barrow, a NEMS employee and the Beatles' publicist, wrote the sleeve notes. The album featured eight compositions credited to McCartney and Lennon on the disc and jacket, although Barrow's notes refer to them as Lennon and McCartney songs. The remaining six songs were covers they performed in their live set. Paul McCartney had gone on record as saying that he and John started to write songs because they'd be in their dressing room listening to the support group and, nine times out of ten, the support group would be doing some of the cover versions that The Beatles were about to do. Funny that, isn't it? The reason that the most successful songwriting partnership in the world was formed was so that The Beatles could do songs no-one else was doing.

For me, the revelation of the first album was the opening song – 'I Saw Her Standing There'. A classic rock song in every sense of the word and a song that could have been recorded by anyone, at any time, and would still have been heralded as a classic. It's just a throat-grabbing, toe-tapping gem and one we stuck into the Nighttime Passengers' set immediately, to great effect I can tell you. So much for McCartney's theory of them playing songs no other groups were! Vincent told me that after seeing how well it went down one night with us – in Manchester of all places – he felt it was the one song that nearly made him give up wanting to write songs.

With 'Do You Want To Know A Secret', Paul showed that beneath it all he really was a bit of a crooner. And then they leave you with a whack nearly as hard as the opening one; their interpretation of the Isley Brothers' standard, 'Twist and Shout', which they recorded at the last minute because producer, George Martin, insisted they needed just one more song. The actual recording you hear on the disc is their first attempt at it. John's voice is all but shot, but he gives it every single ounce of enthusiasm, commitment and passion he can muster.

Can you believe that this is what they were capable of at the end of a sixteen-hour recording session? A session during which the Fabs declined a 'down the pub' lunch break with George Martin and the engineer in favour of further rehearsals. This is The Beatles at their fecking best.

'Twist and Shout' still brings tears to my eyes. Listen to how absolutely tight they were. George Harrison wringing every last note he can from his guitar, swinging his way through the guitar break instead of taking a solo. Paul and George (vocally) egging John on and on, way beyond what is considered humanly possible. Surely some of the most exciting moments *ever* committed to vinyl. And then... then they do that wonderful rundown, just to top and tail it for you. I can still imagine them, even in the studio, doing their trademark low, sweeping bow at the end of this performance. I close my eyes and I'm right there with them. One take was all it took to nail this. George Martin had them perform the song a second time and it was, apparently, still note-perfect, but the first one had the magic you can still hear to this day. One take! Mind you, with the hours they spent playing 'Twist and Shout' and all the other tunes from their Hamburg set, they could probably have recorded a decent version in their sleep.

I noticed, in his sleeve notes, that Tony Barrow boasted the boys had enough original songs to last them until 1975 and with the chart success of this, their first album, it looked like they were going to need all the songs they could write.

I bought my *New Musical Express*, which coincidentally was including more and more about the Liverpool scene, to find the top ten albums on 30th March 1963 were:

1. *Summer Holiday*   Cliff Richard & The Shadows
2. *Sinatra & Basie*   Frank Sinatra & Count Basie
3. *I'll Remember You*   Frank Ifield
4. *All Star Festival*   Various Artists
5. *Girls! Girls! Girls!*   Elvis Presley
6. *Reminiscing*   Buddy Holly
7. *West Side Story*   Soundtrack
8. *South Pacific*   Soundtrack
9. *Please Please Me*   The Beatles
10. *Out of the Shadows*   The Shadows.

The Beatles were in the proper charts; the album charts. The singles' charts were great but with The Beatles, scoring two top-twenty chart entries, well that could have been a fluke. But *number nine*, first-week entry, on the album charts! Now that was the business. Just *the* business. And there was more to come!

The following week, The Beatles rose to number six. Then to number five. I must admit I thought it was peaking at that point, although our friend at NEMS told us they were having trouble getting enough stock to meet the incredible demand, so perhaps EMI were out of stock. The following week, it went to number three. Agh!! Then number two; but sadly the following week it stayed at number two. I was finding following this chart stuff very nerve-racking. I mean, if someone had asked me three months ago if I'd be happy to see The Beatles' first album reach the top twenty, my answer would have been an unequivocal yes. But then it went into the top ten and you wanted more, you know? Then the top five would be great, and then it achieves the number three spot and you feel it would be great if it were the second bestselling album in the country. Then it reaches number two and you start to long for the numero uno spot. And now here we were, going to suffer the ultimate indignity of the staid Cliff and the Shads keeping the Fabs, as they were now known locally, from the coveted number one spot.

But not to worry because the following week, May 11th 1963, The Beatles had *the* bestselling album in the country with *Please Please Me*. Their first album had reached the number one spot in the national charts. I wondered, as I walked around Liverpool on that day, what each of The Beatles and their manager were doing then. Were they sitting down together, reminiscing about all the hard times they had been through together? Was John wishing his best mate, Stuart, were still alive to savour and enjoy the pleasure of it all? Was he wishing, too, that his mum were still alive to see that he'd made something of his life after all? The banjo lessons hadn't been in vain. Or was he thinking of his newborn son, John Charles Julian Lennon? Was Ringo thinking back to his time with Rory Storm and the Hurricanes? Was George thinking about purchasing an expensive Gretch Guitar? Was Paul thinking about his mum, too? About how proud she'd have been of him? Was Brian Epstein thinking about his ever-growing empire?

The truth was they probably didn't have time to be thinking about anything other than getting through another busy day. Yes, Brian Epstein did now have a large roster of artists, but none of them meant as much to him as The Beatles did. He certainly wouldn't be happy for them to rest on their laurels. No, he'd be busy planning the next part of their rise because, nice and all as a number one album in your own country was, there was still the rest of the world to consider, and at that point few people, if any, outside the United Kingdom would have heard about Liverpool's Fab Four; John, Paul, George and Ringo.

In the immediate future, they were about to commence their first UK package tour as top of the bill: a bill that also featured Roy Orbison, and Gerry and the Pacemakers. On top of that, they had secured a weekly radio show, Pop Go The Beatles, for the BBC. Not bad for a group who, a year before, didn't even have a proper recording contract.

Chapter Sixteen

Naturally enough I bought a copy – from NEMS coincidentally – of the very same Beatles' album, *Please Please Me*, for my new girl-friend. Her name was Eleanor Rigby and the Fabs wrote a song about her. No, just kidding, but I thought it would get your attention.

Mind you, to me, six months previously, the chance of Marianne being my girlfriend was as likely as the chance of me meeting McCartney's song character. Marianne Burgess and I, to use my mum's quaint term, started to 'step out'. Actually, truth be known, we did more stepping in, if you know what I mean! I'm ahead of myself here, so let's go back a bit.

As you know, Marianne and I shared that fully clothed night of closeness and the following morning we bade our goodbyes. I felt close to her and I hoped she was going through a similar feeling. In her case, I imagined she was having reservations about getting involved with someone again so soon after the break-up of her situation with the Married Man, so I didn't want to push.

However, the following day I received a call from our Kathleen, which went something like: 'So, lover boy, I hear you and Marianne Burgess, ahm… "spent the night together" as she put it,' our Kathleen began, impishly.

'What? She said that?' I couldn't believe that Marianne and Kathleen had had such a conversation. Equally, I was deliberately trying not to say a lot because I was in the neighbours' (downstairs) flat, taking the call. They were nice about it and I tried not to abuse their hospitality too much, so that I could keep this line of communication open for the Nighttime Passengers.

'Nothing to worry about, Theodore. Actually, she said you behaved like the perfect gentleman Mum and Dad brought you up to be. I was proud of you. And guess what? Your gallant behaviour scored you major brownie points with Marianne. You'll never realise how much a girl sometimes just needs to be held close; how important it is for us and how heart-warming it is when we find a man who is happy to do just that.'

'Yeah well, don't tell my mates, it'll ruin my reputation. Mind you, forget that, I don't really have a reputation,' I replied, trying to be flippant but to imply that I didn't really want to discuss this matter on the phone, particularly on my neighbours' phone. Our Kathleen picked this up, I think, because she said:

'Look, we'll have a nice cup of tea and a chat about this some other time. In the meantime, Marianne said she forgot to give you her phone number and asked if I could casually find a way of passing it on to you without making too big a deal about it.'

'Very casual, Kathleen,' I joked, but couldn't carry the humour for too long. 'Did she really say that? You know, ask you to give me her number?'

'Yep!'

'Far out,' I said, no longer able to contain my excitement.

'So, are you going to take down her number or are you going to chant Beatle sayings like "far out" at me?'

'Oh sorry. Yes. Just a minute,' I said, committing to paper Marianne Burgess' telephone number. From the minute I scribbled it on the top of a page of an old *Daily Mirror*, it burned its way into my brain as effectively as the results of a branding iron: '940 1948'.

I immediately went out and ran up the road to a phone box. Realising that I didn't have any money, I raced back to my flat for four pence, grabbed a jacket, returned to the red romancing house and dialled her number. I heard her voice and, in my excitement, I pressed button 'B' instead of button 'A' and all I got was my money back. I repeated the procedure, pressing the magic button 'A' this time. The hungry phone box swallowed up my coins and I was connected to Marianne Burgess.

'Marianne?'

'Theo?'

That was promising, she recognised my voice immediately.

'Yes. Hi.'

'Hello, how are you?'

'Yeah, I'm fine, how are you?'

'Great, thanks for ringing,' she said.

She was thanking me for ringing. I continued, encouraged.

'Look, I was wondering, could we go out again sometime?' I felt myself doing some severe butt-clenching. Not the most romantic way to ask someone out. What would I do if she said no? I'd kinda have to say goodbye and set the phone down, which would be very embarrassing. I should have talked about The Beatles, or her teaching, or Kathleen, or something else for a while and then asked my big question. That way, it wouldn't look so rude if I finished the conversation quickly. It seemed like she was taking forever to answer my question. Was she thinking of a nice way to say no? A way to let me down gently? A way not to offend her best friend's brother?

Shit, I thought, I'd completely misread the situation. Marianne Burgess had said out of politeness to our Kathleen to pass on her number to me. She was saying that because I hadn't been a complete monster with her the other night. She had said to my sister to casually pass the number on to me. In other words, don't make a big deal of it. And I had. And now I was about to pay the price.

'Yes Theo. That would be very nice.'

'You would?' The words of disbelief had left my lips before I had a chance to think about them.

Marianne Burgess laughed. In my mind, I could see her face, lit up with laughter, and I could hear an electric crackle in my ear. Then the pips went. Guess who didn't have any more money with him.

'What's your number, Theo?'

I repeated the number, twice, and the line went dead. There were two other people waiting outside the phone box and they were both performing the unsynchronised Liverpool shoe shuffle – not as yet an Olympic event but practised for hours every night around the city's streets. The queue consisted of a girl in her early twenties with a beehive hairstyle and the trademark Woodbine barely hanging on her lips. Every time she took a puff, without removing the ciggy from her lips, the wind caught the smoke she'd just blown out and blew it straight back in her face. I figured she wouldn't notice me place my finger, and not the handset, back on the receiver. The other member of the queue was an acne-ridden teenager. He looked like he could have done with a warm jacket. I figured both of them were about to indulge in some love-torn coin popping and weren't in need of the emergency services. At last I had an opportunity to take my revenge for all the nights I'd had been left shoe-shuffling myself on the footpath.

The phone rang once and they both stared into the box. It looked as if Miss Woodbine would have liked to trample carelessly over my carcass as she wrestled the phone from my hands. I didn't care. I was back in contact with the voice. The voice of Miss Marianne Burgess. It's funny the way some voices just do it to you. Do you know what I mean? Usually with me it's Irish or French girls. I hear the female tones of either of those two countries and I have to admit I'm putty in their hands. Marianne Burgess' voice had the same effect. It wasn't that she sounded like she was from Ireland (which would have pleased my mum and dad a lot). It was more like... well, do you remember Barbara Parkins from Peyton Place? I mean, she was neither French nor Irish, but she had a voice that sent me to heaven every single time I heard it.

It's like when you're sitting with your parents watching TV and a naughty bit comes on. You feel self-conscious and uncomfortable because *you* know *they* think you don't know about all of this; you know, the naughty things that men and woman do to, and with, each other. But you don't want to leave the room 'cause it's unusual for such juicy stuff to be on TV and you don't want to miss it. You endure the embarrassment and the red, blushing face.

Well, with Barbara Parkins, it was exactly the same. I'd hear her voice and I'd be embarrassed about my thoughts. Obviously no-one else would be aware of my discomfort because all she would be doing would be something as innocent as asking for directions, or the time, or whatever. I, however, would be miles away, in some other place with Barbara. The only clue for my parents would be if they happened to look at me and see my beetroot face. But in all of this – be it naughty pictures on TV or a voice that sends pleasant resonance from your ears right to your toes, and causes tingling vibrations through every inch of the journey – we always seem to forget that our parents were once sons and daughters themselves, and went through the exact same embarrassment.

'Theo?'

'Yes, Marianne.'

'Ah, good. Where were we?'

'Well, I'd just asked you out and you'd said yes.'

'True.'

'Ahm, so, ah... well, I suppose I should ah.... I mean, you've probably got things to do so I should, you know, let you go,' I spluttered.

'Yes, well, I suppose...'

I could tell she was now feeling a bit awkward. I felt I'd better get off the phone before I outstayed my welcome, if indeed I hadn't already done so.

'Well, okay. Goodbye then,' I said.

'Okay, Theo. Is that all?'

'Yes, ah... I'll go now. Look, thanks for ringing me back. But, ahm, goodbye.'

'Theo.'

'Yes?'

'Are you sure there's nothing else?'

'No, it's okay, I'll leave you in peace. I'm off. Okay, goodb... '

'Theo.'

'Yes, Marianne?'

'Are you sure you're not forgetting anything?' she interrupted. God, I thought, she must want me off the phone pretty quick to be that blunt.

'No, no that's all. Sorry. I'm off then. Bye.' I was about to set the phone down; in fact it was about six inches away from my ear, but I could still hear her voice, so much smaller now.

'Theo,' she was shouting.

'Hello?'

'You're still there,' she seemed to be saying and appeared to be breathing a sigh of relief.

'Why, yes. Yes I am.'

'It's just that...well, Theo, when a boy asks a girl out on a date they usually... ' she started, but didn't finish her statement. She didn't need to, the penny had dropped. Dumbo!

'Sorry. God, sorry. How... absolutely... '

'No, it's fine,' she laughed, 'I find it kind of charming.'

I forced a laugh then. 'When would you like to go out?' I added to my laugh, expecting a reply of something like, 'How about Friday fortnight?' and then the eighteen days of misery would start.

'How about tomorrow night?' she said.

'Great!' I replied, in disbelief.

'I'll meet you in the residents' lounge of the Adelphi Hotel.'

'Okay, that's good for me.'

'I'll see you there at eight, Theo. I can see I'm going to be the one who has to do all the organising.'

I attempted another laugh. It was difficult because I'd got the shivers in the telephone box. Some gang or other had obviously chosen this particular telephone box for target practice because most of the glass at ground level was shattered to smithereens about my feet. The winds of the Mersey were freezing my whatsits off. I started to regret keeping Miss Woodbine and Mr Acne out in the cold.

'Yes. Musicians, we're all the same, Marianne,' I replied.

'I hope not, Theo. I hope not. Anyway, see you tomorrow at eight. Okay? Bye.'

'Bye,' I replied and, a few seconds later, I heard the click of disconnection.

Had she implied by her 'I can see I'm going to be the one who's going to have to do the organising' that we were going to be going out together? No, not possible. I was just reading too much into the situation. Anyway, not something to worry about at this stage. Be thankful for small mercies, Theo, I said to myself as I exited the well-aired phone box. You're going on a date with Marianne Burgess.

Chapter Seventeen

The problem with fantasising about someone for so long is that you overlook their real qualities. I've not been shy in revealing to you that Marianne Burgess was my dream girl during all this time. We are led to believe that Brigitte Bardot was John Lennon's dream girl during the same period. The main difference was that John ignored his dreams and married Cynthia. I, on the other hand, was about to go out on a date with my dream girl.

I arrived at the Adelphi at seven-forty. Actually, truth be told, I arrived there at seven-thirty but I realised that this was just much too keen. Added to which I didn't fancy sitting in the bar by myself for thirty minutes, so I strolled down to Lime Street Station, which was bustling with activity. It was bustling with commuters, all busy going somewhere or coming back from somewhere. Wouldn't it just be great, not to mention damned convenient, if someone somewhere could just redistribute the jobs or living arrangements. That way, everyone could stay put; save themselves a lot of money, not to mention stress, from all the travelling. But the human's sense of adventure prevents this and, at the same time, all the travel continues to make the world go round.

I people-spotted for a time, about five minutes or so, and then returned to the hotel. I was conscious of my dress-sense, or lack of it, as I mixed with the Adelphi crowd. I was dressed in black leather jacket, blue Levi jeans, white T-shirt (I was freezing in it but our Kathleen said it 'added to your boyish charm' – her words not mine) with pointed-toed, black leather shoes. It was kind of the Jimmy Dean look if you were American, but more like a sailor in civvies if you were a Scouser. I'd just washed my copper-coloured hair, with the result that it had taken on a life of its own, leaving me halfway between my old DA teddy boy hairstyle and the Astrid-inspired Beatle-cut. The Liverpool water is very soft and great for washing your hair. After a wash, your hair looks full and healthy. Sadly, in my case, it was still curling up in places I didn't want it to curl up at, if you know what I mean.

I was five-feet-seven and not destined to add any more height to my slim frame. I don't really know how I kept so slim. I'd inherited my mum's sweet tooth and was always shovelling sweets, chocolate and cakes into my beak. My favourite was Fry's Chocolate Cream. Our Kathleen reckoned it was the skin-beating on my drum kit that kept my weight down. She shared the same sweet tooth but found the only way she could keep her weight to a socially acceptable level was to stop eating entirely for two days every week. To me, she looked brilliant, or 'Fab'. We're all the same I suppose; more conscious of our curves than those around us are.

Anyway, there I was, dressed in my coolest gear and mingling with all these well-to-dos in the city suits, complete with bowler hats and brollies. The waiters and waitresses were running around in their cute black-and-white outfits, trying to keep the very busy residents' lounge happy. Why had she suggested the residents' lounge at the Adelphi? Had she been here before? With him? God, had she stayed here with him? That would be obvious, wouldn't it?

I could imagine her saying to me automatically, just like she would have said to the Married Man: 'Okay then, see you in the residents' lounge at the Adelphi' without thinking and then, realising she'd put her foot in it, been too scared to backtrack, preferring instead to leave the arrangements as agreed and hope I saw nothing strange in them.

But how could you fail to notice the grandness of the residents' lounge at the Adelphi Hotel? The hotel preserved a lot of what remained from a long-gone era. It was built as a service to those about to undertake the long passage to America, or for those who had just arrived, weary, from those far-off shores. Then, for some reason, Southampton became the designated port for the American traffic and the Adelphi, like a true Scouser, took the loss on the chin and developed a different clientele. It became *the* place to stay at the turn of the century: a time when classes were separated by those who wanted to enjoy the pretence of a country mansion but couldn't afford to live in one, so their trip to the Adelphi served as their daily, weekly, monthly or annual shot. The fact that they could afford to do so, in turn, separated them from those who now served these pretenders their afternoon teas, complete with scones, jam and fresh clotted cream; or coffee or even a bevy for that matter.

I found a quiet, secluded table with two comfortable seats, in the far corner. No room to accommodate unwelcome guests. Equally, perhaps a little too remote to catch the waiter's attention. At this point, I could have done with some Dutch courage. It was about seven-fifty and I started to get a fit of the 'God, she's not going to turn up' shakes. She's just being polite. She'd have a good excuse she could give to my sister to protect their friendship. Perhaps she'd even relented and gone back to the Married Man. This was their place, wasn't that my theory? Were they upstairs at this moment, wrapped in each other's limbs in adulterous passion? Oh God, please wipe these thoughts from my mind. Give me nicer ones to play with during the final ten minutes of being stood up.

Yes that's better, thank you. She did say that she liked my eyebrows and eyelashes. Our Kathleen said they were my best features. She also said (frequently) that I was the sort of person who would grow better looking the older I became. Did that mean I looked crap at this point in my life? Was I destined to have to live in limbo until I was as old as George Bernard Shaw, and incapable of doing anything, before I became attractive? 'Boys have other forms of attraction,' Kathleen had replied. What? Was that in general or was she referring to me?

And what were they, these other forms of attraction? I'd always been led to believe that girls liked older men because they knew what to do. They knew about important things. How not to come quickly, for instance. Now that has to be the big secret of life. How do you prolong the inevitable? In fact, sometimes you felt so excited you thought you were going to send another pair of pants to the cleaning bag before you even had a chance to get near the object of your lust. I'm convinced that's the main, and most successful, form of birth control: premature ejaculation. My personal secret, just before the tremors of the body-quake start, was to imagine the Queen sitting on the bog. Frightfully disrespectful I know, but it always won me thirty seconds or so.

So, Marianne Burgess had been with a married man. She'd know lots of secrets, wouldn't she? What would she even want to bother with a boy for? And where on earth was she? It was five minutes to eight and she still hadn't arrived. This was unfair. Why did it always have to be this way? If only I didn't want to go out with her so badly, it would be okay. You know, then I could be more casual with her. Come to think of it, I probably would be having more luck with her if I were being casual. The boys in the group were always mouthing on about, 'Treat them mean and keep them keen.' That would be so stupid if it wasn't so true.

At last I managed to get the waitress's attention, and ordered a half of Guinness. By the knowing smile she gave me, I figured she was aware that I'd been stood up. Did they go off into the kitchen area and say, 'Do you see that poor soul over in the corner? He's just been stood up.' The world seems to be full of nothing but embarrassing situations. And here comes another one.

It was one minute to eight o'clock and Marianne Burgess still hadn't arrived. She was now entering the zone where, pretty soon – by the end of this thought in fact – she would officially be late.

Seven minutes later I was thinking: This is not funny any more. I *have* been stood up, no joke. I just had this feeling, which had started at seven-forty-eight, that she wasn't going to show up. That was nineteen minutes ago and then, at least, I still had a little hope and the comfort of the eight o'clock zone. Now all I felt was empty.

Obviously she had thought better of it and was prepared to accept the static she would suffer from my sister for not turning up, rather than suffer an awkward evening with me. God, she must really have gone off me. What happened to my great eyebrows and eyelashes? I felt this pain in the small of my stomach and my throat felt dry. I was feeling sorry for myself, very sorry for myself. My heartbeat wouldn't slow down to my command: I was having a panic attack. I felt like swigging down the remainder of the Guinness and heading off. I would be comforted better in my loneliness by walking around the streets of Liverpool than I would be by sitting here in this bustling lounge surrounded by couples, old and young, all enjoying themselves. I felt like crying out, 'Mother, I don't want to feel this pain in my heart!'

As I was choosing my exit route, a vision of beauty caught my attention, and that of most of the other males – not to mention females – in the room. A stunning woman, dressed in black with thick, waist-length, straight hair, entered the lounge. The brightest red lipstick you have ever seen highlighted her near-white face. She carried her black raincoat over her right arm and in her right, snow-white hand, she held the smallest of handbags, more like a large purse.

You could hear the casual conversation in the room fade as, one by one, people turned to stare at her. Those who didn't spot her immediately, turned to see what it was their partners, lovers, wives or husbands were staring at. As this magnificent woman walked further into the lounge, I had forgotten all about being stood up. Then I realised this woman looked like she was heading to my corner of the room. I'd better find something else to do with myself,

I thought, as my staring was verging on rudeness, and then I realised that the woman was smiling at me. God, smiling straight at *me*. Then, of course, I realised the stunner was none other than Marianne Burgess, *my* date for the night.

I held out my hand awkwardly to greet her. She very gracefully took it in her own and I could feel her pull me towards her as she pecked me on the check. I felt very chic, I can tell you. No-one but she and I would have been aware of how subtly she had manoeuvred the kiss. As we sat down, she used the thumb of her right hand to remove the evidence of the kiss from my cheek. I would have proudly worn it for the rest of my life. I took her raincoat and hung it over the back of my chair.

'I'm so sorry I'm late, Theo,' she smiled.

Who was late? Hey, I hadn't noticed, had you?

I loved this woman with all my being; how could she be late? I'd been infatuated by her up to that point, but now that she was here, with me, and we were sharing a private conversation, just the two of us, the dreaming was over. I loved her. I mean, who wouldn't?

She was dressed in a knee-length, black, figure-hugging skirt, which made sitting on the low chair awkward. When she opened up her high-neck jacket – a black, oriental affair buttoned the whole way up to just under her chin – she revealed a white, silk, well-filled blouse, which showed just a hint of her white bra. Maybe I just imagined that, as I felt it would be too rude to stare. She wore black silk stockings and black, patent leather, high-heeled shoes. Her skirt rose above her knees as she crossed her legs. I tried not to look, but I did. The swish of the stockings rubbing together gave me no other option.

'It's okay, honestly,' I replied.

'Good, thank you. You could have made me feel bad. I'm usually a great time-keeper and like to be on time but, apparently, there was a bit of an incident on one of the earlier buses and now they're all running late.'

'What would you like to drink?' I asked, feeling foolish for all of my earlier thoughts. She was safely with me and I felt great.

'I fancy a glass of wine, don't you,' she inquired, spying the end of my glass of Guinness.

Then, in five seconds, she did what it had taken me ten minutes to do earlier: she made eye contact with one of the waiters, nodded at him and he was at our table in two seconds flat. She ordered two glasses of some kind of white wine, and some nibbles.

'I love it here, don't you?' she began.

'Yeah, it's quite magnificent.'

'It's so lovely. I've been coming here with my parents as a special Sunday treat since I was a wee girl,' she said, solving another of my puzzles.

'What does your dad do?' I asked, before I was aware I was asking her a question.

'He works for the Electricity Board. He's been there all his life and he's got a great job. He's there for life now,' she replied, as our drinks arrived.

'Does he enjoy it?'

'I think he likes the company; I mean the company of the men he's been working with all his life. He gets on great with everyone and has a good time. I don't think it's exactly stimulating because he keeps warning me not to be like him. He wants me to continue my education for as long as I can, to give myself the choice of jobs later down the line. He keeps saying that he *has* to do what he does.'

'Have you any brothers or sisters?' I asked, out of interest.

'Just one, a brother, Jonathan. He's three-and-a-half. My parents married quite late in life. There's a bit of a dark cloud over the early part of their married life that neither of them will go into. Anyway, I was quite a different delivery for my Mum. She nearly died. They waited ages before trying again. She'd always dreamed of having a house full of screaming kids, but had to settle for the two of us as my Dad wouldn't let her risk it again.'

'Did you find it lonely growing up by yourself?'

'No, not really. I had loads of friends and my Mum always used to encourage me to invite my friends around. She always made them feel very welcome, you know? We'd pretend to be up in my bedroom doing our schoolwork, but instead we'd be having a bit of a hoot. My Mum would know, like, she just wouldn't let on. My Dad was more concerned about my schoolwork though; he'd always want to check my homework and stuff. He's a good, loving Dad and all that but, as Mum says, "He's not scared about cracking the whip whenever he has to." She always laughs at that point, but I can tell you, some of the times it was no laughing matter. He never hit me or anything; well, apart from a smack on the leg now and again when I needed it. He was very strict and he'd make sure I'd done all the things I should have before I got any treats.'

'What? Did you have a hard time at school or something?'

'No. No not at all. Schoolwork always came easy to me. But my

Dad would always tell me that you can't just rest on your laurels. You've always got to be thinking about the next step and it's always going to be a harder step, if it's worth taking at all. He also taught me how to enjoy schoolwork by not being scared of it. He would say, "Look Marianne, whether you like this or not, you're going to have to do it and do it for the next few years of your life, so you might as well make it your friend and enjoy it." And I did, and he was right, it worked. I wasn't scared of it; I did enjoy it and consequently, I became good at it. Seems too simple to be true, but it was.'

'Aye, always listen to your Dad, that's what I say. Are you and your father quite close then?' I ventured.

She thought for a moment before answering; not a long time but just enough to suggest she wasn't as tight with her father as, say, our Kathleen was with my dad. Asked the same question, Kathleen would have broken into a warm smile, maybe even a full-blown laugh, and then proceed with a full repertoire of little anecdotes that would reveal just how close they were. Marianne, on the other hand, said:

'Well, we're close, yes, though maybe not as close as we were when I was growing up. My father is one of these men who loves hanging out with his workmates. To him, that's a big thing about his work, you know, the social thing. Don't get me wrong, he never neglected my Mum or me. When I was growing up, before Jonathan, there was always the three of us, but Eric, his mate, was always around, dropping in for a cup of tea or just to collect my Dad to take him down to the Legion, so I suppose my mother and I grew close because we were always together by ourselves.'

'That makes sense. Yeah. I suppose that means that Jonathan would be the apple of his dad's eye. Probably spoilt rotten, I would guess, although I was always told that it was meant to be "Daddy's girls" and "Mummy's boys".'

Marianne sighed. 'I suppose so, but if I'm honest I'd have to say that my mother is probably equally close to both of us, Jonathan and me.'

I suddenly realised I knew nothing about this girl, this woman. I had thought about her so much over the past year or so but that's all I'd done; think about her and what it would be like to be with her. I'd thought about her in various stages of undress but I'd never really thought about *her*. She'd always have this romantic cloud of mystery hanging over her, like a troubled soul, in love with a married man. I'd think about how sad it was and how I wanted to protect her, to save her, but I didn't really know what the person I wanted to save was like.

True, she was my sister's best friend and I could have asked our Kathleen all about her, but I'd never considered doing that. Why? Probably because I'd never really considered her as a person before. But now that she was here, before me, large as life and definitely thrice as pretty, I had to deal with it, or drool like an idiot and get dumped after a few nights, when she saw how shallow I really was.

'But enough about me, what about you? Obviously I know all about your family through Kathleen, but what about you? Have you ever considered being a carpenter like your dad?'

I have to explain here that although my father was an electrician by trade, he was a carpenter in his spare time. It was kind of like a hobby but much more than that.

'I'd love to have the same passion as he has for creating things out of wood. He just loves working with wood, you know. It was always the same when I was growing up. He used to have a rickety old workshop, down on the allotment, and I would spend many an hour there with him amongst the smell of wood shavings, glue, paint and, best of all, the smell of his honest sweat. The mixture of those workshop smells always reminds me of my childhood and I would question him incessantly about everything under the sun. Fortunately, God has blessed him with the patience of a saint and he would answer each and every one of my questions. That's where my real education took place,' I answered, happy to reminisce. I paused to enjoy the memory and take a sip of wine. It wasn't really my kind of drink, wine that is, but it seemed better at the time to be sociable and join Marianne in her chosen drink.

'But no, I never really considered becoming a carpenter. Well, that's a bit of a lie. When I was young and I used to have such great times with my Dad in the workshop – just the two of us and all his wonderful stories – I used to think that that was perfection. That was the way a father and son should be, together like that, so close I could smell his sweat and hear him think. So, for a good number of years, I thought that's how I wanted to be with my son. That's how close I wanted to be with my boy when I had one. Then I realised I couldn't ever be a carpenter. Apart from anything else, I don't really have the gift in my hands that he has. And really it's their fault; the drumming that is, it's my Mum and Dad's fault. From a very early age I was always listening to music. There was always music on around the house. My Dad would have all his

cronies round and they'd have a Guinness or ten, then the old
battered guitar would come out and there would be a bit of a
singsong. Add to that the records that were always around our
house and I suppose it became inevitable that I would develop a
passion for music. Both my parents can sing and play guitar. Well,
my Dad plays guitar and my Mum plays piano,' I replied, conscious
that maybe I was chatting too much. But Marianne just smiled at
me, encouraging me to continue, so I did.

'That was when I first heard the blues, you know. Not John Lee
Hooker, or Muddy Waters, nor Lighting Hopkins or Sonny Terry
and Brownie McGee, but my Mum at her piano in the front room,
when she thought no-one was listening. She sounded sad, very soulful, and she was just making it up as she went along. I assumed it
was always about some unrequited love or something but she'd
never talk about it. I'd go in quietly and encourage her to keep at it,
but she'd come out of her mood and change the tune; start to send
herself up with a few Irish diddley reels, and she was great at those
too. So they were always encouraging me to take up something in
music,' I said.

'Why the drums?' she asked.

'Don't you mean "*But* why the drums?"'

'Well, I suppose I did actually,' she smiled, exposing that twisted
tooth again.

'I don't know really. I started off on piano and a bit of guitar, but
I just love rhythms. I would always keep the beat to the song. And
then the skiffle craze came along and the drums were what I wanted
to play. You know, just to get in a group. All the other gigs were
taken. There was too much competition being a guitarist so I joined
a group on drums, not meaning to do it seriously, just as a bit of a
lark, and I seem to have stuck to it,' I replied, being as honest as I
knew how.

'And it's good for getting girls, I hear.'

'So they tell me, but you'll have to point a few in my direction,' I
said, regretting the words the minute they'd left my big beak. God,
I didn't want her to think I was after anything in a skirt.

'I would have thought you were more of the serious type, Theo,'
Marianne Burgess replied, putting my record straight for me.

'Yeah, I suppose so.'

'So what happened to you and Colette then?' she asked, as she
drained the remains of her wine. I ordered another round before
replying.

'Well, we were in a relationship where both of us were honest with each other from the beginning. We knew and accepted that it wasn't love but we liked each other a lot and we made a pact that, for as long as we were with each other, neither of us would be unfaithful to the other. It was meant to keep things less painful. We had a laugh along the way and then it was time to end it,' I said, twitching nervously in my seat. This was going somewhere I didn't particularly want it to go. Pretty soon, I'd be faced with telling her a truth I didn't want her to know. The alternative was to tell her a lie.

'Who ended it?'

'It just kind of ended itself. It was time for each of us to move on. You know, it was over,' I struggled.

'Okay I hear you,' she replied, in a quieter voice, 'but was she happy to break up as well?'

'Ahm, no, not really.'

'Was it painful?' she continued, in her quieter voice.

'I think… yes, it was. She felt let down.'

'But you said that you were both loose about it.'

'Yes, but she was disappointed. She admitted she wanted something to happen between us. And it was sad because we'd been all adult about it at the beginning, trying to avoid any horrible endings.'

'Ah, yes, horrible endings,' she sighed, as the wine arrived and she insisted on paying her round.

When the waiter had left us to our secluded corner, I ventured, 'Are you, you and the Married Man, definitely finished?'

She smiled, a smile of hurt, 'He's got a name too, you know. He's called Ken. And yes, it's definitely over, forever, between us.'

'Has he tried to get in touch again?' I continued, chancing my arm.

'Yes Theo, he has. But I'm strong-willed. When I decide something, it's hard to get me away from my course or to change my mind. In time, he'll either find someone else to be unfaithful with or he'll try and repair his marriage,' she said, into her drink.

'What about earlier boyfriends?' I asked.

'Theodore Hennessy, you are persistent,' she laughed. 'Actually, Ken was my first serious relationship. Before that, it was always fumbling around with spotty boys. No-one in particular. And you?'

'No, nothing serious,' I replied, and then added a wee bit too quickly, 'so far.'

'So,' she began, expansively, 'we're both footloose and fancy-free.'

'I'll drink to that,' I smiled. By this time, the wine was beginning to go down easily. By the fourth glass it was positively free-falling down my throat. By the time we reached her flat, just after midnight, we were both flying and uninhibited. We kissed just inside her front door. She struggled free and ran into her flat. I followed and we had another kiss; a long and lingering one. A kiss I was happy to just get lost in. She broke it off with:

'Let's break for some air.'

'Good idea,' I lied.

Marianne went to get another couple of glasses of wine. This new supply of alcohol wasn't going down as well as the Adelphi special. She suggested coffee, I opted for tea. We were there, sitting in her living room, when she said:

'Theo, look, I like you. I think I like you a lot.

My face must have showed my disappointment because she quickly added:

'No, I'm not about to say this is going too quickly, that we should slow it down and let it happen naturally. I don't like to be as calculating as that. I like it to happen when it is ready to happen. What I am saying is that I want us both to be in control of our senses the first time we make love and I think, just now, we're both too far gone and pretty soon we'll just... you know... end up making love. And I'm scared that we'll... well, at worst I'll forget what it was like.'

Here was Marianne Burgess, the girl – or woman – who had turned every single head in the Adelphi residents' lounge, admitting to me that she had considered it. Not only had she considered it but it seemed that she'd also decided that she was going to make love with me. Now you should realise at this juncture that I would have been happy, as in ecstatic, just to be able to go out with Marianne on dates – you know, a boyfriend-girlfriend kind of thing. Go to the movies; kiss and fumble in the back row; go for long walks; talk about our future; save up to buy her an electric hair drier for Christmas; to officially be her boyfriend and she my girlfriend; and to be chased from those milky-white thighs with a gentle slap and a "No Theo, it's too early, I'm not that kind of girl".' In a way, I suppose, I even wanted her not to be that kind of a girl. I mean, I could deal with it of course, but do you know what I mean? And here we were discussing the main event, the event some of my mates had to wait months, if not years, for.

'Yes,' was the only word I could find in reply.

Right then, I sobered up by about fifty percent, but she was right: we were too drunk to enjoy it properly. It was also quite exciting to have met a girl who thought about these things and didn't need to be drunk to do the wild thing. Here was a girl admitting to me that she enjoyed doing the wild thing but she wanted to be sober in order to ensure she did enjoy it. She bypassed all the traditional fumbling around because she'd made her decision that she liked me enough to make love with me. Having made that decision, she wasn't going to put me though months of hell, even though I will admit here that sometimes those months of hell have their own particular brand of pleasure. But the thing I liked was that she was not going to make love as a favour to me. She wanted to do it as well.

Now was she so liberal with everyone? Our Kathleen said not and our Kathleen would know. Had her relationship with the Married Man given her this adult attitude? Was it an adult attitude? No, adults would all say, with one voice, 'Wait until you are married.' No, it wasn't an adult attitude, it was a mature attitude and I respected her for it. I also loved her for having the confidence to speak her mind.

'Good,' she smiled, and kissed me again. This time it was a very long, gentle, lingering kiss where her lips were just brushing mine. She held my face in her hands. She was sitting in my lap, her skirt riding way above her knees, occasionally affording a view of something shocking like the top of her stocking. In a way it was a very passionate kiss; in another way, it took the heat out of the situation and cooled us down a bit.

So, we fell asleep on the sofa in each other's arms. We woke up with the birds at about six-thirty and it was daylight outside. We showered, separately, went to her bed and made the sweetest love I ever dreamed it was possible to make. It was perfect, like our bodies were just meant to be together. There was no awkwardness, no clumsiness; it was all so natural and, as I caressed her perfect body, she fell asleep in my arms.

She fell asleep with her face leaning against my shoulder, looking up at me. She had a gentle smile in her sleep and her lips were just slightly parted, enough for me to make out the outline of her twisted tooth; the same twisted tooth that, a few minutes before, I had caressed lovingly with my tongue

Chapter Eighteen

The other great thing about Marianne was the fact that she liked The Beatles. You notice that I didn't use the word 'loved'. I didn't say she 'loved The Beatles'. It was she who made the distinction. She said she liked them but she didn't love them. She saved the word 'love' for other things. It's the same as when people won't use the word 'genius' to describe someone who's brilliant. And therein lies the problem, I suppose. Someone who is brilliant isn't necessarily a genius, but someone who is a genius will be brilliant. Marianne's logic, not mine, but I have to agree with her.

'Liked' was enough for me at this stage. The way I felt about Marianne, I wasn't sure it mattered really. Mind you, with the way The Beatles were doing, it didn't really matter a lot what Marianne, or even I, thought about them.

Their third single, the harmonica-led singalong, 'From Me To You' – released in April 1963 – went straight to number one. It was heart-warming to see The Beatles at number one, even though it wasn't with the best of their material. Kind of like marking time, if you ask me. Maybe they agreed because the boys and their producer didn't include this song on the *Please Please Me* album, selecting instead only the first two singles, 'Love Me Do' and 'Please Please Me'. They were one of the first recording artists to treat singles and albums as separate pieces of work. The Beatles kept the majority of their subsequent singles from their albums. They preferred to give the fans, who were buying everything released, value for their hard-earned cash. Singles cost six shillings and eight pence, and an album would set you back thirty-two shillings and sixpence.

The album, *Please Please Me*, stayed at the top of the charts for all of April, all of May and all of June. To maximise on this, Brian Epstein had the boys work everywhere and anywhere. He was worried only for their safety. On more than one occasion, he even tried to buy them out of a gig that they had vastly outgrown since the time of the original booking. They did every TV show, every radio show and every gig it was humanly possible to do. While on

the run with all of the above, they talked and joked with every journalist thrown at them, and smiled and grinned and posed for every
photographer with a camera. They appeared to be gluttons for
work.

June 26th 1963 was a monumentally important day for The
Beatles. In the evening, they played at the Majestic Ballroom in
Newcastle. After the gig, back at their hotel, John and Paul took up
their guitars and together wrote the song that was to become *the*
Beatles song; the one which would spearhead their launch around
the rest of the world.

To many people, even today, 'She Loves You' is The Beatles at
their best. The press particularly loved the 'Yeah, yeah, yeah' phrase
and trotted it out in headline form at every possible opportunity. By
now, television crews were following them to every gig. Their
charming wit and irreverence was becoming their trademark. They
were nobody's fools, mind you, and everyone was loving them for
their honesty and natural humour. They were using the old system,
extremely successfully, to launch a new sound: the sound of the
youth of the United Kingdom.

This historic song was recorded in the Abbey Studios on
Monday 1st July, during afternoon and evening sessions. The
sessions were produced, as ever, by George Martin, who had just
returned from holiday to find his diary very full with recording
sessions for several of Brian Epstein's groups. It has to be admitted
that on 'She Loves You', his work is not as evident as it is on other
songs.

This is the one song that benefited the most from all the hours
they had spent on stage in Hamburg. This song showed that they
had been subconsciously noting why the classic covers they
performed, in that small club off the Reaperbaun, went down as
well as they did, and why they were encouraged to 'mach show' by
their employers. 'She Loves You' turned out to be the perfect crowd
pleaser and would have fitted seamlessly into the Hamburg show.
Every artist The Beatles praised and covered would have been
proud to put their name to this dance-floor filler.

The royalties would have come in handy, too. Chart-wise, this is
The Beatles' most successful single. It was released on 23rd August
1963 (*Please Please Me*, the album, was enjoying its uninterrupted
fifteenth week at the top of the charts) and entered the charts at
number one.

The Beatles were number one again!

It stayed at number one for four weeks then dropped while, first Brian Poole and the Tremoloes had a number one with 'Do You Love Me', and then Gerry and the Pacemakers with 'You'll Never Walk Alone' – another Merseybeat performance. Then something quite extraordinary happened: The Beatles reclaimed the number one spot. This was unheard off in the British charts. Yes, some singles slipped down for a week and went back up, but never before had a single reclaimed the top spot after nearly two months. This was due, in no small way, to the fact that The Beatles were coming above ground at last. Everyone in the country was loving them now.

They even appeared on the most important TV show in the country, Sunday Night at the London Palladium, causing scenes of chaos outside the hallowed theatre. It was on the Monday morning following this appearance (Sunday 13th Oct) that the press invented the word 'Beatlemania' to (successfully) describe what was happening in the country.

'She Loves You' was one of the songs they performed that night and on the receiving side of the TV, in my mum and dad's house in Southport, you could feel the sheer excitement. I'd brought Marianne around for Sunday lunch to meet my mum and dad. I mean, they already knew her as our Kathleen's best friend. However, now we were dating properly it seemed appropriate for her to meet the folks officially. I'd done the same at her house the previous week and everything had been fine. I think her mum was a wee bit hesitant, you know: 'Is this boy really good enough for my Marianne?' But it went fine and after the hard bit was over; her dad invited me to the pub with him and his mate, Eric, so Marianne later surmised, 'He must really like you.' But it wasn't too bad really. I'm sure my mum was the same with all of our Kathleen's suitors.

As expected, my mum and dad made her feel very welcome and, more importantly, didn't fuss over her. We had a great day, I have to admit. All of Liverpool knew our most famous and loved sons were on the TV with Bruce Forsyth that evening. Brucie had become a household name through the success of Sunday Night at the London Palladium. Personally, I much preferred Norman 'Swinging (thumbs up) Dodgy' Vaughan. We had a full house of friends and neighbours who were, as yet, to subscribe to the moving-picture box in their living room.

The Beatles were top of the bill – and why wouldn't they be – but Brucie brought them out at the beginning of the show, something they had never done with the star attraction before. The Palladium went wild when the 'moptops' walked on stage. Brucie announced, 'If you want to see them again, you'll have to wait forty-two minutes.' I bet there was a big surge in the nation's demand on electricity as everyone went off for a cup of tea.

Not in our house. My dad had a supply of Guinness in for the chaps and Kathleen had brought some white wine for the girls. My mum and her cronies dipped into her Christmas stash of sherry. And we had a right merry time. My mum kept saying the craic was great and it was like this every night in Ireland; a bit of an exaggeration I thought, but I knew what she meant.

The Beatles came back after the final adverts and, following Brucie's countdown of 5-4-3-2-1, went straight into 'From Me To You'. Our house, as I'm sure did every house in the 'Pool, went berserk. God, they were great. I was so proud that I could feel a lump rising in my throat. Marianne must have seen that I was getting a bit emotional because she came over to me, took my hand and said, 'You Irish are all the same. It doesn't take much to set you off, does it?' I couldn't reply and she just squeezed my hand.

I think Paul introduced the next song. I couldn't really tell because of the noise both in the Palladium and in my house, but the camera was on him and his lips were moving. The song was 'I'll Get You', which was the B-side of the fabulous 'She Loves You'. Then it looked like Paul, John and George were saying something, then just George by himself, and then it was Ringo, masterly on his tom-toms, leading them into 'She Loves You'. And that was it. The entire nation went la-la. I'm sure of this if our house was anything to go by. Totally la-la.

The bedlam generated by the end of the song was amazing. A bit more horsing around between John and Paul, including a request for the screamers to quieten down. They didn't. The boys started into 'Twist and Shout' and Beatlemania was launched for evermore.

Neil Aspinall and his assistant (and former Cavern doorman), Mal Evans, would have had their work cut out for them getting The Beatles out of the Palladium that Sunday night. Argyle Street and Great Marlboro Street were streaming with thousands of Beatles fans, or so the newspapers told us the next day. The Beatles had arrived, and BIG TIME!

'She Loves You' went back to number one for the last week of November and the first week of December. It was to enjoy a stay in the charts of a staggering thirty-three weeks. Eight whole months in the charts. Can you believe that? By the end of November, it was the biggest-selling UK single of all time. 'She Loves You' was knocked from the number one spot by another record-breaking single; yes, you've guessed it, yet another Beatles' hit. This time it was with a song called 'I Want To Hold Your Hand' – the first single to have an advance order of over one million copies in the UK.

In the middle of all their touring, The Beatles had been popping into the studio at every available opportunity to record the new songs that were to make up the next album, *With the Beatles*, and the new single, 'I Want To Hold Your Hand', which had 'This Boy' on the flip side (the B-side). Until The Beatles came along, artists had used mostly throwaways for B-sides. However, The Beatles, with their songwriting pride, changed all this. With 'This Boy', they surpassed even themselves. A beautiful, poignant song with three-part harmonies, another of their trademarks. If you get a chance, please listen to this song and hear how absolutely wonderful the voices of John, Paul and George are when they blend together.

'I Want To Hold Your Hand' was no slouch either: another true Beatles song and a fantastic record at that. It was a real throat-grabber, which defied you not to listen to its infectious charms. It was to stay at number one into the New Year and became, at the expense of 'She Loves You', the biggest-selling single in the UK. (A record it continues to hold today if you qualify it as the biggest-selling *non-charity* record in the UK.) But the success of 'I Want to Hold Your Hand' was to have far-reaching ramifications. It was the first Beatles song the Americans were to take to their hearts. However, that's further down the line.

The sleeve of *With the Beatles* shows – courtesy of Robert Freeman copying an Astrid photograph – that visually, the boys had well and truly arrived. The photo shows they had class, style, original hairstyles and, added to that, the fact that they were incredibly photogenic. I think that if that sleeve were to have been designed a bit later in their career – at a time when EMI listened to everything The Beatles had to say – you would have found the white strip at the top of the sleeve would also have been black, and the title would have been more subtly placed. Small complaint.

At this stage, they had everything. Paul and George were beautiful-looking boys, a fact our Kathleen and Marianne kept repeating to me. Liverpool, having been a successful trading port for centuries, enjoyed a rich mixture of blood and races in its sons. I think George, and particularly Paul, bore testament to this with little oriental hints around the eyes. Look at those early photographs; they looked gorgeous. I also liked John, but perhaps he came across a wee bit too threatening to the girls. In fact, I liked Ringo too, for that matter, but let's just say he and John were handsome, where Paul and George were beautiful-looking. Hey, don't blame me. My sister drilled all this into me, time after time. She'd always say that no matter who you were, if someone as delicious as George Harrison or Paul McCartney came up to you and asked you out, you just *couldn't* possibly refuse them. I didn't question her any further on the matter. I'm not sure I wanted to know.

On top of all that, they could play. For me, Ringo's drum-work made 'She Loves You' the great record it is. They had great songs; they made great records. They had a resourceful, organised manager; a musical record producer with exquisite taste; and an efficient, hardworking and fiercely loyal road crew in Neil and Mal. Their perfect team was finally in place; they were ready to climb any mountain.

With The Beatles knocked *Please Please Me* (the album) from the number one spot, ending its thirty-three week reign. That same week, The Beatles were numbers one and two in the singles charts and numbers one and two in the album charts. I thought they might be peaking. Everything was perfect; surely they couldn't go any higher?

I wasn't to know then that this recent burst of songwriting was showing the way of things to come and not the end or pinnacle of their career. But just look at the great songs on that album: 'All I've Got To Do', for instance. In fact, all *I've* got to do is mention the title of one of their songs and I bet you can hum the melody. How about 'All My Loving', and George's Harrison's songwriting debut, *Don't Bother Me* – well worthy of its inclusion on the album? Then you also have *Little Child* and the song Paul and John wrote in the back of a taxi, 'I Wanna Be Your Man', which Ringo sang on The Beatles' album and The Rolling Stones recorded as their first single. I think that was just incredible. London's big hope, The Rolling Stones, had to come to Liverpool and The Beatles, for their first top-twenty hit. Personally, I always thought The Stones were overrated and that they had ungraciously dumped their most talented member. But then, in those days, you were either a Beatles' fan or a Stones' fan; few, if any, were both.

The Beatles were obviously working their way through their Hamburg set list; I'm talking now about songs they covered for the new album. These were songs they'd been performing live, night in

night out, before they'd any of their own songs in the set. They
successfully nailed these often-played cover versions, none more so
than *Money*, which showed why it was such a popular song when
they played it in Hamburg, and then later at the Cavern. Chuck
Berry was also introduced to a wider UK audience with The Beatles'
version of 'Roll Over Beethoven'. 'You Really Got A Hold On Me',
with George Martin playing piano on a Beatles' record for the first
time, shows an incredible vocal performance from John and Paul,
selling you instantly on Smokey Robinson's song as if it were their
own. No mean feat, I can tell you.

I'd say that *With The Beatles* was the most popular Christmas
present in Liverpool that Christmas. I bought a few copies, I know,
including one for Marianne and one for our Kathleen. If they'd
those copies today and in mint condition, with the signatures of the
four principals, they'd be worth a fortune. But then that's not what
The Beatles have ever meant to me. Sure, I've got lots of rare stuff
that, if I wanted to trade in, I could pick up quite a few grand for,
but they're not really worth those thousands to me simply because
I will never sell them. I didn't buy them as an investment; I bought
them out of passion and out of love.

And people say to me that I could still re-buy the albums and
make a profit but it wouldn't be the same. My Beatles stuff is part of
a time (the '60s) and a place (Liverpool), and they are treasures I
hope to pass on to my children some day so that they can see – hopefully to some degree – what I was doing and what was happening
when I was young. The Beatles will never mean as much to them but
it's important, historically, for them to see where the music scene in
Britain came from. It will be equally important for them, emotionally, to see what played such a major part in my life. I'm not sure
The Beatles' music changed my life; perhaps it did, but it was definitely the soundtrack during my formative years. I know that Irish
traditional music plays a similar part in my father's life and because
of that, I can't help being moved when I hear him sing 'The
Mountains of Mourne' or 'The Homes Of Donegal', or feel the fire
in my belly when I hear the pipes start up a jig.

But with The Beatles and their records, and the rarity value and
all of that, I think what I'd like most is that people in the future – my
children perhaps – will actually listen to Beatles music and hear the
value in the songs. Hopefully, for some people, those songs will be
enough for evermore. That kinda sounds like an ending, I know. It's
just that, in 1963 and with The Beatles comfortably nestling in the

one and two spots in both single and album charts, one could certainly be forgiven for thinking that things couldn't get any better. Oh how wrong we were.

Chapter Nineteen

In the wake of The Beatles' phenomenal success, the talent scouts from London duly signed anyone in Liverpool found with a guitar around their neck. These talent scouts were very easy to recognise; they all wore suits, shirts, ties and deaf aids. Even the Nighttime Passengers were signed up. That's a bit unfair, I know. We were okay, I suppose. It helped if you only listened to our stuff, but when you played it back-to-back with The Beatles, it was… well, let's just say it was in a different league. Nonetheless, Pie Records in London, who didn't have The Beatles, adopted us as their Merseybeat representatives. They should have known better.

We should have known better too; the first thing they had us do was change our name. We'd built up a very healthy following around the North West (of England, that is) using the name Nighttime Passengers, but the man from Pie – forever to be known as the Pieman – said it wasn't international enough. He continued, spade at the ready, digging his own grave: 'You know, boys, we want to launch you on the international stage. All these Liverpool groups are okay, but they're not going to travel well with this funny accent. Do you know what I mean?'

So we became known as, and please don't laugh, The Aunts. The Pieman said it was a play on the word 'ant'. Get it? You know, the way the Fab Four had made a word-play on another insect. Yes… well, with Pie Records behind us, we were sure to travel far – in the direction of a cow's tail. I couldn't abide it, to be perfectly honest. Vincent McKee was all for it. He'd got a bunch of songs (four of which I had co-written with him) and he was mad for the studio. And, you know what? We were spending more and more time away from Liverpool and consequently, for me, that meant more and more time away from Marianne. She and I were getting on great and I didn't want anything to ruin what we had, so I left the group.

It's funny – not funny ha ha but more funny peculiar – how easily you fit into a relationship. Take Marianne and me, for instance. Now you all know how much I wanted to be with her, how much I wanted to get it together with her, and I suppose for all of that it could have been a disaster. You know; you're so into someone, so attracted to them and then they say, 'Yes, okay, let's get it together; let's make a commitment to this.' Then the chase ends. Hopefully the romance continues, even gets better, but then you have to deal with everything else. Mainly living with them. You think: How long is this going to last? Then you think: How long do I want this to last? And you worry a wee bit about things like that. Then you worry about your parents and then you worry about her worrying about her parents. Then things start to settle into their own groove. Then you start to make decisions about your life, which in turn involves this other person.

I should say here, in fairness to Marianne, that I didn't leave the band to stay with her. She was not part of my decision-making process and was quite shocked to find out that I'd actually quit the band. I did check with The Aunts to see if they'd be okay if I continued using the name Nighttime Passengers for a new band I was thinking of putting together. They were fine with that and I received two-hundred-and-eighty pounds as my share of the signing-on fee with Pie Records.

I decided not to have the new band as a co-op group, with everyone having an equal share and an equal vote. My dad had been telling me about how some of the Irish show bands do it. They have a bandleader who pays the musicians a guaranteed weekly wage plus some kind of bonus system, and then the leader pockets the rest. That seemed like a darned good idea to me, so I hired a bass player, Rory Jones; a rhythm player, Big John Cotton, who also handled the lead vocals; and a lead guitarist, Brian Batchelor, who was really a mod before his time. Brian and Rory did the backing harmony vocals and, in no time at all, we had the old Nighttime Passengers' set off better than ever. We were now (on the posters and adverts) the *New* Nighttime Passengers.

Well, what can I tell you? We were playing as much as we wanted to. I handled all the bookings myself and I immediately stuck the fee up an extra ten pounds a night. That covered the band's wages. I paid them two pounds and ten shillings a night and if we worked six nights or more in a week, I paid them another couple of quid as a bonus. Lucky for me it was a day rate and not per show because we (well, I) started to stick in a few doubles (two shows on the one day), so basically I was raking it in. The audiences seemed not to care about the change in line-up. That might have had something to do with the fact that Big John Cotton wore the chiselled features the wee girls were going for.

Pretty soon we were getting so many requests for gigs that we just couldn't keep up. I started passing some of the spare ones on to mates who were in bands and they would drop me a few bob for doing so. One band in particular, The Gibbons, told me that they had reached the position where I was putting in more gigs for them than their manager was so would I take them on full time. Well, the circuit was there and I knew all the promoters well. I was out and about most evenings and it was dead easy after our gig, particularly if it had gone well, to chat up the promoter or club owner into taking my other band, The Gibbons.

The Gibbons paid me twenty percent of their fees. I think they were getting about fifty pounds a night at that stage so that was bringing me in an extra fifty a week; cash, that is. I was spending most of my afternoons on the phone getting work for the New Nighttime Passengers and The Gibbons, and do you know what came next? A mate of one of the guys in The Gibbons was also in a band and his band, Simon and the Saints, wanted to know if they could go on my books. I didn't know what my books were but I supposed they meant could I also get them bookings, so I did.

There was a bit of pressure on me now to give up playing drums with my band and be a full-time agent or manager. I enjoyed playing too much to do this, although it would have given me more evenings with Marianne. We talked about it, a lot, and she felt I would regret it if I gave up playing. 'Besides,' she said, 'I'm happy to have you out from under my hair most evenings. I can get on with my studying.' Her finals were coming up and she was quite worried about them.

This was fine. We were getting on well and I loved her. She never really expressed her romantic feelings much. She once told me a story about when George Bernard Shaw got married. He (supposedly) said to his new wife, 'I love you. I mean it, but I've said it now and I'll never say it again,' and he didn't, say it again that is. Mind you, I suppose it all depends on whether you believe the story and I think Marianne certainly did. I assumed Marianne had told me this because she wanted me to know that as far as she was concerned, what was important to her was what she felt, not what she said.

We talked about our long-term plans, but always in very general terms. We talked about children. I told her that I wanted nothing more than to settle down in a few years' time and start a family. She knew from our conversations that I felt strongly about it. It might have just been because I was from such a wonderful family and my sisters and parents were such a continuing joy to me. I also know that sentiment was beginning to grow a little unfashionable in the '60s, perhaps even with Marianne, because she would always talk about such situations in the third person. You know, like she knew I was going to settle down and have a family but thereby implying it would be with someone else.

She didn't exactly say that in so many words but she'd say silly things like I was going to make someone a good husband with all my family values and upbringing and that I would be a great dad. To be perfectly honest, I never really made an issue of it, although I thought it a little odd. But you also have to realise that I was young and I had a stunningly beautiful girlfriend whom I lusted after terribly, so dirty nappies and crying babies weren't really high on my list of priorities.

In a way, I assumed her hesitancy was some kind of test. You know, she was a girl so naturally she wanted babies but she never spoke about it enthusiastically, just to see how bad I wanted to have them. God, please don't get me wrong. I don't for one moment subscribe to that theory, you know, that women sit around all day thinking about having babies. And if I even dreamt such a thought I knew for a fact that our Kathleen would jump right into the dream and beat the living daylights out of me. No, I meant my theory as to why Marianne Burgess remained so distant on the subject: I decided it was so that I would commit myself, or not, before it became an issue, thereby preventing me from throwing it up in her face at a later date. You know the sort of thing: 'If I hadn't been tied down with the three kids and the HP I'd be off with my own successful pop group by now.' She'd say, 'But for heaven's sake, Theo, you're only a drummer.' Then I'd say, 'Ah, but look at the Dave Clark Five.' You see? I'd got all the answers worked out. The Dave Clark Five ace was never one I got to play. Our Kathleen thought he looked cute but she had this theory that he didn't like girls. Me and our Kathleen and all our theories!

For all our theories, I'd have to say that I was right to have one about Marianne and children. I just should have thought it through a bit more as I was way off base. But it's that thing, when you think something is wrong, it invariably is. That's my theory. No matter what the other person says about it being all right or that you're just imagining things, it's all rubbish. Believe you me, if you think something is wrong, something *is* wrong. The trick is working out exactly what. Then, if it's fixable, you can work as a couple at putting it right.

We were a good couple, seldom argued, and on the rare occasion we did it was never in anger. I enjoyed our love-making. Marianne had this big thing about remaining special for each other. Never taking each other for granted. Always putting that extra effort into turning out well for your partner. Never leaving things – mostly underclothes, I think she meant – lying around the flat. (I had moved in with her, by the way.) That was a real passion killer for her, she claimed. She was always going on about how important it was for us to remember how special it was on the first date. She wanted it to always be that special. 'I always want you trying that hard,' she would say. And she told me I was to remind her if she wasn't trying as hard as I thought she should have been.

But I'd no need to. Sometimes I felt that I loved her more than she loved me, but she was very fond of me, that I could tell. Indeed, that was the phrase our Kathleen used all the time, 'You know, Theo,' she would say, 'Marianne is very fond of you.'

She began to say it so much I wondered if she was trying to give me some kind of clue. If she was, I chose to ignore it. Things were fine as they were, no need to rock the boat. And a pretty darned fine boat it was too. We were a great couple; we looked good together. Marianne was good for me. She helped me get my act together in the appearance department. She made me go to the dentist for the first time in years, and she styled my hair to suit the type of growth I had. She encouraged me away from dark clothes (I figured this was because she always wore black). Generally, she seemed happy. Now and again, I would see her apparently under a dark cloud when it looked like she was miles away, dealing with her demons. I hoped her thoughts were not about what it might have been like, should she and the Married Man have managed to get it together. By the way, we never discussed Ken, but there was always something there, lurking beneath the surface with her. When I'd confront her about it she would always laugh off my concern with a, 'Oh, I'm behind in my studies again' or something similar and we'd fall back into our routine. But, as I keep saying, when you're thinking something is wrong, something *is* wrong. It may not always be something obvious but it's always worth putting your mind to it. Usually you don't because, like Marianne and me, you get distracted from your niggles by enjoying being together.

We were together in my parents' house again, to watch The Beatles on TV, this time on the Royal Variety Performance when John made his famous 'Those in the cheap seats clap your hands, those in the expensive seats rattle your jewellery' quip. Apparently, this was a very watered-down version of what he had planned to say to the audience: an audience that included the Queen Mum. Poor Brian Epstein must have been having kittens backstage. It was another great night but I felt Marianne was bemused by my hero worship of The Beatles. I heard my mother tell her, 'Ah well, it keeps him off the streets,' so I figured they were discussing me and my love of The Beatles. It was an important weekend for me because the following Monday morning was the official opening of my own agency.

I was doing so much booking work for the three groups that it seemed a logical step. I hired a top-floor office on Whitechapel. Five fecking flights up and no lift! The street premises below sold coffee beans amongst other things and we had this hypnotic aroma permanently floating around our offices. Basically, I had one room with a large partner's desk (which I assumed the office had been built around 'cause I couldn't see any other possible way of getting it into my small room). I had space at the other side of the desk for a secretary. I interviewed several on that first Monday morning and eventually settled on Christina Castle, a school-leaver with excellent qualifications and a big smile.

By Tuesday, we were a team, Christina and I, sitting around our big desk with three telephone lines and six phones. We were all set to go. By Wednesday afternoon, I had decided it was a disaster. By then, I had logged three calls. Two from Marianne and one from our Kathleen. Not exactly the perfect start to my independent business.

By Thursday morning, I realised what the problem was. Thursday was Marianne's day to stay at home and study and, at about eleven, she rang me in a panic. The phone at home was ringing off the hook; everybody in the world was ringing through to the only number they knew, my home one, wanting to know where I had disappeared to. I immediately set Christina her first task: to go out and buy the office a large telephone book. When she returned, I gave her my list of telephone numbers from my pocket diaries, my small telephone book, the backs of photographs and business cards; all over the place, in fact. A weird and wonderful system that I alone understood.

I had her write up all these contact numbers into our new green book and, as she did so, I had her ring up each number listed to introduce herself and my new company – KOPACE – and to give them our telephone number. By Friday, it was business as usual and Marianne and our Kathleen – and Kathleen's new boyfriend, and potential future husband, Tom Heaney – came round to the office late on Friday to help us christen it. The New Nighttime Passengers came around as well but my other two groups were already on the way to their gigs: The Gibbons in Newcastle and Simon and the Saints in York.

We'd a grand old opening. Christina didn't drink so our Kathleen, good soul that she is, nipped down the five flights of stairs to get her a bottle of orange juice. They got on great immediately but Marianne and Christina seemed a wee bit distant with each other. Apart from that, there were no worries. KOPACE was in business and everybody was happy, particularly the members of the New Nighttime Passengers who'd just been given a raise to five pounds per gig.

It's funny how I fell into that, I mean into being an agent. It's not what I'd intended. I'd wanted to be a drummer. Heck, I'd nearly had a chance to be in The Beatles if only... blah, blah, blah. You know the story by now, don't you? Well, not really, because now I was an agent it (The Beatles connection story) seemed to be developing with some recent embellishments. Anyway, it was not to be taken too seriously, as you know and, as my mother had a habit of saying, 'A miss is as good as a mile.' Conversely, I suppose it could be said that 'A mile is a small distance on a hundred-mile journey,' or equally, while we are on this track, 'A bird in the hand moans a lot!'

In my own little world, KOPACE was to do as well for me, expectations-wise, as NEMS was to do for Brian Epstein. I just thought, on that Friday night – the night we officially opened the office – that I should be feeling a bit better about everything. I suppose it's that feeling that every time you reach a goal and stop to look around you, you realise that, in reality, you've achieved nothing, whereas when you're striving to reach your goal, you're too preoccupied with the journey to worry about it. I suppose the secret is to always keep shifting your own goalposts.

Chapter Twenty

Brian Epstein certainly knew how to keep shifting his goalposts. We all should realise, here and now, that there was a plan in place. 'The Plan' was either one of Brian Epstein's or, more likely, one of Brian Epstein's and The Beatles together. Either way, they had the basic ingredients to make the plan work.

Here was a group of four working-class boys who were embarrassed neither by their roots nor their accents.

They looked good.

They looked different, thanks to Astrid and Stuart.

They could write superb songs.

They could sing well and played together competently as a group.

They had a distinctive, infectious, original sound.

They gave a good interview.

They liked each other; yes, they could argue but, importantly, they were very good friends, one and all.

They were big music fans and had an excellent knowledge of recording artists, particularly American ones, 'cause they absolutely loved American music.

They were not scared of hard work.

They loved what they were doing and, while on stage, they were not scared to show they were enjoying their own music.

They benefited, generation-wise, from perfect timing.

They had a manager with superior organisational skills, a theatrical leaning, a vision and an unequalled love for his charges.

Band and manager had something to prove.

There was a plan.

And the plan had to do with how good they were and how confident they were about their own abilities. They often said that the advantage they had over Elvis Presley was that they had each other. So first, with management in tow and freed from their commitments in Hamburg, they played Liverpool until they were the biggest and the best in the city. Then they spread out into the county and did the same as they had done in Liverpool; playing clubs until they were too big for them. Then they'd move to concert halls and, when they'd consolidated that county, they'd move on and do the same in another English county, and then the same in Scotland. In each place they visited, they spread the news of The Beatles and left the Merseybeat after them.

When they'd worked the length and breadth of England, they did the same in Sweden, then France, and then on and on but always the same – moving out and up from their centre. And so far it was working, working great. They were, literally, selling millions of records. Everyone wanted a piece of them.

Now – and here's one of their biggest secrets, I think – they made a brave decision in that they would only work in America on their own terms. This, I believe, was more of a band decision than a management one, although both were equally committed to it. The Beatles had seen how all the big UK stars, like Adam Faith and Cliff Richard, had gone to America, cap in hand, saying basically, 'Please, mister, give us a chance.' Then these acts would play third or fourth on a really terrible bill, making no headway whatsoever, before returning to England with their tails between their legs.

The Beatles decided this approach was not for them. They declared they would not visit America until they had a number one hit single over there. A big corner to back yourself into, particularly when you consider that EMI could not even convince the company that they owned in America – Capitol Records – to release the first three Beatles singles over there. Instead, George Martin persuaded a small label – well, two in fact, first Swan Records and then VeeJay Records – to release the Beatles singles. All to little or no reaction.

I thought 'She Loves You' would have worked in America and launched their career over there but no, they were still not receiving a favourable reaction from the US branch of their record company. Capitol Records – and historians seem to have forgotten this fact – point-blank refused to release the Beatles records in the United States of America. Obviously Brian Epstein and George Martin were tirelessly working away in the background to try and rectify this situation, but the boys maintained their 'we won't go there until we're number one' stance. It was surely a bit of the same Scouser logic as used in dealing with women: 'Treat them mean and keep them keen.' The only difference was that The Beatles were not dealing with a woman; they were dealing with the biggest, most powerful, fecking country in the world.

'I Want To Hold Your Hand' changed all of this. This Lennon and McCartney original song, which I still think they wouldn't have gotten to if they'd not written 'She Loves You', clicked with the Americans. I mean, it was probably a lot to do with the song but also, I imagine, a little to do with the fact that The Beatles were officially bigger than sliced bread in the UK. They were even on the national news most nights, for heaven's sake, and surely even those 'capital' people at Capitol Records could no longer ignore this fact. Swan Records and Veejay Records were trying hard, but they were small labels and it would have been a bit like David taking on Goliath, and having to use a grape in his sling instead of a stone.

The Beatles were in Paris, playing for a few nights at the Olympia, when they received the telegram informing them that they were number one in the States with 'I Want to Hold Your Hand'. By treating them mean, The Beatles had made the Americans very keen and they were now about to go where all other (UK) artists had failed. They were now ready to commence the next part of their plan.

After Paris, they returned to London for a couple of days' break before heading out to the States. I think they all, bar George, stayed down in London. From what I heard, George probably wished he'd stayed down south as well. There were lots of George sightings going on by Beatles fans during those couple of days. You'd be walking down the street and all of a sudden a tribe of wee girls, all screaming at the top of their lungs, would fly by you with the word 'George' not far from their lips. Three or four minutes later they'd rush past you, heading in the opposite direction. Mind you, that was heaven compared with what was to happen to them in America.

They flew from a fan-packed Luton airport on 7th February, 1964. They knew they had quite a fan base here and they liked their UK fans, so they were expecting them to show up and say goodbye. As they flew over Manhattan they all looked in wonder, viewing the famous skyline for the first time (well, except for George who had been over a few months earlier to visit his sister). What The Beatles weren't expecting was the greeting they received on arrival at JFK Airport in New York. It was packed with their new American fans, all screaming their heads off. Beatlemania had hit the shores of the USA, too. They were rushed, probably jet-lagged out of their brains, into a press conference at the airport, where they put up with the incredibly stupid questions with a great deal of charm and humour.

There was a bit of, 'Well, why do you think you are going to succeed over here when all your limey mates before you have failed?' This question wasn't actually asked, mind you, but it was implied. The answer should have been, were they not so modest about their own work, 'Well, number one, people like our songs and number two, we're ready.'

You see, to take on the world, you first have to have a team capable of taking on the world. The Beatles, the four of them – with their built-in songwriting team of Lennon and McCartney; manager Brian Epstein and all his NEMS people; their producer, George Martin and their faithful, hardworking road crew of Neil Aspinall and Mal Evans – were ready, willing, able and well-equipped for the long and winding road. I know I've mentioned that to you before, but I do feel it's worth repeating because I think it is too often overlooked how great the team were. What the Americans didn't realise was that America wasn't the end of The Beatles' journey: a mistake all other UK artists had been making. Conquering America was merely another step along the way. A large step, I grant you, but a step nonetheless.

They had a day to decamp and catch their breath, listen to themselves on the radio and do a bit of shopping. They were in the land of their musical heroes and I imagine they were as happy as pigs in body refuse. They were holed up in their hotel for most of the time, listening to the thousands of fans continuously screaming, several floors below.

Then it was down to the NBC studios to do the Ed Sullivan show. This was the American version of Sunday Night at the London Palladium, and then some. Brian Epstein had been working on this engagement for some time and had brought Mr Sullivan over to England to see his boys in action. Being the canny man he was, Mr Epstein had not gone for the usual 'fly in – TV appearance – fly home' approach. No, The Beatles' manager thought it would have more impact if he could get the boys to feature on this very prestigious TV show on two consecutive Sunday nights. That's exactly the deal he struck with Ed Sullivan. The Beatles would go to America and stay there for a week. They would do the Ed Sullivan TV show on Sunday 9th and Sunday 16th February, and they would also pre-record a slot for a third show. For this, they would be paid $10,000 plus all expenses. I tell you this because, in later years, people pointed to this as an example of the, supposed, bad deals that Brian Epstein made on behalf of The Beatles.

I don't hold with this theory myself. He was in uncharted waters. Everyone who had gone before him had failed, and failed miserably, in terms of what The Beatles and their manager were to achieve. Brian Epstein realised that the secret of doing a deal was to first make the deal, to get agreement. No need for chasing those last few pennies. It was more important to make a deal, any deal, that would expose The Beatles and their infectious music to the world. Look after the pounds and the pennies will take care of themselves. The exposure that he had secured for his artists on their first American visit was priceless, worth the weight of the Cavern Club in gold – literally.

Brian Epstein was aware of the importance of this first American visit. He said afterwards in interviews that, for him, the turning point in the career of The Beatles occurred the minute they stepped down from the aeroplane at JFK. When he saw the fans waiting for them in America, of all places – the country that had some, if not all, of the greatest music acts of all time – he knew his dreams could be realised. Now all of America was being turned on, big time, by the music of four working-class lads from Liverpool. He knew then that their plan was working, working beyond all of their wildest expectations. Now, his prediction that The Beatles were going to be bigger than Elvis Presley didn't seem so silly after all. And guess what? Even the great Elvis Presley and his manager, Colonel Tom Parker, could see the writing on the wall; they sent the boys a telegram of congratulations via Ed Sullivan, who duly read it out on primetime American TV before The Beatles' performance.

They went straight into 'All My Loving', which had the studio audience of 728 going absolutely ape. They followed with 'Till There Was You' and completed their first spot with 'She Loves You'. Then there was a break during which several other artists, including Tessie O'Shea, performed and then The Beatles returned, towards the end of the show, to perform 'I Saw Her Standing There', and concluding their first American television appearance with their current number one single, 'I Want To Hold Your Hand'.

It later transpired that The Beatles' Ed Sullivan appearance captured the biggest TV audience in history, with an estimated 73 million people sitting around the family television in just over 23 million homes. Another point worth mentioning here is that when The Beatles were actually on TV, the American police reported the lowest rate of crime incidents in recent history across the country, proving that it didn't matter if you were good folks or bad folks – you liked The Beatles!

The following morning they caught the train to a snowbound Washington DC. An ideal journey, you would have thought, for the boys to put their feet up and have a bit of a rest. Wrong! Not so for The Beatles. The train was an ideal opportunity to entertain the American media and the carriages were packed with press, radio and TV types, all looking for their exclusive interviews.

The Beatles' first American gig was at the Coliseum Theatre in Washington DC, and the first song they played live in concert to an American audience was 'She Loves You'. The Fabs were dressed in identical silver suits with black velvet collars. Paul was on his trademark Hofner bass guitar, played through a Vox Bassman 50-watt amplifier; George was on his Gretch guitar through a Vox AC30 amplifier; and John was on his Rickenbecker guitar through a matching Vox AC30 amplifier. Ringo had his trusted Ludwig drum kit and suffered most that night because the boys were, for some reason, positioned in the middle of the audience. This meant that at the end of every second song or so, they would have to move the microphones to a new position to face a different section of the audience. Ringo's drum kit was on a swivel rostrum, which unfortunately stuck and required several men to adjust it for its final few positions.

As ever, there were but two microphones at the front of the stage, the idea being that the lead vocalist had the luxury of a lone microphone, while the harmony vocalists shared the other one. They were so well-rehearsed that their stage steps – you know, moving on and off microphone – went like clockwork, as snazzy as any footwork The Shadows could come up with. The Beatles obviously could have had as many microphones as they wanted at the front of the stage, but this arrangement cultivated the closeness of the band members. They beamed from ear to ear as they each, in turn, stood up to the microphone. The incredible thing about watching The Beatles live was the sheer, absolute joy they gave their audience. They moved their audience like *no-one* had done before them. Every time the moptops shook their moptops – like in the crescendo of 'Twist and Shout' or the 'oohs' in 'She Loves You' – the entire audience went berserk.

They returned to New York the following day to make their New York City debut, performing to two houses at the world-famous Carnegie Hall. Capitol Records wanted to record these shows for a possible live album but the American Federation of Musicians wouldn't permit this. Who knows why; probably just flexing their very powerful muscles for the benefit of the limeys. The following Sunday's Ed Sullivan Show was to be broadcast live from the Deauville Hotel in Miami so The Beatles headed there for, they hoped, a bit of rest and relaxation in the sun. This was the first time they'd seen the sun in the winter (probably not true) and the first time they'd seen palm trees (definitely true!).

The Beatles started their second Ed Sullivan appearance with George, Paul and John, all around the same microphone, singing 'This Boy'. Possibly the best Beatles single never released. They'd obviously made a bit of an impact with Mr Sullivan because, in his introduction, he went on and on about how professional they were, what nice people they were, how they were a joy to work with and how the previous week's show had received the biggest audience in television history.

The one sour note on the American visit, and this was to be a wee bit of a sign of some of the absurd things to follow, was when The Beatles were invited to the British Embassy for a reception in their honour. The 'hoorays' were not The Beatles' favourite people, but I imagine Brian Epstein persuaded them that it might be a good idea to have some influential friends stateside, so they went along. Everything was going fine, well… as fine as is possible at such posy affairs, when one of the official guests stepped up to Ringo and cut a chunk out of his hair. John was incensed and stormed out of the reception in anger.

But as I said, it was perhaps an early sign for them of just how crazy it was going to become and, when compared with some of the other weirdness, the hair-cutting, incredibly upsetting though it certainly was – especially for Ringo – was positively kindergarten stuff.

Such scenes were soon forgotten as they returned to England to be greeted with a hero's welcome. Such was their importance that the BBC interrupted the traditional Saturday afternoon sports programme, Grandstand, to include a fifteen-minute segment showing the boys touching down and advising the waiting hordes of media of their views on the very successful American visit.

Chapter Twenty-One

Morning bliss: you wake up beside Marianne. Actually, *you* don't wake up beside Marianne, *I* do. It was a fine, cold, March morning and we snuggled up close to each other, sharing warmth. When you are that close to a beautiful woman, the beast in you takes over. I mean, no matter how civil you want to be about these things, at that stage in my life I just couldn't get enough of that woman. We were at it all the time.

One sad thing though, which I have to report, is that we weren't kissing as much as we used to. Truth be told, we were hardly kissing at all. This concerned me, only because I loved kissing so much, but I put it down to the fact that we were just getting used to each other. Used to each other? After four months? God, at this rate, what would we be like in thirty years' time? The other thing was – and I hope you don't mind me talking about this intimate stuff and all that, it's just that I think it's important – that the subject of love was rarely discussed.

As you can imagine, I'd already declared my undying love for Marianne and she'd mutter things like, 'Yes, me too,' and hug me like she was so moved she meant to say it but she was just too over-come for words. But she'd never actually come right out and say it. Eventually, she started to discourage me from saying it by uttering things like, 'Oh, don't go all soppy on me.' A bit of a passion killer that, as far as I'm concerned.

But I filed her, emotionally, as a retarded George Bernard Shaw – Georgina Shaw for short – and just got on with life to the point where I eventually found myself without the 'L' word in my vocabulary. But hell, I was young and inexperienced and felt that that was the way it was.

Each time I tried to talk about the future, which I have to admit wasn't all that often – we were both still young and had a lot of living to do before settling down but you always want to keep the long eye on it don't you – but anyway, every time I brought it up, Marianne would... well, ignore would be too strong a word but it was pretty close. She'd listen to me, nod every now and again, but would never actually add anything to the conversation. I figured she'd just been through a disastrous relationship with the Married Man and wanted to be completely sure before committing herself to someone else. The conversations would all invariably end whenever the word 'child' was mentioned. Listen, don't get me wrong, I wasn't particularly anxious to start a family but I saw no harm in admitting that, eventually, I wanted to have children. Maybe that had been a dream of hers; you know, to have had children with Ken, but whatever it was, she always behaved strangely when such a conversation developed. 'Strangely' as in pretending the conversation was not taking place at all and either talking about something else entirely, or just getting up and leaving the room without any warning.

I will say that she still took my breath away every time I saw her. She kept the mystery alive by never undressing fully in front of me, and by never going to bed completely undressed; even after our lovemaking she would re-robe. Don't get me wrong; she had a stunning figure and was drop-dead gorgeous, with nothing to hide that needed hiding. She just had this thing about always wanting to be seen, *no* matter the occasion, at her best. I say this not as a criticism but as a compliment. She always smelt wonderful, her breath was always fresh, and every damned thing about her was so appealing and attractive.

Equally, she brought out the best in me. Left to my own devices, I'm kind of okay to wear a T-shirt maybe just one day more than I should. I'll happily let my beard grow for three days before shaving. Mind you, that's to do with something else entirely; the only way I can get a good shave is to have three or four days' growth – a growth worth chopping off. I can't, for the life of me, shave every day as it tears my skin to bits. I also can't abide those electric shavers; you know, the ones 'I hated so much I sold the company'. Sorry, I went off the beaten path a bit there, but I think you know what I mean: Marianne encouraged me to look after myself and take care, and pride, in my appearance.

Now you're going to be thinking that I'm a scruff. Not true. I was twenty-four years old and in a hurry to get on with life so perhaps, before Marianne…well, let's just say that other things concerned me more. The great thing about Marianne was that we'd never argue about it. It wasn't one of those 'Oh, I can't believe you; your hair's always a mess, you're always in yesterday's clothes and you always look like you need a shave' arguments. No, it was more, 'Let me do your hair for you; it really suits your face when its just been washed and combed out,' and, 'Do you fancy wearing your other Levis? They really fit you well,' and, 'You know what? There's nothing that looks as sexy on a man as a Daz-white T-shirt under a black leather jacket,' or, 'Theo, do you fancy having a shave tonight? I love the feel of your skin when it's just freshly shaved.' That was also usually a sign that it was time to go to bed early.

We got on great and became good mates too, but then I'm an easy-going guy. I don't *not* get on with people, you know? I don't get rattled easily if someone is a pain in the neck. I'll leave them alone or ignore them, rather than getting upset with them. Marianne is a little, sometimes a lot, more withdrawn. She can pick up on bad vibes from some people and it does upset her. The mixture of our two personalities worked, though; we thoroughly enjoyed each other's company. And there was no dirty linen aired in public (I do hate couples who behave like that with each other) because there was no dirty linen.

I always thought I loved her mainly because my feelings towards her after our lovemaking where as strong, if not stronger, than they were before. That was my only guide, I'm afraid. Slightly naive I know, but there you go.

Before I started going out with her, I always wondered (as you do) what she did with her long, waist-length hair when she was making love. Mystery solved! She didn't do anything with it at all, apart from sometimes gathering it up, winding it around and placing it over her shoulder, or to the front, like a large ponytail. Mostly she just let it go where it wanted and sometimes she'd let out shrieks of pain when it had gotten caught somewhere underneath or between us. Other times, she'd let it hang free from above as she performed 'Marianne's massage'. But that's another story and there are children about.

Wednesday morning, we're in our usual position, Marianne with her back to me and me stroking her back. She loved that, having her back stroked. On the few occasions I worried about the fact that we didn't kiss a lot (part of the same worry was the lack of the use of the word 'love'), I thought she might like this position – for us just to lie together – because it was not conducive to kissing. So anyway, I'm stroking her back gently as she awakes and one thing leads to another and we end up doing the wild thing. She goes for a shower immediately thereafter and I lounge on in bed, enjoying my customary extra half hour or so. She usually comes up before she leaves for college with some tea and toast and plants a peck on my cheek as she bids me goodbye. This morning, for some particular reason – I don't know why – I decide to get up early. I have my shower, pull on a clean pair of jeans and a red pullover (a loose one my mum knitted me for Christmas), go downstairs into the kitchen and Marianne's there at the table, white as a sheet, reading a letter.

'What's the matter, Marianne?' I ask. I have to say I'm not, and never have been, someone who calls their partner 'sweetheart', 'honey', 'honey-bunch', 'diddums', 'darling', 'love', or 'lover'. These are mostly names boys give to girls and I know (from Kathleen) that girls favour some additional names of affection like 'teddy bear'. There's even this girl, in the flat above us actually, who seems to call her boyfriend 'Don't come', for some strange reason. He must be hard of hearing or something, particularly on Sunday mornings, because she persists in shouting out his name! No, if someone went to the trouble of picking a beautiful name – like Marianne, for instance – then I, for one, am more than happy to use it.

She just looked at me with a blank gaze. I mean, she was looking at me but she wasn't really looking at me. She was looking straight through me to the red-painted door of our kitchen. We'd quite a funky kitchen; all the woodwork was painted crimson and all the walls were green. This colour combination brought a smile to the faces of quite a few of our visitors but at this moment, it was producing anything but a smile from Marianne.

At this point, there is something else that I should tell you about Marianne. She can't tell lies. She doesn't know how to fib. So, when I repeated my question, she replied:

'I've just had a letter from Ken and he says he's left his wife.'

'Oh,' I say, seeing the storm clouds gather above both our shoulders.

'He says he wants to see me.'

'Ah,' I say, trying another word from my vast vocabulary of useful words for when you're about to be dumped.

'What should I do?' Marianne asks me.

Hang on a minute, here. Isn't this conversation moving just a wee bit too speedily to its ugly conclusion? We've been together for four months, four fun-packed months played to a Beatles soundtrack. For heaven's sake, we'd just made love and there she was, asking me what she should do. Tear up the letter, pretend you never received it, let's just go back to bed and forget today altogether. That's what I wanted to say. That's what I wanted to do. But then I heard some very sensible words escaping from my lips.

'What would you like to do, Marianne?'

Wrong again, Theodore, you know Marianne can't lie. Ask her a question like that and she's going to tell you exactly what she'd like to do, isn't she?

'I'd like to see him.'

Agh, shot down in flames. I'm in a heap on the floor. No letting me down easy or anything like that. I want to say: What about us? But I'd learnt not to ask questions I didn't want to hear the answers to.

'Theodore, I have to,' she begins.

But hang on here a minute, Marianne. I didn't ask you the question. Come on, you don't need to be so fecking honest that you answer the question you think I might want to ask. She's started so she'll finish.

'It's still unresolved between us. I remember you called him a cheat and you were right. He says in his letter that he was a cheat. He says he was cheating his wife, with me; cheating me by not being with me; and cheating himself by not doing what he wanted to do.'

Pretty heavy stuff for a married man, I think. What's he been doing, reading Edna O'Brien?

'He says he been thinking about me since we split up and he wants to give it a proper chance. He also says he'll understand if I don't go back to him but, either way, he's left his wife for good.'

A simple drummer-cum-agent from Liverpool can't compete with that. Hang on, don't go, there's more…

'Theo, if I do go and see him it'll mean that part of me still wants it to work with him and so, by the same token, it wouldn't be fair if I left you waiting to see if I get back with him,' Marianne began, as I was thinking: Who needs fair? I've mentioned to you before that she had a wonderful speaking voice and it was still hypnotic, even as she was about to put the knife in. 'So, we should split up.'

Part of me wanted to get up on the table, and jump and shout: No, you can't do this. We can't possibly split up. I love you. He's still an asshole. Maybe his wife caught him with the next you and threw him out, so now he's working his way through his old phone book.

I wanted to rant and rave and plead with her not to go, but this was Marianne. I loved her so much I could deny her nothing,

including her polite request to return to her previous lover, and I
heard myself say, 'If that's what you want to do.'

'If that's what you want to do.' The words reverberated like
thunder around the inside of my head. 'What kind of fecking wimp
are you, Hennessy?' I screamed in my mind, while on the outside I
was civil and calm. Then do you know what she said?

'I'd like us to be friends.'

Okay, there is a certain logic to that and I could go along with it.
My life was collapsing before me and I was having this very cool
conversation, feeling like I was dealing with it, until she said:

'We've been more friends than lovers anyway, haven't we?'

What? I couldn't believe she had said that. I could not believe
that Marianne Burgess had actually said that to me. Ten minutes
before that statement, we were in the throes of passion in a pool of
spring sweat. In that spilt second I had a clearness of vision. All the
no kissing, all the avoidance of the word 'love' suddenly became
very clear. It wasn't a flaw in her personality. It was a lot simpler
than that. Marianne Burgess was simply not in love with me, and
probably never had been. I was a good guy, I was fun to be with and
we had a great time hanging out together but I was just compan-
ionship for her until the real thing came along or, in this instance,
came back again, or equally, until something better came along.

I was gutted. I felt empty to the pit of my stomach. For something with so much potential to end with so little – nothing to be
exact – was totally unpalatable at that point. And yet, for all this
hurt, I couldn't feel badly towards her. I still loved her, I suppose,
and now I would have to teach myself how not to love her.

'I'll move my things out immediately,' I said, grand-standing a
bit.

'Oh, Theo, don't be stupid. Of course you won't. Take your time
to find somewhere else. You can stay here until you do, of course
you can.'

There was just something in the way that Marianne Burgess said
those words – so calmly, so collectively, so precisely – that made me
believe this was a scenario she had thought about a lot. It was just a
wee bit too pat; do you know what I mean? And it hurt.

Marianne Burgess rose from the table with a new resolve. She
had made some decisions. She came over to me and hugged me. Still
no kiss, not even a farewell one.

'Will you be okay, Theo?' she whispered.

'I'll be fine, Marianne, I'll be fine,' and then after a few seconds, 'but I do think it will be better if I move out today. If I hang around here it'll just be too painful.'

She just hugged me some more but she seemed distracted in a way, like her mind was on something, or someone, else. Hey, and how could I blame her? She was off to chase her own dream now, having starred in mine for the past four months.

And so, at eight-forty-five on that cold, March, Wednesday morning, Marianne Burgess walked out of my life.

Chapter Twenty-Two

So, the evenings that were once ours were now our own. To be very honest with you, I felt completely lost and very much alone.

We'd never discussed it to a conclusion but, to be perfectly honest with you, I felt that I was going to be with Marianne Burgess for the rest of my life and so I hadn't considered any other options. The other thing I found weird was, you know, when you're with someone and you're in a relationship, you feel wonderful; you feel ten-feet tall, like you could walk on water. In the early days I'd find myself sneaking off to a telephone box and ringing her, just to hear her voice and reassure myself that we were a couple.

At that stage, I couldn't imagine it being any better than it was. The point when you're getting to know each other in every way and you haven't yet given her a reason to start to compile a 'things I don't like' list about you. Oh yeah, and that's another thing, you know? Like all the times you are about to make love and you can't, for whatever reason: 'It's too late,' or 'We've got to go out in five minutes,' or 'They'll be here in a couple of minutes,' and you reply, 'It's okay, we've enough time, I only wanted to do it twice.' Ha, ha, ha. But all these lost opportunities would be excused with, 'Oh, don't worry, there'll be lots of other times.' And now that you know there won't be – lots of other times, that is – you feel regretful and slightly dejected, not to mention totally pissed off.

As I said, when you are stepping out with a girl and doing the wild thing regularly, you feel great. Conversely, when you're not, you feel crap and fear that you'll never do it again. When Marianne Burgess and I split up, it all happened so suddenly that I felt shell-shocked, but in a strange way I still felt okay. I thought: You know, I should be feeling a lot worse than I do. Hey, maybe it's going to be all right and it's all for the best. But I think I was suffering from a delayed reaction. The more the realisation of what had happened hit me, the worse I felt. I also thought, a lot, about the little or no kissing and the lack of the use of the 'l' word and figured that if I'd been sensible instead of blind, I probably could have seen it coming.

I moved back in with my parents. I mean, I could have moved in with our Kathleen but I just didn't feel up to it, to be honest. The great thing about parents is that they are not scared to leave you alone when you want to be alone. And I wanted to be alone. I often listened to The Beatles' 'This Boy' and 'If I Fell' over the coming months. I threw myself into the KOPACE Agency thing and went around looking for new groups to sign up, but you know what it's like; too many oysters and not enough pearls.

Brian Epstein had *the* pearl and good luck to him for being smart enough to spot it.

Our Kathleen wasn't, it transpired, as shocked as some about Marianne Burgess and me splitting up. All she would say was that she had always felt the thing with the Married Man had never been properly resolved and we'd maybe gotten together a bit too quickly for our relationship to have had a chance of working properly. I encouraged her to tell people that Marianne Burgess and I were finished. It's just that awkward thing of when a couple split up and you're the one who was dumped: you have to go out in public and admit the 'It's my fault, I'm a failure' kind of thing.

Some people eat a lot when they split up with their lover; some cry; others, delighted at their new-found freedom, go out and try and bonk their brains out; some sleep too much; others drink. Me? I played my drums a lot and listened to loads of music, mainly The Beatles and Ray Charles. I took some comfort there. I suppose that's the great thing about being a musician at such a time; you have the release for your blues. The blues makes *your* blues *the* blues.

Other times I'd go out drinking with mates, supposedly on the pull. One night, Vincent was back up in Liverpool (The Aunts had moved down to London). He was feeling happy; his songs were getting covered, including one we'd written together. He suggested we write some more together. I was game, so we went out to the Adelphi Hotel to celebrate. After a few drinks, a couple of girls – well, hookers actually – at the next table were giving us the not-so-expensive look. Thankfully, we took no comfort there.

But I was looking again. Five weeks after that fateful Wednesday morning, girls were catching my attention again. I didn't notice it at first, honestly. You've been staring at good-looking girls – and Liverpool is full of beautiful-looking girls, roses of England one and all – for a week, unwittingly, and then you catch yourself doing it and you chastise yourself with a: 'No, Theo, you're not over Marianne Burgess yet.'

And I wasn't. Truth be told, I was still madly in love with her. I was thinking that perhaps now I could qualify for Kathleen's 'the thing with blah blah blah is that it was never resolved, you know', only instead of saying 'the Married Man', she would substitute my name. I wondered did they, Marianne Burgess and her Ken the Married Man, refer to me as 'the drummer'? Could I win her back? Should I try? I was scared that if I did, I would look bad in her eyes. I was sure that, to her, I would come across as a pathetic, lovesick moron.

You can be so cruel to yourself when you're down, can't you? I kept taunting myself with the: 'You know what, Theo? She was with you for four months. She lived and slept with you for four months. She gave you a chance and if you had been anyone special, she would have stayed with you. Consider it. You had the advantage. When Ken wrote that letter, you were in residence, he was not. He was playing away. Mind you, it seemed like he always was fecking playing away. But, with Marianne, he must have been at a disadvantage, yet she still chose him over you so you're no big shakes, are you?'

As I said, girls were catching my eye again. I'd find myself queuing at the bus stop just because I'd seen a beautiful girl already standing there. This one time, I kid you not, I actually got on a bus after an absolute stunner caught my attention. I followed her to the top deck and sat behind her. I was trying to work up the courage to sit in the empty seat beside her but I've never been any good at that; you know, chatting a girl up from zero. Besides which, people on buses and trains protect themselves behind this incredible invisible curtain and, should you speak to them, they look at you as though you're just out of the loony bin for the day. But then I thought: 'Feck it, I've got nothing to lose,' and I was about to sit beside this Brigitte Bardot look-a-like when she got up and hopped off the bus. I wondered did The Beatles realise that there was an English version of their French Goddess, every bit as stunning as the original, roaming around the streets of Liverpool on the top of double-decker buses? Honest to goodness, I kid you not.

Okay, I will admit that I did pick up a few judies after our Nighttime Passenger gigs and did the business. Mostly they were forgettable and left me feeling disgusted with myself. It was as if I was being unfaithful to Marianne Burgess. One night, out at Southport, I picked up this girl: Janice Callaghan she was called, and a redhead at that. My mum always told me to beware of people with red hair. Anyway, Janice was a bit of a hoot and she liked a laugh; she must have done, she said, as she went out with me. So, we're getting on like a house on fire, only I'm thinking a house on fire is surely the makings of a disaster. But people do insist on saying that, don't they? 'Oh yes, they're getting on like a house on fire!' I didn't fancy being burnt to death with someone, no matter how much I liked them. Janice was a good laugh though, and she gave as good as she got. I do like that in a girl.

We went for a walk on the beach and retired to a rain shelter for some horizontal recreation. Well, we were at it on the bench in the shelter and I imagine her back was sore 'cause the bench was hard and cold and, to be honest, my heart wasn't really in it. We were at it for a while, quite a while in fact. Eventually the death rattle arrives and we're all done and dusted. We were rearranging our clothes into a well-known fashion or saying when she says:

'If I'd have known what was, eventually, going to happen, I'd have baked a cake.'

I say, 'What?'

She says, 'If I'd have known you were coming I'd have baked a cake.'

'Very droll,' says I.

'Well, for a time there I wasn't sure if you were doing what I was doing or if you were drilling for oil,' says she.

I was going to say something nasty but instead I said, 'Look, I'm sorry.'

'It's okay,' says she, as she lights up a fag. 'What's her name?'

'Marianne,' says I.

'When did you split up?' says she.

'Five-and-a-half weeks ago,' says I

'Oh, is that all? Ah, don't worry about it, you'll be over her by the time you're twice married,' says she.

We both laugh.

'So what about yourself?' says I.

'Oh, I'm looking for a feller,' says she.

'Really?' says I. I liked this girl's honesty. 'And how are you getting on?'

'Well, it's like this,' says she, looking at me and nodding negatively, 'When looking for a feller, it's easier if you find a feller who is also looking.'

I liked Janice. You couldn't help but like Janice; she was very dry-humoured and very quick and, bit by bit, she coaxed the

Marianne Burgess story out of me. Any prying I did into her romantic life was greeted only by another question about Marianne.

'Aye, giving it to the married men. It should be illegal,' says she.

'Sure it is,' says I.

'Aye, but as yet not punishable by death,' says she.

'Oh, I think that could be easily arranged,' says I, and we both
have a great laugh.

We took some comfort in each other's arms for the next few
months. I never knew what deep and dark secrets she hid. I could
have easily started going out with her, serious like, but she didn't
want to know. She said I still belonged to someone else and was
going to be no use to anyone, emotionally, until I resolved that for
once and for all. So we drifted apart, occasionally bumping into
each other, and quite pleasant bumping it became too!

Chapter Twenty-Three

Well, if what was left of my personal life was disappearing down the plughole, I imagine The Beatles had absolutely no personal lives to speak of. It was work, work, work and then some more work, as they became more and more popular. They couldn't even venture out in public alone any more: they'd be mobbed. They even had to plan elaborate Houdini-type escapes from their gigs now. And, just like Houdini, they sometimes appeared to be within inches of death. They'd use vans, ambulances, lorries, cars and limos. They'd dress up in long coats, caps and beards or commissionaire uniforms, even surgical gowns, in order to effect an escape. Not since Colditz had such complex planning been called for. On more than one occasion, The Beatles tried to casually walk out of the venues in ones and two, as if they were theatre staff.

As all this was going on, Mr Brian Epstein was putting the final touches to the next part of The Beatles' master plan: the making of a movie. This step, using the silver screen, would expand their ever-growing audience even further. The Beatles were all big movie fans and, on more than one occasion, had made Mr Epstein aware of their ambitions in that area. He, in turn, had persuaded United Artists to offer The Beatles a three-picture deal. The deal was done primarily because the film company in question, United Artists, also owned a record company of the same name. United Artists, the record company, were more in touch with what The Beatles meant in Europe and they were keen to secure the soundtrack rights to the movies. Anyway, for whatever reason, work was about to commence – this would have been early March 1964 – on their first movie, A Hard Day's Night. What an innovative venture it was to turn out to be.

Ringo has always been credited with coming up with the title, but John Lennon had recently published a book of craziness, *In His Own Write*, in which there was a story called 'Sad Michael'. It's on page thirty-five (they were short stories, *very* short stories) and a line from that story goes, 'He had had a hard day's night that day,

for Michael was a Cocky Watchtower.' Maybe Ringo turned it back
on John but it doesn't really matter because The Beatles' first movie
still became A Hard Day's Night.

Dick Lester was selected to direct the film, and that was okay
with The Beatles because he'd worked with the Goons – the arche-
typal bunch of crazies – and he'd recently directed a short movie
with his holiness of zaniness, Mr Spike Milligan. Funny, but I
always consider Victor Spinetti to be the director of this movie, only
because he plays a director in the movie. But that was in front of the
cameras. Behind the camera was Mr Dick Lester and a very good
job he did too. Yes, Dick Lester *was* the director and just to prove it,
he hired Welsh playwright, Alun Owen (another choice endorsed by
the Fabs) to do the script. Owen was clever, very clever. He hung out
with The Beatles during a few days of their mad and chaotic life.
Owen then went away and came up with a script that was utterly
magic, in that he captured the essence of The Beatles' spirit and their
individual personalities perfectly.

The Beatles, Dick Lester and entourage spent the next couple of
months travelling around various locations in the UK, and then
completed the (film) studio work in the Twickenham studios, a
place The Beatles would return to frequently over the years for
video clips, recording and film work. Any time The Beatles were not
needed on camera, they would nip back into Abbey Road Studios to
continue working on the soundtrack album, *A Hard Day's Night*.

During these and earlier recordings, The Beatles had produced
two new tracks for their next single, 'Can't Buy Me Love'. The
single shot straight to the number one slot and was the second single
to have a million copies, presale, in the UK. In the US of A, it was the
first single to have a staggering two million ship-out figure. A few
months previously the Americans hadn't wanted to know about
The Beatles; now the Fabs were already breaking industry records.
As per the norm, The Beatles were giving value for money with
another class song, 'You Can't Do That', on the flip side.

So, while The Beatles were working on their movie, one of their
classic singles was out there working hard for them around the
world, maintaining and building their profile. 'Can't Buy Me Love'
has quite sad memories for me, if I'm being perfectly honest. It came
out right at the time Marianne Burgess and I split up and the sentiment of the A-side cut me to the quick every time I heard it. The B-
side didn't comfort me much either because she had *done that*, if
you see what I mean. The Beatles' hectic lifestyle was certainly not

taking any of the edge off the young songwriting partnership; indeed, if anything, it was adding to it.

At this point they were probably just writing for the sake of writing: no longer needing to prove a point, like trying to secure a record deal or to score a hit record. They were in a creative cocoon now, as writers, free from all pressures, apart from the probable self-imposed one of wishing to become better writers. And they rose to the challenge big-time. John and Paul knew they had this large and expanding audience awaiting their work and, unlike some who would have buckled under the pressure, they used it as a watershed from which they would produce some of their best work.

That's one of the things I always find amazing about The Beatles; how their success, instead of destroying them, drove them on to greater artistic heights. I had thought they'd peaked with 'She Loves You'. To me, at the time of its release, that was the perfect pop single. I couldn't see anyone, even The Beatles themselves, bettering it. How wrong could I be? I had only to wait until the movie and the movie album were released to be proven wrong. It's also worth noting that I was happy to be proven wrong in this case.

I considered sending a copy of 'Can't Buy Me Love' and 'You Can't Do That' to Marianne Burgess. But, and I kept going back to this point, I didn't because I thought she'd be disappointed in me for being so petty. Why was I still so concerned about what she thought about me? I mean, 'You Can't Do That' was more tongue in my cheek than a dig at her, and she did like The Beatles so why not?

Well, why not indeed? Simple. Because she disappeared from the face of the earth after we split up. Our Kathleen told me this. She, as a friend, tried to get in touch, only to find that Marianne Burgess had moved out of the flat that she and I had shared. I was thankful for that small mercy because I couldn't bear it if I thought they – Marianne Burgess and Ken the Married Man – would be doing all the things they were doing in the place where once we had done all the same things.

Kathleen wondered whether my ex had moved into her current lover's flat, but she didn't think so because she was sure Marianne would still have been seen around Liverpool by one of the tribe. Perhaps they'd moved to another town or city, Kathleen offered, and I remembered something about her wanting to go on some course after her exams were over. Anyway, as my mum always said, 'Out of sight, out of mind.' Who was she kidding? Certainly not me, although I pretended otherwise. And the opening of the movie helped with this pretence.

The Beatles had not been in Liverpool for ages and they decided that as well as having a premier right smack bang in the middle of London – at the Pavilion in Piccadilly Circus – they would also have one in Liverpool. Politicians were keen to jump on the bandwagon and it was decided to hold a civic reception for them at Liverpool Town Hall. The streets of Liverpool were lined for the Fabs on this day, Friday 10th July, and the premier was at the Odeon Cinema. I had four tickets and I told Christina, my secretary, to take the day off, close the office and bring her boyfriend to the movie.

I think that at that point, with all my post-Marianne Burgess erratic behaviour, she thought I was totally crazy. However, she didn't argue with me, even though she knew she'd be the one who'd suffer the most when she had to catch up on the office backlog the following Monday morning. I brought Janice in from Southport, booked us a room at the Adelphi and we had a grand old time. She said I was starting to get the hang of it, you know, diving for pearls, by this point.

But back to the movie: what a movie. I went back to see it three more times over the next seven days. For me, you can't separate the music from the movie, and 'If I Fell' and 'I Should Have Known Better' were in my all-time top five Beatles songs at that point. What were my favourite five Beatles songs then? Okay, as you've asked, I'll tell you.

1. 'She Loves You'
2. 'If I Fell'
3. 'I Should Have Known Better'
4. 'This Boy'
5. 'Can't Buy Me Love'

I mean, not necessarily in that order and not necessarily not. What about this song or that song, I hear you ask. Well, different strokes for different folks.

After the movie came out, the Fabs were compared to the Marx Brothers. I think that was only because there were four of them and they were funny. They were very funny and very natural. It would probably have been very different if there had not been four of them. No matter how big it was all getting – and forget the fact that they were making their first motion picture – they were still John, Paul, George and Ringo from Liverpool. If one of them suffered a slight attack of the delusions of grandeur, the other three were happy to remind them how silly they were being; particularly John, who had been seen in Hamburg, on more than one occasion, playing guitar and trying to sing while wearing a toilet seat around his neck.

They didn't quite go to those lengths to get laughs in the movie but a lot of their scenes and set pieces were to be blatantly nicked over the following years for pop videos, movies, TV and such like.

A Hard Day's Night still stands as the best Beatles movie made and a yardstick all other music films fall miserably short of, relish judies and all. It sucked you right out of your cinema seat and into the train with them, as they pulled out of Paddington. Just as you are thinking: 'Cor, that blonde sitting there amongst the schoolgirls looks very beautiful,' you get the feeling George Harrison was experiencing the exact same feeling. In fact, George liked the blonde so much he later married her. Patti Boyd was her name.

It was the first time in my life I had been to a movie where the audience, usually docile, reacted vocally and energetically to everything that was happening on the screen. Then, when they performed 'If I Fell', I was in heaven. It was so inspiring and so completely uplifting. I immediately thought of Vincent and him saying when he heard that song for the first time that he wanted to give up songwriting forever. I know that if I ever dreamed about writing the perfect song, I would have felt I'd written it if that song had been 'If I Fell'. I couldn't wait to go out and buy the record and listen to that song, nonstop, for a week. Then they hit you with 'I Should Have Known Better': totally glorious. It was a song that exactly summed up my sentiments about Marianne Burgess.

Paul seemed to be the least comfortable on the big screen. Most of his solo performance apparently ended up on the cutting-room floor. Supposedly he had this big scene with a Shakespearean actress in her rehearsal studio, but his performance was considered too self-conscious for the final cut. Also dropped was a sketch with 'peelers' chasing The Beatles around the streets of Notting Hill Gate. Ringo, on the other hand, seemed to have the critics in a bit of a tizzy over his performance. You know, the bit where he goes off on his own and walks along the riverside. That was one of the last scenes to be shot and Ringo claims that he'd been out on the town all the previous night – he came straight from clubbing to the movie set – and he felt rough, to say the least. The cameras started rolling and he wandered around looking lost, deep, thoughtful, soulful and concerned, when in truth he was hung over. But they say that's what makes great actors, don't they? People who can take life's experiences and use them for their performance, although I don't think they meant it quite the way Ringo achieved it. Anyway, as I said, the critics loved Ringo's performance and predicted big things for him although I, for one, wasn't sure there could be anything bigger than being in The Beatles.

Chapter Twenty-Four

People were having a hard time believing just how big The Beatles actually were. If I tell you that at the end of March 1964, the top five singles in the *Billboard* singles charts (USA) were:

1. 'Twist and Shout'   The Beatles
2. 'Can't Buy Me Love'   The Beatles
3. 'She Loves You'   The Beatles
4. 'I Want To Hold Your Hand'   The Beatles
5. 'Please Please Me'   The Beatles

No, stop a minute. Please read that again, one more time, just for me. The top five singles in the most important record chart in the world consisted entirely of Beatles records, and all of them Lennon and McCartney compositions at that. It is worth dwelling on this achievement a wee while longer. It was to be the only time in the history of the American charts that this phenomenal feat has been accomplished.

On top of that, they also had additional singles at nos. 16, 44, 49, 69, 78, 84 and 88. And, on top of *that* – that's if it needed topping – their current American album, *Meet The Beatles* (with sales in excess of three-and-a-half million copies) had just become the biggest-selling album in American recording history. Can you imagine any artist in the world doing that today? Impossible, I tell you, impossible. I'd say someone would have as much hope of achieving that as I had of getting back with Marianne Burgess.

Time is cruel. I was at that stage where I was remembering all the great times we had had together. Like when we went to a toff's party; they were all dressed up like Mr and Mrs Moses, but we just danced our brains out, ignoring everyone. Or the times we went to see the Fabs at the Cavern. Or like the times we'd stay in bed all day Saturday and then be too exhausted to get up on Sunday. Or like the time we took her four-year-old brother, Jonathan, to Southport and I swear we had more fun in the amusement arcade than he did. Or like the times when I was away from the flat for a night with the band and I even took to wearing her denim shirt just to have her fragrance with me.

For the life of me, though, I couldn't recall one single bad or unpleasant time together to counter all this lush. I mean, that says it all, doesn't it? We always got on well. This 'Ken the Married Man' thing had patently been brewing beneath the surface all the time and all it took was a catalyst (the letter) to send her true feelings exploding across our breakfast table, metaphorically speaking of course. I couldn't really settle down into another relationship. I'd meet people and think, 'This is it. This is the one to make me forget about Marianne Burgess', and they wouldn't, simple as that. I suppose the mere fact that Marianne Burgess was my gauge was going to ensure it was never going to happen. So, the more it didn't happen with other people, the more I thought about Marianne Burgess. Our Kathleen thought it was unhealthy. I'd have loved it to be different, but it wasn't.

'So how's your band doing?' our Kathleen asked one night, when I was around at her flat.

'Which one?' I replied. I suppose I was a bit too blasé for our Kathleen.

'The one you play in, remember? You're meant to be a musician as well as a money-grabbing impresario,' she snapped, cutting me down to size. I was in her flat, as I said. It was a really comfortable place and I liked being around there but she was making me feel acutely uncomfortable.

'Yeah, Kathleen, we're doing good, working all the time.' I tried to row back to her shore; the safety of dry land was much more attractive to me at that stage than inhabiting my little island with thoughts of only Marianne Burgess for company.

'What about a record? Have youse got into the studio yet?' she pushed, betraying the influence of my mother with her use of the word 'youse'.

'What have you been going to? Bleeding night classes under Brian Epstein or something?' I snapped. She was beginning to bug me now. We had a habit of doing this to each other. One of us would take the other for granted and so the other one would, ever so politely, dig up a raw nerve or two.

'Well, I see all these other groups, not half as good as the Nighttime Passengers, with record deals,' she lectured.

'What, like The Aunts?' I joked.

'Well at least they're up off their asses and having a go.'

'And struggling to find gigs, and at half the price we're already turning down. Once you shoot for the stars, Kathleen, if you don't reach them there's no parachute strong enough to break your fall.'

'What are you talking about, Theo? Parachutes? Are you that scared of not making it? At least Vincent and the boys can say they've had a go. All you can say is that you're the big fish in a little bowl.'

'Geez, Kathleen what's the problem with you? Why are you on my case? Boyfriend gone and left you or something?'

'No, Theo. I can keep my partner, which is more than you can say.'

Ah, now that was cruel wasn't it? So far below the belt she'd untied my laces. The conversation was in free fall, so I thought I'd better get out of there.

'Now that's not fair, Kathleen. You know she left because of the thing with Ken the Married Man,' I pleaded, wanting a truce rather than a victory. I hadn't the heart for this.

'Oh, did she now?' Kathleen said, with a cross between a tease and spite in her voice.

'Yes, in fact. We loved each other and that was enough. But then Ken came back on the scene again and it wasn't enough any more,' I replied, not really wanting to be drawn too far into this, but at the same time my stubbornness refused to give ground.

'Well, Theo, I hate to have to be the one to tell you this, but someone has to. That wasn't the case.'

'What wasn't the case, Kathleen? She didn't leave me for Ken? God, I was there when the letter arrived. I saw how she reacted. It was like they'd never been apart. Her time with me seemed to count for very little. Honestly, Kathleen, it was all over in ten minutes. I'm not kidding.'

'Theo, look at the situation. She's having an affair with a married man. She feels bad about it at the best of times. She's pretty much an outcast.No-one likes a husband-stealer. She figures he's not going to leave his wife. That was thanks to a conversation with yourself. You come along. She likes you. You're her own age, you're unattached and you play in a band, which opens up a whole new and exciting world for her. You make her laugh. Christ, Theo, she hadn't laughed since she met the bastard. She wants to love you. She wants it to work with you. She goes into the relationship wanting it to work. She hopes she might be falling in love with you and you go and smother her love by loving her too much.'

'Sorry? I was loving her too much?'

'Yes, Theo, too much,' Kathleen continued, full of rage now and not about to pick her words carefully to spare my feelings. It was like one of those conversations you keep telling yourself you must have with a friend and you avoid it because you don't want to hurt them, but because they are your friend, you feel they should be told the truth. If it were the other way around, you'd want to know the truth. And then this person, unfortunately me in this case, gives you an opening and the whole sordid thing comes spilling out. She saw the hurt in my eyes but now she'd gone this far she was going to see it through.

'You were her little puppy dog. Everything she wanted to do, you wanted to do. It was as though you'd lost your personality completely. Like you'd decided: "This is it. This is who I love. This is now my life." And you loved her so much you smothered her and any love she felt for you completely disappeared. You became a very boring person. I mean, just look at yourself, sitting there, king of your own little sandcastle and slagging off Vincent McKee because of his group and how crap you think they are. It doesn't matter whether they're good or bad, only that they are out there trying. And I know Vincent; if it doesn't work with The Aunts, he'll have a go with some other group. Theo, life is not about meeting someone you think you love, someone you think you want to be with for the rest of your life, and then giving up on everything except that person.' She paused and smiled, more to herself than me. She looked like she wasn't finished with her lecture, so I held my counsel.

'I knew you always loved the movies, Theo, but I didn't realise you bought into them in such a big way. Life doesn't always end with "and they lived happily ever after." We'd die of boredom if it did. It's about each person struggling in their own way for greatness in their work, in their relationships and in their life. That's what makes life worthwhile. That's what gets you up in the morning.'

'And here's me all this time thinking it was my Mickey Mouse alarm clock!' I tried a bit of comic relief but she wasn't having any of it.

'I'm serious, Theodore, deadly serious.'

We both sat in silence for some time, quite some time actually. The only sound was the sound of her clock ticking away the time, which passed. I had to say something. I didn't want us to end the evening on an argument.

'And she really thought I was boring?'

'Yes, Theo, in the end she did.'

'She told you this?'

Our Kathleen hesitated, seemingly considering her words.

'Yes, she did. I mean, as you were going along, she would say little innocent things like, "I wish Theo would let me love him" or "He always wants to do what I want to do".'

'And that's a fecking criticism? I thought I was being considerate.'

'Theo, it's boring to get your own way all the time. As a couple you have to have equal parts, equal bits of give and take.'

'Why didn't you tell me?'

'It's easy when you sit back and look at it, and put together all the conversations. With the advantage of hindsight, you can see what was going wrong. Apart from that, you wouldn't have thanked me for my views, would you? I hope you'd have told me to mind my own business, and then gone and done something about it. She doesn't *not* like you, Theo. She wasn't happy about splitting with you but she got the letter from Ken and, suddenly, he appeared to be the more attractive option so she took that route. And even then, she told me she couldn't believe that you didn't try and stop her. From the way Marianne puts it, you very nearly helped her pack her bags. She couldn't believe that you didn't even put up a fight.'

'She couldn't believe I didn't put up a fight? Now that's going a wee bit too far, Kathleen. I can't play those kinds of games. Was I supposed to know that Marianne leaving was a bit of a showdown to see if I would fight for her? Drumsticks at dawn on Kingsway? I don't think so. She received the letter, she told me what she wanted to do, and I respected her too much to put her through any more grief.'

'Hang on, Theo, that's what I'm trying to tell you. Next time, don't be so respectful. Geez, even if she was hellbent on leaving you for scumbag Ken, her ego was still going to want you to like her enough that you would at least put up a bit of a fight for her.'

'So that's what it was all about, her ego? She wants me to love her, but not too much; she wants to leave me but she's not happy leaving me unless I put up a fight to show her I still want her to stay? For Christ's sake, of course I wanted her to stay,' I gushed, my voice cracking. I could feel tears rise up in my eyes. 'Of course I fecking wanted her to stay, Kathleen. I loved her more than... more than I wanted to be in The Beatles.'

'Wow… hold on here, boy, don't go too over the top.'

I couldn't continue talking for fear of crying. Kathleen Hennessy had (what was known in family circles as) 'given Theo a good talking to' in the hope of making me see sense and wise up. In reality, all she did was make me realise exactly what I'd lost. It's funny, I was sad about splitting up with Marianne Burgess and all that, you know, feeling blue like they sing about in the songs. But until the end of the conversation with our Kathleen, I hadn't realised the magnitude of my loss and how much I missed my ex.

Love is a word we all use to describe an affection of convenience but with Marianne Burgess, I had found my soul mate, the other part of me. Very few people ever succeed in doing that. Yes, they find someone they are attracted to and they settle down, have kids and live (mainly) happily ever after. Fill in your own missing bits and all the adjectives you wish to use but, for me, with Marianne Burgess I had found the missing part of the puzzle of my life. Perhaps if I had been clever enough and realised what she was, maybe I could have become the same in her life and perhaps then we would have been one. Of course, I knew that we wouldn't live happily ever after. Of course we'd go through all the human crap, but if the spiritual unit had clicked, it wouldn't have mattered. You wouldn't notice it, you'd just get on with life. But I'd fecked up.

I'd had such a chance and it had been overwhelmingly big. What I didn't realise was that I could have picked it up with my fingers. Our paths had crossed and we hadn't connected and the chances of our paths crossing again were… well, I figured I'd have to have the luck of the proverbial cat's nine lives just to be in with a single chance.

My other problem was an equally serious one. After Marianne Burgess, how was I going to be able to have a relationship with a mere mortal ever again? If our Kathleen knew I was having such thoughts, she would have sent me home with a clip around the ear. If I'd known who was waiting for me around the next corner in life, I would have walked home that night, not slouchy and sad, but with an extra spring in my step.

Chapter Twenty-Five

Before that was to happen, there were a few action-packed months for both me and the members of Liverpool's finest. While I had been contemplating my navel I had also been doing a few other things, like having Christina go out and buy a box of our Kathleen's favourite chocolates – Raspberry Ruffles actually – and deliver them with a thankyou card from me. They were waiting for our Kathleen when she returned from work the following evening.

Now where was I? Oh yes, while I'd been doing that, John, Paul and George were having to do without Ringo. Having to do without him to the point that they had to replace him. Here, listen, I'd better explain.

Okay, remember that The Beatles had spent 33 weeks at the top of the album charts with 'Please Please Me'. The next number one, as I mentioned, was *With The Beatles* and that stayed at the top of the charts for 21 weeks ('Please Please Me' remained at number two for the first twenty weeks of this run). So, by that point, The Beatles had held the number one spot in the album charts for a staggering 54 weeks: that's a fortnight over the year! They were then knocked off the top by The Rolling Stones' first album (no doubt helped greatly by the success of the Stones' cover of John and Paul's 'I Wanna Be Your Man'). The Stones were number one for 11 weeks (the first seven with The Beatles at number two) and were then knocked from the top spot by – you've guessed it – The Beatles and their soundtrack album, *A Hard Day's Night*. This album was to hog the number one slot for the next 21 weeks.

I know a lot of the stuff here is bordering on the train-spotterish. I did say *bordering*! But the thing is, when your (my) social-cum-romantic life is non-existent, you (I) tend to take your (my) pleasure and satisfaction from the things you (I) support. In a way, by taking pleasure out of someone else's success, you make your life more interesting. You've got something to talk to your mates about with enthusiasm and in Liverpool, it was either The Beatles or football. I think you know, by now, where my loyalties lie. Right, enough said.

Now when you walk into a pub, a football terrace, or a club like the Cavern, and you see and hear all the fan(atic)s going on and on about our particular passions (non-romantic), you can either view us as a load of sad bastards or people with great interests in their lives. But really, do you think it's healthy to take so much pleasure from every award your favourite group wins? From every chart record they set? From every box-office record they break?

Don't get me wrong. I'm not putting myself or other Beatles fans down, here; I know, from my point of view, having something as powerful a force as the Fabs in my life, *especially* at that point (considering, as I say, the lack of any other activity with Ms Burgess), was definitely positive. I know a few of my friends, who didn't have such a powerful distraction with music or, say, football (but definitely don't mention train-spotting or I'll strangle you), became couch spuds. Consequently, they became socially unattractive and were in danger of remaining couch spuds. It's just that when I look at other fan(atic)s, well, I find it quite sad the way they all run around together, getting excited about seeing a bluetit out in Woolton. It's not even that bluetits were rare, particularly on the frosty winter mornings, but they took such pleasure out of being the first one to spot it. Sometimes I felt – just sometimes, mind you – that there but for the grace of God go I.

When The Beatles climbed to number one in the charts, what did it mean to me? I mean, really? I wasn't on a percentage; I wasn't even a relation of someone who was on a percentage. I didn't help them make the record; I didn't work for their management company; and I didn't work for their record company. Hell, I didn't even work in a record shop that sold their records. At least I would have had some connection, were that the case. But at the same time, when they did get an album or a single to number one, I felt such a sense of pride it was quite overwhelming. On the other hand, when someone knocked them off the number one spot – as invariably must happen – I felt sick to the pit of my stomach. I openly berated any of my mates who had unwittingly purchased the said offending record. It's just that The Beatles were *our* band. They were four ordinary Scousers who were, at first, up there with the best of them, and then later in their career, way up above where anyone had ever been. They had such a strong connection with their fans; they all, to a man, were forever showing consideration to and about their fans so it was hard not to get carried away on the wave of it all.

I mean, it was hard not to, wasn't it? Look for yourself: by the end of March there were Beatles effigies in Madame Tussauds and, as well as hogging the top five singles in the American *Billboard* singles charts, the Australian singles charts read thus:

1. 'I Saw Her Standing There'   The Beatles
2. 'Love Me Do'   The Beatles
3. 'Roll Over Beethoven'   The Beatles
4. 'All My Loving'   The Beatles
5. 'She Loves You'   The Beatles
6. 'I Want To Hold Your Hand'   The Beatles

So it came as no surprise that Mr Epstein planned a tour of Australia and Japan, before which they slotted in a quick trip to Denmark and Holland. Poor Ringo was suffering from tonsillitis and had to have an operation. George said that if there was no Ringo there was no Beatles so they shouldn't go. But the dates were sold out and it was decided, not by The Beatles, to have a 'dep' in to replace Ringo for the trip. Ringo was pretty depressed about this and probably imagined a Pete Best coming up on him. Guess who they got to replace Ringo? No, not Theodore Hennessy. (Remember I had missed meeting someone who had missed meeting George in the Les Stewart Quartet by two weeks?) No, nor Pete Best. In fact, one Jimmy Nichol. Jimmy had recently recorded for Tommy Quickly, with George Martin producing. (It was George who, along with Brian, persuaded the other George to work without Ringo and if the stories floating around Liverpool were true, quite a bit of persuading was required.) Jimmy was also familiar with the material because he also recently worked on a Beatlemania album for a small label.

The Beatles' first show with Jimmy Nichol was in Copenhagen and they got by (just) but the boys were missing Ringo, especially as his stage suits were too small for Jimmy. With Ringo still in hospital, The Beatles-minus-one moved on to Holland where they were greeted by thousands of fans, for once not lining the streets but the canals.

During all of this running around, recording and making a movie, the Liverpool hit-factory of Lennon and McCartney also managed, in the first six months of 1964, to write songs that, along with other popular Beatles tunes, were covered by other artists. Let's see: there was 'I'm In Love' plus 'Hello Little Girl' for the Fourmost; 'A World Without Love', a number one hit in the UK charts for Peter and Gordon (who also had another Lennon and McCartney song, 'Nobody I Know', for their follow-up). Then there was 'Bad To Me', 'From a Window', 'I Call Your Name', 'I'll Keep You Satisfied' and 'Do You Want To Know A Secret' for Billy J Kramer and the Dakotas. Then there was the aforementioned 'I Wanna Be Your Man' for the Rolling Stones; 'Like Dreamers Do' for the Applejacks; 'Love of the Loved' and 'It's For You', especially for Cilla Black; 'One and One is Two' for the Strangers (with Mike Shannon); and then jazz diva, Ella Fitzgerald, covered 'Can't Buy Me Love' to top the compliments.

Now it was time for their first trip to Australia. They stopped off in Hong Kong on the way and picked up a few presents for Ringo, who was flying via San Francisco to meet them. Jimmy was still in the party as they wanted to make sure Ringo was fully fit before he rejoined them on stage. None of them, though, could have imagined the greeting they were to receive in Adelaide. Three hundred thousand people lined the streets to greet them. A warm welcome back for Ringo, or what? John, Paul and George made such a fuss over him that he need never have worried about being haunted by the ghost of Pete Best. Jimmy did the first gig though, and then it was back to the Fab Four and business as usual.

When they returned to England it was time to spend some of their hard-earned money. George (Harrison) bought a bungalow in Esher, the stockbrokers' belt; with his new bank balance he should have felt comfortable there. We heard it set him back £20,000. John bought a more expensive house than George's, but then John had a family as well and needed a larger home. Paul bought a house as well. He made his dad give up the job he'd kept for forty-eight years and bought him a horse to keep him occupied in his retirement.

It was also a time for The Beatles to catch their collective breath; get ready for a tour of England; write some new songs; record a new single ('I Feel Fine' backed with 'She's A Woman'); and record a new album (*Beatles for Sale*), which would turn out to be the album that ended part one of their recording career.

Then they were back off to the States again for the largest tour undertaken by a British artist. I would just love to have found a way to go to America; not just to see them but because it was such a larger-than-life, romantic country and it seemed such a perfect place for someone like me. America, it seemed to me, was set up for people who wanted to enjoy life and buy clothes; books; records; memorabilia; gadgets; musical instruments; food; sweets and ice cream. They had lots of television channels, and the programmes ran all day and well into the night. They'd places that served breakfast all day long. Apparently, the waitresses were even polite to you. It was a consumer-driven nation. It appeared as though the police were your friend and protector rather than your master and ruler. It seemed, to me at any rate, to be a country where the entire nation was the cast in a continuous movie – that's in colour by the way, not black and white like England.

If I had gone to America, I would have seen The Beatles playing to between 14,000 and 32,000 people per night. They were still having fun, still working just as hard and still trying to dodge the 'Jelly Belly' sweets thrown at them. This turned out to be a regular occurrence each and every night, ever since George told fans that they were his favourite nibble. The Fabs returned to the UK to enjoy a week's break before starting another UK tour, in Bradford. TV, press, radios and concerts, on and on until late November, when they released their next single. It was originally to have been 'No Reply' but this made way for the more innovative 'I Feel Fine', with John Lennon inventing and using guitar feedback for the first time. Thanks to John's invention, Jimi Hendrix was to have a career. McCartney's belter on the flip side proved he could rock it out with the best of them. The single was another million seller and went straight to number one.

Beatles for Sale, released shortly thereafter, also went straight to number one. To me, it's an uncomfortable album. I mean, there has to be one of their early albums that you like the least, doesn't there? Well, this is mine. I don't really know why; it seems rushed, not in the recording but in terms of the marketing, you know? It appears that when they were putting it together, the priority was to get it out in time for Christmas. Were The Beatles trying to give us a clue as to their unhappiness over its untimely release with the throwaway title?

It shouldn't really be my least favourite of the early albums because it has some classic tracks on it. You can see why 'No Reply' was a contender for a single, as must have been 'I'm A Loser' and 'Eight Days A Week'. Maybe it's just that I felt sorry for them. They looked so tired on the front picture (another Robert Freeman photograph) of this, the first gatefold sleeve I can remember.

Just supposing that you took the Lennon and McCartney songs from this album, got rid of the six covers, and allowed the chaps time to come up with another six originals. I think it would have been up there and a major step towards their future work, as opposed to a stopgap. My point would have to be that if they had been afforded the time to make this a more rounded album, what would the future albums have progressed to?

But then again, that's stupid and a very 'fan' thing to say, isn't it? It's kinda like saying, 'Can you imagine how much more fun you would have if there was daylight all the time?' But, as I say, I'm a fan and make no apologies for it. It appeared to make being a fan more valid, as well, when you were prepared to stand back and look at the stuff with a critical eye. Or should that be ear? I felt it made your praise more valid when it wasn't unconditional. But for all that, you know what? Just listen to John's singing on 'Mr Moonlight'. It's breathtakingly brilliant. This is how I imagine they would have sounded on stage in Hamburg. That's Paul, adding a bit of tension on the Hammond Organ. They also got around to covering a Buddy Holly song, 'Words Of Love'. Buddy Holly was one of their favourite acts, mainly because he used to write all his own songs. Performance-wise, I've never seen him live but I've watched clips of some of his television appearances and, if they are anything to go by, he's so camp he makes Elton John look like John Wayne!

There were six covers on the album, including George Harrison singing 'Everybody's Trying To Be My Baby' by Carl Perkins (this was the third Perkins' tune they had covered, giving him the top honours in The Beatles' covers department). I don't know if it was intentional but, what with 'Everybody's Trying To Be My Baby' and Ringo's reading of another Carl Perkins's song, 'Honey Don't', the *Beatles for Sale* album had a distinct country flavour. Incidentally, the third Carl Perkins song that The Beatles covered was 'Matchbox', which appeared only on an EP, *Slow Down*. The EP, their fifth, was released and charted well in 1964. But then, everything with The Beatles' name on it was charting strongly at that point. *Beatles for Sale* knocked *A Hard Day's Night* from the top of the album charts on December 12th 1964. Just to show you how much the chart had changed since they first entered it, some eighteen months before, the top ten that week was:

1. *Beatles for Sale*   The Beatles
2. *A Hard Day's Night*   The Beatles
3. *The Rolling Stones*   The Rolling Stones
4. *12 Songs of Christmas*   Jim Reeves
5. *The Kinks*   The Kinks
6. *Pretty Woman*   Roy Orbison
7. *Moonlight and Roses*   Jim Reeves
8. *The Animals*   The Animals

9. *Five Faces of*   Manfred Mann
10. *Aladdin and his Lamp*   Cliff Richard and The Shadows.

The following week, my dad was happy because Mr Val Doonican was in the top ten. But the chart shows how, following The Beatles' lead, beat groups like The Stones, The Animals, Manfred Mann and the superb Kinks were making heavy inroads into the charts. *Beatles for Sale* enjoyed a relatively short (for The Beatles) stay at the top (six weeks in fact), but it was to return for another three-week stay shortly thereafter.

Something else was happening at that point. A chap called Bob Dylan appeared on the scene. His career launch was helped by praise from The Beatles (particularly John Lennon and George Harrison). Both he and The Beatles demonstrated that songs could now be used to put your point of view across; that's as well as for the listeners' enjoyment, of course. The Beatles and Dylan were to give songs and songwriting a credibility never before experienced.

However, instead of resting on their laurels, the next batch of Beatles songs were to show a major leap forward in the songwriting department: a feat I, for one, would have argued impossible a few months before.

Chapter Twenty-Six

It was coming near to Christmas again. Nearly another year had ended and I hadn't heard from, or about, Marianne Burgess for the best part of that year. Sad to report, there wasn't a day that passed when I didn't think about Marianne Burgess. That was, of course, until I met an American girl called Susanne Quinn. Now there was a one-woman whirlwind, if ever I saw one. My memories are of it all being pretty calm but then, equally, I remember John Lennon, while reminiscing about the early Beatles days, saying that if you're going to be in a storm the best place to be is in the eye of the hurricane. He claimed that's what saved The Beatles.

I met Susanne – she hated to be called Susie, so I didn't and I won't – at the Empire in Liverpool. The Nighttime Passengers – we'd long since dropped the 'New' as, in point of fact, none of the promoters had ever bothered to use it , though they mostly remembered to lose the second 'T' – were on a multi-act bill that toured several venues in the North West. Anyway, we were due on stage about midway through the first half, but we were getting twice the money that the act closing the first half was getting. I should know: I booked them for the promoter.

Anyway, I'm talking to our Kathleen backstage and I catch sight of this beautiful woman, dressed in brown slacks, a fawn suede, well-cut jacket and blue blouse. She's talking to a member of one of the other groups. I'm trying hard to have a conversation with Kathleen but I can't take my eyes of this blonde stunner. The guy she is talking to points to me and she looks over and smiles. I assume she must be a friend of Kathleen's 'cause she's also smiling at my sister. Anyway, she appears to thank this guy and then makes her way across to Kathleen and me.

'Hi. Are you Theodore Hennessy?' she starts, immediately betraying her thick New York accent.

'Yes. Theo will do, though,' I reply, offering my best smile and hoping to impress my sister with the 'Hey look at me, I'm hungry for life. Look Kathleen, it's me going for it' look.

'Wow!' was her only reply.

'And this is my sister, and my keeper, Kathleen,' I say as I introduce them. Kathleen shakes her hand and offers the American the
biggest Irish smile seen outside the homeland. Oh, I almost forgot,
at the same time she kicks me on the shins.

'Wow!' the American says again.

This is getting boring. I give her one of my well-practised, agent
'Can I help you?' looks.

'Oh, Geez, forgive me, but you look so… ' she hesitated.

I imagined she was going to say I looked so like Brando, or James
Dean, or even my own favourite, Montgomery Clift. But no.
Instead, she says:

'… so Irish.'

'Aye, it's all to do with my parents, you see.'

'Gee, are they real Irish?'

'Well, yes, they are actually.'

'Incredible. Far out. So are mine; well, my grandparents on both
sides were, actually. So that makes my parents second generation
and me third generation. Listen, I'm sorry to be so rude but I was
talking to the promoter, you know the guy in the tux at the main
door?'

'You mean Harry?'

'Yeah, Harry. A bit of a sleaze. I think he was trying to pick me
up.'

I thought, I'll forgive him for trying! She wasn't beautiful in the
way Marianne Burgess was classically beautiful. The American girl
was plainer in a way but, at the same time, she made the most of her
looks. Susanne had shoulder-length blonde hair, which she kept
pushing behind her ear. It might have been that her horn-rimmed
glasses gave her something to hide behind, but she was physically
more confident than Marianne; more body aware and body proud.
Her slacks left nothing to the imagination. One by one, I noticed the
musicians from the other groups slowly happen past our corner, in
order to gain a vantage view of a rare American behind. I can tell
you, they were very rare in Liverpool in those days.

'Anyway, I asked him if he knew anyone who was Irish and he
said yes, in fact he did, a good friend of his, blah, blah, blah, and he
sent me backstage.'

I said a prayer of thanks for my four grandparents to have had
the good taste to (a) have been born in Ireland, (b) have had my
mother and father and (c) to have allowed them to meet so that they

could marry and have me, so that I could run wild about Liverpool
for a few years and then meet this delicious goddess, and so on.

'Do you know Kevin Barry?' she asked, her New York tones
tending to make a question out of everything she said.

'Not personally,' I replied, as my shin took another crack from
Kathleen's vicious left foot. With my pointed-toe, Cuban-heeled,
Beatle boots I could have returned the compliment, and more, but
I'm not sure our visitor would have appreciated such drastic action
and there were certainly enough musicians loitering around with
intent should I fall from my current state of (Irish) grace. Okay, I
thought, I get the message. I've got to try harder. It was a bit weird,
though. Our Kathleen was continuing to hang around, although
not taking any part in the conversation. Obviously, she felt her role
was one of official observer so that she could tell me (later) where I
went aground, should that prove to be the case.

'You see, I'm a singer and I've been trying to get the proper
words to that song about Kevin Barry and a few others, blah, blah,
blah. All Irish, in fact. Guess what?' she beamed, and before I'd a
chance to guess what (regretfully) and receive another kick (thankfully), she continued, 'I'm off to Dublin at the weekend.'

She must have seen and heard my chin hit the floor because she
smiled, laughed and said, 'But I'm coming back next weekend.
Anyway, I wanted to know where to go in Dublin and who to try
and see. That's why I've been trying to meet someone Irish to find
out where to go and blah, blah, blah. That's how I came to be talking to the sleazebag at the door, blah, blah, blah.'

'Ah,' I said, entering into the flow of the conversation as one
does, thinking that there must be lots of American sheep with
speech impediments.

'So?' she said, getting into my monosyllabic variation on human
communication.

'Well, let's go and have a coffee,' I ventured, not *exactly* as
smoothly as Michael Caine but come on, it's hard when your sister
is standing right there taking notes on your technique, or lack of it.

'No, silly. Where do I go in Dublin?' she giggled. 'Geez, you
Liverpool boys are all so funny. Not at all backward in coming
forward.'

This from the girl who had walked straight up to me without any
introduction and started a conversation, and was obviously not
(yet) put off by conversing with a strange guy, even though his sister
was present! Hey, perhaps that's it; perhaps the fact that our

Kathleen was present gave her the confidence to continue the conversation.

Mind you, if she thought Harry was a sleazebag, there was no chance for the rest of us. Harry was just that wee bit more direct and honest with girls than we were. Well, he had to be, he claimed; when you're a married man, you can't waste time chatting them up over a couple of weeks just to get nowhere. His technique was to see if they were prepared to 'come across' – as he so eloquently put it – before he agreed to go out with them. And it seemed to work; his technique that is. Yes, he did get a slap on the face every now and then but, equally, he'd often return from the back of the ballroom wearing a large grin and some telltale sign or other – like his shirt sticking out or something equally unsubtle – which would prove to all of us that he was on to something, or just had been, if you see what I mean.

'Look, ahm, our Dad's got loads of mates in Dublin. I'll check with him, if you want, and find out all the places to go. I know there's this one guy, Johnny McEvoy, who you should go and see.'

'Oh, I know him; he used to be in the Ludlows. That song of his, *'Murshen Durkin'*, is great, and I love his version of Johnny Cash's *'I Still Miss Someone'*,' Susanne gushed.

'And he's quite cute.' At last, my sister had decided to join the conversation.

'Yes he is, isn't he?' Susanne Quinn replied and they both enjoyed a few seconds of (girls-only) giggling.

'Now, what about that coffee you were promising, Theod... sorry, Theo, or has a girl got to die of thirst around here?'

By then, we (the Nighttime Passengers) had our own roadie, Mike, a burly but friendly Scot. Mike's presence meant I didn't need to worry about my gear any more.

'Great, let's go,' I said. 'I know this great little coffee bar, it's... well, I'll show you.'

Susanne linked arms with our Kathleen and they trouped off as though they'd been friends for life. Kathleen looked back as me as if to say, 'I'm sorry for cramping your style but I've no choice,' and she rolled her eyes heavenwards the way my mum would do whenever my dad was being impossible in company. It was always a very friendly gesture; more like, 'Oh, your father's off again!'

By the time we were out on the street our American friend, in order (I'm sure) to further forge Anglo-American relationships, interlinked my arm as well, creating the filling in a Hennessy sandwich.

'So, Theo, tell me, do you know any of The Beatles?'

'Does he know any of The Beatles?' our Kathleen replied, with a knowing grin.

Please don't! my eyes screeched at her.

'Does he know any of The Beatles? Hah, he nearly *was* a Beatle, weren't you Theodore?'

'No!' our American friend screamed, so loud that everyone on the street, and there were many, turned to stare at us.

'Well, not really,' I began, trying to get away from this story.

'Not really, Theodore? Surely you're being too modest by far.' Kathleen teased. I thought: Just wait. Just you wait, Kathleen Hennessy.

'I think it's so cute the way she calls you Theodore. That's such a sisterly thing to do. It's a beautiful name too: Theodore,' Susanne said, and she pronounced my name like it was a question: 'Theodore? Tell me your Beatles story. Oh please do.'

So, I decided it would be better to tell her the story outdoors rather in a packed cafe with lots of Scousers eavesdropping. I repeated my story about having to leave The Blues by Three just before Christmas and how they replaced me with two people: another drummer, and a vocalist called Paddy Shore. And how Paddy went for an audition with the Les Stewart Quartet and how, a wee while after that, George Harrison joined the quartet. And how, if I had stayed on and met Paddy Shore I, in turn, might have met George Harrison and perhaps, when they (The Beatles) were replacing Pete Best, I might (just might) have got the gig.

'Wow!' exclaimed Susanne.

'Oh, and there's more, Susanne. Tell Susanne why you had to leave The Blues By Three, Theodore? Wait until you hear this, Susanne. He's such a romantic, my brother,' Kathleen revealed impishly.

'Kathleen!' I repeated my dad's trick of breaking her name into three syllables when she was annoying him: 'Ka-th-leen'. She was certainly annoying me now.

'Oh, go on Theodore, tell us why. Oh please do?' Susanne teased. Either she was picking up on Kathleen's mischief or she was sending me up as well. If this were the case I was doomed, dead in the water, which would be sad as I'd never been with an American girl before. Come to think of it, I'd never been with a Scottish, Irish, French, German, Welsh, Dutch or Italian girl either. I think you get the picture, though. I'd never been with any girls before who weren't English. Top of my wish list, though, were Irish girls, then French and, maybe it was just that night but American girls had just entered my top ten – first week, straight in at number three. Good first-week position if you're Gerry and The Pacemakers; a disaster if you are The Beatles. Anyway, if our Kathleen had blown my chances with a girl who would not only be my first non-English girl, but also my first from that magical place called the United States of America, then I swear to you, she was dead meat!

'He's too modest; I'll tell you. He'd just gotten himself a new girl-friend and he only had enough money to buy either new skins for his drums or a Christmas present for her.'

'And he bought his girlfriend a present and had to leave the group and missed his chance to be in The Beatles,' Susanne inter-rupted our Kathleen with full vocal excitement, for all the street to hear. Beetroots are pale compared to my cheeks on that night, I can tell you. The American broadcast continued, 'How sad, how romantic. Oh that's so beautiful, Theodore. You're a wonderful human being and she's such a lucky girl. What's her name?'

'And there's more.' Our Kathleen, not content with her handi-work so far, was up for more.

'There's more?' Susanne gushed in disbelief. They were both sending me up something rotten now.

'Yes,' Kathleen said. She was having trouble stopping herself breaking into an uncontrollable fit of the giggles now. I knew her laughter dam was about to burst and I was about to join her; the whole farce had now become too amusing for words. 'This girl, she packed him in two days later, on Boxing Day. Do you have Boxing Day in America? You know, it's the day after Christmas over here.'

Susanne told us that our American friends celebrated Christmas Day and then went back to work the next day. That seemed weird to me, you know; Boxing Day was at least as important as Christmas Day in that I needed that extra day to recover from all the food my mum always made us eat on Christmas Day. My dad always called it St Stephen's Day, but that's another story. In the meantime, our Kathleen held the floor and boy, was she milking it.

'Well she packed him in, ditched him on Boxing Day and kept the present.'

I felt that Susanne Quinn was about to say, 'Oh that's so sad,' but our Kathleen's laughter dam burst and she got the predicted fit of the giggles. As usual I joined in, which in turn had Susanne joining in louder than the two of us (Hennesseys) combined.

'That's cruel, Kathleen,' Susanne tried to say through her laughter, 'to laugh so at your brother's misfortune.'

'Oh,' Kathleen began through her subsiding giggles, as she considered the American's words before continuing, 'I'm not sure his fortune has been missed.' And she winked at me, the way brothers and sisters do. She was such a hoot, our Kathleen, and usually at my expense, but even for her this was a big one. I was going to get my own back, of that I was certain.

I got my revenge, in a way, about one-and-a-half hours later, only our Kathleen was not present (thank goodness). I got naked with my first American girl. Just in case any of you think there may have been any pervy things going on, I feel I should tell you that Susanne Quinn got naked as well, and with her first second-generation Irish boy, if you can get your head around that concept. I had too many other things on my mind at the time to bother thinking about it any more. 'Blah, blah, blah' indeed, as they say in America.

In one of the lull times (as there has to be) you climb the hill, get to the top, and you try to stand on the top for as long as possible. Invariably, you fall down the hill and have a wee rest, and then you start to climb the hill all over again. When I was young, I used to think it would be great to be able to stay on top of the hill all the time. But now, I think it would just be boring. It's the contrasts that make it all the better; well, from my point of view anyway. I have to say, though, that in the early days you'd fall down pretty quickly before you even got a chance to take more than a few steps up the hill. 'What on earth is he on about now, father?' I hear mother say. 'It's probably the X-certificate bit,' my dad would reply dryly, as he waved the newspaper about a few times, pretending to remove the creases so that he could concentrate on an article but, at the same time, clocking what page she was on in order to revisit it later.

I had to stop myself there for a moment, you know. I was in full flow, as I'm sure you can tell, and I'm talking about getting it together with Susanne; then I had a flash of Marianne and Ken the Married Man. Can you see where I'm going with this?

Yes, Susanne was an American and they were always meant to be more liberal with their favours than the English, but I remember how shocked I was when I first found out from our Kathleen that Marianne was actually going with a married man. I couldn't believe it really. And in a way I still can't believe it. You know, now that I've got to know her and all that. She's not exactly what you would call wild. Neither is she a slag. She's not a judy – you know, someone who'll drop them for a pack of Woodbines. She's a good person, comes from a good home. She loves her mum and her dad and her brother but, and I keep returning to this point she was still having sex with someone before she was married. What would have happened if she'd got pregnant? Would I have thought any the less of her? Would Kathleen? Would my parents? If Marianne and I had wanted to marry, would my parents have been against it because of that? I keep saying how much we were all meant to have a virgin bride, yet we were all out running around trying to get naked with as many girls as possible. Good girls weren't meant to do that! And yet I was always happy when I met a good girl who did. Yes, you're one hundred percent correct; my new friend from the USA. America was another country; another country I was eager to learn all about. I was also eager for another bit of hill climbing.

'So, tell me about California?' I said, noting that we had at least another forty-eight states to work our way through.

Chapter Twenty-Seven

The Beatles were conquering America at the same time as I was having (lots of) fun being conquered by an American. Following *Beatles for Sale*, things slowed down, but only a wee bit. They had four long-playing albums, five extended-play EPs, eight singles and one feature film out there working for them, so they still had a profile – a major profile.

It was time for the second movie, and although this was to produce a couple of Dylan-influenced ace songs, it would also sour them from making movies. For some reason, Alun Owen was *not* brought in to do the script. Big mistake. Whereas Owen had discovered that the secret of transferring The Beatles onto the big screen was to let them be themselves, the scriptwriter for Help wanted them to be actors. Wrong! Big mistake!

They were happy to be themselves and because they had such powerful charisma, their magic came across naturally on the big screen. Now, in Help, they were being asked to act. Now, also, a bit of behind-the-scenes cheekiness came into play. The Fabs had never been to the Bahamas before, so they requested a few scenes be shot in the Bahamas. They'd never been skiing before, so they requested that a few scenes on the piste (as it were) be written in. They were now well capable of flexing their new-found muscle, and so off they went to Austria.

This is all small cheese, you know, because I still loved the movie when it came out. I didn't go back and see it as often as I did A Hard Day's Night, though. I saw it only once, in truth, but it still made the hairs on the back of my neck stand up. Equally, that could have been Susanne, up to a bit of mischief with me in the back row.

It should be reported that we were getting on very well, Susanne and I. She'd realised, and later reported, what Kathleen had been up to and said she loved me for going along with it and showing such restraint. She had other qualities, as well you know, but more about them later. Anyway, back to The Beatles.

The next song we were to hear from them was 'Ticket To Ride'.

The B-side was another classic ballad (in the style of 'This Boy') called 'Yes It Is'. This April 1965 release shows how wide the boys were preparing to cut their cloth. It was a musician's kind of single, as well as being very commercial. Ringo's drumming was fantastic with some very cheeky bits, lots of triplets and all that, but don't get me started on Ringo's drumming or I'll never stop. Paul added lead guitar breaks at the end of the middle eight sections. Another first for The Beatles: double lead guitars. 'Ticket To Ride' topped the charts both in the UK and the US of A. You see, with my new live-in American connection, I was kept fully abreast of The Beatles' American activities.

After rejecting the first suggestion for the movie title, Eight Arms To Hold You, The Beatles eventually agreed on Help. They were asked to write a title song, and John went away and did just that. He was in what he called his 'Fat Elvis' period – although the rest of the world had yet to notice an ounce of fat. This song was a departure (encouraged by Dylan's songwriting) from their usual boy-girl love songs. It was a cry-for-help song, much more confessional and auto-biographical than before. I said this was John's song, and in fact it was. At this stage, John and Paul were writing as much apart as they were together. They would still work on each other's songs, and encourage and support each other, and all of the songs (as they had previously agreed) would be published and credited under the Lennon and McCartney banner.

Outside influences were beginning to take effect and they were probably forcing The Beatles to become introspective. George refused to allow them to be part of a ticker-tape parade in San Francisco. His point was that it seemed just a few short months since the very sad death of John Kennedy and the young George Harrison didn't want either himself or any of his mates to become targets. In Canada, a bunch of crazies had assumed (incorrectly) that Ringo was Jewish and threatened to kill him on stage. The show went ahead, but the boys wore their brown suits that evening. People were forever trying to get near, and touch, The Beatles. It was as if they had the power to heal, which was ludicrous, but even more ludicrous were the endless queues of people afflicted with one ailment or another. They turned up in droves, wheelchair-bound, seeking The Beatles' attention. I'm sure the boys felt sad for the poor people in the wheelchairs. I'm not so sure they would feel as sorry for the people using the excuse of pushing the wheelchair to gain access to places they were neither liked nor wanted.

Everyone had a story to tell The Beatles. Everyone had a reason and an excuse as to why they should have an audience with them. The *fans* were okay. They knew their place and they kept their distance, on the other side of the stage, the other side of the radiogram and the other side of the cinema screen. It was the high-ranking police officers with their wives or the dignitaries or the hotel managers, with their 'You want to meet The Beatles? Hey, no problem, just follow me.' It got to be so bad that the only place The Beatles could enjoy any peace was in the bathroom of their hotel suite.

So, you're in the middle of all this weirdness, you know? You're on stage trying to play in your group, the best band in the world, and you just can't hear a thing with all the girls screaming. Not a thing. George Martin once compared the noise of the audience screaming to the sound of a Boeing 747 taking off. You know what? I think he may have been exaggerating – the noise of a 747, that is! You're a musician and you can't hear yourself, or your mates, playing your music. It was all pretty weird. Then they were at this party where they met Bob Dylan, their hero. He turned them on to grass (cannabis) and they were able to look at everything differently. They were able to escape while still being there. They were able to report back to their songwriting muse with a new vision. And although *Help* is a patchy album, it shows the seeds of the new vision. I always thought that between the tracks of *Beatles For Sale* and *Help*, there was perhaps one amazing album. Again, that's stupid I know; nobody else was in the same league and here I am, nit-picking.

If John brought the plaintive *Help* song to the album and movie of the same name, Paul wasn't exactly slouching around in the background, feeling pissed off and sorry for himself. No, he brought the classic 'Yesterday'. The most covered Beatles song ever and quite possibly the most covered song of all time, with over 2,500 versions in existence.

This was a true solo effort. Just like he and John (together and separately) had done in the past, Paul played an acoustic version (voice and guitar) of his new song to producer George Martin in the control booth. George Martin liked the song (and Paul's acoustic performance) as it was; quite a lot, in fact. He didn't hear anywhere for Ringo to add drums. For that matter, he didn't really hear electric guitars on it either. He told Paul to go down into the studio and perform it just like he had done in the control room. They would record it and see what else was needed.

They recorded 'Yesterday', voice and guitar, as per the expert record producer's advice, and then they decided that the only instrumentation required to enhance the song was a string quartet. George Martin did the arrangement for the quartet and the song was completed, done and dusted, no fuss no bother, and the first solo recording by any of The Beatles was in the can. It was, in fact, released in America under the name of Paul McCartney and was a number one hit, selling way over a million copies. Paul picked up quite a few awards for 'Yesterday', including the Ivor Novello Award for the most outstanding song of the year. Not bad for a song that started life under the title 'Scrambled Eggs' and was turned down (for recording purposes) by both Chris Farlowe and Billy J Kramer. On the other hand, such luminaries as Otis Redding, Nat King Cole, Perry Como, Cilla Black, Pat Boone, Marianne Faithfull, Tom Jones, Smokey Robinson and the Miracles, not to mention Frank Sinatra (who I just have), recorded it.

It wasn't released in the United Kingdom as a single, but Paul did perform it on ATV's Big Night Out during a Beatles performance, when George Harrison introduced it as, 'For Paul McCartney from Liverpool, opportunity knocks.' Following the performance, when the rest of The Beatles rejoined Paul, John quipped, 'Well done, Ringo Starr!'

The last two songs to be covered by The Beatles appeared on *Help*. First, there was Ringo singing 'Act Naturally', a song written by Johnny Russell and Voni Morrison, which was a hit for Buck Owens and contained the classic lyrics: "They're going to put me in the movies. They're going to make a big star out of me. I'll play the part and I won't need rehearsing. All I gotta do is act naturally." And Ringo did – act naturally – which was why he was so great in the movies. The other cover was the final track, with John singing another of their early stage numbers – a Larry Williams show-stopper called 'Dizzy Miss Lizzy'.

George Harrison had two songs on *Help*. The first one was 'I Need You', which featured a wah-wah pedal (volume-control foot pedal) for the first time. George was bearing his soul in public on that tune. His second *Help* song was the ripping 'You Like Me Too Much', with John, Paul and George Martin all on piano. The other Lennon and McCartney songs are all beautiful, vintage songs, which you felt sure were your friends the very first time you heard them. For instance, every time I listen to the lovely, gorgeous, delicious 'I've Just Seen A Face', I just melt. And the voices! The blend of the voices. Yeah, yeah, I know, 'Here he goes again about the voices.' Sorry and all that, but I personally feel that that 'extra voice' – the sound of John, Paul and George singing together – played a big part in their success. Other groups, like The Hollies and The Beach Boys, had close harmonies but to me, both those groups lacked the soul of The Beatles. The lift The Beatles give their records when those combined voices hit you is incredible. It's like moving up another gear. Even when it's a bit wavy, if you know what I mean, it's still so soulful. Technically on the button, yet it still manages to sound effortless.

'Another Girl', 'You're Going To Lose That Girl', 'The Night Before', 'It's Only Love' and 'Tell Me What You See' all show the band and producer growing in stature as performing artists before your very eyes and ears, with Lennon and McCartney on safe lyrical ground. As usual, they had you wondering which of your ex's their lyrics might apply to. Equally, I could always hear references to Marianne lurking in there somewhere. That's why The Beatles' songs had such strong universal appeal. We could all relate directly to what they were writing about.

But with 'You've Got To Hide Your Love Away', John Lennon was again digging deep into his inner self. You can see Bob Dylan sitting on his shoulder, egging him on to write lyrics that were honest; so honest, in fact, that with all the potentially revealing stuff, if it had not been hidden in a wee three-minute pop song, it might have hurt someone. Was this a song, I wondered, about the time he had married Cynthia, and the fans weren't meant to know about it in case it would harm the group's career? I'm not sure this was something they should have worried about because Lennon didn't really receive that kind of attention from the fans. He was too scary and hard for little girls to dream about in the way they certainly dreamt about George and Paul; but had someone told John to hide his love away?

It was around this time that The Beatles were each awarded the MBE and a big fuss was made of it. Some thought that what they were doing was great for England and they deserved every award possible. However, a few of the old soldiers, who had risked their lives for the same country, felt that awarding the MBE (Ringo reported he thought that stood for Mister Brian Epstein) belittled the award. Either way, The Beatles were bringing millions of pounds into the country and deserved some kind of recognition for the good they were doing for the economy. Of course, that's not to mention the fact that they were giving the nation's youth something inspirational and home grown to look up to. Perhaps John had even been persuaded to hide some feelings about that little episode, too. Equally, it could have been about someone else he was seeing at that time; someone he wanted to keep secret from his wife. Or, I suppose, he could have been, very subtly, telling his manager to be discreet about his sexual preferences? I tend to think the latter myself. Either way, it was a hit song for another of Brian Epstein's groups called Silkie. John and Paul produced their record and Paul also played guitar at the session.

Both singles, 'Ticket To Ride' and 'Help', were also on the *Help* album, even though we all knew that The Beatles abhorred this practice of having the fans pay for the same song twice. It was probably put past them with "We've got to have them on the soundtrack album; they're in the movie." Either way, it was the last time this practice was to be allowed. Well... at least until the next movie album, that is. *Help* went to the top of the album charts in the middle of August and stayed there for eleven weeks. The Beatles' reign was continuing, unabated.

Chapter Twenty-Eight

You've probably been hanging around here, waiting for me to tell you more about Susanne Quinn's other qualities. Well, don't get your hopes up too much. I'm not ready to tell you about nights spent swinging from chandeliers, although... just kidding. Honest!

No, all joking aside, I soon discovered that my current American girlfriend had a great voice (kind of raspy), played guitar, wrote these incredible 'story' kind of songs, and floored me every time she lifted up the guitar. I felt a bit of a conflict of interest coming on, you know? We were stepping out and it was going great. Kathleen loved her and told me she thought I had my act together this time. I hadn't thought about Marianne Burgess for a long time. Well... that is unless you count the times, every day, when I thought to myself: 'Self, you know what? You haven't thought about Marianne Burgess yet today,' thereby thinking about her, if you see what I mean. But let's not dwell on that one.

So, as well as dating Susanne Quinn, I also had a professional interest in her. I knew a good song when I heard one and I remember the first day I discovered she could sing *and* write songs. Before then, to be honest I treated it as a bit of a joke. You know, 'You can sing and write songs? Gee, great, I'll have to hear them sometime.' And then, one Sunday afternoon, she got up from our bed, put on a T-shirt, got out her guitar, sat on the end of the bed and sang me her songs.

After the first one, I thought to myself: 'Self, you know what? Everyone has at least one great song in them, and obviously it's her best song because she started with it.' Seventeen songs later, my jaw is on the floor. She was quite drained. I mean, she'd been singing these great songs, some of them pretty intense I can tell you. She wanted to get back into bed and have a bit of a cuddle. With Susanne, a bit of a cuddle meant the race of the fiddler's elbow but I wanted to hear some of her songs again. We compromised. What a compromise.

An hour and twenty minutes later (it's worthwhile pointing out that this time included a snooze for an hour or so – that's just in case any of you were beginning to think I knew the secret of the hovering butterfly; well, apart from the fact that you should never take the wings in your fingers), I persuaded her back *out* of bed (it's a knack of mine). She played me the songs again and I swear to you, I heard at least five hits in there.

Susanne Quinn had this mystical air about her when she performed her work, like she was going somewhere for her performance. I was thinking that if I could get someone to cover some of these songs, Susanne would do well. She didn't want to perform them herself, she said. She didn't fancy dressing up the way pop girls dressed up and being made up the way they were made up. She was blind as a bat to boot, and had to wear her horn-rimmed glasses all the time. Well no, not *all* the time.

Susanne was happy to write her songs, though. I was convinced that if other people heard what I had heard – you know, the voice and guitar version – there could be an audience for that as well. Dylan was doing well and Joan Baez was also shifting quite a few albums to the same audience. But Susanne Quinn didn't want to know. It had taken her five weeks to work up the nerve to play me her songs in the first place. To get her to know her audience was going to take too long, if you see what I mean. At that speed, she could play to about ten people a year, maximum.

In the meantime, I had the songs. I could spend some time working on persuading her to be a performing artist at another time. In the meantime, I had this little niggle at the back of my mind that the better I did my job, the more popular and successful she would become, and the greater the choice she would have of men. Very insecure I know, but remember, I was still smarting over the loss of Marianne Burgess and she left me for a broken-down relationship with a rickety old Married Man. Actually, that wasn't quite the case; he wasn't old and he wasn't rickety but he definitely *was* married. This was all small potatoes though; whatever he was, or wasn't, she had still left me for him.

And what about contracts? Did I sign my girlfriend to a contract? I know she was an American and they do everything, including marriage, by contract but this was different. Did I think she and I were going to last happily ever after? Oh, please don't tell our Kathleen I said that or she'll go off on one of her 'Happy ever after is only for the movies, Theo. You have to deal with people, deal with life. Stop dreaming, darling baby brother' speeches. But did I think that what I had with Susanne Quinn was going to be happy ever after? To be quite honest, I didn't think about it at all. It was fun. We had fun together. Love wasn't discussed much, if ever. Perhaps only while doing the wild thing in fact, and that's something else again, isn't it?

But we got on great together. As she was a foreigner, so to speak, my friends became her friends because she had no English friends at all. She'd talk about her American friends intermittently and she'd tell me all the places she would take me when we made a trip to US of A. I tried to see if there was a 'him' looming somewhere in the background. That would have made sense, wouldn't it? You know, she'd been in a disastrous relationship and fled the country when it broke up. However, this would appear not to have been the case. No, Susanne was into her music, had been all of her life, and wasn't particularly into American men. To be perfectly honest, she wasn't really into men much, full stop. She had a love of all things Irish and claimed she was as surprised as I was when we ended up in bed together the first night. She claimed she had wanted to keep clear of men for a time as she thought it would just slow her down in achieving her musical goals. She just thought our Kathleen and I had been so funny and charming that she had let her defences down, seeing the way my sister was winding me up and how well (her words) I'd reacted to it. She'd found herself being sucked in and subconsciously attracted to our relationship. The fact that we were family and had a relationship, I mean. I got the picture that she was pretty much a loner and had been all her life. Perhaps that's the basic ingredient for being a great songwriter.

And, she liked The Beatles but she *loved* Bob Dylan. I mean, she was a songwriter so she would, wouldn't she? And she was in good company. All The Beatles loved Bob Dylan and, more than anyone, he was to influence the next and most important part of their songwriting and recording career. Perhaps a wee touch of chemical stimulants had a hand somewhere in there too. It wasn't that they copied him; I suppose it was just that he showed them what else was possible in songwriting.

Getting back to Susanne for a minute, I suppose this difference in priorities – or should I say difference in musical tastes (me The Beatles, her Dylan) – probably made for a better relationship. We could, and did, enthuse about the high points of our favourites to each other and then, when we got tired of that, we'd find something else to amuse ourselves.

She loved my dad and was forever picking his brains about what the good old days were like in Ireland. He had a simple answer for her: they weren't the good old days but they certainly were, for him, the happy old days. Whenever there were any kinds of family gatherings, Susanne always made a beeline for my dad. For some reason, she took to calling him Pa and, because she was a foreigner, he let her. You'd always find them huddled away in some corner for the rest of the evening, laughing, joking and having a bit of a hoot.

My dad was the first person to get her to sing in public. He has such natural charm that it really is hard to say no to him; for him, everything is so natural. He knew from me that she wrote songs. He also knew how brilliant I thought these songs were. To my dad, songwriting and singing had nothing to do with the music business. No, as far as he was concerned, the ability to write songs is a gift: a gift some people had and one that was to be shared with friends and family, at gatherings such as our Kathleen's birthday on September 20th 1965.

Our parents' house was packed with family and friends (no Marianne Burgess, just in case your mind went off on a wander there), and a few people were doing 'turns'; mostly dad's old cronies, who were a few pints of Guinness the worse for wear and didn't know any better. My dad had just done his party piece, 'I'll Take You Home Again Kathleen', to much applause, and tears from my mum and our Kathleen. When the applause died down, to a hush in fact, my dad offered the guitar to Susanne.

'Come on now, Susanne, won't you sing us one of your songs on this grand occasion?'

I could see the look of panic in her face but my dad just disarmed her with his gentle, smiling Irish eyes. With his smile, he offered her warmth, support, confidence and protection. I was about to intercede on her behalf because there were the usual mutterings of 'Yes, sing us a song'; 'Have a go, Susie' (obviously someone who didn't know her); and 'Aye, it's time we heard what the Americans have to offer.' My mother, in her usual considerate role, said, 'Ah, leave her alone will ye?' But my father brought the guitar over to where Susanne sat and said, 'Come on lass, you're with family.'

You could have knocked me over with a Beatles wig (made in America, by the way) when Susanne took the guitar. She had this thing (she did it all the time in our flat) where she wouldn't put the strap around her neck; instead, she'd roll it up and rest it on the top of the guitar, then play the guitar on her knee, swinging around all the time as she played and sang. The thing about Susanne's guitar playing was that it wasn't very ladylike. As she got carried away with her song, whatever song she was singing, she'd just belt away on the guitar louder and louder, making quite a racket. That's how I think she developed her unique vocal style; from trying to be heard above her own guitar playing.

My dad returned to his seat and Susanne started into her song, staring at him all the time. It was as if there were just the two of them there. Maybe that's how she was managing to do it, to sing in public; she was blocking out everyone else in the room, apart from my dad. And what a song. It was a new one – one I hadn't heard before called 'I Need To Belong' – and it was all about friends and family, travelling around and making a connection, or trying to make a connection. It was very moving. As far as the rest of the household were concerned, it was just one girl singing a song. But I, Kathleen, and certainly my dad, realised how honest she was being in her writing – painfully honest. That's the amazing thing about songs: strangers can tune into them if they are a well-crafted slice of life and, at the same time, friends can get something deeper and much more personal out of them. I swear to you, I had a lump in my throat. She sang her song with such passion, I really felt for her there, baring her soul to us all. But she wasn't really; she was baring her soul to my father, the father she was proclaiming she never had.

When she finished singing, she put the guitar down immediately. People were so shell-shocked by the beauty and power of the song that for a time nobody did or said a thing. Then my father said:

'That was magic, just magic,' and started clapping his hands. Soon the whole room was doing the same and there were shouts of 'Give us another one.' But my dad knew what she'd done and how much courage it had taken for her to do it, so he announced:

'Nagh, fair play. Susanne's done her turn. It's time for someone else now,' and he passed the guitar over to an Uncle Paddy who he knew would positively hog the instrument for the rest of the evening.

And that's how Susanne gave her first public performance: in my parents' living room. You're probably thinking: Okay, if she was that good, how come I don't know the name Susanne Quinn? Well, I can tell you that you do know her songs; you've heard them performed by lots of other people, of course. She did make one record. She produced it herself, played guitar and had a friend on flute. Oh yes, she also used a string quartet to back her on a few songs.

She also did a few club gigs around the North West. She would bring the house down every time, but then she reached the point where she thought the business side of the music was in danger of ruining her songwriting. She kinda went along with my dad on that one. Songs, she figured, were for singing to friends, and for sharing emotions with them. Repeating a song thirteen times on the trot for a television camera was not how you protected the magic. Answering stupid questions from spotty newspaper herberts about your favourite colour, food and drink didn't help you dig deeper into yourself. And, as a writer, you needed to be able to dig deeper into yourself to find a way of understanding yourself and to communicate, through words and music, your deepest thoughts. Thoughts that were not meant to be shared with a BBC radio interviewer, who would stop you halfway through your deeply confessional song with a 'Sorry, love. Larry didn't like his announcement and we have to do it again. Okay? From the top then, love, on three. One, two, twee.'

However, I loved her for it, because you know what? She didn't complain; she just said to me quietly one day that she didn't want to do that any more. It was alien to her and she felt there was a danger it might destroy her ability to write songs, and that's what she loved doing and all she wanted to do. She would do the occasional folk-club gig because there would always be a respectful, knowledgeable audience and it was a good way to air a new song before offering it to someone. Her gigs were rare, though. She didn't want to travel the length and breadth of England in vans, cars or trains; it just wasn't human, she claimed, and this was from someone who liked to travel.

Then came December, and Christmas was looming. The Immigration Department had tracked Susanne down and advised her of her illegal status, now that she'd been in the country for more than six months. We discussed, but never really considered, marriage. I mean, we got on great and we had mighty fun, but that was it. It sounds so negative when you put it like that, but it isn't meant to be. It was a joyous union that we had, a celebration of a time in our lives. Sadly, we could both tell that the time was passing and, equally, it would be destructive to hang around after the little directors in our head were running around yelling, 'Cut. It's a wrap. Let's set up the next scene!'

Christmas is hard on my relationships with women. Another Christmas had arrived and another relationship was over but this time, I wasn't sad. No, perversely enough, I was happy; happy to have been lucky enough to have met, and managed to spend some time with, someone as magical as Susanne Quinn.

I had turned twenty-five. The '60s had reached their halfway point: a point completely unrecognisable by any of those who had stood staring into the '60s from the end of the '50s. All around, it was time for the next step. First footing was going to mean something entirely different for me this year. I knew not where I was going but, perhaps for the first time in my life, I felt excited rather than apprehensive about what was to follow.

I wonder if The Beatles were as excited about the future? They certainly should have been.

Chapter Twenty-Nine

It's not hard to imagine what it would be like to go, for instance, to the Kop and stand at one end (the home end, say), and have a mate of yours stand at the opposite end. Then, just as Ian St John scores a goal and the entire place goes mental as fifty-six thousand fans start screaming like they've won the pools, you shout – scream even – at the top of your lungs. What do you think the chances are of your mate hearing you? Just to help the argument along here, you can use a 100-watt PA system to amplify your voice. I don't know exactly, but I imagine it would have been at least one hundred times easier than hearing The Beatles performing to the biggest paying audience in history (56,000), creating the largest box-office gross receipts (US$ 304,000) and collecting the highest fee up to that time (US$160,000).

Ed Sullivan introduced them to the biggest American audience ever for a music event and the band launched into 'Twist And Shout'. It was lucky that people came to *see* The Beatles, not really to hear them. They could have done that in the comfort of their homes. They could see John Lennon without his guitar for the first time (he later confessed to feeling naked without it) as he played the organ during 'I'm Down'. John was always saying that he felt safe on stage once he and his guitar were plugged in. In all the madness, his guitar was his safety line. George Harrison was so amused by seeing John playing the organ with his elbows that he couldn't get to grips with his guitar solo, but it mattered little as no-one was able to hear them, least of all the boys themselves.

They said, in television interviews, that they were very nervous at this gig but they certainly didn't look it. They were having, or appeared to be having, a ball up there. And if the fans couldn't hear them, they knew when the songs had finished because The Beatles took their famous low bows. Obviously, this is all second hand as I wasn't there at the time and had to wait, with the rest of country, until the TV special from Shea Stadium was broadcast in England. Another excuse for a bunch of my mates, and Susanne and our

Kathleen, to pile into my parents' living room and scream our heads off at people screaming their heads off.

It was on this trip to the US of A that The Beatles went to Graceland to meet Elvis Presley. They were surprised to see and hear him watching television while playing bass guitar, loudly, through an amplifier. They were all very impressed by the meeting; he'd been a real hero to them. Elvis' success was the benchmark Brian Epstein had set his sights against, so it was natural they should be excited by meeting the 'King' for the first time. Our Kathleen found this weird. She could understand me liking The Beatles, or even Elvis, but she couldn't, for the life of her, come to grips with a group as great as The Beatles having artists they in turn would look up to; artists such as Elvis in the early years and, nowadays, Bob Dylan.

Elvis and his posse were friendly to Liverpool's finest, although it was later claimed his paranoia over their unprecedented success resulted in a call from Elvis to the CIA, to see if he could have The Beatles barred from the USA. This wasn't to prove necessary as events were already gathering at a pace of their own, which would see them staying at home of their own accord.

The thing about The Beatles was that they were a cracking live band. They were a rock 'n' roll band who knew how to rock 'n' roll. All of them were great musicians, a fact usually ignored. Ringo, for instance, claimed that the only reason he accepted The Beatles' offer to join the band was simply because they were the best musicians in Liverpool, and he wanted to play with the best. In all the times I've seen them live, they were always tight. Sloppy playing in The Beatles was as rare as rocking-horse droppings. But now, because neither the band nor their audience could actually hear the playing, they were losing their edge. This fact depressed them considerably because they were proud, and rightly so, of their reputation.

You still get a lot of talk today from musicians all over the world – lots of great musicians – claiming they took up their instruments because of The Beatles. I can't count the number of people I have met, particularly from the States, who took up playing the guitar because of George Harrison. George was the first musician whose guitar became an extension of his body. You got the impression he rarely put it down. His excellence was second to none. His single-mindedness on mastering all things stringed enabled him to keep coming up with original and innovative guitar breaks, solos and introductions. Not for George Harrison a band-cliché guitar sound or style. Whatever the song needed to make it work was what he delivered. Nothing was so simple or so complicated that he wouldn't have a go at it. That was also part of The Beatles' magic as a group. They were fearless in their approach to their song settings. If the song required a ballad setting, a blue ballad backdrop was called to play. If it was a rocker, they rocked it out with the best of them and, if the song worked well within a country style, then The Beatles would draw proudly on their country roots.

However, a new wave of bands were coming up, like The Stones, The Animals, Them and The Kinks. I'd like to add the name of one of my bands there but that would just be out of vanity and would detract from all those other bands. All of those bands were into songs, good musicianship and they shared, with The Beatles, a desire to be great. The Beatles simply felt that if they stayed on Brian Epstein's never-ending gig circuit, they would lose it; lose their magic and lose it for good. Although their final gig was still a bit in the future, we were getting the impression they were now concentrating on what they enjoyed most – writing and recording songs.

Between 'We Can Work It Out' in December 1965, and the release of 'Paperback Writer' on the 10th June 1966, we experienced the biggest gap so far between Beatles' singles. Quite a gap musically, too, and a gap that included the recording of both *Rubber Soul* and *Revolver*. This was a time when band and producer were rising to a creative height as we all sat around at their feet, waiting to be turned on. I'm talking musically here, of course.

We, the world outside their window, didn't know what was going on in The Beatles' camp. We didn't know that 'Day Tripper' was about taking drugs. We just knew it was a very catchy song composed around a bass riff. Even the great Otis Redding recorded 'Day Tripper'. His amazing brass section punched out the riff just like he would do on any of his own soul classics. Otis scored another UK top ten hit with his version. But lyrically, it could have been about a girl, a tease who only took you halfway. Equally, if the rumours were true, it could be about Paul who was supposedly the last and most reluctant of The Beatles to indulge in drugs. Perhaps he was being slagged off for only being a day-tripper. In John's eyes, Paul might have only been a day-tripper as far as drugs were concerned, but he still knew how to pen a cracking tune. The other side of this double A-sided single – the first of four double A-sides from the Fabs – was Paul's 'We Can Work It Out' (with John co-writing the middle eight). We all thought it was a song to, and about, Jane Asher. Now there was a beautiful girl. I always thought she was up there with Barbara Parkins; stunning, delicious and very much her own person. Again, on record, The Beatles were at full power and they'd produced yet another million-selling number one single. 'We Can Work It Out' was also a top ten hit for Stevie Wonder and it proved to be another Beatles' song that artists such as Dionne Warwick, Deep Purple, Sam and Dave, Humble Pie and Johnny Nash were all eager to cover.

This single, 'We Can Work It Out', with 'Day Tripper', was also the first single to have a promo clip (video). Again, necessity proved to be the mother of invention. The Beatles just didn't have time to travel all around the world, appearing on television to promote their new single, so they came up with a novel idea. They would make their own little mini television show featuring, in this case, visual performances of both titles on the double A-sided single; make lots of copies of their visual performance; and send the copies to television stations around the world. The video was making the tour for them, as it were. The clips were used first by Top of The Pops in the UK, and the Ed Sullivan Show in the US of A, where The Beatles (mostly Ringo) also recorded a special (spoken) introduction for the clip. John played keyboards on 'We Can Work It Out' and also in the clip of the same.

Rubber Soul now appears to me like a flawless gem. The Beatles, in their development, were giving a credibility and a much-needed fullness and roundness to the art of making albums. Most artists, and certainly all record companies, saw albums as an excuse to bung out the last few singles, plus a few filler tracks, in order to relieve the fans of their hard-earned dosh. The Beatles, on the other hand – perhaps driven on by their frustrations at not being able to show the world how great they were on stage any more – made their albums into their current 'show'; the new (and only) way they could communicate with their audiences around the world. Beatles' fans were experiencing a never-before-considered value for money. The singles would be released before (but never on) the albums, and would serve as a trailer or sampler of what the boys were up to on their recent work.

Purely and simply, *Rubber Soul* is a beautiful album. I have to say I loved it when it came out and I played it to death – each play revealing something extra for me – and I still love it today. It's one of my favourite Beatles' albums. That the album should have these qualities was quite remarkable, especially when you considered it was recorded under the pressure of time, and the looming and ginormous (my father's word for something which is a cross between gigantic and enormous) Christmas market.

This was The Beatles' brave new world and their first step into it showed them on an album sleeve (photo yet again by Robert Freeman), looking stronger, fresher and more like men than before. John, ever the one to challenge, is the only member looking you (the camera and the audience) in the eye. No band name on the sleeve; they were so popular now, worldwide, that it wasn't necessary. The photo is elongated because when the photographer was showing the band slides for the sleeve, the backdrop tilted backwards and they were all so excited by the distorted image that they shouted, 'That's it, that's the sleeve. We'd like it to look like that.'

The title came from Paul McCartney and was coined to describe 'white Anglo-Saxons' playing American soul music: in some circles, a contradiction in terms. In fact, a few of the cynics even went a step further, suggesting that Mick Jagger's particular interpretations were more akin to 'plastic' soul. But *Rubber Soul*'s fourteen songs were purely and simply the results of four chaps from Liverpool, with their producer, hitting their stride and leaving the pack behind. Interesting to note as well that the suits were going; the various shots on the back of the sleeve show The Beatles dressed casually, comfortably and as individuals for the first time.

The album started off with 'Drive My Car'; The Beatles having fun and happy not to take themselves too seriously, with their funny backing vocal lines, 'Beep beep' and 'Beep beep, yeah.' The second song is the ground-breaking 'Norwegian Wood (This Bird Has Flown)' in which John is dealing with an (alleged) romance with a journalist who was (apparently) giving him a hard time and not letting him have it all his own way, if you see what I mean. Anyway, whatever went down (including the fire of vengeance), he hid it in a song to protect his wife from what was going on. At the same time everybody was saying, 'Who do you think that's about?' so he might have been better served to do it straight. You know, they do say the best way to hide something is to put it right under their nose. Then again, this was from the pen of a man who'd already confessed 'you've got to hide your love away'.

'Norwegian Wood' was definitely a song inspired and greatly influenced by Dylan and his 'It's quite easily done, you just pick anyone and pretend that you have never met' period. It's easy to be flippant about John's words of confession now, but we have to remember this was a time when divorce was a taboo subject and one

that still carried a cloud of shame. In most cases, we are merely talking about a son or daughter in a family. But John was one of the four
sons of an entire nation: a nation who thought they knew and
owned him and who, in their fickleness, would send him to
Coventry for betraying poor Cyn. To add insult to injury, there was
also 'a poor wee wain' (Julian) involved. This would have made
Cyn tarnished goods and she'd have found it difficult, if not impossible, to find another man to take both her and the child on. So,
forget Coventry, the nation would probably have sent one of their
four favourite sons to Birmingham!

So, to this twist (lyrically) you add a heart-tugging melody,
George Harrison's new-found love of Indian music, and a unique-
sounding Indian instrument, a sitar. And what do you have? A
Beatles track in a class of its own. Abbey Road Studios must have
been a very exciting place to be for the next few years. You had The
Beatles and all their influences, new and old; George Martin, with
his vast wealth of classical music and experience making records;
plus a team of engineers being continuously pushed to the limits of
experimentation and development by the five principals, forever
requesting: 'Could you now find a way of making this sound like
that?' It was a melting-pot that inspired greatness from all those
involved. The rest of us could only look on in awe.

While The Beatles, under great time constraints, created and
worked away in the studio, they had outside the doors of Abbey
Road, a tribe of people awaiting their new works and words. The
Beatles were the leaders of a new breakaway generation. It was a
generation that knew not what they wanted, but only that they
didn't want to do it the way it had been done before. The Beatles, as
I have said, were the leaders and, as leaders, we all assumed they
would have the wisdom to reveal, to us, the answers to our ever-
growing list of questions.

Hey, and you know what? Influenced, no doubt, by their new-
found stimulants, they were prepared to have a go at least in giving
us 'the word'. 'The Word' – the song and the message (on *Rubber
Soul*) – was LOVE. And that was fine. We could deal with that and
get on with it until, that is, they came back with their next message.
'The Word' (the song) was a daring attempt, by John, to take us to
where The Beatles would eventually, and more successfully, take us
with 'All You Need Is Love'. 'The Word' was just a wee bit
awkward, but then it was a very big step that John was encouraging
a frightfully stiff nation to take.

'Michelle' is the 'Paul' song on a predominately 'John' album. It's very much in the vein of 'Yesterday', with The Beatles singing part of the lyrics in French. Perhaps they were trying everything they knew to get a message to Brigitte Bardot. Not surprisingly, it is the most covered song on the album, with both the Overlanders and David and Jonathan gaining simultaneous chart success with it.

George showed his songwriting was developing perfectly. I mean, it must have been really difficult for George in those days. You are in the same band as the best songwriting team that, quite possibly, the world has ever known, and you've got to bring your songs to the same table as those guys. Add to that the pressure that you don't have a John or a Paul (like they had each other) to help you finish a difficult bit, or even co-write it. The fact that the man managed to get songs on any Beatles albums at all is a major achievement in itself and George still had a few classic surprises up his sleeve. George's two tunes on *Rubber Soul* were 'Think For Yourself', with Paul playing a fuzz bass, and 'If I Needed Someone'.

The Hollies covered 'If I Needed Someone' but George criticised their soulless version and, to show you the power of The Beatles at the time, the record was a flop. (The Hollies' previous single reached number four in the charts and the one that followed 'If I Needed Someone' reached number two.) The Hollies demonstrated perfectly what I was trying to tell you about the magical blend of Beatle voices and how it contributed immensely to their success. The Hollies also worked on close harmony arrangements and, technically, they probably were perfect but, perhaps because they were trying so hard to get it perfect, the majority of their singles sounded like vocal exercises, whereas the Beatles' blend appeared to be so effortless, yet still powerfully soulful.

Rarely were The Beatles more soulful than on 'In My Life'. This is one of my all-time favourite songs, written mostly by John, with Paul adding the middle eight after John had completed the rest of it in his house. They rarely sat down and wrote a song together these days, although both would still make valuable contributions to each other's material. George Harrison claims this was one of his favourite Beatles' songs and you can tell by his economic melodic contributions that he was obviously inspired by the whole senti- ment. Lyrically speaking, this song started out as a trip through Liverpool, reflecting on all the childhood places like Penny Lane and Strawberry Fields. For whatever reason, the lyrics didn't sit comfortably with John who chose instead to bare his soul, leaving the vivid Liverpool scenes to the future with 'Strawberry Fields Forever' in his case, and 'Penny Lane' from Paul's recollections.

'In My Life' (the record) shows just how important George Martin had become in the Beatles' creative processes. His superb baroque piano break is the final piece in the beautiful arrangement that elevates the record into the rarefied land of Beatles' classics. Martin's piano playing was recorded with the tape running at half speed and then replayed at full speed, giving a kind of harpsichord effect. It's a very moving song and one that never fails to tug at the heartstrings. I think it's because we can all put ourselves in the position of the song's commentator, trying to accept life's disappointments and lost loves – in my case, Marianne Burgess. For some reason, every time I hear this song I think of her as a mysterious and graceful lady of the lake. I haven't a clue why I imagine her in those settings but there's something awkwardly elegant about her long, slender neck. The angle at which it protrudes from her body gives you the impression of someone floating by, or floating way off into the distance. It's like I can only stare after her, in her wake, as there is nothing whatsoever I can do to stop her. Again, as with all the great songs, it's short and it's simple, no space wasted on repeating lines. George on guitar and John and Paul on vocals bring it to a very moving climax.

Listening to *Rubber Soul* – as, in fact, I do while writing this – it sounds like a masterly piece of work with all the songs working together perfectly, each one in its right place. This was still a George Martin chore although by now, The Beatles were taking more of an interest in the post-recording process of mixing and sequencing the songs. Mixing down the songs in order to achieve the perfect balance between instruments and voices is a very skilful process. Should, say, a guitar, piano, drums or voice be out of balance with their counterparts, the net result can ruin the flow of the song. The song only works as a record if nothing is allowed to distract you from its natural rhythm and flow. Equally, if the songs are not placed in the correct sequence the album can drag, lose its pace and become unsatisfying. This vital work is what George Martin and his Abbey Road team were masters at, as is evident by how much we still love and enjoy The Beatles' albums.

It should not be forgotten here that we fans sometimes grow out of our once favourite music. For whatever reason it just doesn't move you and, with the passing of time, it becomes dated. The sounds become annoying rather than offering the pleasure they once did. In the case of The Beatles, at least for me, this is never the case. I love all their albums (all the ones I consider to be true Beatles albums, but I'll get into that more later), without exception. The recorded works pass the test of time and remain classics. This is quite incredible, especially when you consider how antiquated the recording equipment and procedures were in the early days. Equally, it must be put down to the quality of the songs, their performance and the manner in which they were committed to tape.

Actually, that was a bit of a detour there. What I was starting to say was that it appears on *Rubber Soul* as if all the songs were written around the same time and came together to make this album. But such was the pressure of getting the record ready for that all-important Christmas ship-date that as they neared their deadline The Beatles, and their producer, realised they only had thirteen songs instead of their traditional, value-for-money, fourteen. So, they retrieved (from the vaults at Abbey Road) a song they'd recorded for *Help* but, for whatever reason, hadn't included it on that album. The song was *Wait* and they did a bit more work on the vocals. Then, as if by magic, they had their album completed *literally* within minutes of their deadline.

The album, their sixth, went straight to number one in the charts only ten days after they had finished recording it. I bet that would have brought smiles to the faces of all the EMI bods now that their Christmas bonuses were assured, thanks once again to George Martin's Liverpudlian discovery. You'd think EMI would have looked after Gentleman George Martin properly, wouldn't you? No way! Profits are profits and although The Beatles were filling the EMI coffers by millions upon millions, their producer was still a salaried member of EMI staff and shared none of these profits. Somewhat disgruntled, George Martin left to set up his own company and studio, AIR, and continued to work with The Beatles as an independent producer.

Brian Epstein, for his part, chose this time to renegotiate The Beatles' record royalty rate. EMI, hoping to keep their most successful breadwinners happy, hiked the royalty up by a staggering 650%. What this did, of course, was to make The Beatles less dependent on the phenomenal income their continuous touring generated. Sadly for Brian, this also served to lessen his role in the most successful entertainment act the world had ever known.

Chapter Thirty

I was dreaming a lot at this stage, I seem to remember.

The dreams I dreamt were quite unpleasant. I was living in a large city and for some reason I would have the same vivid dream, each night, of people coming to us and telling us that there were others on their way into the village who wanted to kill us, so we all had to leave quickly and go with them. And, like sheep, we would go. Instead of hiding and taking cover, we would do as they commanded and then find ourselves running along the beach, trying to get away from these destroyers. The next second I'd be indoors, climbing up to a top shelf (no kidding!) and pretending to be an ornament in order to escape the threatened wrath of the mysterious people.

Our Kathleen wanted to know what I was on. Simple answer: nothing. Then, as now, I've always got by with Guinness and a wee drop of wine now and again. I've got nothing against chemical stimulants; it's just that I don't need them and I worry about taking something that would make me lose control of my senses. I mean, I accept that can happen if you drink too much Guinness too. But then, getting blotto has never been a recreational pastime of mine either. I kept wondering if the dream had something to do with that, you know, losing control. I mean, the difference between 'there is someone coming to do you harm' and you are either left to your own devices and confidant you can protect yourself, *or* you bow to the authority of someone else and hope you will be okay. But what if the authority has an ulterior motive such as culling the population, and these people who herd you to supposed safety are in reality the death masters come to expedite the proceeding with the least possible inconvenience to the masters?

All pretty weird I know, and I'd try and talk to our Kathleen a lot about it but she said, and kept saying, 'Get out of the house a bit more!' I kept replying that I did get out of the house a lot but she said no, she didn't mean it like that. I could only assume she meant mentally.

I suppose it's when you're in love with someone – Marianne Burgess being the case still under discussion – and the relationship fails, you immediately try and fill the vast void with someone else (Susanne Quinn in my case), and by becoming involved in a relationship you are not allowing yourself to deal properly with the loss of that love. In a way, you are just delaying this process until a time you feel more able to cope with it. This is all very subconscious, don't you see, and you don't willingly or knowingly make any of these decisions.

When it had been resolved that Susanne was going to America, and thereby ending our relationship, I began to find myself thinking a lot about Marianne Burgess again. Susanne hadn't yet left for America but at least we had made all our decisions and were civil to each other. No, that's not quite true. When I say we were civil to each other it implies, in a way, that there was a strain between us and we were trying consciously to be nice, or civil, to each other. This was not the case. We were mates and would become friends if time and distance would allow it. But we had mutually agreed it was time to move on.

In a way, I suppose I was clearing out my mind and therefore allowing, or encouraging, myself to think about Marianne Burgess. The problem was that I realised, and accepted, that I really had been in love with her. The bigger problem was that my feelings hadn't really changed; I was still in love with her.

'What is love, Theodore?' I hear you ask. 'What do you mean when you say you were really in love with her?'

Yes, thanks. Thanks a million! Ask an easy question, why don't you? Love is personal. It is the state you find yourself in when you are attracted to another human and words fail you. I couldn't get Marianne Burgess out of my mind. It still brought a lump to my throat every time I thought about her. When we'd been going out together and I would see her again after a break of a day or night, I would literally have to fight to catch my breath. I felt as close to her after making love as I did before. I cared about her as much as I cared about my mum and dad and our Kathleen, and my other sister, I suppose. She (Colette) was older than Kathleen and I and we weren't really close, but she was family.

Marianne dumped me for a married man and I still couldn't feel badly towards her. She was the only person in the world I would consider lending my Beatles records to. I could talk to her forever. We never fell into a routine. I liked her. I know that probably sounds a wee bit funny; boys like girls 'cause they can get into bed with them and do naughty things together, but that's not what I mean. I mean I liked her as a person. I admired her views. Mind you, we didn't agree on everything but that was okay because it meant we had more than a few healthy discussions.

We all have this suit of clothing we wear above, or below, our normal clothes. This is the suit of our individuality. You know the sort of thing: do you care about your parents? Do you give money to charity? Do you let people know that you give money to charity? Are you capable of being faithful? Do you like books? Music? Films? Football? Ballet? Brain surgery? Train spotting? Are you ambitious? Do you seek wealth? Do you care about what's going on in the world or are you just preoccupied with your own little space? And so on. All the thousands of preferences, thoughts and ideas, which, when placed in a certain combination, create our own uniqueness. And I liked the person Marianne Burgess was. She didn't think ill of people. She didn't harbour bad thoughts, even though she probably had reason to with the Married Man and how he had treated her before we'd met. She hadn't been just feminine company for me. She was a mate and I was really missing her as a mate... that is, of course, as well as all the other ways I was missing her.

And then there is sex, so let's talk about sex. The sex had been great, but Marianne Burgess had this big thing that it always had to be special. She once told me that an aunt of hers, who was only in her mid-thirties, had claimed that she and her husband, Marianne's uncle, rarely made love any more. Neither of them felt like it. No big thing, she claimed; she and her husband still liked each other, it was just that for them the mechanics of where all the body parts fitted together was functional rather than sexual. This aunt had had a few sherries and she went on and on, telling Marianne about her breasts sagging, her bottom falling and her husband developing a beer belly. She also told her that, at about the same time, he lost his will or interest in pleasing her and they were no longer attracted to each other in that way. The aunt said she couldn't see how a man and a woman could live together, share the same space continuously and not lose it; the desire for each other. When the moans of pleasure become the grunts of annoyance at not being able to find, or give, relief, the writing is on the wall and not just the bedroom wall.

So, Marianne Burgess' big thing was that she wanted us to keep it special, to make an effort to keep it special. Like keeping our space in the flat private from each other. Marianne felt that there

were few things, if any, as sensual as underwear, filled with the
body's erotic mysteries that is. But scattered around the bedroom
floor, crumpled up and a day or two old, they were a complete turn-
off. Marianne Burgess said that we wouldn't make love every single
night. Equally, we wouldn't not make love every single night. It
would happen if, and when, it was right. Try to recreate the first
time when you didn't know whether or not it was going to happen,
but you just wanted it to happen. She would ask me to remember
how much I wanted to make love to her the first time, before I knew
it was definitely going to happen. She claimed she had felt the same
way: where your behaviour to a potential lover is lots of things but,
above all, considerate. Her thing was to always want to be that
considerate to your partner. In a way, you have to feel that if you
play your cards right you end up making love. Equally, if you don't
– play your cards right, that is – you won't. Above all else she
wanted to keep the spice in our relationship. It was as though she
needed me to always want her as much as I had first wanted her. She
need not have worried on that front. I found her to be the most
sensual, provocative, creature that'd ever walked the face of the
earth. I wanted her so much it hurt. Physically. Yes, I don't mind
admitting it. And the bittersweet thing was that I still did.

The funny thing was, though, the last time we made love, on that
fateful Wednesday morning, it was beautiful; it was great. What
more can I tell you without blushing. We didn't know it was to be
our last time. It was just another time we had come together to share
the pleasures of each other's bodies. For me, it was like, you know,
you have this secret vision of whom you would like to make love to
because you think it would be the best: an actress, Barbara Parkins,
in my case. But the image is preserved because you don't live
together. It's just an illusion you pull from the heavens when you
need it. Well, with Marianne Burgess, my dream, my illusion and
my lover had been one and the same.

If I'm being very honest, I'd been thinking about her when I was
with other girls, even Susanne, which is dog-doo, I know. However,
now that I had considered it – now that Susanne Quinn and I were
not in a relationship and I was dealing with the loss of Marianne
Burgess – I was, little by little, accepting these things and coming to
the conclusion that I shouldn't try for relationships with other
women. The way I felt, it was going to be too destructive. I felt I was
in danger of permanently damaging my feelings and my ability to
understand them.

On the *Rubber Soul* album, Paul McCartney, with a little backup from John Lennon, sang that love had a nasty habit of disappearing overnight. The song was 'I'm Looking Through You' and I was beginning to accept it was true; the man knew what he was talking about. But how on earth did any member of The Beatles have time to fall in love, let alone deal with, consider and articulate any thoughts on it? Paul, in that song, was dealing with the stunning Jane Asher leaving to go to Bristol on an acting job. She was going against Paul's wishes, it transpired.

These thoughts, and others, filled my mind as I walked from a meeting at the Adelphi Hotel. I'd written a few songs with Vincent, and his publisher had caught the train up to Liverpool to discuss a deal with me. I was feeling quite happy because he'd also let it slip in the conversation that they'd persuaded a group – he wouldn't tell me who, only that they were big – to record one of the songs. The song in question was one I particularly liked and was proud of my contribution. Surprise, surprise, the song was about Marianne Burgess. The lyrics were mostly mine and the music was mostly Vincent's. The song was called 'I'm Thinking Of You (Again)'. I liked the brackets idea; it's like giving people two thoughts to ponder, not just the one. It's like 'I'm thinking of you' is to say, 'Oh, you know I'm thinking of you,' and the answer usually is, 'Oh, are you dear? That's nice.' But when you add the word 'again', especially if in a bracket, (I think) it implies an obsession of some kind. Don't you think? Not really? Oh well, never mind. Lennon and McCartney needn't worry about my efforts then; their mantle is safe.

Anyway, I was walking along feeling quite chuffed with myself; in fact, I was whistling 'I'm Thinking Of You (Again)'. You really don't think the brackets imply an obsession? No? Humph! Sorry, back to the story. A very catchy melody, Theo, I was thinking, that will do well on the radio. When all of a sudden I hear from behind me:

'So, which cream has this cat been licking?'

I turned around to see John Lennon, and you know what else he said? I'll tell you. He said, 'I really think that those brackets around "Again" imply an obsession, and a great obsession at that!' No, just kidding! But I tell you, if it had been John Lennon I probably would have been less shocked than I was when I turned around to discover the speaker was none other than the very beautiful Marianne Burgess. But she was looking distinctly different. Picture me speechless, because I was. Marianne Burgess had cut her long, beautiful hair into a French bob. Her new look made her look older, more sophisticated and damned more attractive, if that was possible. She looked a little world-weary however, but even that added to the intrigue.

'Have you heard the new Beatles album?' I blurted.

'Theo, I haven't seen you for ages, we… well, we kind of, you know, dissolved and disappeared out of each other's lives and now I meet you by accident and you don't say something like, "Where were you?" or "How are you doing?" or "I see you've had your hair cut," or even, "Leave me alone, I never want to see you again." Any of those I would have been expecting, but never did I expect you to ask me if I'd heard the new Beatles record. It's good to see you haven't changed,' she smiled warmly, revealing instantly that although she may have changed her look drastically, she hadn't gone the full hog and had her twisted tooth seen to.

'How are you doing?' I ventured. It was still one of those conversations that could have lasted for only another thirty seconds and then we'd both go our way into oblivion. Equally, it might have developed into a chat.

'I'm… ' she paused, 'I'm okay, Theo, you know.'

I smiled. As I smiled, I considered my teeth. How did they look? Fine, I hoped. Did I hope that because I wanted to kiss her? What an absurd thought. I thought about the coffee I'd just been drinking at the Adelphi and how it might have stained my teeth. I found myself closing my mouth and wiping my teeth with my tongue.

'You're growing your hair.'

'You've cut yours.'

'Yes.'

'It looks great, Marianne. You look great.'

'Yours looks like George and Ringo's on the *Rubber Soul* sleeve. I see they made a mistake on the sleeve, though,' she offered.

Great, she had got the album. I don't really know why I thought it was great that she had bought a copy of *Rubber Soul*, but I just thought that it was.

'What? What was the mistake?'

'They forgot to put The Beatles' name on the jacket,' she claimed.

'I don't think they forgot, I think it was intentional. The Beatles' photograph on the jacket lets everyone know it's The Beatles, and their faces are so well known around the world that everyone knows who they are. What do you think of the album?'

'I love it, Theo, I really do. Every time I hear John singing 'In My Life', I think of you.'

I didn't really grasp what she had said. I just took it for shared enthusiasm. 'It's a great song, isn't it? I just love it. Brilliant!'

'I love it that you're still so enthusiastic about them, about their music. It's so... so you.'

'Where have you been, Marianne?'

'Have you got an hour?' she said with a laugh.

It was one of those things people say for effect in a conversation, obviously not actually meaning it literally: 'Do you have sixty minutes to spend with me so that I can tell you this long story?' You just mean that it's a long story. But I had my opening and was about to jump into it when I heard our Kathleen's voice in my head, reminding me that I had been too 'into' Marianne Burgess and it hadn't been appreciated. So I held back my feet for once, thought first, and then said.

'Not really, but how about a quick coffee?'

'Yes, that would be nice,' she replied, and we headed back to the Adelphi.

Chapter Thirty-One

Four coffees later we ordered our first glass of wine. The thing about wine is it loosens the tongue; make tongue plural in our case. There was a buzz from the residents in the residents' lounge of the Adelphi, although I wouldn't have liked to place a bet on how many of our noisy company were actual residents. A noisy room does give you a certain degree of privacy, though.

'So, how are you and Ken getting on?' I offered to the room, so noisy it was like a bingo hall before the caller arrives. I had rephrased the question in my mind a few times. I couldn't get the one with 'Married Man' past my censors, nor would they go for 'ahm... what's his name?' I didn't want to be facetious. I didn't particularly want to score points with Marianne Burgess. She looked stunning but not in the way she used to look stunning. Gone was the all-black look. Today she wore cream slacks, a white shirt (looking dangerously like a man's shirt to me, but I was hopeless at all that; you know, what side a lady does her buttons on, what fingers all the various rings go on, and so on – I always lean on our Kathleen for all that stuff), and a well-worn suede jacket. As I mentioned, her hair was shorter, barely shoulder length, and she had the minimum of make-up on; just a bit around the eyes and a bright red lipstick. Now there's a point: talking about all things feminine, is lipstick called lipstick because (a) it comes in the shape of a stick or (b) because it sticks to the lips? I don't know the answer to that question myself, but names of things have always interested me. Things like the first meal of the day being called 'breakfast' simply because you were breaking the fast you had enjoyed during your sleep. A nice wee descriptive word, 'breakfast', isn't it? So why isn't lipstick called 'lip covering' or even 'lip-artificial-colouring-to-give-the-appearance-of-sexual-arousal-in-the-female-species-stick'?

'Oh, ahm...that didn't really work out,' she replied.

'What?' I replied, at a volume that turned each and every head in the high-ceilinged and beautifully decorated residents' lounge. The same lounge that, when newly built, would have hosted passengers (first class) nervous about their imminent sea journey to America, or relieved by their safe return: either way, in need of a few stiff drinks.

Marianne Burgess looked like a little, lost girl as she raised her wine glass to her lips to spare her some embarrassment. I followed suit and when our audience discovered there was not to be an answer – at least not an answer shared with them – bit by bit, and decibel by decibel, they returned to their own conversations at their original volume.

'Sorry,' I whispered.

'It's okay. It was quite amusing, in a way,' she said, as she smiled at me.

'So what happened? Where did you go? Why didn't you call me? When did all this happen?' I gushed.

'Goodness, Theo, such a lot of questions. Let's see now. I sent him back to his wife when I realised how stupid it all was. I went to teacher training college in Manchester. I didn't think it was fair to call you. It all happened about three weeks after you and I split up.'

'All just as simple as that?' I pushed, as I caught the waitress's attention and ordered two more glasses of wine.

'No, not really. Look, this is awkward. I'm not sure I'm ready for this, Theo. I didn't think I'd meet you for ages yet,' Marianne Burgess replied, taking several different stabs to try and find a direction from which to answer my question.

You know, it *was* awkward. I mean, when you are sitting with the woman you once loved, still love in fact – a woman you have shared the greatest pleasure known to mankind with – and you are merely talking to her, well it is difficult. You are no longer privy to the secrets of her delicious body, yet you know all these secrets and you would have surely discovered more had the relationship not been prematurely terminated. So, in effect, you have to be very careful with your language and even more careful with your body language. I mean, she carried it off absolutely to a tee. An outsider looking at us – well, looking at her – would never have guessed we were anything more than friends.

'It's funny,' I began, my thoughts surfacing into the conversation. 'I was just thinking, earlier today in fact, that I missed so much having you as a mate.'

Now you see, there's a perfect example of what I was just talking about. In the old days, she would have looked at me coyly and said, 'Do you always *have* your mates?' Yes, she would have used italics in her conversation. She still managed to surprise me with her reply.

'I've missed you too.' Her words hung in the air above us, visible to no-one except us. But she had let the guard drop, if only a little. 'It was all so sudden, impulsive. I can't believe we finished so quickly.'

'There seemed no other way to do it,' I replied. 'I felt you had made your decision and I thought it would be less painful for the two of us if we moved on immediately. Also, if you and I had had a winding-down period, so to speak, it could have made it awkward between you and Ken.'

'I don't mean to be rude, but that's just such a flipping stupid thing to say, Theodore. Why would you want to be so accommodating to another man?'

'I wasn't. I was being accommodating to you, Marianne.' I replied quietly. The wine arrived and she drank half of hers in one gulp.

'Yeah, well, it seemed to me like you couldn't wait to get rid of me. I was hurt Theo, hurt that you didn't put up a fight,' she said in the pause, just before she completely drained her glass of wine.

'I can't believe you're saying this,' I said. We were both sitting on our own half-sofas. There were three of them and one hard chair around this basketwork table with a glass top. I was now leaning on the arm of my sofa closest to her. She, in turn, was very close to the arm of her sofa nearest to me. We were so close I could smell her. Indeed, we were close enough to talk at a volume that could not possibly be overheard.

'We were together, getting along just fine, I thought. He sends you one letter and you go all misty-eyed and then you're off. Yeah, Marianne, I didn't think I could compete with that, so what was the point? You knew I loved you, but if that wasn't enough then que sera, sera.'

Marianne Burgess ordered the next round of drinks, even though I'd done as much damage to my glass of wine as my mum would to my dad's Guinness. (My mum's tipple was sherry.) She looked at me as if deciding whether she could, or should, or *would*, tell me what was on her mind.

'You loved me too much, Theo. You wanted too much from me. For you, our love was everything. Nothing else mattered and that was destructive. In that world everything has to be perfect, and nothing's perfect, Theo. We still had our lives to lead. But you wanted too much of us. The problem was that the more you wanted from us, the bigger the disappointment was going to be when you realised that we weren't living in a fairytale world and we weren't going to live happily ever after.'

She saw from my face that she was hurting me and she leaned across to take my hand.

'Theo, when it's as great as it was between us, you can't want too much. Most people never feel in their lives what we had, but equally you can't waste it, and I was scared. I was really scared. Scared of you becoming a lapdog. You were substituting our love for the beans-and-chips diet you told me you and Vincent used to live on. You can't live on love, Theo. Your love could only end with me letting you down. I'd too much to live up to. I didn't want to disappoint you. Ken's letter gave me an out, or at least a way to readdress our situation, but before I'd a moment to think about it that morning, it was all over. Our relationship was over. I'm not really sure what I wanted, but I was shocked when it all ended so quickly. However, I should also say that, hurtful though it was, it was probably for the best.'

I was still speechless so she continued: 'I asked Kathleen about you and she told me to leave you alone, and let you get on with your life.'

'When did you see our Kathleen? She didn't tell me that she'd seen you. All these people, walking around, deciding what was best for me behind my back, really makes me sick.'

'Ah, don't be mad at Kathleen. It was only the day before yesterday and I just got back at the weekend. I asked her not to tell you I was back. I wanted to get ready for you before I met you again.'

She was still rubbing my right hand in both of her hands, across the top of the sofa arms. She used to do that quite often when we were walking, or listening to music, or listening to the radio, or watching the television round at Kathleen's or my parents' house.

'You see,' I began, not really sure what I was going to say but feeling a need to say something, 'I don't figure it the same way you do. I thought we were in love. That was fine, that was enough for me. For me that was, and is, the starting point. No matter what is wrong, if we start on the basic premise that we love one another, we can work out everything needing to be worked out. Now I accept, thanks to our Kathleen, that I didn't have my act together and that my failings were evident. That's fine, I can deal with that. *We* could have dealt with that, because all it took was for her to sit me down and say blah, blah, blah and I'd have thought about it and accepted it. Now maybe it would have been a different matter if she had said it when you and I were together; maybe I would have thought she was talking rubbish and still felt it was all wine and roses in our corner of the garden. But I'm sure that if you and I had talked about it, I would have looked at it differently.'

'Yes, great Theo. It's all very easy with hindsight. But when you are right bang in the middle of the hurricane, it's a different matter. I didn't know what was happening or what was going wrong. Hell, I didn't even know if anything *was* wrong. I just used to have the overwhelming feeling that you felt we were in love and that that was enough for you, but it wasn't for me. I was happy to be in love with you but I also wanted to have a life. I wanted *us* to have a life. Your love was so sure and so strong it frightened me, Theo. Sometimes I worried that I might not love you as much as you loved me and I thought that was a big sin, the greatest sin. But I realised after we split that I did love you.'

'You did?'

'What? Love you or realised I loved you?'

'Both.'

'Yes… both. This is confusing.'

'Ah, no. It might have something to do with the wine and the lack of food in your stomach,' I replied, saddened that the conversation had gone off the rails. She'd just been about to say something about 'love' and 'me' and how the two words fitted together.

'I'll drink to that. Where's the waiter?'

'God, it is true what they say about students.'

'What's that?'

'You know, about the drink and stuff?'

'Theo, just a bit of Dutch courage. I've been working up to meeting you and what I was going to say for ages; how I was going to pick my words very carefully, and then I met you by accident. Anyway, where was I?'

Good, I thought, she's obviously got something she wants to get off her beautiful chest and wants to get on with it.

Might as well help her along!

'You were just getting to the point where you had realised that you had been in love with me. Why didn't you contact me then?'

'Well, I had thought about it to be honest, but then someone told me about your American singer. God, you didn't hang around long in sackcloth, did you?'

'Susanne Quinn's her name. Hey, you were gone for good. Ken had left his wife for you.'

'Ken's an idiot. Just because you have a wife and two children does not mean that you are blessed with any intelligence. I used to think that when I was young, you know. I would look up to all these people getting married because I thought they all needed to be worldly-wise before they were allowed to get married. When they had children, well, goodness, I thought they were up there with the disciples. Wrong! Ken was just playing with people's emotions, including his own. That's when I started to think about you again. I'd compare the two of you and I couldn't believe I'd made the choice I made. I still wasn't sure I'd made my choice though; I kind of had a feeling that you being, being so... so... so accommodating forced me into it.' She gave me a reproachful look and dropped my hand in search of her wineglass.

'Relationships either work or they don't. You can't really force them, can you?' she continued, after a sip. 'Some are natural like ours was and some are not, like the one with Ken, for instance. You know, when it's just natural to be together and hang out, as you used to say. Then you have the one where you're always wondering if your partner is okay, and then he says, "And what would you like to do now, dear?" Ken started to treat me like I was "the wife, the wee wifey indoors". I didn't realise that some men don't think of their wives as humans.'

'Oh come on, Marianne.'

'Honest Theo, I kid you not, even a little. I've worked out that's why they are unfaithful. They don't think that their wives are human. They think that "the wee wife" is an appliance. She keeps his house, cleans his clothes, feeds him, looks after his offspring and provides sexual relief – usually in a state of kinky undress, but that's another story. So, after a month of this I was running up the walls. I couldn't believe what I had let myself in for. I couldn't believe that I'd actually longed for that, you know, to be with him all the time; all those tearful, lonely nights by myself while I awaited a visit from "him on high", "he who must be obeyed". Then he started to do the same thing again, only this time I was the "wee wife". I was the one being cheated on. I was the one being told all these stupid stories.'

'What? He started to cheat on you as well?' I asked, in disbelief.

'Well no, not quite, but all the signs were there that he was about to. And I was angry. I wasn't jealous, I was mad. Mad at him for being a shit. Mad at myself for losing something special,' she said, in a very quiet voice. After a time, she added, 'Losing someone special.'

Someone special. Was that me? And if it was, did the fact that she had lost me meant that she figured that she had lost me forever? What were my feelings in all of this? Would I have gotten back with her then if I had the chance? I didn't know. That's why I was asking myself the question.

The problem with going out with someone you love and then splitting up is that if you get back together again, surely you must keep thinking that you are going to split up again. You know, you keep thinking that your original thoughts about this being forever was wrong and so you can't really trust your feelings. Would such doubts sour the love and have you split up again anyway? Or would you just be so happy that you would put up with anything again just to be with this person, despite all the pain you'd felt over losing her?

Could it ever be a true relationship again? The thing about relationships is not to get too preoccupied with them. You can't spend all your time sitting around, contemplating your navel and thinking about your relationship because if you do, you are not really in the relationship, you're around it – and that can't be rewarding. Don't you see now there was a lot of baggage, and dealing with baggage is not a genuine emotion. It's like you either *live* your life or you *think* about living your life. One of those is a waste.

'So, what happened?' I asked, innocently.

'Ah, now there's a story.'

'Yes?'

'Well, he liked to give these dinner parties. One night he was due to have his boss and wife around, as well as some chap from Holland and his wife. Ken and his boss were apparently trying to set up some kind of deal with the Dutch. They wanted this chap's company to handle the European distribution rights for their stuff.'

'What is his stuff?' I interrupted. Now that it appeared Ken and Marianne Burgess were no longer an item, it was harmless in putting some flesh to the bones. 'What does Ken do?'

'Oh, didn't you know? They manufacture tops for milk bottles.'

'What?' I said, in disbelief.

'Oh yes, Theo. It's very interesting, very exciting. Did you know that they can do three different coloured bottle tops. I know this to be a fact. Ken brought them home for me to have a look at,' Marianne Burgess said and then broke off into a fit of laughter. I'd caught up with her in the wine stakes and found it equally hilarious.

'So anyway, back to the story. I decided to show this Dutch couple what domestic family life was like in England. I cooked the vilest meal I could think of; I mean just rubbish – eggs, sour milk, rhubarb, bacon, ham, peppers, cabbage. It was *the* most unlikely concoction you can imagine. I'd been saving up leftovers for weeks and everything went into the pot. And I do mean everything. On the night, I built up the meal by saying that for our Dutch friends I had cooked a favourite traditional English meal, Kop Kurrie, and I would serve it in a traditional English housewife's costume. So they were all sitting around the dinner table, guzzling down their wine, and I walked in carrying this big tray. I was dressed only in stockings, a suspender belt, black bra and panties, high-heeled shoes and a large smile.'

I couldn't believe what she was telling me. Marianne Burgess, dressed like that in company? Wow, she must really have been mad. Oh yes. When she said 'suspender belt', I thought of it as another of those names, you know, like lipstick. So-called because of the use of suspension, but something like 'a garment of limited material but high sexual stimulation' might have been more appropriate.

'What happened?' I asked, anxious as the rest of you for her to reveal the rest of her story.

'Well, because of the build-up I'd given the costume and how much Ken liked me to dress up in it, Ken and his boss went as red as the beetroots on the top of the Kop Kurrie. Mavis, the boss's wife, got the joke; she'd obviously been in the same situation herself, lots of times, and I don't mean the dress.'

'I know,' I said, unnecessarily.

'So, I brought over the meal, set it down and dished out a big portion for everyone, except Mavis and me, and I winked at her as I was dishing out hers. Well, you should have seen their faces as they started into the food. The Dutch couple tried to be polite and eat it, but it was vile. I kept saying, "Come on now, eat up everyone, there's lots more." Ken didn't know where to put himself, he couldn't shout at me, his pretend-wife, sitting there dressed as a tart, in front of his boss. But I had one final act planned. I went over to Ken's side of the table and said, "Oh dear, you're too full to eat the beautiful dinner I've just cooked for you. We have another tradition here," I said to our guests. "When the man of the house does not eat his dinner, it has to be poured over his head," and I did just that. I poured it over his head and all over his best suit. I felt so great. I'd already packed my bag and I went upstairs, put on some clothes and left them all with their chins, lots of chins, hanging down on the floor.'

'Funny, Marianne. Remind me never to make you mad. A wee bit strong for someone you *thought* was *considering* cheating.'

'Actually, he had been cheating, all the bleeding time we were together, with his secretary. But at least one of them was going to be out of a job following the evening of the Kop Kurrie. I mean, he must have thought I was stupid. It was so obvious he was cheating. He didn't even bother to try and hide it. Maybe he didn't think that he had to 'cause I wasn't really his wife. God, what a disaster,' and then, without batting an eyelid, she asked, 'So how are you and the American getting on?'

'Ah, she's gone home.'

'What, to America?' she asked. I thought I could see a little bit of relief in her magic, smiling eyes.

'Well, that's where Americans have a habit of going home to,' I replied, deadpan.

'Come on, Theo. You know what I mean. Tell me what happened.'

'Well, her visa ran out and she needed a permit to stay here. Her choices were either to marry or to go home.'

'Did you think of marrying?'

'No. I mean the visa thing probably made us look at what we had, which was really a friendship thing, and that was fine. Perfectly fine when both parties are taking it like that. And we did. And we are. And we are still friends and still will be friends. I wish her well and she wishes me well, I'm sure. She is a great person and I'm sure she will meet someone and get on with life,' I said. In truth, what I was about to say there was, 'and live happily ever after,' but I remembered the first part of our conversation and opted out.

'Did she know about us?'

'Yes, Marianne, she did.'

'Mmmm!' she said, as she looked at her watch.

The question I wanted to ask her, the one that was screaming to be asked, was, 'What about us?' but it wouldn't fly. I just couldn't make it fly.

'So what are you doing now, then?' I asked her instead.

'I'm still at teacher training college, but I've got two weeks off. Another one and a half left.'

'And then you go back to Manchester?'

'And then I go back to Manchester. So Theo, what are you doing?'

'Well, the agency is going very well and my group, the Night...'

'No, no. I meant romantically.' she interrupted.

'To be honest, Marianne, I've come to the conclusion that I was only delaying dealing with losing you. I've been going out with these people either to fill the gap or to avoid the pain. But after Susanne, I decided it was time to face up to it, deal with the pain and get on with stuff. That's really where I'm at, not really looking for someone.'

'That's when it's most likely you're going to meet someone.'

'Nagh, I think you have to be able to pick up signals as well as give them out. At the minute, my receiver is turned off. And you?'

'Well, kind of. There's this boy at college. I like him, I think.'

She liked him, she thought. She'd just scored two direct hits and she *liked* him, she *thought*. Shit, I thought, I could use italics as well.

'And is it serious?' I asked, crossing my fingers, legs, eyes, mind; anything, in fact, that I could find.

'Well, I suppose I'd have to say that it is,' she replied, sheepishly.

'That's a strange way to answer the question,' I said, quietly.

'Well, it's just… it's just… I… what I mean to say, Theo, is that he has just asked me to marry him.'

Chapter Thirty-Two

Sounds to me like time for the adverts. You know, you're in the middle of watching No Hiding Place on the telly and, just as Inspector Lockhart discovers, while questioning a husband and wife, that the husband is not, in fact, the husband (and the daughter he thought was his daughter is in fact the daughter of his best friend), they leave you hanging in the air as someone comes on singing that, "Johnson's are the polishes for furniture and homes because they shine so easily". I don't have any adverts for you, unless you want to buy some of my records. I've got a garage full of them and that *definitely* is another story. No, I think it's time for another musical interlude with The Beatles. And *what* a musical interlude we have for you.

'Paperback Writer' was written mostly by Paul McCartney, with a little help from his friend, John Lennon. The song was meant to be about John Lennon the author. John's second book, *A Spaniard In The Works*, was to be published on June 24th, two weeks to the day after the release of this new single. 'Paperback Writer' was another story-song with references to a few characters, including one whose name sounded not unlike how Paul's name would have sounded were it to be recorded backwards. Paul was trying to show that The Beatles could compete with his current favourite group, The Beach Boys, on vocal harmonies. He didn't have to try to show he was a great bass player; it is more than evident with his playing the classic bass riff that this song is based upon. The flip side was *Rain,* which showed the hints of psychedelic influences creeping in, especially with the first use of vocals recorded backwards (perhaps how the above-mentioned character name originated), and was yet another number one single. More's the reason to celebrate.

If *Rubber Soul* was a 'John song-led' album, then *Revolver* is a 'Paul song-led' album; and a damned fine album at that. To be honest, it took me a while to get to grips with the music on *Revolver*. Now, when I look back on it, I keep thinking it had something to do with the sleeve; *Revolver* is my least favourite Beatles sleeve. I have to admit, I'm not a fan of black-and-white photos, artwork or movies at the best of times. Add to that the fact that Klaus Voormann's artwork (literally) leaves me a bit cold, and you end up with a sleeve I had to get beyond before I could enjoy the music within. They say perseverance pays; well it did with this album. It's now up there in my top three Beatles albums.

The album starts off with a George Harrison song, 'Taxman'. At this point in their career, The Beatles were paying tax at a staggering rate of 19 shillings and 6 pence (97 and 1/2 new pence) in the pound. Newly-wed George, tongue firmly in cheek – for it was he who signed (on behalf of The Beatles) the cheques to the Inland Revenue – was having a bit of a go at our taskmasters. George and his new bride, Patti Boyd, took a holiday in Spain with Brian Epstein. Brian obviously gave his client a bit of a pep talk about the old songwriting, because George had an unprecedented three songs on the *Revolver* album and, spurred on by the confidence of this, he was writing and stockpiling a lot of the songs that would make up his first solo effort, *All Things Must Pass*. His other two *Revolver* songs 'Love To You' and 'I Want To Tell You' sound perfect under the Beatles umbrella, proving that no preferential treatment was afforded to the Lennon and McCartney songs.

Paul had written another song, 'Woman', for his mates Peter and Gordon, and he had the song credited as Bernard Webb to see if the song could be a hit merely on the strength of its quality, rather than through the Beatles connection. He needn't have worried because it was a chart success both here and in the States. As a songwriter his future was secure, even outside of The Beatles. His songwriting for the band was still on the rise and a long way from peaking, although some of us wondered if he would ever be able to better 'Eleanor Rigby'.

'Eleanor Rigby' benefited immensely from George Martin's exquisite string arrangement, using a double string quartet or similar. Lyrically it's one of Paul's best works, taking us right into the middle of this mini-movie, during which all these characters come to life through the words and the music. This is very important in trying to create a story in a song. You don't have the luxury of time and pages to fill out all the subtleties of the scene and the characters. The melody of a song and the mood created by the vocalist, however, will certainly take you to a place that words rarely can. When I listen to this song I always think of Marianne Burgess.

With the song you discover, through the lyrics, all about the soul and life of one Ms Rigby and how all may not be as it seems. You see this girl, perhaps beautiful, picking up the rice in a church where a wedding has taken place, and you get to go behind the beauty and see some of the troubles. Marianne Burgess was still, in a way, a mystery to me. Yes, we'd spent time together; yes, we'd shared some intimate moments, but I always kept thinking there was a lot more there, like I'd not even scratched the surface and that perhaps I should have tried. Had there been things she hadn't told me? Were there questions I could have asked her that would have unlocked the secrets? I tried to imagine the various scenarios that might apply to her; perhaps Ken The Married Man had something on her, something he could blackmail her with to ensure she kept running back to him. But what could he possibly have on her?

This was an image I kept coming back to a lot because, as I said, every time I heard 'Eleanor Rigby' I thought of Marianne, and I was hearing it a lot as it was yet another Beatles song that proved very popular with other artists. At least two hundred artists covered it, including The Supremes; The Four Tops; Johnny Mathis; Vanilla Fudge (whose dramatic sound worked well on the song); Ray Charles (who scored a UK top thirty hit with it); and the soul queen, Aretha Franklin, who enjoyed a USA top thirty with this unique song.

As I mentioned to you earlier, *Rubber Soul* was to be the first step in substituting a new medium to fill the impending gap that would be left in their lives by not touring. Despite this new-found space, they were still under pressure of time, release deadlines, televisions and concerts, as they completed work on *Rubber Soul*. Not so with *Revolver*. This album was recorded between 8th April 1966 and June 22nd 1966, which was towards the end of a gap that would prove to be their longest break from gigging since the days of The Quarry Men.

Originally in this period, The Beatles were meant to be working on their third movie; the movie that was to be based on the novel, *A Talent for Loving*, by Richard Condon. This movie was to have had a country and western feel, and the boys were meant to come up with some country songs to reflect this. The Beatles (particularly Ringo, who was looking forward to playing a Mexican) liked the book and gave their nod to the project but they were very disappointed with the first script presented. The project moved onto the back burner, and eventually it was dropped altogether. This in turn allowed the decks to be completely cleared and so, with trusted and creative producer Gentleman George Martin, they started work on the new recordings, which were to produce the 'Paperback Writer' and 'Rain' single and *Revolver* album.

Revolver is The Beatles at their creative peak; three years and a million planets from *Please Please Me*. I suppose that *Rubber Soul* showed us they were capable of scaling incredible heights but with *Revolver*, they created an album against which all future albums would be judged. In the middle of this creative whirlpool, you had the four musicians themselves; George Martin; their engineer, Geoff Emerick; Lennon & McCartney, the world's finest songwriters; George Harrison, proving the finest didn't have a monopoly on Northern songs; studio electronic experimentation; stimulants (chemical and otherwise); an explosion in the fashion and pop-art worlds; the frustrations of touring and living continuously in a fish bowl (yes, it was a *gold*fish bowl, but it was not rewarding); and, on top of all of that, you had a host of emerging artists such as Dylan; The Beach Boys; The Kinks; Spencer Davies Group; Jimi Hendrix's Experience; and Ulster's finest, Them, chomping at the bit. All were ready and willing, but unable to steal The Beatles' crown.

Hell, some of them even tried with songs from the *Revolver* album. Cliff Bennett and The Rebel Rousers recorded 'Got To Get You Into My Life', with Paul producing their version of his Tamla-influenced classic. This was yet another hit with another Beatles song; number six in the UK top ten during late Aug 1966 (around the same time The Beatles held the number one position with 'Eleanor Rigby'). On the Beatles' version, the brass section is from Georgie Fame's band, The Blue Flames. This punchy song proved that The Beatles could do what the rest of the English artists were failing miserably to do – reproduce the American soul sound. The Beatles' version was released some years later as a Beatles single in the US of A. It was at the time of the Charles Manson thing and he was giving heavy publicity to 'Helter Skelter'. Good old Capitol Records stuck 'Helter Skelter' on the B-side of 'Got To Get You Into My Life' to capitalise on the Manson profile. It reached number three in the American charts.

Paul McCartney has often said how much he loved The Beach Boys; particularly their song, 'God Only Knows'. This influence he proudly demonstrates with the beautiful 'Here, There and Everywhere'. I love listening to this song; there is so little instrumentation on the record that all you really get is the song itself. Again, I hate to be boring, but that incredible blend of Beatle voices!

It was no surprise that someone with a voice as pure as Emmylou Harris would record this song and, in so doing, enjoy a UK top thirty hit.

Marianne Burgess' four-year-old brother, Jonathan, loved 'Yellow Submarine', which was another track on the *Revolver* album. This song, purely and simply, was written and recorded for the enjoyment of children. Jonathan could sing this song from start to finish, making a brave attempt at all the silly sounds in between as well. This was the first time we were to hear Ringo singing on a Beatles single (another double A-side and another number one single). The vocal chorus is provided by Mal Evans, Neil Aspinall, Brian Jones, Marianne Faithfull, Patti Harrison and George Martin, with John keeping them all in time by blowing bubbles with his latest musical discovery – a glass, water and a straw! The kids around the streets of Liverpool had their own version of this song. It went: 'We all eat Stork margarine, Stork margarine, Stork... ' I think you get the picture!

The influence of chemicals is rarely more apparent than on 'She Said She Said', a 'John' song and definitely a drug song. Peter Fonda had dropped a tab of acid, in The Beatles' company, and felt he'd died. As he came down from the influence of the drug, he ran around saying he knew what it felt like to be dead. Definitely a good lyrical idea, which John immediately picked up on. Peter would know what it was like to be dead, wouldn't he? I mean, unlike his dad, he'd been acting like a stiff for years, hadn't he? Ouch!

The songs on this album, one after another, were brilliant – truly brilliant – and for some reason they all work well together. I can't imagine anyone being brave enough to put 'Yellow Submarine' on a record that shares gems like 'Here, There and Everywhere', not to mention 'And Your Bird Can Sing'. But I believe that was part of their secret: they weren't musical snobs. They were, first and foremost, songwriters in the classic songwriting tradition. Songs were meant to be about entertainment, about consoling you, about comforting you and about making you laugh. Songs were not written as a way of making money. Yes, a by-product of successfully writing songs was that they generated income, but this was mainly because the songwriters were being successful at their art. They were communicating with people and people responded. People liked the songs so they bought them. It is that simple. Really!

I mean, just look at all the other stuff that was being put out at the time; look at all the other groups. Why, out of all the Liverpool groups, all the British groups – all the artists in the world even – why, out of all of that crop, would The Beatles be the most successful and sell the most records and, even after all these years, *continue* to sell the most records? Because they had *great* songs. Yes, they also made cracking records; they'd a brilliant producer; a highly competent manager; a superb road crew; they looked cute; played as well as anyone else in the land; and were professional, very professional. But all of this would have been meaningless if they hadn't had great songs as their foundation. They certainly wouldn't still be selling records today, in the volumes they do, because of fashion, 'coolness' or clever marketing: I mean, when was the last time you saw an advertisement for a Beatles record? For that matter, certainly none of today's sales are as a result of Radio One airplay. But people, old and young, still react to the phenomenal body of work that they left and it will, I believe, serve as their testament for evermore – and a bit more than that.

Even today I'm finding *Revolver*, perhaps more than any of the other albums, to be maturing with age. Every time I put it on, I know and savour the joy in store for me but it's not a nostalgic thing. The record still excites me, still involves me, and still pulls me into the songs. As one song finishes, I can hear the opening bars of the next one before it even starts.

The songs are like old friends; friends you still enjoy rather than tolerate because of your joint history. 'Dr Robert' comes on and I immediately think of John Lennon and his search for Dr Robert, the New York City doctor who kept all his friends from being ill by keeping them high. Or there's 'For No-One', a 'Paul' song that was a personal favourite of both John and George (neither of whom actually played on the track). Its innovative French horn solo was hummed by Paul to George Martin who, in turn, scored it so that Alan Civil could play it.

Even the song that *Revolver* closes with, 'Tomorrow Never Knows', leaves you hooked, intrigued and hungry for what they were to do next. It's an experimental song, written by John, with a little help from The Tibetan Book of the Dead, some chemical substances and a few influences from Dr Timothy Leary. The magic is that, no matter how alien all of the above might have been to you, the song is structured, and the record produced, in such a way that it carries you along on John's journey of discovery. Funny how, in the middle of all these illustrious people, places and things, it would be the down-to-earth Ringo who would come up with the most

cosmic song title on the album. He'd been meaning to say 'tomorrow never comes' but his tongue flipped the 'comes' to 'knows' and
John had the title for his enlightening song journey.

It certainly wasn't a song like Paul's 'Eleanor Rigby'. Neither
would it ever achieve anything like the latter's 200 cover versions,
but the variety it offered to *Revolver* along with, say, 'Yellow
Submarine', is what entertained us, and is what made The Beatles
the complete band. And just in case we thought we had them sussed,
they had another major box of tricks they were waiting to open for
us.

Chapter Thirty-Three

Back to Marianne Burgess' ever-growing box of tricks. What's a man meant to do when he hears news like the news I had just heard? It was just before summer time in 1966 and Marianne Burgess (new, shorter hairstyle and all) had just announced to me that she was considering getting married. Now, I bet you were all thinking: Oh, it's okay. She's just considering it. She won't possibly go ahead with it. Wrong! She was very serious about it. She *told* me she was very serious about it and our Kathleen told me that she felt the marriage would go ahead.

Kathleen felt that Marianne, after the trauma of her relationships with Ken and with me, was happy to have a regular boyfriend at last. A boyfriend who hoped to become a solicitor, settle down, get married and have a couple of children. The attraction for Marianne Burgess was apparently the fact that, emotionally, he wasn't going to be too demanding. If anything, Marianne was just another item to be ticked off on the would-be solicitor's shopping list of life.

I took the train to Manchester, armed only with Marianne Burgess' college address. I didn't have a lot of time to spare as her college term was about to finish and she hadn't yet decided what to do with her summer break. She needed money and was considering taking a working holiday in Jersey. I arrived at Salford Teacher Training College at about eleven-thirty. How do you find a student? Simple! Then, as now, you visit the bar. Wrong! Marianne was nowhere to be found. I sat in the bar, by myself, all lunchtime. I was twenty-six at that point but felt, for the first time in my life, incredibly old amongst the youthfulness of the next generation of teachers. They were all terribly busy, wearing scarves (yes, in the summer) and they were confident, not to mention noisy.

I went to the bursar's office to try to find out more about Marianne Burgess' whereabouts. I was met by a very official 'No, we don't give out that kind of information to strangers.' However, as I was walking down the footpath, dejected and miserable, a wee girl came running after me, shouting, 'Mister' in a Scouse accent. I recognised her as the girl I'd just seen working in the bursar's office. She knew Marianne Burgess and, as a fellow Scouser along with Miss Burgess, felt I was legit. Marianne Burgess was on day release at a local primary school, gaining valuable classroom experience. She would, however, be returning to the campus around four, or shortly thereafter, and I was reliably informed that she would, in fact, be in the bar at six, where they (she and this girl) had planned to meet for a drink.

'Are you Theo?' she asked, when she'd imparted all her valuable information.

'Yes. Guilty,' I replied, somewhat taken aback. 'How did you know that?'

'Well, I am her friend as I said, and I know Kathleen, your sister,' the wee girl smiled.

The 'wee girl' turned out to be twenty-eight years old and was called Annie Roche. Annie was going to look like a schoolgirl for the rest of her life, which would surely have been an annoyance in her early twenties and would be a compliment in her thirties and forties.

'Is she okay?'

'Yeah, she's great. And you?' she replied, with an air that suggested, 'I don't really know you, but I know *of* you, and I'm not sure I want this conversation to go on much longer.'

I wasn't exactly sure how much she knew about me and I wasn't about to start off a conversation with, 'Of course, you know Marianne and I were lovers.' Yet at the same time I wanted to try and find out something about this new solicitor bloke and how he'd managed to sweep Marianne off her feet and, more importantly, just how close he and Marianne Burgess were.

'Well, you know, I've had better times,' I shrugged.

'I've seen your band, you know. They're very good.'

'Thank you, thank you very much. Where did you see us play?' I asked, feeling a little uncomfortable. I'm not very good at accepting compliments, you know. I mean, if Annie had said that to our guitarist, he would had whisked her off to the bar with a 'And what exactly did you like about us?' and then would have proceeded to agree with absolutely everything she said.

'You did a bop at the teacher training college in Leeds. My boyfriend comes from Leeds and we were there for the weekend. It would have been October last year. You certainly kept everyone on their feet,' she smiled a distracted smile. She kept looking over my shoulder towards the bursar's office, giving me the distinct feeling that I was detaining her from her work.

'That's very kind. I remember it, actually. It was raining, very hard in fact, and it took us ages to get back home. It was my turn to ride shotgun and keep the driver awake,' I offered, trying desperately hard to find a way of moving the conversation to a more personal level – a level where it would not be considered inappropriate for me to inquire about Marianne Burgess and her new boyfriend.

'It's funny, you know. Kathleen had told me about you and the group, but it's that thing, you know, you feel if you know someone in the band they can't be any good. But musicians have to be someone's family, someone's friends. I mean, even The Beatles have relations, don't they?'

'Yes, contrary to popular opinion, musicians are humans,' I said, hoping my smile would show I wasn't meaning to be rude.

'No, no, I didn't mean that. It's just, well… it's just this thing about the fact that stars are, you know, they're not really real. You know? Do you know what I'm on about or do you think I'm mad?' she gushed.

'No. I mean, yes. Yes, I do know what you mean,' I stammered.

'It's just that I've seen you on stage with a great group and I'm sure, because of that, you look different to how you would have looked if I'd seen you before I saw you on stage. You appeared bigger; but you're quite small in real life,' Annie offered. She was circling her point, but circling it well. I knew exactly what she meant. Ringo Starr was five-feet-seven but because he was a Beatle, you expected him to be ten-feet tall (at least) and because he obviously wasn't, he looked tiny on the street. The other three Beatles were five-feet-eleven, give or take a layer of hair. Visually this was pleasing and it gave The Beatles (on stage) a uniformity similar to three full pints of Guinness. The other thing about Ringo is that he is one of those people who are just genuinely great blokes. A great geezer, a chap; you know, whatever. A nice fellow but again, that's not something you'd expect from a show-business type.

Anyway, I was still trying to come to grips with the fact that I 'looked smaller in real life' when Annie made her apologies, saying, 'Look, sorry, I've got to get back to work. It really was nice to meet you. Perhaps I'll see you later in the bar, with Marianne?' she held out her hand for me to shake.

'That would be great,' I replied as I shook her hand, thinking it also might be convenient if she were there, just in case Marianne Burgess' future betrothed arrived in the bar. I crossed my fingers, wishing that he would soon, hopefully, become her ex.

I had an hour and a bit to kill but decided not to wander around the streets. I didn't want to get caught in one of the city's infamous downpours. I don't mind a drowning now and then but I didn't want the discomfort of damp clothes to distract me from my meeting with Marianne.

I suddenly got an attack of the panics. What happened if she saw me and got mad because she felt I was bothering her? Hell, maybe even embarrassing her if the solicitor was around. How would she explain me away? Ah well, not to worry, I was here now and going for broke. I suddenly realised I hadn't a clue what I was going to say to her.

I visited a bookshop and bought a copy of Dick Francis' paperback *For Kicks*. I'd already read his first, *Dead Cert*, which was a great read, and I was looking forward to spending time with his new one. I couldn't really get into it, to be honest. Nothing to do with the author; it was just that I kept thinking about Marianne and what I would say and wondering if maybe I was mad to be there in the first place.

Anyway, I was looking at the pages and not the words when my corner of the bar seemed to go darker. I automatically looked up to see what had happened and there, standing in front of me, was Marianne Burgess. She was smiling and it was like I could see right into her eyes, they were sparkling so much. Well, I thought, at least she's not mad at me. She couldn't possibly be, with a smile so warm.

'And to what do I owe this pleasure, Theodore Hennessy?'

What can you say? How can you answer that question? Should I tell her I was on a raiding mission into enemy territory, way behind the lines, trying to save this doll from a life of possible misery? Did I say 'doll' there? I mean, did I think 'doll' there? If she knew I was calling her 'Doll', even in my thoughts (capital 'D' or not), she'd send me packing back to Liverpool with my tail between my legs.

'I don't want you to marry your man,' I said, calmly. It was a simple thing to say, I know, but that was why I was there. I could have beaten around the bush for a week or three, but that was what I had come to say and that was what I wanted to get through to her, so feck it, why not just come right out and say it? Why not?

The smile disappeared from her face. In a split second, Marianne went from looking radiant to looking like someone whose picture would fit perfectly on the sleeve of a Leonard Cohen album.

'You'd better get us a drink.'

I did. I got a bottle of wine and two glasses – something that had previously been unheard of in the students' union. I realised it was a little too extravagant in those circles but I didn't want us stopping our conversation every few minutes (a bit of an exaggeration, I know) for refills. Marianne Burgess (unlike everyone else in the union) didn't seem to notice my gesture; she seemed to be fighting with her own distractions.

'Theo, why are you doing this?'

'Because I love you.'

I had a whole speech planned in answer to her inevitable question but I realised, when I finished those words, they were the four words I would keep coming back to. That sentence was, for me, as complete and perfect a four-piece as The Beatles were. Marianne Burgess obviously expected me to continue because she kept looking at me, neither a smile nor a frown on her face.

She looked very 'studenty': you know, plimsolls; yellow, figure-hugging slacks; white blouse; and her well-worn suede jacket. I was still getting used to her shorter hair but it definitely gave her the look of learning, if you know what I mean. She was more of a Friday type of person now, and less of the original Sunday type she used to be. She was so beautiful as she sat there, staring at me, this weird man who had come to encroach on her happiness and peace of mind. When I first had the idea of trying to come and see her, I talked it through with our Kathleen, as I do most things, and she warned me to be careful I didn't send her running straight into the solicitor's waiting arms.

The thought of such a possibility knotted up my stomach. Thinking of her, looking like she did then, in anyone else's arms, was just…well, it was just that the way I saw it, we were *sooo* meant to be together that her, or me, being with anyone else was breaking some balance of nature. In all of this there was such a thin dividing line between us being together forever and Marianne Burgess seeing the sense in that, or, on the other side, her thinking I was a pest and wishing me out of her life. But it was so close, as Kathleen had said, that I could just as easily have driven her away.

But it was the strangest of things; I could see the whole relationship so clearly. I doubt if I ever had a clearer vision of what had to be and what should be. It was so obvious to me and I knew if I could just get her to share that clearness of vision, even for just a split second, I'd be safe. If I could achieve this then everything would be fine for us. Don't get me wrong; I'm not for one minute suggesting that it would be happily ever after for us. No, as Kathleen pointed out, that was not a possibility; but if we were tight, then it wouldn't matter about all the shite. We'd get through it. We could do anything as long as we were together.

Equally powerfully, I felt that if we didn't get together then neither of our lives would ever be complete. I know that sounds such an egotistical thing to say, but it's how I felt. I mean, I'd even thought it through to the point where I'd considered that she and this solicitor of hers just might marry and if that did happen, I was prepared to sit around and wait for it to go wrong (as I felt it must). In the meantime, the only thing that was important was that I remained cool so that, when they did split up, it wouldn't be out of the question that we would get together again. Yes, a bit of damage would have surely been done, as there must have been when I dated Susanne and she dated Ken and then the solicitor. This turbulence might take away from our specialness. But, on the other hand, it might not. It was just so obvious to me, why bother with other people when I knew in my heart she was the one for me?

'Well, get to the point, Theo, why don't you?'

'I know, I'm sorry, Marianne. I don't want to scare you, but that is at the heart of why I'm here.'

'You can't love me, Theo.'

'I… what? Why?'

'Well, if you really loved me, you wouldn't want to spoil my happiness.'

'Wrong! I wouldn't want to see you ruin your life, and I don't.'

'How dare you,' she snapped, with as much anger and venom as she had displayed in all the time we had been together. 'You… you decide that you know what's best for me and that you want to save me from myself. How dare you. That's so insulting to me. And then you profess to love me.'

'Look, I'm sorry… '

'And stop saying you're sorry, it's so pathetic,' she interrupted. As you can see, I was going down really well here, and 'down' was the operative word. As they say in show-business circles, 'Let's hope the second house is better than the first.' It couldn't get much worse.

'Okay, feck it, Marianne, I'm not sorry; I'm not one wee bit sorry. It's just that it's so clear to me that we should be together.'

'What? We should be together because Theodore Hennessy says we should?'

'No, because it's meant to be.'

'Because it's meant to be? What on earth are you on about? What on earth do you mean, "because it's meant to be?" You know what you do when you say things like that? You scare me. You scare me, Theo, and that's a fact. Why are you so damned sure that we are meant to be? You know, maybe we *were* meant to be,' Marianne added, and paused to think about it.

Encouraging, I thought.

'And maybe we weren't. Maybe we were meant to be together and we blew it because we didn't keep it together when we had the chance, and now I'm meant to be with someone else and yso are you. Ever considered that option, Theo?¨

'No, not really. Look I accept it was my fault, my fault entirely, that it didn't work out the first time. And in a way it might have been that you were my dream, or my illusion, and when you actually stepped into my reality, I couldn't deal with it properly. You know, in dreams and illusions you don't have proper conversations about the weather and dirty socks and the jam being nearly finished and you're being nearly out of loo rolls. No, you talk about physiology and theories and the furtherance of mankind and saving the world. But now I accept that there is a life still left to lead when you fall in love. I admit I haven't always thought that. I admit I thought you fell in love and that was it. And especially you, Marianne, I idolised you. I thought you were so beautiful that if I squeezed you too hard you'd break. And when you left, I realised that wasn't the case.'

'And while we're talking about that, how come when I left you let me go, if you loved me so much?'

'I didn't want to ruin it. I still wanted you but I didn't want us to end up fighting and hating each other. And you know what? When someone says they want to go, you assume they mean it. I didn't want us to fall out. I suppose, even then, even as it was happening – us splitting up, that is – I wanted another chance. I wanted to try again.'

'You see, that's the scary thing about you, Theo. I think you have this thing, you know, that you are convinced that sooner or later we are going to be together.'

'I'm not convinced of it but I will admit, it's what I want and what I hope for.'

'But don't you see, that's all too much for me. It is, really. It's too much pressure to put on a relationship. Don't you see that?'

'No.'

'With Brian…' she began

'Brian?'

'Yes, I told you about him.'

'Yes,' I grunted.

'With him, it's all so simple. With him I get the feeling that when we're not together, he's getting on with his life. We could marry and I'm sure it would be fine. He'd take care of me; he'd look after me. He wouldn't hurt me. He wouldn't smother me. I'd be fine with him and I'd be able to get on with living my life and doing my things as well.'

'Do you love him?'

'That's none of your business.'

'Do you love him?' I persisted.

'He's a good man, Theo. He's honest, he's kind and he might just be the best man I've ever known.'

I was sick of hearing about his qualities; it was time for another 'Do you love him?'

'I *like* him. There are different kinds of love, Theo.'

'Oh, Please! We're not talking about a fecking cat or a pony here. Do you love him?'

'No,' she uttered very quietly. I didn't feel like it was a victory, and it wasn't. She started to cry, softly. Marianne Burgess rarely cried in my company. I was proud of that, in a way. I'd always felt that her time sitting alone at home, waiting for the Married Man to come calling, was a very dark and sad time for her, so I had always wanted to make her smile; I wanted her to be happy. Of course, you know how successful I was in my endeavours: she left me. And now I had made her cry. She was crying here, in front of me, in the students' union. I went over to her and held her in my arms and she sobbed gently.

'Please stop crying, Marianne. I didn't want to hurt you,' I whispered, as I rocked her gently. She clung tighter to me. She sobbed gently for a time and we said nothing. Then, she started to search in my jacket, the way she used to do. She would never tell you what she was looking for; she would just keep searching through all your pockets until she found it. On this occasion it was a handkerchief, which, luckily enough, was a clean one. She claimed it and dried her eyes. She blew her nose at the precise moment Annie Roche walked into the bar. Annie took one look at us, in each other's arms, turned around and walked back out again.

'No, Theo,' she began, after perhaps four minutes of silence between us. 'I don't love Brian.'

I have to admit, I breathed a major sigh of relief.

'I mean, how could I?' she continued. 'I'm in love with you.'

It was as though I'd swum through the stormiest seas and fought off the wildest animals; I'd won all the battles and saved something so precious I couldn't find words to describe it, or what it meant to me. Now I was swimming to the shore with this...this prize in my arms, and I was exhausted and wondering what I would do with it now that I had found it.

'But it will never work between us,' Marianne Burgess announced.

I could feel the winds gather and troubled waters brewing again.

'But... I... you... oh... ah...' I spluttered.

She raised her fingers to my lips, her eyes pleading with me, beseeching me to stop.

'Please don't hurt me any more, Theo. Please leave me here and let me get on with my life. I can't take this any more. You want too much from me and I don't have it to give, Theo. I love you. I've said it. I've admitted it to the both of us. But I will never say it again. I know it can never work. Too much has passed between us and your love is too pure for me. I'm not what you think I am. You still have this illusion of me but it's not me, Theo. It's still an illusion. We can't do this to each other any more. It's too destructive. That's why, and please don't get upset again, but that's why I like Brian. He's safe. He won't cause this turmoil.'

'But you love *me*?'

'There are other emotions, Theo. Emotions that allow you to still breathe freely without having to feel a non-stop pounding in your chest. A pounding so forceful that you feel that some time soon it is going to explode right through your chest. And I just don't want that continuous pain. It's too draining. There's nothing left any more, nothing left for me, and I need to find something for myself.'

I felt she was getting a bit too dramatic now. I mean, if she wanted to give me the elbow all she had to do was say 'Shove off!' Had I done all this to her? Was I causing her all this pain? Wasn't love meant to be a thing of joy? Wasn't it meant to be a continuous

pounding in her chest? Perhaps her bra straps were too tight, I
thought, but I didn't consider it would further my cause to offer
this solution to our evident problem.

'Please don't come here again, Theo. Let's part and hope that
after we've dealt with all of this we can still be friends.'

Oh no! She wasn't going to ask me to her wedding, was she? I
couldn't really get into all this. Was this an intellectual way of letting
someone down? Tell them you love them, and then throw in, 'Oh
and by the way, I never want to see you again'? I have to tell you I
was totally flabbergasted. Winded. Gutted. Speechless. Hurt.
Numb.

Bottom line? I'd made my pitch and she'd shot me down.

Bang! Bang! She'd shot me down.

Chapter Thirty-Four

Yes, you're right, it is time for another chapter; another chapter in my life, and time for the Fabs to move on as well.

Although not a deciding factor in how things turned out for The Beatles on the live stage, it surely was an ominous sign when the year started off with the closing of the Cavern Club in Liverpool, with debts of £10,000. The Cavern had been their (and my) old stomping ground and a name synonymous with The Beatles. Throughout the year (1966), quite a few things were happening that would, once and for all, put the final nail in The Beatles' touring coffin.

The year started off with a May 1st appearance at the *New Musical Express* Poll Winner's Concert at the Empire Pool, Wembley. I'd intended to go down to London for the concert. It had been so long since their last appearance and I was anxious to hear what the new songs were like. If *Rubber Soul* had been anything to go by, I was in for a treat. Assuming, that was, that they would perform some of the new material from the current recording sessions. Sadly, I didn't make it; at the last moment we got a great payday for the Nighttime Passengers. Sad, because the Wembley show was, as it turned out, their final English concert appearance:a prelude to a world tour, but their final UK appearance nonetheless.

First stop on their world tour was Japan, where they were to perform five shows in three days at the hallowed Budokan, starting on June 23rd. So hallowed was the venue, in fact, that a number of people complained (publicly) about The Beatles being allowed to perform there. It's hard to appreciate now, in these more liberal times, just how difficult and dangerous it was for The Beatles to be in that environment. I suppose something similar today would be the power and corruption of the Chinese government in their treatment of their own people in the Tiananmen Square incidents. That might sound a little (or even a lot) extreme but basically, The Beatles were prisoners in their own hotel, trapped on the eighteenth floor, with the lift stopping at the seventeenth. They were rushed in

armoured cars to and from the venues and were not allowed out.
Traders, however, in the name of international commerce, were
allowed to visit The Beatles in their hotel rooms to sell their local
wares. The world never changes in that respect. Countries who
once were at war with each other, at a cost of tens of thousands of
lives, are prepared to forget about the past in the name of the dollar
or the pound. Quite disgusting if you ask me, and please remember
never to get my dad started on that one.

So, it was all a bit hairy, but that's not the really important thing
that came out of the Japanese gigs. It just may have been due to the
fact that the Japanese where incredibly (bow, bow) respectful or,
equally, it may have been the 3,000 armed police packed into the
Budokan for each Beatles performance, but the audience were
incredibly polite. And quiet! And when you have a quiet audience,
you create a situation where the band is able to hear themselves.
Hear themselves, in fact, for the first time in years and they were
very depressed about how bad they sounded. They hadn't realised
they'd become quite so bad. Out of key, out of time and maybe even
out of song. Strike one.

Strike two came when they visited the Philippines on what was
to prove to be their final world tour. We all know the grossness of
Imelda 'I can't possibly find a pair of shoes to match my underwear'
Marcos and her husband, 'the Prez', with his poor line of ill-fitting
shirts. We now know what they were up to. We now know who was
paying for all those shoes. We all know *now* who was paying for the
lifestyle of the rich and infamous. But back then, they were a well-
loved couple of chancers who had the support of their nation. So the
Prez's missus announced to the press that she would be attending all
The Beatles' concerts and that The Beatles, in return, would be
attending the palace to have tea and finger picks (with any luck it
wouldn't actually be someone's fingers) with her and four hundred
or so of her good (personal) friends. The only problem was that
everyone neglected to inform The Beatles, who were enjoying a
well-earned sleep, that the carriage had arrived.

Brian Epstein refused to wake his charges from their slumber
and, as my mum always says, there is no wrath quite like the wrath
of a woman scorned. I'm sure my mum would have added a few
notches on the wrath-o-meter when the woman in question also
happens to be a dictator. Then a few more notches on top of that to
account for the fact that the humiliation was public. The old palace
press machine sprung into action, whipping up a storm amongst the

fans. There were riots and protests and a whole hullaballoo. The Beatles' security was withdrawn. The promoter of The Beatles concert at The Rizal Memorial Football stadium in Manila (he who had neglected to advise The Beatles of their audience with her royal shoeness) is a gentleman whose name bears repeating here just in case you should ever meet him – a Mr Ramon Ramos. Mr Ramos refused to pay Brian Epstein the vast funds due to The Beatles for fulfilling their side of the contract and selling 80,000 tickets over the two shows on the one day. Blood is thicker than water; and royal blood is even thicker than that.

And there's more. The tax authorities contacted Mr Epstein and informed him that The Beatles and entourage would not be able to leave the country until he paid income tax on their sizeable fee. The same authorities were not interested in small technicalities, such as the fact that he hadn't yet been *paid* the fee, nor was he likely to be, plus the fact that the contract with the promoter called for said promoter to pay any and all taxes. Brian Epstein eventually paid this bribe – sorry, did I say bribe? Of course, I meant tax – and he organised a TV interview from his hotel to tell The Beatles' fans the Liverpool side of the story. The good thing about Beatles fans is that they can think for themselves. That is, when they are allowed to receive and digest all the information. Unfortunately, the country was hit by a freak electrical storm for the entire (exact) time Brian Epstein was on the TV and The Beatles' story was never heard. Surprisingly (surprising, that is, if you were a monk in the Himalayas), the electrical storm disappeared as quickly as it arrived – the second Brian finished on air actually!

The Beatles were still under siege in the hotel and made a quick getaway, minus security, to the airport. They were caught up by an unruly crowd who manhandled them and in the scuffle, several of them were hurt. Brian Epstein, for one, was thrown to the floor and sprained his ankle. They had been advised that they would be shot at as they made their way to the aeroplane and literally had to run for their lives. But their ordeal was not over yet. The authorities advised them that when their plane had landed, a few days earlier, the proper paperwork had not been completed and so, as they had not officially entered the country, they couldn't possibly leave it. There was a tense hour while Mal Evans and Derek Taylor returned to the airport to (successfully) negotiate their release.

It's a hoot, isn't it, that these banana republics can treat people in this way and get away with it? Funny the way the local faithful changed their tune years later, when they realised exactly what had been going on. The only problem is that these people make you so mad you want to act with the same insanity you are accusing them of. Anyway, as the plane was taxiing up the runway, Mr Brian Epstein would not have been winning any popularity competitions; he was bearing the brunt of the blame for the entire incident. Strike two.

There's more, still more, as if more were needed. Earlier in the year, in London, John Lennon had been giving an interview to a friend of his, Maureen Cleave of the London *Evening Standard*. John had been studying religion a lot recently and in the course of the interview, he alluded to the fact that Christianity was on the wane (a fact) and that The Beatles were more popular than Jesus (a fact). This was all very well in the current 'love culture' in England, but some of the Bible thumpers in the US of A took exception to it.

The problem with churches is that although they may not be popular, they are powerful – very powerful. Soon, public Beatles-record-burning sessions were going on all over America, organised and promoted by radio stations in these God-fearing states. Some radio stations even chose to ban playing Beatles records. It's worth pointing out here that they'd never played, nor were they likely to play, Beatles music in the first place. But a bandwagon is, as we all know, a gravy train. Also, it's very interesting to note that the record shops in these bonfire areas were doing an amazing trade in Beatles records prior to the local torching. If there is a God, we were all amused to learn which side She was on when we heard that one radio station, a Radio Klue in Longview, Texas, was struck by lightning. The flash from the heavens not only burnt out the transmitter, closing the station down, but it also stuck the news editor, leaving him in need of his brown trousers. This bolt from our maker came, incidentally, the day after the same station organised their own Beatles-record-burning session.

Needless to say, with all these nutters running riot, the tour was fraught with incidents. The most frightening of these probably took place in the Memphis Coliseum on August 19th, when six local Ku Klux Klan members threw rubbish at The Beatles on stage, as they performed. Someone also threw a firecracker on stage during the performance and The Beatles instinctively looked from one to the other to see which of them had been shot. In spite of all of this, the true measure of the fans' feelings at this time was demonstrated by the fact that *Revolver* was number one in the charts and showed no sign of slipping.

By the time The Beatles reached their final date on the American tour, at Candlestick Park in San Francisco on August 29th 1966, they had decided it was to be the final gig of their career. Sad, very sad, but then none of us would have wished them the lives they were being forced into. Most important was the fact that if they hadn't taken such a drastic decision, their music would most definitely have suffered. It's hard today to realise exactly what such a decision meant, or could have meant, to their career. Then, in the '60s, touring was everything. Touring *was* your career. Turning their back on touring could have meant the end of The Beatles. At this point, however, the musicians were so fried by it all that to end the touring was the only option. Strike three and out!

Brian Epstein was devastated and heartbroken by their decision. He knew that, in a way, it meant less of an involvement from him in their career. The boys made the music; he looked after the concerts and television appearances, both of which were now non-existent. Brian Epstein twice attempted suicide in 1966. Had this been a call for help? Was his personal life a mess? Had he been unable to fill the dramatic void left in his life by the shift in The Beatles' priorities? Who knows? But whatever it was, he'd obviously been unable to achieve the same fulfilment from the host of other artists he represented as he had from The Beatles. There was talk of deals going wrong and all that, but I think it was all idle gossip from those jealous at not being involved with The Beatles, and, as I mentioned before, he was *the* first pop-group manager. He paved the way that others are still following. He was efficient and honest; he shared The Beatles' vision; he had a tremendous flair; he was a brave tactician; and he had class – loads of class.

My dad always says, 'Making money doesn't take class but spending it does.' I don't know how my dad knows about these things but he obviously does.

Chapter Thirty-Five

'You're doing it again.'

'I'm doing what again?' I asked.

I was in our Kathleen's house. It would have been during the first week of June; we were listening to *Revolver* and having a glass of wine. We were a few songs beyond 'Here, There and Everywhere'; I think it was John singing 'And Your Bird Can Sing' because I remember the line: 'And your bird can see but she can't see me.' I've never been able to fully get a grip on that lyric but I thought that if 'your bird' was our Kathleen then the lyric was spot on because she sure as hell could see me, and see me better than anyone else could.

'You're being a wimp again,' my sister, the oracle on human relationships, persisted.

'Kathleen! God, I've tried, you know I've tried. It's not going to work, it's as simple as that.'

'Well, if you really believe that then don't come around here, whingeing about your lost love.'

'Geez, who's rattled your cage?'

'Theodore, look at you, look at us. We in our mid-twenties and neither of us have a partner. God, it's terrible. I'm going to be left on the shelf.'

'Kathleen, I hate to bring this up at a time like this, but if I'm in my mid-twenties, that would make you twenty-eight and correct me if I'm wrong, but surely that's late twenties.' I now knew where her venom was coming from and I was sure as hell going to turn it back on her, calling me a wimp indeed!

'Yeah, okay, rub it in why don't you. But look, seriously, from the way you've told it to me, I'd say that what she wants is for you to sweep her off her feet; not give her a choice in the matter.'

'That's not the way I picked it up. She seemed pretty convinced to me that she wanted to marry the real wimp and inherit the boring lifestyle to go with him. I'm quite disappointed in her, to be honest. I'd have expected her to want more, if you know what I mean. That's a bit of a letdown,' I whined into my wine.

'Ah, you're just trying to find something negative about her so you can channel your anger into that and make it easier to deal with the fact that she's chosen one wimp over another.'

'It's just that she's the one, Kathleen. I don't know why I'm so convinced about it but she *is* the one.'

We consoled each other for a while and opened another bottle of wine. At about eleven-thirty, her doorbell went.

'Aha! Who's the midnight caller, Kathleen?'

'You go, Theo. If it's that bastard Ernie, tell him the Mersey's an illusion and if he jumps in he'll be fine.'

'I'm not going to deal with any of your exes. Do your own dirty work in your own house,' I said, slumping further back into my chair so that she'd get the idea.

'I'll remember this, Theo. Just you wait and see if I don't.'

With that she rose from her chair and made her way, very unsteadily, to the hallway, leaving the living-room door open. Then I heard a female voice I thought I recognised, say:

'Kathleen, I've got to talk to you about Theo.'

I froze in my seat and eavesdropped as the voice of Marianne Burgess apologised profusely for calling around so late.

'Come on in, Marianne,' Kathleen said warmly. 'Ahm, I should warn… '

'Theo!' Marianne half shouted, Kathleen's warning arriving too late.

'Marianne,' I said. 'Sorry.' I'd maybe had a bit too much wine at that stage.

'Okay, youse two, I'm going to finish off my wine and then go to bed and I want this sorted out between you. The only topic I ever discuss with either of you these days is each other, and even if neither of you can see it, it's blatantly obvious to me, and anyone else not in need of a white stick, that you're meant for each other.'

'Look, I'm sorry to interrupt you two. I'll go. See you some other time, Kathleen,' Marianne began awkwardly.

'No you won't. If you go, we'll just discuss you until we are so drunk we fall asleep and both wake up with sore necks. And if Theo goes, then you and I will just discuss him and how lousy he is in the sack.'

Marianne Burgess and I shouted simultaneously: 'Kathleen!'

'Just kidding, Theo. Sorry Marianne, but I'm too drunk to care. I'm off to bed. Sort it out. BOTH OF YOUSE, SORT IT OUT ONCE AND FOR ALL!'

With that she waltzed off out of the room in a very flamboyant, but potentially very dangerous, walk-cum-jog, missing the television by not more than two inches. Marianne and I jumped up, me to catch the television and Marianne to catch Kathleen but we only managed to catch each other, landing in a heap in the middle of the floor. All that remained of Kathleen in the room was her scent.

For some reason, the two of us lay on the floor in each other's arms. It was more like a Brian Rix farce than a romantic scene. So much so that we both started laughing, quietly at first but then louder and louder until Marianne Burgess got the giggles. There were lots of open mouths and twisted teeth, and me being over-whelmed by this woman's natural beauty. To kiss her seemed the most natural thing to do. So I kissed her. That's all we did, I swear. It wasn't like I tried something and got knocked back or anything like that. No, it wasn't that kind of a moment.

'I thought I would feel better when you left me in Manchester and we…and I… ' she searched for the proper words.

'You got me out of your life?' I volunteered

'Yes, something like that. But I felt worse. So I thought I might feel better if I told Brian I would marry him.'

'You told the solicitor you would marry him?'

'Yes,' she replied sheepishly, 'I told you I was going to.'

'You also told me you didn't love him.'

'Yeah, I did. That's so bad that you should know that about him. That was so unfair and unkind of me to do that to him, behind his back. But you got me so mad, Theo.'

'You're actually going to marry him?' I asked, picking myself up off the floor, physically and literally.

'I've told him I'm going to.'

'But are you?'

'Theo, we've been through this.'

'Yes and you've just told me you're doing it to make yourself feel better. Did it make you feel better when you told him that you would marry him?'

'No, it didn't, if you must know. It didn't in the slightest. I felt great and excited all day leading up to it – you know, telling him I was going to marry him – and then when I told him, I wondered, 'Is that all there is?' I had thought, naively, that I would feel better when I knew I was going to be married. I expected to feel healed. I really expected to have felt like I'd arrived somewhere. Instead, if felt like I *had* arrived somewhere but there was no-one there wait-

ing for me. And I thought: Oh, is that all there is to it? She paused
and looked at a religious picture Kathleen kept above the mantel-
piece. She smiled, more to herself as if in private amusement, then
continued:

'I remember once I went to an evangelist meeting and the
preacher got us all worked up about being saved, about accepting
God into our lives and into our hearts. He made it seem like if we
did one little thing, then everything would be great thereafter. I was
about twelve and I wanted to stop feeling so hurt all the time. I
wanted to stop being a child and grow up. I thought grown-ups had
it made; that they never felt as bad as children felt, or at least as bad
as I felt. I wanted something in my life to take away that hurt and if
God was going to be the one to take it away then I was going to take
Him into my heart and into my life. Not just take Him in, but
welcome Him in,' Marianne Burgess reminisced. Unlike me, she
had not risen from the floor. She was still sitting there, knees
hunkered up under her chin and arms wrapped around her legs and
her long, green dress. She had on a bum-freezer black jacket; a
black, high-collared blouse; and black, half-heeled boots, which
disappeared under her green skirt.

She seemed to have gone off into a trance, so I felt compelled to
ask, 'Were you saved?'

'Well, it was getting to the end of his sermon and he was saying
that at the end, all those who wanted to be saved should put their
hands up and someone would come along and take care of them. I
wanted to be taken care of. I was nervous because all our neighbours were there and all the shopkeepers who owned the shops my
Mum did her shopping in. I was nervous. The preacher was a kind
man, I remember, and he had a very sexy voice. Men of God
shouldn't be allowed to have voices like that. It confuses the wee
girls. It makes their emotions run riot in their bodies, which have
started screaming for womanhood while their brains remain in a
childlike state. I found my hand going up as if controlled by its own
mind, somebody's mind but definitely not mine. All these people
were turning around to look at me by this stage. They were all
thinking, but not saying, "Marianne Burgess, you wee hussy, what
are you doing?" But my hand remained firmly up. I was going to be
saved. And heaven help me, I needed saving. Soon, someone came
along and brought me and three others to the front of the marquee.'

'Really?' I asked in disbelief, not at her going up to the front of
the marquee, but at the whole scene.

'Yes. I remember we all got down on our knees – three girls and a boy – then the man with the sexy voice came and laid his hands upon our heads, two at a time, and asked us if we were ready to take God into our hearts. We all answered yes. I mean, at that stage we weren't going to say no and run away. We were being saved; we were doing a grown-up kind of thing so we had to act like grown-ups. He said to each of us in turn, "Congratulations. You're saved," and then, in turn, each of the elders – including my Dad's friend, Eric – came up, shook our hands and offered their congratulations too.' She paused at this point.

'And you know what, Theo?'

I know what, I thought, but my eyebrows obviously replied 'What?' because she continued:

'I didn't feel a thing, nothing at all apart from feeling very let down. Empty perhaps, as well. Nothing. God had not saved me. What was wrong with me? I thought that maybe it took time, this saving thing, so I went home. Each morning, I woke up hoping to feel saved. I woke up feeling that way for twenty-two mornings: I counted them, Theo, believe me. And on the twenty-third morning, I woke up with the curse and I knew for definite that I hadn't been saved,' Marianne said, as she hugged her legs tightly, so tightly that she was squashing her magnificent breasts against her legs. I was becoming distracted and I knew I shouldn't be.

'So, in a way, I suppose I was a fool for thinking that I'd feel better after I'd told Brian I'd marry him. I mean, I'm not an unintelligent person. Why would I ever tell someone I would marry them just to make me feel better? What a stupid thing to do.'

'You won't get any argument from me on that one.'

'Thank you, you're so considerate,' she replied, sarcastically.

'It's the Irish in me.'

With that she laughed, so loud that I thought she would raise our Kathleen from above.

'What? It wasn't that funny. It wasn't funny at all, in fact.'

'No, sorry. It's just when you said that, I got a flash of the Irish in me,' she teased.

'You didn't tell me you had any Irish relations,' I offered, innocently.

'No, silly, I meant you,' she laughed, coyly.

'Marianne Burgess! No wonder you were beyond saving, with a mind like that.'

'Oh come on, Theodore, Mr High and Mighty. I saw you

staring at my breasts,' she teased.

'I… ' I began, starting to lie but then thinking better of it. 'Well, now you come to mention it… '

'I know you, always trying to be subtle about it but it's never far from your mind. Maybe we weren't able to deal with the love stuff but we certainly always had fun in bed.' She was not going to let me off the hook so hell, I thought, I'd go with the flow.

'Yeah, you know me, Marianne. I may not be the world's best lover…' I said, offering her my hand to help her up from the floor. In reality it was an offer of another kind as well but this way, refusal would not offend because all she had to say was that she was happy on the floor. She took my hand, finger by finger, as I continued, 'but number five is not too bad.'

She laughed so much that she let go of her grip on my hand, lost her balance and fell back onto the floor with a thud. I went over to her, to see if she was okay. She caught me by the neck of my denim shirt and pulled me towards her delicious lips, whispering, 'Let's see if we can't move you up to number four.'

Hey, I'll take all the practice I can get, particularly when it's with Marianne Burgess.

Chapter Thirty-Six

I bet you're thinking, If he's spending all his time chasing this woman, what's he doing about his career? What's he doing about the agency? And I wouldn't blame you for asking. If it was me out there, that's what I'd be thinking. Before I get into that though, I think it's only proper that I should tell you a little more about the night in our Kathleen's flat. You know, when Marianne Burgess and I did the wild thing on our Kathleen's floor. Well, on her carpet actually. Swear you won't tell her?

It was great. What can I tell you? In fact, it was better than great. It was months (thirteen to be accurate) of pent-up emotion and, quite frankly, lust. We stayed most of the night and went for the big three: once for us, once for her and once for me. The final one, perhaps the best, was at Marianne's instigation, which was why I thought it was very funny – as in funny peculiar – when she started feeling all guilty. I mean, once, yes, okay, for old times' sake and all that; twice because the first one was so exquisite; but the third one, well, that showed there was something more than just the lust or the devilment or the wickedness of doing it (a) on my sister's living-room floor and (b) when Marianne was (supposedly) seriously considering marriage to someone else.

I've never come even close to being able to figure out women; I mean that in the nicest possible way but I have to tell you, I was shocked (and concerned) when Marianne started going on about 'what she'd done to Brian'. I was about to remind her that she hadn't been doing anything to Brian, just in case she hadn't noticed, but I thought I might be on a bit of a sticky wicket there. Well, you would, wouldn't you? You've just made love to the girl you're convinced is your soul mate and she immediately starts talking about another boy; so it's not really the correct time to be fickle, is it? Add to that the fact that if I'd sent her out of the flat in the early hours of the morning in tears, she probably would have run straight back into Brian's arms – probably even his bed – for the first time (she assured me that they'd never made love and I believed her).

So, I tried to console her (unsuccessfully), dressed myself (quickly) and went out into the morning air with her to catch a taxi (successfully). She insisted on dropping me off; I assumed she didn't want me to know where she lived. I asked about seeing her again (well you would, wouldn't you?) but she said it was wrong, all wrong. She went on about how much she loved me; how I wasn't right for her and that was because she loved me; and that there was something about her I didn't know and I never would know, but to please leave her alone. I mean, *me* leave *her* alone?

As you know, I'd all but given up on her and, well, I'd been to that movie before. The last I saw of her that morning was her crying and waving out of the back of the taxi; a dark green, clapped-out Austin Princess. Again, I was left feeling empty and more than a little confused.

If we were to finish – and it seemed as sure as the double beat on the big drum in a marching band signalling the end of the tune that we were – then that had been a pretty spectacular ending, don't you think? The camera would pan up to rooftop level to reveal me standing there, alone and dejected; as dejected as the chap in the poem: 'Here am I, sad and downhearted, paid a penny and only farted.' No, sorry. Seriously though, it's only bravado, please believe me. The camera would show me, hands in pockets, standing there, looking at her as she stared at me through the back window of the taxi. The credits would come up as I turned and walked away. Before the taxi reached the end of the street, a Coronation Street-type street, I'd kick a can – an empty Heinz baked-beans can – which had earlier served as someone's football. The Beatles' version of 'I Should Have Known Better' would fade up on the soundtrack and there wouldn't be a dry eye in the house.

I'd now reached the stage where I was morose and moody, but I was quite enjoying being alone with my thoughts. I suppose what I'm saying is that I was happy being unhappy. You know: 'Poor me, I'll never find anyone else I'll love as much as I loved her. I'll never, ever go with another girl again. She'll be sorry when she sees what she's done to me, but it will be too late,' and on and on. Well, not too much, because I had work to do and I had about two-and-a-half hours in which to freshen up and get ready.

The Nighttime Passengers were going into the studio for the first time that morning. Vincent and I had written four new songs especially for this grand occasion and we'd even secured the services of an American producer. Well actually, he – Hank (Henry to his friends) Travener – was over to produce some new London band (he'd never tell us which one) and the deal had fallen through. We were lucky enough to scoop him on a good deal. Well, at least that's what our A & R guy (it stands for 'artist and repertoire' – the artistic liaison, if you will) at the record label told us. The thing about Hank was, well, he kept the sessions going really well. You know, there was lots of fun and everyone was made to feel good. Every time we'd hit a problem in the recording, he'd come up with the 'Oh, don't worry, we'll sort it out in the mix.' We believed him. The major problem was, it didn't. I mean he didn't – work it out for us in the mix.

In fact, he didn't even try. He just fecked back off to the States, leaving all the tapes in a mess. Now they say every cloud has a silver lining and this one had, too. I knew what I liked about records; I knew how to construct a good song. Hey, I'd listened to The Beatles a lot. I didn't for one moment share their gift, but they were showing us all how to do it, nonetheless. So, later the next week, we went back into the studios, this time with me and Vincent producing. It was a giant step, but not really too much of a risk because we were writing a lot at that stage and a few of our songs had been minor hits, so we already had a bit of a name. Vincent was pleased about the times we met up in the studio; it always gave him a chance to get up to date on the romantic comings and goings of our Kathleen.

Rather than write the whole thing off, the record company, although still not prepared to put us in a proper studio with a proper record producer, gave us £350 to go back into the studio and see what we could come up with. The first thing Vincent and I had to come up with was another £73 pounds each, to pay the eventual studio bill. Yes, you're right, for a so-called agent I wasn't doing such a great job for myself. My first producer's job had left me £73 out of pocket.

However, Vincent and I did receive a one-and-a-half percent royalty, which was three-quarters of one percent each. This was a princely sum in those days, but the record company felt they weren't giving away anything in order to (potentially) get themselves out of a jam. The sessions went well and were great fun. Just to show you how professional I was prepared to be, I got a session drummer in for the day, feeling that I would compromise my role as co-producer if I was also a playing member of the band.

One of the songs we cut that day was 'How Many Times Do You Want To Break My Heart'. You recognise it? I thought you might. It was one of our biggest hits. Yes, I *did* produce that; well I co-produced it and co-wrote it with Vincent McKee. The song was all about you know who. What started out to be one of my late-night thoughts of self-pity about Marianne Burgess turned out to be a reasonable hit. Luckily enough, it was to be one of those titles that, as you say it, reminds you of the main melody line. Yep, you're correct, it was a lesson we took right out of the Lennon and McCartney songbook.

The dep drummer we had for that day's recording with the Nighttime Passengers, Wally Siemons, was a good guy and a great drummer. I hired him for the band to allow me more time to write songs with Vincent and we were hopeful about having to accommodate some production requests. In effect I was giving up drumming, much to the disgust of our Kathleen. 'Just you wait and see,' she said, in one of her weekly berating sessions. 'You won't meet many girls in the studio.' To her, life was one great dating opportunity.

But I was busy, you know. KOPACE was going great guns. We now had two agents working for us and Christina really ran the whole show for me. Occasionally, she would rattle my cage so that I'd pretend to be angry to get a point across to a promoter or a client. I was writing songs with Vincent; I was also writing songs by myself, all about Marianne Burgess. No-one was allowed to hear them until they were ready for recording. While we waited to get production work, we would hire wee studios and a few musicians so that we could make demo tapes of our new songs. By now we had a London music publisher, LSP (London Song Parade), eager and keen for our new tunes. Like The Beatles, we had our own publishing company, TheoVin Songs, within LSP. Unlike The Beatles, we owned our own copyrights outright, which, in pure and simple terms, meant that we owned our own creative material. I thought it was obscene the way Northern Songs was bought and sold from under The Beatles' noses. I don't care what excuses were offered; it should never have been allowed to happen. The Beatles' publishing administrators already had their pound of flesh (and then some), and in my book, naive though it may be, they were taking their large cut from Beatles songs in order to protect the writers against the very thing that eventually happened.

Vince and I owned TheoVin Songs on a 50/50 split. Right from the beginning, we agreed that we would not chase the high advances but would forgo them in order to receive the highest royalty rate possible. To be quite honest, LSP didn't put up much of a fight. I'm sure they didn't think Vince's and my humble endeavours were going to mean anything, but we had a couple of songs on The Aunts' albums (that's as well as Vincent's own songs with The Aunts, which were covered by a separate deal). The record was due to come out any day soon and so a deal had to be done quickly. To be honest, they nearly bit our hands off when we said we weren't after advances. They just saw it as a way to get the copyright for free. We agreed that LSP would administer TheoVin Songs for ten years. After that, we could do whatever we wanted. I think they felt at that point that the songs would find a resting place on the scrapheap. Best deal I ever did and not a single solicitor in sight!

I gave our Kathleen 5% of my half of TheoVin Songs. She cried when I told her. She cried even louder when she received the first cheque. My mum was real proud of me for doing that. I mean, I must admit I didn't do it for any reason other than I really like my sister. She's a good person and she is the only one who won't let me get away with anything. She keeps pushing me. She keeps encouraging me, though I must admit her sights are set on quite a high level. Any time The Beatles achieve anything, she's on my case. Silly things like, 'So when are the Nighttime Passengers going to make their first movie?' or, 'Can't you and Vincent write a song for Cilla Black?'

This was after she had heard Cilla's cover of 'For No-One' (from the *Revolver* album) and our Kathleen thought it was time Cilla had more of a girl's song to sing. I told her to ring up Vincent and tell him. She did. Vincent thought she had a point and so we duly wrote a song that had the working title of 'Kathleen's Song' (in fact, that's what my mum still calls it). Actually, my first attempt at a title was 'Forget Ferrying Across The Mersey, Why Bother? With Brian Epstein as My Manager I Can Walk Across It'. Conceptually, a bit of a tongue twister I know, but we eventually settled for 'Don't Come Back (I Don't Want You Anymore)'. I loved the brackets and again, surprise surprise, it was about Marianne Burgess.

Anyway, we sent it to NEMS and they sent it back saying 'Thanks but no thanks'. At least they replied and at least they didn't keep us waiting for months. So, we sent it to LSP and they gave it to one of their producers. He gave it to a drummer friend who played it to the piano player of another group who, in turn, played it to an arranger on a session who forced his then producer to listen to it, and they cut (recorded) it on that very session. As you know, it was a hit for Francis Ford (whose real name, by the way, was Windeline Grommas). It only did okay in England but it did brilliantly in France, Germany, Switzerland, Austria and Italy, and gained numerous covers over there.

So, you see, if it hadn't been for our Kathleen, the song would never have been written in the first place. I suppose, if you take that to its logical conclusion, I should have been paying Marianne Burgess 5% as well. But if we had been so friendly that I would have been in a position to offer her a part of my company – as well as my personal company – I wouldn't have been mad at her, or mad enough to write the songs. Actually, mad is the wrong word there. I wasn't mad at her, not really. I was blue because of her and, because I was blue, I could write these songs. I keep thinking that if I had been happily settled down with someone at that point, I wouldn't have been able to write those songs. That's the magic of writing songs; it helps you deal with stuff. And – here's the important bit – you can deal with it successfully.

When I spilt up with Marianne Burgess, I finally accepted the fact that there was a good chance she was going to marry Brian the Solicitor (incidentally, have you noticed how her boyfriends seem to have those kind of medieval names like John the Tailor, who obviously eventually became John Taylor and so on, only in her case it was Ken the Married Man, Brian the Solicitor and Theo the Drummer?). Sorry, I digressed there for a bit. Where was I? Oh yes, when I accepted the fact that she was going to probably marry this legal eagle, I took solace in songwriting. I dealt with it by writing songs about it, about us, about her and about the break-up. Some I wrote with Vincent but mostly I worked by myself; the songs were unheard and I found a comfort in them. Some of the songs may seem to be sad songs, but to me they are not sad because they are about me dealing with a situation and trying to understand it. I suppose what I'm trying to say to you is that I needed to write the songs. In another, more cosmic, way the songs wrote themselves.

I've tried on many occasions to write a song about this very subject. I don't completely understand it all myself; I can't seem to grasp it, hard as I try. It's like the song is right there by my ear and I can't sing it but I can't help listening. I never get it though, no matter how much I keep listening.

Did I want Marianne Burgess to hear these songs? Well, I suppose that's why I wrote them but you see, once I had written them she was hearing them. I mean, the whole motivation behind

'How Many Times Do You Want To Break My Heart' on one side
and 'Don't Come Back (I Don't Want You Anymore)' on the other,
was the fact that they were statements to her. Part of the magic of
being able to make the statements was that she couldn't answer me
back and therefore couldn't hurt me any more.

    Or so I thought.

Chapter Pepper

Just as I was starting to become a wee bit proud of my songwriting, The Beatles were starting to work on a project that would make me and every other songwriter in England, with the possible exception of Ray Davies, want to pack up writing songs forever.

They – The Beatles – ended 1966 with touring forever a thing of the past. They then had a sabbatical, which afforded John the time to act in director Dick Lester's film, How I Won The War. George visited India for six weeks, during which time he studied yoga, Indian culture in general, and the sitar in particular. Paul (along with George Martin) composed and recorded the soundtrack music for the film, The Family Way. And Ringo, more chilled than the others, did not feel the need to fill the space so enjoyed a well-earned rest. Suitably refreshed they, along with producer George Martin and engineer Geoff Emerick, regrouped at Abbey Road Studios on Thursday 24th November 1966 to commence work on what is arguably the most famous album ever released. In its own way, *Sergeant Pepper's Lonely Hearts Club Band* is proving to be as popular and enduring as any of the works by the accepted greats such as Beethoven, Mozart or Bach.

For the first time, The Beatles were not under the pressure of an album delivery date. Brian Epstein had already advised EMI that there was no chance the new album would be released in time for the extremely lucrative Christmas market. The EMI bods ensured their bonuses by putting together the *Oldies But Goldies* compilation album and shipping it in time for the Christmas rush. The one good thing about *Oldies But Goldies* is that, with the inclusion of the track 'Bad Boy', it brought the UK and USA up to date with each other for the first time. The Americans – remember the 'capital' people at Capitol who didn't want to put The Beatles' music out in the first place? – well, they were releasing an average of three albums for every two albums released by The Beatles in the UK. They would cull tracks from various albums, singles and EPs to create their own additional releases. Brian Epstein was negotiating a new contract with EMI. The contract, which was eventually signed in January, tied John, Paul, George and Ringo to EMI, both as members of The Beatles and as solo artists, for the following nine years. Needless to say, at a greatly increased record royalty rate and with the assurances that all future worldwide releases would be identical to the official UK releases.

So, as I say, for the first time they had no pressures or deadlines to work under. In a way, this time in the studio was as much for The Beatles to see if, creatively speaking, they could exist as a studio identity as well as (hopefully for EMI and the rest of us) producing a new album. Towards the end of the touring, all four Beatles hated the live arena, although it did give them a natural base and a basic need for the band. Paul was the last to admit this. It should be said here that they really were very lucky to escape that particular (Philippines) experience with their lives, not to mention their sanity, and it speaks volumes for them as humans that they did in fact escape with the latter firmly intact.

They were no longer the moptops, singing comforting songs about boys and girls and lost love. They collectively grew their hair, beards and/or moustaches. The identical suits had made way for casual, colourful, vibrant clothes. Gone were the painfully youthful looks of George and Paul. The craziness had made them all older (naturally), more experienced (definitely), and wiser (noticeably). Yes, wiser... but still human. Their experimentation with drugs was opening their minds and, creatively speaking, inspiring them to different heights. Musically, by their own admission, they could not play successfully while under the influence of chemicals. Invariably they would have to re-record music recorded while under the influence, no matter how great they thought it had sounded at the time.

Now they were all gathered together in Abbey Road Studios, London NW1 to create music, which, for first time in their career, they would not have to attempt to perform live. They had an open canvas upon which to paint their weird and wonderful new pictures, drawing from a palette full of colours they hadn't even known existed five years before. There were no restrictions, barring the limitations of four-track recording machines. One of the things I still find incredible about *Sgt Pepper's* is how they managed to make an album so rich and textured using only four tracks. Admittedly, they had magicians – George Martin and engineer Geoff Emerick – continuously mixing down the tracks to free up space for the ever-increasing wave of ideas thrown at them by the four principals.

How it works is this. Say you record a four-piece string section; to give each of the instruments clarity, you record each on their own track. Then, when you complete the recording, you mix them all down to levels sympathetic with each other onto one track, freeing up the remaining three. Now it sounds quite simple when you say it like that but, at the same time that you are mixing down, you have to try and look into the future and see what else you, or The Beatles, can add so that you leave space in the audio 'picture' for such eventualities. George Martin was the master in this area and his engineer, Geoff Emerick, was able to deal with everything thrown at him. Necessity *is* the mother of invention and it was probably during these sessions that people started to dream of eight-track or sixteen-track machines, or even 'How about a thirty-two track machine?' Today, even the thirty-two track jobbies can be slaved up to produce... well basically, whatever you need in multiples of thirty-two.

But in all of this, the funny thing was, I think, that even if they had an eight-, sixteen- or thirty-two track recording machine instead of the standard four-tracks, I doubt that *Sgt Pepper's* could have turned out any better an album than it did. Of the several Grammy Awards (record industry's Oscars) *Sgt Pepper's* won, there was none more deserving than the one to Geoff Emerick for Best Engineering.

I mentioned at the beginning of this chapter about *Sgt Pepper's* proving to be as popular and as lasting as some of the great classical composers. I didn't mean I felt it was *better* than any of their works because I think that would be as stupid as saying that one of those great works was better than the others. No, I meant that The Beatles had put something, a work, out there into the world and the world had reacted to it and adopted it now and forever (well, we'll see, or at least our children will see!). But like the classical composers, Liverpool's finest – ably aided and abetted by George Martin – were creating 'sound pictures', using everything available to them. Unlike the greats they were using voices, natural and traditional instruments and unnatural (or synthetic) sounds.

In November 1966, the introduction to the first song they recorded, as part of these sessions, was played on an instrument never used before in recording. It was a Mellotron, an electronic instrument and the forerunner to the synthesizer, which used pre-recorded tapes. These tapes were activated by the use of a keyboard creating an electronic version of strings, brass, voices – anything, really, which you chose to pre-record. In the case of the song in question, the classic 'Strawberry Fields Forever', they used it to 'recreate' a flute sound. This song was written by John when he was on the set of How I Won the War. Although Neil Aspinall was with him and Ringo came to visit his mate, John was homesick. 'Strawberry Fields Forever' is a song about John's long-lost Liverpool. Strawberry Fields is a neighbourhood John lived in for a time and often, you have to leave a place to discover its real beauty, which is exactly what John Lennon was doing in this song.

I was lucky; it might have been because of my mum and dad, but I did see the beauty and enjoy the delights of Liverpool, and that was one of the main reasons I chose never to leave. Mind you, if I thought leaving would have encouraged me to write a song like 'Strawberry Fields Forever', or the equally incredible 'Penny Lane', I'd have been on my bike ages ago.

John wrote a song, 'Strawberry Fields Forever', about Liverpool, which prompted Paul to write a song about Liverpool, 'Penny Lane'. Both were totally different. John's lyrics were surreal and ambient; Paul's lyrics were real and, as usual, very visual. As with 'Eleanor Rigby', Paul was creating a socially observant mini-movie, with well-rounded (perhaps real) characters, all set around Liverpool 18, and a day in the life of the famous barber's shop, Bioletti's. "*In Penny Lane, the barber shaves another customer*", Paul sings and immediately you're right in there with him, off on this wonderful trip. And you know what? They both complement each other. These two songs, written by the best writers around, show in their diversity the magic of The Beatles. These songs were like chalk and cheese – one an electronic production and the other a very clean recording of natural instruments – but in a way they still worked together as comfortably as Laurel and Hardy.

They worked so well together, in fact, that EMI, anxious for a single, nicked them and rushed them out as a double A-sided single (The Beatles' third). In a way it's ironic, not to mention sad, that it should have been this single – perhaps one of the best singles ever released – that would be the first single since The Beatles hit the top with 'Please Please Me', which didn't reach number one in the UK charts. Sadly, it peaked at number two. It would have been their thirteenth number one so perhaps part of the secret of the chart failure lies there. I mean, could it really have failed to make the number one position just because it would have been their thirteenth number one single? You figure it out, I know I never could. To add insult to injury, it was kept from the number one spot by the 'singing grin and haircut', performing *Please Release Me*. The Beatles made yet another innovative video clip for their two Liverpool tracks. Ground-breaking again in that this was not a performance piece by the band but, in fact, a very surreal film with a running, jumping and spooky Beatles. John Lennon was wearing in public, for the first time, the glasses he'd been wearing for so long in private. In the '60s, glasses and wives were bad for the image so both were kept (equally) in the background. This made for strained relationships and even more strained book reading.

It's all over, the critics cried. They're finished. My dad always told me, when talking about others in public, to use only the sweetest of words. 'You may have to eat them someday,' he'd reminded me. Well, the critics' words were anything but sweet, but if the excitement generated at Abbey Road was anything to go by, then the critics were all going to be sitting down to an unpalatable feast six months later.

Sergeant Pepper's Lonely Hearts Club Band was always meant to be a concept album or a theme album of some sort; of that there is no question. Some of the rumours around Liverpool at the time were that it was, in fact, meant to be an album with songs all about Liverpool. The third song they recorded was 'When I'm Sixty-Four', a Paul McCartney Indigo Jolliphant vaudeville-type song, which they had been performing (during equipment breakdowns) as early as the Cavern days. Now Paul's dad had just celebrated his sixty-fourth birthday and so it was duly dragged out and recorded for the Liverpool album. Then EMI released 'Strawberry Fields Forever' and 'Penny Lane' and, as The Beatles didn't like fans having to buy their songs twice (as singles and album tracks), those two pivotal songs had to be withdrawn from the album's shortlist.

In times of trouble you could always leave it to Paul to come up with an idea or, as on this occasion, a concept. And he did. The San Francisco scene was just starting up and all the bands over there had these weird and wonderful names like Big Brother and The Holding Company, and a few cods had even put a group together called Country Joe and The Fish. Inspired by these names, Paul suggested – and the others agreed – making up a fictitious band and having the album as the showpiece of this imaginary band. They could make it a real show so that the show could go out on tour and they could all stay at home. Great idea! So, what would they call the band?

Sergeant Pepper's Lonely Hearts Club Band, of course. So they did and the rest, as they say, was 90% perspiration and 10% inspiration.

The title track showed The Beatles to be a group as tight and as rocking as any other band out there. It's also a very exciting track that actually pulls you into the show. The whole project was gathering steam at this point and cameras were recording their every studio move for a possible television special. The other revolutionary idea they came up with was to segue the songs one into another. It was a show, after all, and there was no need or reason for disruptive breaks. 'Sgt Pepper's' (the song) melted into the next track, with audience noise (this was actually lifted from The Beatles in concert at the Hollywood Bowl), so effectively and (not to mention) excitingly that you couldn't see the join. The next song was 'With A Little Help From My Friends', written for and about Ringo (we assume). Ringo took on the character name, Billy Shears, for his place in the band.

There, sadly, the original idea ran out of steam. The remaining songs, except the reprise of 'Sgt Pepper's Lonely Hearts Club Band', have no link to the original concept. They were all exceptional but in no way connected, except that they all shared a 'show' kind of feel, don't you think? We are left with another of those 'What would it have been like if they'd stuck to their guns?' questions and it doesn't bear thinking about really, does it?

'A Day In The Life' is a Beatles masterpiece in anyone's book and displays some of the most soulful singing John Lennon ever performed. John took his inspiration from two newspaper stories. One, a Beatles friend and one of the Guinness heirs, Tara Browne, had been killed in a car crash; and two, a story about how many holes there were in Blackburn, Lancashire. There was a natural gap in the middle of John's song and he, at the time of original recording, didn't know what he was going to put in. They recorded the song, leaving a gap with Mal Evans counting 24 bars and setting an alarm clock at the end of the break, so that everyone would know when to start playing again.

So, John had a beginning and an end to his song but he didn't know what to do in the middle. Paul McCartney, on the other hand, had this little bit of a song; you know, probably the middle of something he would eventually finish. But why not use... ? Why not indeed, and they did, but because he sang "I'd love to turn you on", the BBC banned the song from airplay (as they did another song on this album), effectively causing the television show to be doomed to the shelves. But at least they now had the basis for the song. That was one of the good things about The Beatles in the studio. They would always go with the best idea for a track, no matter who suggested it; there was none of the 'It's my song and I want… ' – that was for later, when there was no Beatles.

Anyway, one of the things they did record for television was the orchestra recording their contribution for inclusion on this track. The Beatles wanted an orgasmic orchestral climax on the end of the recording of 'A Day In The Life'. They wanted all the instruments to start on their lowest (deepest) note and work their way up into a frenzied crescendo as the musicians hit their highest notes simultaneously. The Beatles asked the orchestra, all forty of them, to dress up in dinner jackets, but also to wear something silly to add to the party atmosphere at the recording. They also invited some of their friends and so, people like Mick Jagger were to be filmed sitting around at The Beatles' feet during this historic recording.

Mal Evans and Neil Aspinall were still just as invaluable to The Beatles. I'd imagine they thought that the end of the gigging would also be the end of their career with The Beatles. Not so. They were needed just as much in the studio as they were on the road. They were trusted members of The Beatles' entourage at a time when trust was worth more than its weight in gold. In order to achieve the BIG piano note (E major), which concluded 'A Day In The Life', John, Paul, Ringo and Mal all had to hit *the* note simultaneously, on separate pianos, while George Martin added weight on the harmonium.

Now they had the beginning and the end to their album. All they had to do was fill in the middle bits. 'Good Morning, Good Morning' is a 'John' song and inspired by a Kellogg's TV advert, with the Sounds Incorporate lending their brass section. The Sounds Incorporate were the top instrumental unit of the day and frequently toured as back-up band for American soul artists touring the UK without their own bands. They were also managed by Brian Epstein and occasionally toured as an opening act for The Beatles.

They recorded 'Only A Northern Song' as George Harrison's composition for *Sgt Pepper's* but, for whatever reason, it didn't make the cut and didn't actually surface until the *Yellow Submarine* album a few years later. George did, with help from his Indian friends (there were no other Beatles on the recording session), record 'Within You Without You'. This track, as you well know, did make the historical album.

'Fixing A Hole' was apparently the easiest song on the album to record. John Lennon bought a circus poster advertising a circus appearance in Rochdale in February 1843, and pulled all the performers mentioned on the poster into a song, as you do, called 'For The Benefit of Mr Kite'. George Martin, under instructions to come up with something 'fairgroundy and circusy', secured library sounds of the same, cut the tapes up into little pieces, threw the fragments into the air, picked them up from the floor and stuck them all back together again to create bizarre sonic mishmash. Then he added some of his own harmonium playing to the song, completing yet another unconnected scene in the magical show.

If George Martin was happy with his work on 'Mr Kite', he was somewhat put out when an impatient Paul decided that, rather than wait for his producer to return from a function, he would hire Mike Leander to do a string arrangement for his current song, 'She's Leaving Home'. It was the first time strings were to be included on a Beatles record that were not arranged by George Martin. The arrangement is good, although somewhat more predictable than George Martin's arrangements, and the recording was completed with only John and Paul on vocals. It was yet another of Paul's 'story-in-a-song' songs, and very effective at that.

'Lovely Rita', 'Getting Better' and 'Lucy in The Sky With Diamonds' completed the songs for the album. 'Lucy' was the second track to be banned by the BBC. The title was not, in fact, about the drug LSD (Lucy/Sky/Diamonds) but was John's son, Julian's description of a painting he had brought home from school. Again, with 'Getting Better', we see the alternative side of The Beatles with positive Paul singing 'It's Getting Better All The Time' (referring to his progress with learning to drive) and dour John countering with 'It can't get much worse.'

All good stuff and they had the album completed; apart, that is, from one little addition. The final recording for *Sergeant Pepper's Lonely Hearts Club Band* was carried out on Friday 21st April 1967, when they recorded a high-pitched, 15-kilocycle whistle (a noise only dogs could hear) and placed it just after the aforementioned single (multi-tracked), E-major piano note that was to fade for ever and ever.

Over five months, The Beatles spent a staggering 700 hours working on their masterwork. A long time in those days, but these days it's probably about the length of time it would take the Spinal Tap drummer to get his drum sound correct. Back then, however, EMI owned the studio and none of the recording costs were billed to the artist. I wonder if it was around that time that record company accountants considered that perhaps they should start to bill the band for their studio time? We'll never know.

The sleeve of this album is possibly the most famous album sleeve in the world. It was Paul McCartney's idea, although some of the people he hired to do pieces of the work on it would later claim credit. It was the first record sleeve to contain printed lyrics. Brian Epstein was so worried about the sleeve that, at one point, he suggested it might be an idea to release it in a brown paper bag so as not to offend. In the cast of characters adorning the sleeve, John Lennon wanted to include Hitler and Jesus. EMI refused, and further requested that Gandhi also be removed. Neil and Mal went around all the libraries collecting prints of the various celebrities and a genuine fairground painter, Joseph Ephrgave, painted the famous drumhead. I wonder where that is now? Who has the Sergeant Pepper drumhead?

Sergeant Pepper's Lonely Hearts Club Band (or PCS 7027 as it was known to EMI's accountants) was released on 1st June, significantly enough, in the year of the 'Summer of Love' (the capital L is intentional). The pirate radio station, Radio London, played the entire album on air, claiming a first for both themselves and The Beatles. In England, with pre-sales of a quarter of a million copies, *Pepper's* shot straight to the top of the charts, where it remained for twenty weeks. It then dropped to the number two position for eleven weeks and returned to the top during the first week of 1968 for a further two weeks.

It is the biggest UK-selling album ever! That is, by anyone before or since, with sales now approaching a staggering four-and-a-half million copies. Around the time of the release of *Sgt Pepper's*, EMI announced that The Beatles had sold (across all their records, and counting each album as six unit sales and a single as one unit) 200 million units!

I think it is interesting to note the top ten records (singles) in the week that *Sgt Pepper's* was released.

1. The Tremeloes   'Silence is Golden'
2. The Kinks   'Waterloo Sunset'
3. The Mamas & The Papas   'Dedicated to the One I Love'
4. Procol Harum   'A Whiter Shade of Pale'
5. Beach Boys   'Then I Kissed Her'
6. Jimi Hendrix Experience 'The Wind Cries Mary'
7. Engelbert Humperdinck   'There Goes my Everything'

8. The Supremes	'The Happening'
9. The Who	'Pictures of Lily'
10. The Dubliners	'Seven Drunken Nights'

Equally interesting to note is that the number two single was written by Ray Davies who, with his consistently insightful songs, was proving to be the best English songwriter who didn't come from Liverpool and wasn't a member of The Beatles.

In America, with pre-sales of over a million copies, *Sgt Pepper's* went straight to number one and remained in the charts for over two years. It has now sold over twelve million copies in America. At this point, worldwide sales must be approaching the thirty million mark for this phenomenally successful album.

During the summer of 1968, I was in Ireland – Northern Ireland – visiting my mum's relations. I'd bought the record before I left for Ireland but hadn't had a chance to listen to it too much – preoccupied as I then was with Marianne Burgess – but I had liked it. Then, one Saturday evening, I was at this party in Cookstown, Co Tyrone, in a church hall. All the walls were covered with colourful posters and streamers, and coloured balloons were hanging about everywhere. The music was great and, as they say over there, the craic was ninety. People were laughing, joking and dancing; some were sitting around on the floors, drinking and having a good time, and then someone put *Sergeant Pepper's Lonely Hearts Club Band* on the PA system. This is a true story by the way!

One by one, the party people stopped talking and chatting and the noise and bustle of the party died down completely, until the entire party was being seduced by the beautiful and inspiring music. People were smiling and loving it, and happiness was spreading from one to another with the same power that panic can move through a gathering – as if by some instinctive communicative thing. Only this was a good feeling, a great feeling. Every new track drew everyone deeper and deeper into this new world. Our new world, a world created for us by The Beatles. It was like everything they had ever done had been leading up to that point. Every note of music they ever played and every song they ever composed had been in preparation for this moment, the moment they captured with *Sergeant Pepper's Lonely Hearts Club Band*. It didn't matter that perhaps the *Revolver* album might have been a better album. It didn't matter that touring had nearly destroyed the band – our band. It didn't matter that I didn't have someone (Marianne) there with me to love and share this with: there was already more than enough love in the air and all of it created by The Beatles. All that mattered was that they had fulfilled their promise. This album wasn't a great album because it sold lots of copies. The album sold lots of copies, purely and simply, because it was a great album. Maybe even the perfect album.

And the thing about the party that night in Cookstown was that we were all sharing it, sharing the pleasure. And as it was being shared, the pleasure grew. When John Lennon started to sing 'A Day In The Life' I swear to you I felt shivers run down my spine, the hairs on the back of my neck stood up and my throat went dry. I could feel my nostrils tightening as though tears were going to flow. Not one person felt any different, I bet you. No-one moved a muscle for fear of spoiling the mood. As the last note, the E major, drifted into silence everyone was left stunned, speechless. It was like a mass turn-on but instead of the buzz being induced by a (potentially harmful) drug, it had been induced by the show that The Beatles had wanted to present to us, possibly for years. The show they knew they could never do on stage but felt they could do by sending it out to us in the form of *Sergeant Pepper's Lonely Hearts Club Band*. I know that probably sounds like I may have been indulging in some of the harmful chemicals I alluded to, but I wasn't. I never have and I never will; I've never needed to. But you really had to be there, in Cookstown, to know what I'm on about. All I can tell you is that as we strained to hear the disappearing E major, there was such an incredible feeling of elation. Everyone clapped their hands, no-one knew what else to do. We just clapped and clapped and then clapped some more.

You'll never meet anyone who can tell you what it was like at the first ever performance of the 1812 Overture. But I'm happy to say, with my hand on my heart, that for me, what they felt could not have compared with what I experienced listening to The Beatles' 'meisterwork'.

It was never the same. I never, ever experienced that buzz again. I don't tell you that with the slightest regret. I am proud to have been alive in that time and to have enjoyed that once-in-a-lifetime experience. I still love, and enjoy listening to, the record. It may just have been the communal spirit between everyone at the party, that summer evening in Cookstown, that made it as special as I remember it, but whatever it was, it certainly wasn't going to be an experience that could be repeated frequently, if ever. And it all came from the music; the music of The Beatles.

Chapter Thirty-Eight

I settled down to think about myself at this point. You have to at some stage, don't you? The whole *Sgt Pepper's* thing was a complete revelation to me. The problem is, you can look, search or struggle (or even all three) for something for so long you eventually have to admit to having lost the plot. The search becomes the issue more than what you are searching for. But I kept getting back to the fact that music was a real healing force and that you owed it to yourself to at least put yourself in a position to enjoy it.

Feeling I had but simple needs didn't really help matters. I mean, it's one thing to have simple needs and to be able to say, 'Well, I could give this all away and drop out anytime.' Dropping out was the big thing then. 'Drop out, turn on and tune in' was the key phrase, all the rage, thanks to Timothy Leary. I had KOPACE, and KOPACE had given me freedom (as in financial freedom), but at the same time, the cost of this financial independence is that you take on responsibilities for other people and for your artists. Probably, in a small way, I was feeling some of the pressures Brian Epstein found himself under.

The difference was, of course, that I didn't really see myself as a businessman. I was an artist, or so I thought. I found myself under the gun on two fronts: delivering as a songwriting partner with Vincent, *and* keeping KOPACE going. In both instances, I had people to share the load but I got to the point of thinking: Why bother? Why am I doing this? I don't need to any more. I had simple needs and more than enough funds to support them, but our Kathleen assured me this was a delayed reaction to accepting the Marianne Burgess situation.

I had worked hard to reach this station, only to find when I arrived there was no-one to share it with. No-one even for a chat. The way I felt, I didn't really want to try to get it together with anyone else. What was the point? I mean, I'd made up my mind who I wanted to be with for the rest of my life. It was now blatantly obvious, even to me, that this was not going to be a possibility. To accept anything less than that would have been cheating myself and, I figured, hurting myself. So, if I were in tune with my true feelings, to go with anyone else, knowing the way I felt about Marianne Burgess, would have been a sham.

I was still in a bit of a tizzy, you know? Marianne Burgess had told me she *did* love me. Okay? Good so far? But then she also told me she was going to marry someone else, a man she *didn't* love. How was I meant to live with that? Was all of this because I hadn't told her I wanted to marry her? It was impossible to fathom. I recalled her saying at various times that she wasn't what I thought she was. What was that all about? What did I think she was that she wasn't? Was there a mystery lurking there somewhere?

This phrase played on my mind a lot. She wasn't what I thought she was. I thought she was beautiful and to me, she was beautiful. I thought she was sensual. Again, in my book, she was *the* biggest turn-on, full stop! I thought she was training to be a teacher. My trip to Manchester proved this. I thought she was considering marrying someone other than the man (she claimed) she loved. Now maybe there was something there. I hadn't met him, had I? But why would she lie about him? What good would that do, particularly when it was hurting me so much and pain like that could only (eventually) kill love?

What else was there about her that *wasn't*? Kathleen knew her before I was interested. Kathleen did love me and would never knowingly hurt me. I mean, she would hurt me by being honest with me if she felt I needed to know something. I thought of everything I knew about Marianne. About her mum and dad, both of whom I didn't really know well. About her brother Jonathan – whom I'd spend quite a bit of time with when Marianne and I were going out. We got on great. He'd been a little distant at the beginning but then, to a four-year-old, a 'friend' of your sister's (and who is an old person and not part of your weird and wonderful imagination) is an outsider. He did learn 'Yellow Submarine' with me and, much to his sister's amusement, we would frequently sing it while out on walks with her. Sometimes I would catch her looking at us – Jonathan and me, playing together – with that lost-world look about her. Then she'd catch me clocking her and she'd snap out of it, pretending that she'd been 'miles away'.

I wracked my brains and could not come up with a single thing. Perhaps I had just been concentrating too much on her words and I had either picked them up wrong or she had done a Ringo on me and twiddled her words around. These were thoughts I shared only with our Kathleen during our numerous late-night chats. I'll let you into a secret at this point. I even daydreamed of trying to fix up a joint dinner with Marianne Burgess and Brian, and me and our Kathleen, in the hope that Brian would fall for Kathleen and I'd be left with Marianne Burgess. I even ran that plan past Vincent McKee but he was disgusted at the idea. Well, he would be, wouldn't he? He and our Kathleen had started to become friends – nothing more, mind you, just friends, but that was enough for him to persuade me away from the double-date plan. No, I quite simply had to accept that the fact that she wasn't *really* interested in me for some reason; whether Brian was around or not. She had already admitted she loved me and didn't love him, so what kind of dilemma must she be in?

Kathleen encouraged me not to give everything up and drop out. She said I would later regret it and, worse than that, would be unable to get it all back again once I took my foot off the pedal. She assured me that I was going to meet someone. There was going to be someone there for me. Just because there was no-one there when I arrived didn't mean anything. Well, anything apart from the fact that I'd arrived first. Our Kathleen claimed that whenever I met the magical person – whoever she may be – I wouldn't even think of Marianne Burgess, I would just know immediately that this was it. This was rich coming from someone who was older than me and still without the partner to make her own life complete.

'Besides,' Kathleen would repeatedly announce, 'when you're writing songs as great as the ones you are, you don't really want to grow contented and lose your angst and upset things, do you? Think of my 5%, Theo.'

I must admit, I liked the persona of the troubled artist. I, like my heroes, started to grow my hair and a beard. Although the beard was a bit wimpy – you could still see my skin through the bum fluff – our Kathleen said that the long hair suited me.

It was around this time that someone turned on the colour switch over England. I always thought of Liverpool as a very colourful city but it appears in all the photographs from the early '60s as an industrial-looking, black-and-white city. Early 1967, colour took over and we could see what a vibrant city we had, as photos now testify. I frequently considered moving to London – business and all that – but the pull of the Mersey proved to be too strong. At times the temptation was there – you know, as an escape from Marianne Burgess and all those feelings – but each time I got down to it something would get in the way.

Christina had, by that point, met the man who was to be her future husband and she was certainly not interested in relocating, not in the slightest, so we stayed put. KOPACE stayed in Liverpool and I'm very happy now that we did. With England, courtesy of Bobby Charlton, winning the World Cup the previous year, there was a national pride thing going on. People were accepting, for the first time, that England didn't end just north of Watford. The Beatles had a lot to do with that, you know.

Then I started to get mad, I mean really mad. I loved this woman. She loved me. All the rest was just shite and we should be sensible enough to try and work our way through this. What was all this fecking crap about her wanting to marry Brian the Solicitor? I mean, come on Marianne, it's time to get out of the house a bit more. At least let me off the hook. Tell me you were mistaken and you don't really love me. You've had a brain (as opposed to a 'Brian') transplant and woken up to discover you are madly in love with him, you hate my guts, and you are going to marry him. At least I could live with that. Turn a bit of healthy old anger into a life motivation. What was she playing at? I decided to go and have it out with her, face to face, one final time. I didn't tell our Kathleen about my plan, just in case she wanted common sense to prevail. Who needed common sense at a time like this?

This was a time when I would remember fearing becoming a weedy old man living with nothing but my memories, too decrepit to do anything but dwell on the past. I'd be saying 'Why oh why didn't I try?' I liked those words; they sounded like a song title to me. In fact, I liked them so much I wrote a song around them, there and then, and by the end of my song I had resolved – lyrically, emotionally and physically – to go looking for her.

Guess what? Marianne Burgess had disappeared from the face of the earth; well, at least the face of Manchester's rain-soaked soil. It was late August 1967 and she was meant to be back in Manchester getting ready for her final year. I had just returned from my spiritual time in Ulster and was going to give this one last shot for my own peace of mind, although I'd already resolved to get on with my life with or without her. I felt I'd arrived at a crossroads. If I was to progress beyond this point, without Marianne Burgess in my life, I decided I had to give it this one final go. You have to really, don't you?

All Marianne's mum would tell our Kathleen (who I'd now had to recruit) was that Marianne and her brother, Jonathan, had gone off for a time and were not due back for a couple of weeks. Kathleen was also told that Marianne was to marry Brian in the middle of September, a week after she came back. Time was running out. She had to be somewhere.

Then I cheated a bit. I had our Kathleen ring up Colette at Salford Teacher Training College and find out Brian's number. Colette willingly obliged. Proved my theory, Colette did, that girls are so much tighter with each other than men will ever be with each other.

Next came the difficult bit. I persuaded our Kathleen to ring up Brian and say she urgently needed to get hold of Marianne.

'What am I going to say I need it for?' she asked.

'Yes, Theo,' Vincent chipped in, for he was round at Kathleen's as much as I was by then, 'you haven't thought this through properly, man. What is she going to say she needs Marianne's number for?'

'Oh, something girlie. I'm sure you'll think of something,' I replied, practising one of my weakest qualities; being nonchalant.

'Come on, Theo, think of something. I'm not just going to ring him up without a reason. He'll see through it immediately,' Kathleen said.

'Then just be honest.'

'What, tell him that my brother is madly in love with his wife-to-be and wants to steal her from the altar?' my sister said in disbelief.

'No, I meant a more selective form of honesty.'

'Oh, yeah?'

'Yes. Just tell him that you've heard she's getting married and you want to wish her all the best and see if there is anything you can do to help with the preparations,' I replied.

So she did and, surprisingly, he did – give her the number, that is. Our Kathleen rang the number, only to find that it was a wee guesthouse on the front at New Brighton. 'And that, your honour, is how I came to be standing on the door step of the same guesthouse, WindView (and they weren't kidding) at nine-forty that very evening.' Lucky for me they had a room to spare, small but clean, and I checked in.

Next morning, I woke early. Truth to tell, I hadn't slept much. I never have been able to sleep much in guesthouses. The rooms are so small, and they do so much cleaning that the air is always full of cleaning smells. With this unnatural smell filling my nostrils, I always have trouble breathing; it's like the air is contaminated and if I'm not conscious I might lose my breath. Silly, I know, but then again I'm a drummer. I heard the strange noises about the house as the guests and guesthouse came to life. I swore I heard Marianne talk just outside my room. That brought on a major panic attack, I can tell you. Apparently Jonathan was keen to get to the 'side' of the seaside and Marianne was insisting on more practical things first, like getting a good breakfast down them. It was brisk on the beach, she claimed. The northern wind does tend to cut through you if it meets resistance. Marianne won her argument and about forty minutes later, I watched from my window as she and Jonathan walked across the road and over to the sea front. It was quite beautiful, watching them going about their day, happy and totally contented in each other's company.

I still hadn't decided how to play this. For some strange reason, just being this close to Marianne dissolved all the pressure I'd been feeling since learning of her imminent marriage. I didn't know what I was going to say to her or how I could figure out a reason for being there. 'What? You like this place too? I've been coming here for years. You know, every time I want to get away for a break, I always end up here. What a coincidence.' I wasn't quite sure that one would fly! Feck it, I thought, she could only tell me to go, clear off; and this time, with my new resolve, if I was invited to clear off I would. Forever!

So, I crossed the road and followed them down to the beach. They looked great together and seemed very close. At one point, just as I was coming up on them, Marianne hugged Jonathan. She hugged him as if her life depended on it. It was a nice thing to see. As I mentioned, our Kathleen and I have always been that close but it's not typical for brother and sister, I can assure you. Take me and my other sister, Colette, for instance. We do not get on at all. Can't stand each other. That may be a wee bit extreme but it might just seem that way because our Kathleen and I get on so well.

Jonathan spied me first and, without any adult inhibitions, cried out my name at the top of his voice and ran towards me. Marianne looked shocked at first and then, when she realised it was me and that Jonathan was in no danger, she relaxed and smiled. Then she realised, once again, it was *me* and her jaw dropped as if to say, 'What the feck are you doing here?' But she didn't. I picked up Jonathan in my arms. As ever, he pulled at my long hair. It was still strange, outside of pop groups, for people to have long hair and it always intrigued Jonathan. I liked Jonathan. He was cool, and he had a deep logic for one so young.

'I'm sorry, I just had to come,' I started, as Marianne sighed, 'but I'll leave if you want me to,' I offered.

'No,' Jonathan laughed in disbelief,' you're staying with us to play in the water, isn't he, Mari?'

It was interesting the way he hadn't quite got his tongue around his sister's name, but went for "Mari" rather than the easier "Mary".

'Hey,' Marianne announced, a smile creeping across her face to reveal her twisted tooth, 'Jonathan's the boss and whatever he says goes.'

'Perhaps I should try to get him in my corner then,' I replied.

'Oh, he's already in it. He likes you.'

At that precise moment, I wasn't sure whether that was an accurate statement as Jonathan was trying to stretch my nose and find a way of putting it into my ear.

Marianne Burgess looked a lot more serene than before – peaceful even – maybe because she'd made her decision (to marry) or maybe just because this trip to the seaside with her younger brother had been the shot in the arm (tonic, dose of reality or whatever you want to call it) that she'd needed. A child's perspective – you know, down there from three-foot nothing – is totally different to an adult's. I know those of you with children will be saying, 'But of course, Theo.' It's just that firstly, I haven't been around them much in my life and secondly, they all share this beautiful innocence. Jonathan's innocence was just totally overwhelming. He was not aware, obviously, of what had been going on between Marianne and me. More to the point, he was not aware of what had not been going on between us, but we were all together on the beach and so that meant we *should* be together. Only natural. And so say all of us!

'Theo,' he said, as he held out his hand to Marianne, 'you take Mari's other hand and we'll walk to the sea, all of us together,' and he broke into a big grin.

And that's what we did, just the three of us. But it was weird; I was not getting this strange anti-vibe from Marianne that I'd been expecting, along the lines of 'You know I'm getting married, leave me alone why don't you.' No, there was none of that. Instead, she took my hand – the first intimate contact we'd had in ages – and with the touch, her touch, and her fresh, newly bathed smell, she sent shivers up my spine.

As Jonathan ran off to view a shell to our left, Marianne interlinked her arm with mine and we braced ourselves against the strong sea breeze. It was pleasant, exhilarating and very refreshing. I felt good, a sense of goodness I had not experienced since we last made love. I hoped her new-found contentment had nothing to do with her imminent marriage. I hoped she was going to say something about liking me a lot (maybe even loving me) but that, after thinking about this long and hard, she had made her decision to marry Brian and, having made that decision, she was enjoying a calm she hadn't known since she was a child. It was one of those far-fetched fears that you have but when you experience them, you feel it's okay because, in a way, by exorcising them (the fears) they would never become a reality. A cold sweat broke over me. I was convinced this, or a variation on the above, was what she was going to tell me.

'Theo,' she said, in a voice barely above a whisper, 'I want to tell you... I need to tell you... something.'

This is hard for her, I was thinking, here comes the big 'E'.

'I need to tell you that I am in love with you and we need to talk,' she said, eventually.

Okay. First part a bit better than I expected. Now here comes the 'but'.

'But let's enjoy our day with Jonathan and we'll talk this evening. The landlady's daughter baby-sits and we can go out. That is, of course, if you can stay?'

Only for the rest of my life, I thought. Okay, fair dues to her; she was going to let me down easy. She didn't want to shoot me down on the sea front and have me rushing off, leaving Jonathan perplexed. He was very sensitive and would pick up the vibes instantly. Hey, I'd tried. What was I going to lose but a day? Maybe she needed to spend this last day with me as well, for her memories or something. All these thoughts were rushing through my mind as my mouth, of its own accord, said, 'Yes, that would be fab, I'd like that.'

Chapter Thirty-Nine

It is fitting that during this summer, the 'Summer of Love', The Beatles – having reached their artistic and commercial peak, should have been involved in a project that took them, live, directly into 350 million homes over five continents.

The Beatles, as the most famous group ever, were commissioned to write a piece, as England's official representatives, to launch the live television link-up via satellite, in a BBC programme called Our World. In those days, it was a big thing. Television was still considered to be the wireless in the corner, which occasionally showed distorted pictures. It had yet to reach the stage where it controlled all domestic life, and I mean *all* domestic life, as we knew it.

The Beatles being The Beatles and never ones to shirk from a challenge, decided they would do their section live and the live recording would be the official single. John Lennon wrote the song and the backing tracks were rehearsed and recorded at the Olympic Studio in Barnes. On the designated day, June 25th, The Beatles assembled with friends, musicians and the ever-present cameras. The studio was decorated with multi-coloured streamers, banners and balloons. The Beatles themselves were dressed to the nines in their new, vivid hippie gear. Amongst those present were girlfriends and wives, plus Donovan, Marianne Faithfull and Mike Love, with Mick Jagger caught on camera sitting at John Lennon's feet. Mick Jagger seemed to spend quite a bit of the '60s sitting at The Beatles' feet, a position he seemed then, as now, to be unable to rise from.

The message that John and his fellow travellers, of the mind and globe, had come up with was 'All You Need Is Love'. It was probably more of a chant than a song, but a very infectious chant and one with a message, which, if it had been taken to heart, would have made the world a much better place. But even then there were darker powers lurking around the corner.

'All You Need Is Love', live on air and produced by the ever-trusted and inventive George Martin, was released as a single with 'Baby You're A Rich Man' on the B-side. 'Baby You're A Rich Man' might have been written about a trip all The Beatles took to Greece that summer. The intention was to buy an island so that all The Beatles and their friends could retreat there and form a commune. They lorded it up for a week or so on expensive yachts and in exclusive villas and returned to the UK, not having made the purchase but (via Paul's pen) with the B-side of their next single.

The news of The Beatles' imminent demise when 'Strawberry Fields Forever'/'Penny Lane' failed to reach number one in the charts was proven to be premature as 'All You Need Is Love' shot to the top of the charts and remained there for three weeks. In the middle of all this, The Beatles had already commenced work on their next project, another 'Paul' idea. Most of their ideas seemed to originate from the bass player. The recording part of this project took place a matter of only five days after they completed work on the monumental *Sgt Pepper's* recording session. The new project was *The Magical Mystery Tour*. The idea (very hippie) was that they were to get on a bus with a few friends and a few pints of beer, and travel around, having a laugh and recording it all for a film.

Humour was a big thing in The Beatles' camp. They had a great ability to laugh at things, including (it must be noted) themselves. The Beatles frequently portrayed the fun side of life in their music. The main difference between them and The Stones, for instance, was quite simply a sense of humour. I always put that down to being a Liverpool thing.

That summer they also discovered, via George Harrison, the teaching of Maharishi Mahesh Yogi – a guru not a bear, before you jump to that conclusion. Basically, the Maharishi taught those who would listen that one could achieve spiritual enlightenment by meditating – transcendental meditation: ten minutes in the morning and ten minutes in the evening. Towards the end of August, The Beatles and entourage boarded a train at St Pancras for Bangor in Wales, to take instruction in meditation. Sadly, very sadly, while The Beatles were in Bangor, Brian Epstein accidentally took an overdose of pills. Their mentor, manager, partner and friend was dead.

Brian Epstein was thirty-two years old when he died. Some say he was unhappy. He was reportedly very unhappy in his personal life and, let's not forget, we're talking about the not-so-liberal '60s. He was also unhappy in his business life. The Beatles – the musical force that he helped bring to the world – had decided to give up touring. And that had always been his big thing, his big strength,

organising and plotting their rise through concerts – their direct link
to their audience. He had succeeded brilliantly in his endeavours on
this front and, as I keep saying because it bears repeating, he paved
the way for everyone who was to follow.

However, now that The Beatles had, in effect, retired from the
road, they were eagerly jumping to the next phase of their career, or
the recording years, as they are now referred to. As such, at least on
paper, there would have been less need for a manager. But I think
Brian would have reinvented his role as The Beatles' manager, just
as The Beatles were very successfully and creatively reinventing
themselves. He'd been depressed; he'd been given some antidepres-
sants. Sadly, when mixed with alcohol they proved to be lethal.
Such was also the case with several other celebrities, all of whom, at
some stage, were accused of committing suicide. But I would like to
think that people like Mama Cass, Keith Moon, Jimi Hendrix, Jim
Morrison and Brian Epstein – all talented young people in their
prime – were guilty of nothing more than mixing their medication
with alcohol. Fatal mistakes but (just) mistakes nonetheless.

That's a personal view, *my* personal view. I mean, it should be
pointed out here and now, because it's very important and somewhat remiss of me not to have done so before, but these views – all
these views – are personal and may not necessarily agree with those
in circulation. You see, it's all a matter of personal perspective, isn't
it? I'm quite sure that the same story, even told by any of the four
principals involved, would be different. Yes, I'm sure those accounts
would be very different from my perspective. So, this is how I see it
and feel it and recall it. I'm sure that sometimes my views will even
differ from those of the author!

There was no doubt that the death of Brian Epstein left a huge
void in The Beatles' lives, a void they tried to fill immediately by
heading off to India to study further with the Maharishi. The funni-
est story I remember reading about that trip was the one where his
great holiness (or was that wholly pyjamas?) was getting a bit frisky
with one of the actresses and The Beatles were annoyed at his
actions. Mr Yogi asked them why they were so upset and John
Lennon replied that if he were indeed as spiritual as he was claiming, he'd know exactly what was on their mind.

It was also during this visit that John, Paul and George undertook a lot of individual songwriting. These songs were to be the
creative nucleus of the double album called *The Beatles*, aka *The
White Album* because of its unblemished cover. The sole marking

on the cover was an embossed 'The Beatles' and an individual number. Each album was stamped with its own number, making each copy unique.

I wonder who had copies numbered 1, 2, 3 and 4. I know I had copy number 0300801; I still do in fact. I suppose that shows how influential my 'I was nearly a member of the Fabs' line had become. *The White Album* does have its moments, like the incredible 'While My Guitar Gently Weeps'. This was George at his best, aided and abetted by his mate Eric Clapton on guitar. 'Ob La Di Ob La Da' was very poppy, another of Jonathan's favourites and introduced West Indian influenced music to a wider audience; 'Birthday' was very heavy and, along with 'Helter Skelter' and 'Yer Blues', perhaps formed the beginnings of heavy rock and heavy metal music.

'Back In The USSR', influenced by The Beach Boys, set the record off to a joyous, uplifting, in-your-face start. On the other hand, the confused and pointless art-piece, 'Revolution No. 9', very nearly ground the album to a complete halt. If they had at least positioned that particular track halfway into the album, it would have given us a golden opportunity to go off and make a cup of tea.

But don't you see, it doesn't matter that, as George Martin suggests, it could, or should, have been a singles album: a brilliant singles album with all the fat cut off it. It's The Beatles experimenting and flexing their new, independent, individual muscles. At one point during the recording sessions, John, Paul and George were all in separate studios simultaneously, working on their own songs. This probably accounts for the variety on the album. It wasn't enough for them to want to remake *Rubber Soul*, or *Revolver*, or even *Sgt Pepper's* – brilliant and all as those albums certainly are. No, The Beatles preferred, and needed, to head off into uncharted waters rather than paddle around in a familiar pool the way, for instance, the group called Yes did on each and every one of their albums, and the same goes for ELP. The Moody Blues, for instance, spent an entire career trying (unsuccessfully) to get their version of *Sgt Pepper's* right. Electric Light Orchestra, responsible for some of the best 'Beatles' albums The Beatles never recorded, used *Abbey Road* as their template. But The Beatles were different; they had to play on. They had to move on with what little life there was left in the band. So, taken in this context, *The White Album* can most simply be described as an album that The Beatles just *had* to make. It was a case of 'Hang on there for a minute and we'll be right back with you.' Or, as Paul McCartney very succinctly put it, 'It's great. It sold. It's The bloody Beatles' *White Album*. Shut up!'

It was the first album to be released on The Beatles' own record label, Apple, and it shot to the top of the charts all over the world, becoming the biggest-selling double album ever by quickly notching up sales in excess of six million. It was during the making of *The White Album* that Ringo Starr left The Beatles. He said he felt unloved, unwanted and unworthy as a musician and a mate. It was probably hardest for Ringo. Being the nice geezer in the band, he probably didn't know which way to turn when all his mates, the mates he loved, were off in separate studios working on their own versions of The Beatles. He must have felt that there was nowhere for him to turn.

John, Paul and George realised what was happening and went out of their way to reassure him that there would no Beatles without Ringo. The best band in the world needed the best drummer in the world – it was that simple. And, thankfully, Ringo returned to the fold. Returned, in fact, to a studio decorated from top to bottom with flowers, an outward display of an inward affection organised by his three colleagues.

They were back together again and, to some degree, enjoying their time in the studio and their new role as a studio band. The next bit of vinyl available from all good record shops was 'Hello Goodbye', backed by the legendary 'I Am The Walrus'. This was the first of four consecutive 'Paul' songs specially written as a single. 'Hello Goodbye' is an excellent pop song and very commercial, but few people's favourite, I fear. However, its straight-ahead hook took it straight to the top of the lucrative Christmas charts, where it remained for seven weeks: The Beatles' longest reign at the top since the early days, in fact.

It was quickly followed by 'Lady Madonna', backed with 'The Inner Light'. 'Lady Madonna' was not one of The Beatles' more popular singles but it did reach number one, where it stayed for two weeks. It was to be The Beatles' last (and fourteenth) single on the Parlophone label. The other distinction of 'Lady Madonna' is that some people thought it bore more than a passing similarity to Humphrey Lyttelton's 1956 top twenty hit, 'Bad Penny Blues', coincidentally also produced by Beatles producer, George Martin. The other strange coincidence was that one of Lyttelton's colleagues, jazz legend Ronnie Scott, led the brass section on the recording of 'Lady Madonna'. It would appear that the Old Etonian trumpeter didn't come out of the matter too badly; a High Court judge agreed with him and The Beatles had to pay Mr Lyttelton a percentage of their royalties. The B-side featured the first appearance on a Beatles single of a George Harrison composition.

When they'd completed some of the recording for *The White Album*, John Lennon wanted 'Revolution' (No.1, I hasten to add) to be released as a single. Reportedly he was dissuaded from this on the grounds that it was too slow a track. Quite ironic, then, that it should be the B-side for the equally slow, but very moving, 'Hey Jude', which was the first single on their own label and the beginning of a concentrated time for The Beatles and Beatles-related material at the top of the singles charts.

John Lennon and his wife Cynthia had broken up, and Paul McCartney was on his way to see Cynthia and her son Julian (who shared his Beatle dad's troubled looks), probably to console and encourage them (as good friends do). On the car journey, Paul had this idea going though his head: 'Hey Jules (for Julian), take a sad song and maker it better.' You know the sentiment: 'Look, it's bad now, I know, but don't worry, it'll get better.'

Paul changed the Jules to Jude because it sounded more 'country', and pretty soon had one of the all-time Beatles classic singles, 'Hey Jude', which, at seven minutes and ten seconds, was the longest single ever to reach number one. With a total of nine weeks, it was to be The Beatles' longest reigning number one single in the US of A whereas, in the UK, although it sold very well it was knocked from the top spot after only two weeks.

And guess what the offending single was? Mary Hopkins with 'Those Were the Days'. Paul McCartney produced Mary Hopkins' first single for The Beatles' Apple label. He had previously tried (unsuccessfully) to persuade Denny Laine to record this folksy-type song. Next number one single (UK) was from a Sheffield lad called Joe Cocker, singing 'With A Little Help From My Friends', a blistering performance on a very original interpretation of the *Sgt Pepper's* song. This classic single was to launch and sustain a career for one of England's best soul singers. No Beatles activity in the charts for a while now, as the title song from the Clint Eastwood breakthrough movie, *The Good, The Bad And The Ugly* emerged. However, following Ennio Morricone's theme tune, The Scaffold (a Liverpool co-operative of poets with a musical bent), featuring Paul McCartney's brother Mike McGear, reached number one with 'Lily The Pink'.

And there's more! Next single to step up to the number one position was The Marmalade with their version of 'Ob La Di, Ob La Da' – another Lennon and McCartney number one single. The Beatles then undertook a project that was responsible for their next single, 'Get Back', which came crashing straight into the number one spot in the charts, where it enjoyed a six-week stay in the spring of 1968.

As with a lot of the ideas, the one behind the fateful recording sessions 'Get Back', was Paul McCartney's. On paper it has to be admitted that it was a brilliant and original idea. The idea was twofold. Firstly, The Beatles, having invented the term 'studio band', wanted to *get back* to basics. They wanted to *get back* to playing live together. No over-dubs and no hours and hours working on one small part of a track while poor Ringo would get bored out of his Christmas tree reading the papers or playing chess. He would normally do his drum part first (so that they could build the song up from the rhythm track, which would invariably consist of drums, bass, guitar – maybe piano – and a guide vocal).

To achieve this feel, and yet keep it as a special project, involved the second part of Paul's masterplan. They would move into a movie studio and rehearse an entire album's worth of new material. The cameras would be present to catch The Beatles creating their magic, and also present when The Beatles would perform their first live concert since San Francisco. This concert would consist of The Beatles presenting their new album as they recorded it, both visually and audibly. They'd even gone as far as booking the legendary Roundhouse at Chalk Farm, Camden Town, for the concert section.

They moved into Twickenham Studios for what was, sadly, to become the winter of their discontent. Instead of capturing The Beatles' magic, the cameras caught the sad disintegration of the group. There were lots of mitigating circumstances. The principals, who'd been together now for nearly ten years, were drifting apart; the studios were cold and not conducive to creating music; the cameras proved to be an intrusion; Yoko was always around – literally never more than a few inches from John; The Beatles had to come in each day at much too early an hour for musicians to be creative, just so they could fit in with the film crew's schedule; and so on.

Things came to a head when Paul appeared to provoke George Harrison into an argument over the guitar playing. George appeared too weary of the whole situation to even bother getting into the fight, and he replied to Paul: 'I'll play whatever you want. I won't play at all, if that's what you want.'

Shortly thereafter, George Harrison left the band and the sessions ground to a halt. A few days later they all met up in a pub and agreed that they should get back together again and finish the project. They obviously negotiated a better situation and agreed to abandon the coldness of the movie studio for the warmth of their own cosy Apple studios. Alex, their electronic wizard (who, in fact, wasn't) didn't have the studio ready so they brought all the equipment in from outside and set it up. The Beatles also brought in American Billy Preston, on piano and organ, to give themselves a much-needed stimulus, not to mention a wee bit of cement.

They got on with finishing the album, which as it turns out, apart from a few moments, is a sorry album, and should, in truth, never have been released. I'll hear tracks from the albums around this period – *The White Album, Let It Be, Abbey Road, Magical Mystery Tour* and *Yellow Submarine* – on the radio or something and I'll go back to it encouraged by those tracks, but I usually never make it the whole way through the album.

'Get Back', however, does show them as a cracking wee rock group, cemented together, as I've said, by Billy Preston on organ, and shows John Lennon had obviously been spending some time away from Yoko Ono, if only long enough to practice his guitar solos.

The Roundhouse concert never happened. Instead, again for the benefit of the cameras, they performed on top of the Apple Building in Baker Street, stopping the traffic and eventually being stopped from performing themselves by the long arm of the law.

Although the *Get Back* album was the last album to be released, it was not the final album to be recorded. The Beatles, knowing exactly how big a mess the album was, ordered it to be put on the shelves and, although they knew they were going to split up, decided to get together one more time – only this time they would do it properly.

Chapter Forty

As The Beatles were contemplating their end, Marianne Burgess and I were down on the beach.

Marianne Burgess and me on the beach! Hey, not the way you're thinking. Come on now, this is a family book. 'Hello, sweet Josephine and little William, why don't you go out and play in the garden for a wee while. I've got to tell your parents something that is quite sad. You can all come back in for the ending, okay?' Good.

So there we were, Marianne Burgess, Jonathan Burgess and me, Theodore Hennessy. We had a great day on the sea front, an absolutely brilliant day and, true to Marianne's word, we didn't discuss *us* once. Which was brilliant, you know? My dad always says there are those who do and there are those who talk about doing. Well, Marianne and I had done nothing but talk about doing for so long now that talking was in danger of becoming the sum total of our relationship. After a time on that old roundabout, one grows a bit tired. You know, one side is 'I love you and want us to be together' and the other is the 'I love you and don't want us to be together' side. Two entirely different points of view and you're not likely to make much progress together in life starting from those two extremes.

We – a ragtag and bobtail Scouser trio – hung out on the sea front until lunch time. It is incredible what can amuse and occupy a child's mind. Jonathan, who I was pleased to see had a Beatles bob (circa 1965), was happy to investigate the shell collection scattered around the beach. I mean, he made it into a collection by bringing all he could find over to us and continuously advising his big sister that he (she) was taking them all home. We sat perched on Marianne's red tartan blanket and did the 'putting the bigger shells to the ear to hear the sea' routine, even though the sea was but a few feet from where we were. We talked about the fish in the sea for ages, and how they couldn't come out of the sea because if they did they'd die.

Dying? Selling the concept of dying to a four-year-old is not the easiest or the most pleasant thing to do. 'But would you die only for a little while?' 'Is Mari going to die, like the fish?' 'But I don't want Mari to die.' 'But *you* said she *was* going to die.' And then the big ones. 'What's the difference between 'could' and 'would'?' 'Who's God?' 'Why would God want to take Mari to Heaven?' And he was so cute, as well. Marianne told him that if he wasn't careful, while walking along a wall, he'd fall and bump his head and the angels would come immediately to take him to Heaven. 'Does that mean angels are quicker than ambulances?' Jonathan inquired, without missing a beat.

Every answer you give you dig yourself deeper into the hole. After about fifteen minutes of this, I was so far in the hole it would have been quicker to turn around and dig my way out via Australia. Marianne seemed content to let me fend for myself; if she knew the escape routes she was keeping them to herself.

Lunch time, we had fish, chips and mushy peas, with flavouring courtesy of the *Daily Mirror*. We all sat in a bus shelter on the front with our bottles of Coca Cola and devoured our meals. It must have been the sea air but we all appeared to be famished. 'What's famished?' 'Why do they have no food to eat?' 'Could they not just go to the fish and chip shop and buy some?' 'Why does their Daddy not have any money?'

And it wasn't just in the poor countries where there were famines. This was the swinging '60s, where all the window dressings were terribly nice and colourful but, at the same time, the last war was still only twenty years behind us and yes, times were good, but not everyone was back on their feet again. It still was unusual to see barefooted, short-trousered kids; yes, just like those in the Hovis advertisement, but not as well dressed. With the HP man continuously about, there were plenty of houses with shiny new television sets. Some of the same houses would not have enough money to put food on the table, sending the kids out with a jam sandwich or even a butter sandwich with a little sugar thrown in. I was always surprised, in those days, how the church was so powerful and incredibly rich, and yet would seldom use either its power or its wealth to feed and clothe the needy members of its flock. Who knows what the wealth was used for. Costumes? Property? Paintings? Gold-plated fittings? Whatever. The power was used to keep the flock under control, on the pews and feeding the gold-rimmed collection plates.

I was lucky, I suppose, in that my parents, although not exactly rich, never let the three of us go without. I don't know how they managed to do it all the time, but I grew up not thinking or considering whether or not we were rich. As far as I was concerned, we were just a normal family and got on with our lives. More importantly, we were a happy family in the same way as I considered the Burgess family to be a happy family. And here we were together, one Hennessy and two Burgesses, and we were all getting on great.

But I knew I was on borrowed time so I was determined to enjoy myself. And enjoy ourselves we did. Next, we went off to the amusement arcade and Jonathan had a great time. Scrap that, *I* had a great time. Under the excuse of being with Jonathan, I got to go on the helter skelter, the dodgems, the swings, the ghost train (the three of us) and the helter skelter again (another two times). The net result of this was that Jonathan was exhausted by the time we returned to the guesthouse, WindView, and he was asleep – with baby-sitter in attendance – by the time Marianne and I left to go for another walk and find somewhere to eat.

It had been a rewarding day, mainly due to Jonathan, and I felt sad but content as we walked down the sea front, arm in arm, with an independent air. We small talked our way through dinner at an excellent Italian restaurant. I can't recall the name – I wish I could. I really do.

'Let's walk off our pasta along the sea front. The sea air will also give us a good night's sleep,' Marianne Burgess began.

The words 'us' and 'sleep' kept floating around my head, banging against every corner they could find in my wine-dulled brain. I wondered did these words imply anything like a farewell night together? You know, one for old times' sake, to see me happily into my old age. You know the sort of thing: 'I remember the time, back in the summer of '67 – the *Sgt Pepper's* summer – when I enjoyed my last night with… now what was her name? Oh yes, that's it, Marianne. Marianne Burgess. Yes, we'd a great final night of passion.' My nurse, in turn, would say, 'There, there, Mr Hennessy, you're hallucinating again. Here, take your pills and I'll wheel you in out of the cold.'

Marianne Burgess and I walked in silence along the sea front, the waves lapping gently inches from our feet and the smell of salt and seaweed filling our nostrils. Not very romantic I know, but accurate nonetheless.

'Look I don't want to give you grief but I heard you'd finalised your plans to marry and I just wanted to make one last attempt at this, you know? Actually, that's not strictly true. I was in Ulster for a good part of the summer and I had a great time, just travelling around and meeting people, and I did a lot of thinking. I thought about you a lot and I returned with a resolve to speak to you one final time, to try to see if there is some way we can be together and make something out of this. But, at the same time, I've found an inner peace to accept the fact that if we are not going to be together, then at least I have reached a stage in my life where I can get on with things,' I started, breaking the peace between us. We both were, well, not weary exactly, but… relaxed. Yes, relaxed is the best word. We walked on and as we did so, she slipped her arm out from mine and took my hand in hers. It was all a bit surreal to me, to be honest, walking along the beach with Marianne Burgess, hand in hand.

'So, when I started to try to track you down I found out that you had made your plans. I don't know why I needed to explain all that to you, apart from the fact that I didn't want you to think that I had found out you were going to get married and had come along to bug you again,' I said, quietly. There, I'd said my bit and she had earlier claimed that there was something she wanted to speak to me about, so I decided to give her the floor – as they say at the local working men's clubs. And I should know; I'd played my fair share of them over the years.

'Theo, I've been thinking about us a lot as well. I've been thinking about you and I know that I love you. In a way, I suppose, it's because I love you that I know we'll never, ever be together,' Marianne Burgess said, her voice faltering and sounding even more dramatic against the sound of the rippling waves.

'I know that I will disappoint you with what I'm about to tell you, but I feel I owe it to you to tell you this so that you will know why we can't be together. This way, I figure I will be releasing you from your love, a love which I will admit has kept me going on many a dark night,' she continued.

My mind raced ahead of her to the things she could possibly be on about. She's pregnant with Brian's child: I could live with that. She's been excommunicated: the church's loss as far as I was concerned and, as John Lennon observed, they surely couldn't afford to be losing many more of their flock. She wasn't really going to get married; she was going to become a nun. You may laugh but that happened to a friend of mine who met a girl at a dance in Rasharkin, Northern Ireland. It was a blind date. My mate went with his friend, whose regular girlfriend brought along her sister.

My friend and the (holy-to-be) sister got along great. They dated about half a dozen times over the next month and were getting on great, until they were at a dance together and she took him outside. He couldn't believe his luck and not sure he wanted to have such luck; you see, he really liked this girl. There and then she told him, gave it to him right between the eyes. She was to leave home in six weeks to take her vows. My mate was devastated and, to add insult to injury, she gave him a goodbye kiss that night, which he claims was the most sensual kiss he'd ever had in his life, before or since. He didn't know whether it was so earth-moving because the kiss was from the forbidden lips of a nun, or… I don't know why I should have thought about that then and, with that perversity off my mind, I dismissed the idea on the grounds that (I thought) you'd have to be a virgin before they'd allow you to be a nun. I was intentionally keeping quiet at this point to allow Marianne Burgess to make her announcement.

'I love you, Theo, and I love Jonathan.'

'I know, I like him too. He's fab.'

'No, Theo, not like that.'

What? Excuse me. Was she saying what I thought she was saying? No, of course not, idiot (me), he's only four years old for heaven's sake. Wash out your mind with soap and bleach.

'What!' I exclaimed.

'Jonathan, you know…Jonathan is not my brother.'

'He's not?'

'No, Theo, he's not.'

God, who on earth was he? Was Jonathan part of the deal with Ken the Married Man? I mean, that would explain a lot if Jonathan was one of his children, but why was his wife not looking after him. Was Jonathan Ken's son by another woman, and he wanted to hide it from the world and his wife? Believe me, of all the things I was thinking about and considering, one thing (and you have probably guessed it by now) never occurred to me.

'Jonathan's not my brother, Theodore, he's my son.'

'What, Jonathan, your little brother, is your son?'

'Yes, Theo, he is and you'll never realise what a load off my mind it is to finally have told you,' Marianne claimed, as tears started to flow down her cheeks. From the look in her magic eyes, I would agree with her on the relief factor and I figured her tears were tears of joy and not sadness. 'At the time we were together I was trying to find ways not to love you, things like all that stuff about not kissing.

I thought if we stopped kissing, because we both loved kissing so much, maybe we'd not be making love, you know, we'd just be having sex. I also thought that if I stopped *saying* I loved you, maybe I could *stop* loving you and you would stop loving me, and we wouldn't have had to deal with the Jonathan situation.'

'Marianne Burgess, I can't believe it. That's the big thing? The thing that has kept us apart?'

'Yes, and you must swear never to tell anyone. No-one knows but my parents and the doctor.'

'What? You haven't told Brian?'

'No. I've told him that I've agreed to take my brother in with us, to take a bit of the pressure off my mother and father, and he seems fine with that.'

'So you are prepared to live with and marry Brian, and move Jonathan in with you, but you didn't feel you could do it with me?'

'Brian knows what he's getting. I haven't once told him I love him. I haven't once made love to him. And he seems not to mind; he seems to be okay about it. He wants to take care of me.'

'So you're prepared to live in a loveless marriage rather than try with me?' I said, my voice rising a few octaves in disbelief.

'But, Theo, don't you see what I'm on about? I'm soiled goods. I've been knocked up; in the club; up the pole; I've dropped one; had a child out of wedlock; had a bun in the oven. You know, I've heard them all over and over again until they all made me cry. I've committed a sin; I can't even get married in the church. I suppose that's the price to pay for a sham marriage. Kathleen always told me how religious your family are, and how much your mother and father wanted the both of you to have white weddings and live happily ever after.'

'Listen, Marianne, I love you. I don't love a saint. I... love you. Don't you see these are not just words? When I say I love you, I mean I want you, I need you. I need you in my life, I need to be in your life and I need us to be together. I want to care for you and I want you to care for me. This doesn't make any difference. My parents... yes, they do dream about those things but they're certainly wise enough to know that dreams and reality are two different things. God, I thought you were going to die of cancer or something...something drastic. I can't believe you'd been thinking I would react badly to this. And Jonathan's so cute, so adorable, who's not going to love him?'

'You mean you're not disappointed in me?'

'Marianne Burgess, just look at yourself. How could I ever be disappointed in you?'

'Theodore.'

'Marianne. God, it's okay, really.'

'But I thought... '

'Listen. Look around you. Everyone you know has got something they feel bad about, a dark secret they want to keep hidden. But believe me, having someone as beautiful as Jonathan would not trouble anyone I know. You being Jonathan's mother shouldn't be a dark secret. It's a wondrous, joyous thing.'

'But I thought you loved me so much and were so *in* love with me that it had to be a pure love.'

'It is a pure love, but it's a pure love between us. That's the only place it has to be honest. That's the only place we can't cheat, in our feelings for each other, now... today. What would upset me, whether or not I was involved, is if you married someone knowing that you didn't love them. That is a sin, a sin against yourself.'

'Theo... I'm speechless, really. I don't know what to say.' Marianne wiped the tears from her face, finding words to say as she did so. 'In my mind I've told you about Jonathan a million times in a million different ways. I've even started a few times to tell you and each time I've backed away. The last time I saw you at Kathleen's I'd actually gone around to her house to tell her and see if she could help me tell you, but I thought if I did she'd be insulted and I'd lose her friendship as well as a chance to be with you. And all the time you were going to be like this about it. I mean, I suppose I should have known. But it's just that this has haunted me for nearly five years now. Every time I hear whispers, I feel that they are about me. Every time there's a knock on the door I think it's someone come to tell me they've found out about me and my illegitimate child and that I'd have to leave the street. And then you say, "So what!" I can't believe it,' Marianne spluttered as she broke into tears again.

'I thought you would have guessed, you know; older parents; big age gap between me and Jonathan; Jonathan and me always together. I was sure you would guess,' Marianne sobbed.

'But we all believe and accept what we perceive as being the truth. If someone says to you, "This is my brother, Jonathan," you say, "Okay." There's no reason to look for clues and pick up on all the things you mentioned.'

'I've never mislead you about anything else, Theo.'

'I know.'

'Oh God, I've made a mess of everything.'

'No you haven't.'

'Yes I have. I'm getting married in two weeks' time. I'm going to be unhappy for the rest of my life; you're going to be unhappy until you find someone else. It's all ruined. Why's it all gone wrong?' Marianne cried.

'Marianne Burgess, in three weeks' time it would all be ruined. If you think I'm going to stand by and let you ruin your life, Jonathan's life and my life, you've got another thing coming, girl. You're not going to hide your head in the sand. You've been dealing with this for too long by yourself. No more, Marianne, no more mistakes. And before you go worrying again, the only mistake you have made is not telling me about Jonathan in the first place. Okay, now here's what we're going to do. We're going to get back together. Of course, we'll wait until you tell Brian and a respectable amount of time has passed. We will then marr… Sorry that's all wrong,' I stopped and sank to the ground on one knee, took her hand in mine and said, 'Dear sweet woman, can we get married?'

'You mean it, don't you?'

'Of course I do.'

'You don't even know who Jonathan's father is or what happened. How can… ?'

'When the time is right I'm sure you'll tell me all you want to tell me… ' I started, only to be cut off mid-flow.

'No, Theo, it's important to me to get all of this off my chest now. It's taken me a long time to get to this point, you know, of being able to admit all of this to you.'

'So, is Jonathan's father Ken the Married Man?' I offered, assuming I'd found the reason for her continued commitment to him. I was still having trouble figuring out the original attraction, though.

'No. No. No. Of course not,' she snapped impatiently, then paused, acting somewhat annoyed at herself, smiled sweetly at me, and added, 'Never. Never in a million years. Although at that time, I did feel I had some attraction towards older men, even in spite of myself, which is probably why I became involved with him in the first place. It's funny, Theo, it really is. I mean, I can look back on that relationship now and declare, without hesitation, that it was all a big mistake. But, at that time, I was absolutely convinced it was the right thing to do. How could I have been so wrong, Theo?'

I wanted to say, 'Yes Marianne, how could you have been so

fecking wrong? Ken was a first-class jerk and everyone could see it.'
Instead, I elected to be supportive and said, 'Well, considering what
has just come to light perhaps you thought he might make a good
father, you know, already being married and all that.'

'That's sweet of you, Theo, and maybe that's what I was thinking,
about his experience as a father. But now, when I think of the possibility of that man bringing up my child, I break into a cold sweat.'

I hiked up my shoulders in a 'Gee shucks' gesture that I hoped
would get me out of having to respond. I didn't think I could be so
positive a second time. Luckily I didn't need to be as Marianne
drifted into a reminiscing mode.

'Anyway, Eric was a different matter... '

'Not your dad's mate, Eric?' The shock was immediate and
evident. The words just spilled from my lips. Of course it couldn't
have been her father's mate Eric, and I was due a right royal clip on
the ear.

'Actually yes ,Theo, he was my father's friend, best friend in
fact.'

'God,' I shrugged, not entirely sure I wanted to hear any more.

'I was about to say, "It wasn't like that," but then, of course, I
suppose it must have been like that. Eric's been around our house all
the time. There's never not been Eric around. Maybe like an uncle I
never had, maybe not. Ahm, look I'd better just spit this out, otherwise I'm going to splutter around here for ages. Eric was *always*
there, as I say. We always played around, fooled about, just joking
in front of my parents and all. He'd tickle me and that, chase me
around and say I was his little girl. He was very warm and very
friendly, but I was growing up and sometimes, I'd be a bit embarrassed. You know, I wasn't a kid any more and yet, at other times it
was great fun just to get away from the pressures of college and
growing up, and having to pretend to be an adult when your
weren't really, or at least I wasn't really. I... ahm...'

'Look, Marianne, this is all okay. I really don't care what
happened before. For so long I've wanted for us to be together and
it looked like it wasn't going to happen, and all the time it was
because you were scared of this stuff.' I quickly changed knees to
avoid the cramp. I grabbed her hands tighter and could see she was
close to tears. 'Look at me, Marianne. This is all okay, it doesn't
affect us. You don't have to go through this now. You don't have to
go through this at all, in fact.'

'It's okay, Theo, really it is. You're making it okay, but please let me tell you this now, once and for all, and hopefully put it behind us. One Sunday, Eric dropped in to see my Dad. My Mum and Dad were out visiting friends for Sunday tea. Eric didn't know at the time and he started goofing around. I don't know what came over me, I just remember thinking, "I'll show him I'm not a child to play with any more." He was wrestling with me; you know, he'd both my arms and was trying to get a fall, like in Kent Walton's wrestling, pin both my shoulder blades to the canvas (carpet in our case) for a count of three. I just went limp on him and let him push me to the floor and move my arms whatever way he wanted to.'

I was in two minds about what she was telling me. Part of me was trying to live with my 'I'm okay about all of this' promise and the other part was thinking what a pervert Uncle Eric was. I could tell how hard it was for her to tell me about this so I felt it advisable to say nothing and allow her to continue.

'I was wearing a skirt and I manoeuvred my legs so that it rode up, exposing my legs. He could see a different kind of look in my eyes now. It was serious. I was taking the lead. I pulled his head down and kissed him full on the lips. All the time we were squirming around, me underneath him, still under the pretext of wrestling. He worked the lower part of his body in between my legs. He pushed against me. I pushed back. I thought I'd get scared but I didn't. I felt all the time that I was in control and I was. I was seventeen years old and I was dealing with an adult, in an adult world, doing a grown-up thing for the first time. It just happened, Theo. At some point the wrestling stopped, my clothes were all over the place, and we were having sex. It was as simple as that, it really was. It wasn't particularly pleasurable, nor was it painful, it just happened. Afterwards, Eric was not in the slightest put out by it all. He rearranged his clothes as I did the same and asked me was there any chance of a cup of tea. He's one of those salt-of-the-earth types who probably thought he was doing his mate a favour by giving the wee lass a proper seeing too. We only did it on that one occasion. That was the funny thing – he didn't try again and I didn't offer. He was very cool and nonchalant about it at the time, but he wasn't so cool about it when I told him that he'd got me pregnant. He was scared for his life because he probably knew my father would swing for him if he knew Eric was the father. I didn't tell my parents about him, though. There was no point, was there? It wasn't important. Eric discreetly started to come around to the house less and less. He did give my mother a present in the shape of a large cheque when

Jonathan was born. I put it all into a Post Office savings account in Jonathan's name and I 'encourage' Eric to make deposits as frequently as is socially possible. My mother was great about it; after the initial shock, her parental protective instincts clicked in and she cared for me like only a mother could. I could tell how mad my father was from the way he looked at me but he never said a word; I think my Mum had him under strict instructions. My mother and I disappeared to Paisley at the appropriate time and we returned several weeks later with my baby brother, Jonathan. Now you know it all,' Marianne said quietly, suddenly becoming aware of my present predicament vis-à-vis the proposal pose.

'Now listen, in about thirty seconds all this is going to be in vain because I'm going to be drowned. Can we get married?' I pleaded, as the waves inched dangerously close to us.

'Of course we will, Theo. Of course we will. I want that more than anything in the world, for me and you and Jonathan to be together.'

I felt great, spiritually elated and about ten-feet tall. I'd secretly always feared that when I eventually asked someone to marry me I would feel let down, deflated, when it had all been agreed and decided. With Marianne, however, if anything I wanted to marry her more, now that she said she would.

'But what will we do about Jonathan?'

'There'll be no more lies or deceit, Marianne. Living with them nearly destroyed you and nearly wiped us out. We'll tell everyone about it and be proud about him.'

'Oh, I am proud of him; he's such a wonderful boy. And he's a good boy too, Theo. He's got good in him.'

'I know you're secretly proud of him but I want you to be able to show him off as your son. After we're married, immediately afterwards, I'll officially adopt him. He'll be a great brother to our tribe.'

'What? Theo, I know you're Irish but there are forms of contraception you...'

'I know. The best one is you grip a Smartie tightly between your knees. Darned effective but absolutely no fun whatsoever. No, seriously though, I don't want too many really. I thought if we could have three besides Jonathan we'd be...' I started.

'Four? Why on earth do you want four children, Theodore Hennessy?' Marianne gasped, in genuine shock.

'Agh, now wouldn't that be so that I could start my own version of The Beatles,' I laughed, not altogether joking.

Chapter Forty-One

Endings and beginnings; they're the same really, aren't they? They inhabit the same space and one begets the other, as St John the Apostle probably would have said. Marianne and I were ending our 'unable to get it together' phase and starting the 'rest of our life together' phase. The Beatles, sensibly, made the decision to end on a high and not at their all-time low, as with *Let it Be* (which started its life as 'Get Back'). They needed to do this really, to go out on a high, so that they could get on with the start of their solo careers with clear consciences.

Paul McCartney rang up George Martin and told him that The Beatles would like to return to the studios and make another album. He added that they would also like George Martin to produce them. George Martin agreed, on condition that he was *allowed* to *produce* them. They accepted George's reasonable condition and the sessions took place between 1st July 1969 and the end of August that same year.

Apparently, they were happy sessions. Perhaps that was because they'd all agreed and accepted that they were working on *the final* Beatles album. They were aware of their position and their history and, no matter how bad it had become being a Beatle, they did not want to take their last low bow in public on a bummer like *Let It Be*. I was surprised when that album was released, to be honest. I have to believe that had they still been the Fabs with Brian Epstein around, then the *Let it Be* album would never, ever have seen the light of day.

In a way, *Abbey Road* should have been the album to close their account on. It was The Beatles being The Beatles (although conscious of this fact for the first time) and being produced by George Martin. The album shows George Harrison with two of his own compositions – not just Harrison classics but worthy Beatles classics as well. Frank Sinatra always introduced 'Something' (composed by George) as one of the greatest Lennon and McCartney songs. I have to believe his words were carefully chosen.

Hey, and then there's the joyous 'Here Comes The Sun', with
perhaps the best acoustic guitar sound ever recorded. There are
other great songs on *Abbey Road* as well; songs like 'Because' and
'The End', with lyrics as profound as anything The Beatles had done
before. Joe Cocker recorded and had a hit with 'She Came In
Through The Bathroom Window'. The Beatles showed off the
'wonderful blend of voices' thing I'm continually going on about in
'Because'. I think *Abbey Road* is spoilt from being a classic album
only because of the ever-present 'Look, let's not leave it like this (*Let
It Be*), let's show them we can still do it' vibe. Yes they *could* still do
it, and they certainly *did*, but for the first time in their career they
were competing; competing with themselves, but competing
nonetheless. I'm not sure, though, that this is a view the record-
buying public shares with me as *Abbey Road* shot straight to the top
of the album charts and remained there for 18 weeks. It is one of
The Beatles' biggest-selling albums, with worldwide sales of over
thirty million.

    Abbey Road (the album) was sandwiched by two vastly different
singles. Before the album came out, John Lennon rushed into the
studio with Paul McCartney and the two of them quickly recorded
(with Paul taking over Ringo's stool) 'The Ballad of John and Yoko'.
This was The Beatles' eighteenth, and final, number one single. The
'The 'Ballad of John and Yoko' was followed by 'Something'. This
was the first time in ages that an album track was released as a
single. It was issued as their twenty-first single but sadly didn't reach
the top, peaking only at number four. It was the first time one of
George Harrison's songs had appeared as the A-side to a Beatles
single.

    The Beatles had been chasing their tails for several years. They
wanted to be the best group in Hamburg; accomplished. They
wanted to be the best group in Liverpool; likewise achieved. They
wanted to get a record deal; done that, admittedly with a comedy
label but nonetheless they had their deal. They wanted to have a
number one single; there, too, they were successful. They wanted to
be successful in America; they were and how! They wanted to be
bigger than Elvis; Elvis *who*? They wanted to make the best albums
ever made; they managed this not once, not twice, but thrice. You
know the story, though; before the record company crows thrice,
they'll have been denied twice. But denied what? Denied their own
happiness? Denied their own peace of mind? Pretty soon they were
in rarefied air, and what was the only problem? When they got to

where they'd worked so hard to get to, they realised there was no-one else there waiting for them. Heaven was as empty as The Rolling Stones' awards cabinet. It was boring.

Don't you see, they had to split up to protect their own greatness. When you'd created what they had, when you had all those songs and all those records to your credit, where was there left to go? There was absolutely no point in repeating themselves. No point whatsoever. They had enough integrity to suss this.

The Beatles had scored a lot of firsts in their relatively short but meteoric career:
- First to use feedback.
- First to have lyrics on the sleeve.
- First to use a gatefold sleeve.
- First not to print their name on the sleeve.
- First to print *neither* the artists' names nor the album name on the front of the sleeve.
- First to appear on a satellite TV link-up.
- First to use pop promo clips.
- First group to appear at an outdoor stadium.
- First to have their own record label.
- First to use backwards recording.
- First to use non-musical sounds on recordings.
- First to produce a concept album.
- First to develop and use ADT (automatic double-tracking) while recording.
- First to achieve the top five singles (simultaneously) in the USA pop *Billboard* charts.
- First to achieve the top six singles (simultaneously) in the Australian pop charts.
- First to have a million pre-sales for a UK single ('I Want To Hold Your Hand').
- First to replace themselves at number one in the UK Charts ('I Want to Hold Your Hand' replacing 'She Loves You' – December 12th 1963).
- First to have two million pre-sales for a US single ('Can't Buy Me Love').
- First English artists to break into the American market.
- First to own their own shop.
- First to have an entire album played on an English radio station.
- First to produce an album with no gaps between the tracks.

- First to use the wah-wah pedal.
- First to have a fade in a single.
- First to have an EP in the singles charts.
- First to have an album in the singles charts.
- First to have a double EP in the singles charts (and number two at that).
- First to have twelve consecutive UK number one singles.
- First to have eleven consecutive UK number one albums (all their official albums, in fact).
- And, first to split up!

And as all that was happening, The Beatles enjoyed a staggering 333 weeks in the UK singles charts. That's out of the possible 408 weeks, from early 1963 to the end of the '60s. They spend 66 of those weeks languishing in the luxury of the coveted top spot. That 333 figure is a bit cosmic, isn't it, not to mention one hell of an achievement. And, as Jimmy Cricket would say, 'Come here, there's more, there's more!' In the same period, they were in the UK album top ten charts for 356 weeks in total. I mention the top ten here because, in fairness, there was hardly a week when The Beatles weren't somewhere in the charts (top 30) with an album or two. For 158 of the aforementioned 356 weeks in the top ten, The Beatles were number one. For a *further* 70 weeks, they enjoyed the number two position. This was all before the split. Even *after* the break-up, Beatles albums were to continue to set sales records and enjoy chart placings few could dream of rivalling. The Beatles had achieved so much success already, and had even sacrificed part of their lives to do so. They were in a position where they didn't need to do it any more. Ever!

I know that lots of people, and a variety of circumstances, were blamed for the split. One of the more ludicrous suggestions was that they split because the rhythm guitarist's wife stole one of the lead guitarist's digestive biscuits. For me, there are two predominant reasons why The Beatles disintegrated between the making of *Sgt Pepper's* and *The White Album*, and subsequently split up. One, Brian Epstein died and two, John Lennon met the person to whom opportunism was an art form – Yoko Ono. Meeting her wasn't the decisive factor, though. Paul, George and Ringo were all in relationships at that time. Jane, Patti and Maureen respectively had not felt threatened by the closeness of the group, nor did they feel a need to destroy it. However, Yoko clung to John for her lifeblood. Everywhere John went, Yoko went, simple as that. And that

included into the recording studio. For the first time, one of them
had introduced another person into the creative mix. We all saw the
results. Maybe it was because John had Yoko around that Paul
introduced Linda into the mix. And there were others as well –
lawyers, would-be managers and general hangers-on (and I can tell
you, the music business does produce its fair share of hangers-on).
But you can't blame the ship going down on the lifeboats that carry
the passengers to safety.

Brian Epstein's death was to affect the picture more than any of
us could ever have predicted. He and The Beatles had worked hard,
incredibly hard, over the years to set the operation up and, as it
turns out, all they had created was this wealth – a wealth beyond
their wildest dreams. They had created an empire that a whole team
of lawyers and accountants were going to fight over for the foresee-
able future, all with their expensive meters running. Divide and
conquer. The Fab Four had often chanted, in the dingy Hamburg
dressing rooms, that they were going to the "toppermost of the
poppermost", but had found, when they got there – reached the
plateau – that there was no-one else there to play with or compete
with. No, all they found when they reached nirvana was a bunch of
lawyers and accountants waiting for them, all rubbing their hands
with glee.

I would respectfully suggest that if Brian Epstein had been
around, he would have discreetly mentioned to John that Yoko
shouldn't be in the studio. Done at the correct time, the situation
would have been defused and it wouldn't have become a problem.
As it was, none of the other three wanted to say anything. But how
was John to know otherwise? I would also suggest that Brian would
have put a team of people together to give the *Magical Mystery Tour*
that extra bit of something it needed to make it brilliant. I mean,
when you look at it today it looks great... nearly. Don't forget that
although *A Hard Day's Night* looks like it was all very casual, unre-
hearsed and improvised, it was based on a very clever script by Alun
Owen. One of Brian's main abilities was to put together great
people. That's one of the qualities he brought to the table; these
theatrical literary types were the people he naturally liked to mix
with. He was proud of this fact. *Magical Mystery Tour*, at least on
paper, should have worked, but simple things like insisting the BBC
broadcast it in colour were forgotten and it just did not work as well
in black and white. This was an oversight Brian Epstein would not
have made.

Critically, a bit of a meal was made of *The Magical Mystery Tour* special. Come on, it wasn't anywhere near as bad as the press proclaimed. It was just that this was the first time The Beatles had created something that was less than worthy of their genius, and the press – who had been sitting on their wings, sharpening their pencils and waiting – at last had their chance. And how they vented their spleen. Their frustrations at this worldwide acclaimed Northern group – a group previously way beyond their reach – now ran riot as The Beatles showed for the first time that they may be mere mortals after all. To me, though, critics are a bit like eunuchs; they sit around all day watching people do the wild thing, knowing full well they'll never ever be able to do it themselves. All this frustration *must* cause some kind of resentment, don't you think?

Going back to Brian Epstein for a minute, I also think Brian could have contained the solo inclinations of John, Paul, George and Ringo and used them to the advantage of The Beatles, rather than to the band's detriment. Just small but important things, like organising and co-ordinating the sabbaticals, and re-grouping at a time to suit the band's career. Creatively, as I have mentioned, they needed to take a break from each other at the time they did. It was inevitable; of that there was no doubt. But my point would have to be that if Brian Epstein have been around, it would have been handled in a more discreet and friendly way: a way that would have allowed the boys to come back together, albeit several years later, to work on a project.

It had been mentioned many times before that they, particularly John and Paul, had an ambition to create a musical. This could have been the perfect project to regroup for. Can you imagine how amazing that would have turned out to be? There are a few hints lurking around in the body of their work for us to be able to hazard a guess. Like the opening of section of *Sgt Pepper's*, the first two songs were part of something greater. Add to that their flair for all things visual: Paul McCartney's 'Eleanor Rigby', 'She's Leaving Home' and 'Penny Lane'. These were all perfectly executed, story-in-a-song approaches, so there is no doubt it could have been quite incredible. I'm sure Brian Epstein, with his theatrical flair and background, would have been over the moon for such a project to happen. You can't help wishing for what could have been. But then again, as my mum always says: 'Wish in one hand and pee in the other, and see which one fills first.'

More importantly, I feel that Brian Epstein would not have

allowed the publishing situation (Dick James selling his shares of Northern Songs) to become the nightmare it did. Again, Mr Epstein would have contained the situation by buying back, for The Beatles, the shares Dick James wanted to unload. As it is, creative birthrights are currently being bought and sold around the world as we speak, for obscene amounts of money. Yeah, he's correct, he is *bad*, accepted, no argument from me. Personally, I would like to see a situation where one of this nation's genuine treasures (The Beatles' songs) are returned immediately to this country and to their rightful owners. I mean, imagine the fuss people would be making if we were talking about work on canvas or stone, rather than work on vinyl.

But in all of this I'm not, for one minute, suggesting that Brian Epstein was a genius, for this was not the case. However, he really cared about The Beatles and, for me, that is the best quality a manager can possess – to genuinely care about his or her artists. With Brian Epstein and The Beatles, there was never any doubt over this and, quite simply, he would not have allowed them to split up. He did not look upon them as a meal ticket. He would have seen their growing wealth, not as a bigger pie from which to cut himself a more generous piece, but as something to look upon with a sense of pride. He'd have surely viewed it as something to use for the benefit of The Beatles and others. We've seen how each of The Beatles, in latter years, did more than their fair share of benefits and charity work. I'm absolutely positive that Brian would have brought a calming influence and the organisational skills that Apple needed to turn it from a series of harebrained ideas into the true artists' co-operative The Beatles had planned. Well, at least as close to a co-operative as you could get when one party (The Beatles) were paying all the bills.

Far from having nothing to do once 'his boys' had stopped touring, there was a multitude of things for Mr Epstein to get stuck into and get excited about. But no matter what, he would have continued to protect them. They were friends, after all. That's one thing I found touching at the time of his death: John, Paul, George and Ringo all talked about losing a friend. But sadly, Brian did die, and die an untimely accidental death. With his death, there were lots of parties whose prime interest was that the boys, who were once the best of friends, split as enemies. Don't forget: divide and conquer.

I know a lot of people will disagree with me but I think that The Beatles peaked, as The Beatles, with the albums *Rubber Soul*,

Revolver and *Sgt Pepper's*. Yes, after *Sgt Pepper's* they did make more music and, don't get me wrong, great music at that. To me, though, it was not music they made as The Beatles. No, sadly, not as The Beatles but as four artists, starting off on their solo careers. I'm talking here about *The White Album*, of course.

Then there's *Magical Mystery Tour* (which was just an EP) and someone saying, 'We can do it without Brian' and proving that, apparently, they couldn't. However, 'I Am The Walrus' *is* a very invigorating track, lyrically and sonically. 'Blue Jay Way' showed George with nothing to say but play his own individual blend of wonderful blues. And 'Fool On The Hill' was a song all the McCartney impersonators would love to have been able to put their name to. It was an area he'd covered a few times before, perhaps more successfully, but nonetheless the song was still way above the competition. I think, from what Paul was saying in interviews around this time, he considered the *main* competition to be The Beach Boys in general, and Brian Wilson in particular. Equally, he wasn't scared of letting this influence show through in his work.

Yellow Submarine was a great children's video and still is. The actors taking on Beatle accents launched the tourist Liverpool accent on the world. 'All Together Now', a new track made for, or given to, this project was The Beatles being great at being The Beatles.

Let It Be, quite simply, should not have been released. Giving us a free book didn't make up for a shoddy piece of work, particularly when we found out that someone was allowed to interfere with the music (without the composers' permission) after the recording. A couple of good songs, I suppose – yes, of course – but they probably should have been released as part of the 'Anthology' series. But then again, I don't really agree with all of that either. I do see the reason (anti-bootleggers) but perhaps there should have been a couple of great singles albums in there somewhere, instead of the three doubles.

Then again, if there had been (a great singles album), it would have come out at the time. If you want to know the truth, if someone asked me to pick a 'best of The Beatles', it would be easy, very easy. It would be *Please Please Me* as Volume One; *With The Beatles* would be Volume Two; *A Hard Day's Night* would be Volume Three; *Beatles For Sale* would be Volume Four; *Help* would be Volume Five; *Rubber Soul* would be Volume Six; *Revolver* would be Volume Seven, and Volume Eight would be *Sgt Pepper's Lonely Hearts Club Band*. Get the picture?

Chapter Forty-Two

For the first time in my life, I was happy that I had not *nearly* met up with George Harrison in the Les Stewart Quartet. You know, what we talked about, that when they were replacing Pete Best he may have suggested me to John and Paul? I was happy because, if things had turned out that way, I would never have met and loved, and lost, and met and lost again, and met and married one Marianne Burgess. I would never have experienced the joy of being in the life of her special son, Jonathan, and I would never have experienced the bliss of parenthood when she gave birth to our daughter, Kathleen.

Equally importantly, should I have (via the Les Stewart Quartet) met George Harrison and consequently met and joined The Beatles, then perhaps they would never have enjoyed the success they eventually did. Gifted artists, such as The Beatles, are sent amongst us to entertain us and, if we have a heart and a mind to listen to this magic, our lives will be all the richer for it. When The Beatles split up we were all scared that we might have lost our leaders, but that wasn't the point of The Beatles at all. They weren't meant to be our leaders; they were sent to be with us and keep us amused and entertained for that part of our journey, the part where the maximum numbers of paths were crossing.

But don't you see, they had to split up, not only to seal their greatness but for their own self-preservation. And after all the joy The Beatles gave the world, who would begrudge them a wee bit of their own happiness? My dad – who wasn't a hippie but could, and should, have been one – put it best: "A meteor can't burn that bright forever. Eventually it will explode, destroying everything." The Beatles stopped when they were burning brightest. They'd been burning so bright they'd been lighting up an entire decade – the '60s. They managed, somehow, to stop before the explosion, thereby destroying little. Little, that is, apart from their own nervous systems, as George Harrison has often said.

They released one final single; actually, *they* didn't release any further records officially as The Beatles. At least one member that we know of (Paul) did not agree with re-mixing or adding strings, or any of that stuff. But they were so busy with their own solo work at the time that they didn't bother to try and stop the accountants putting together the *Let It Be* package. I think they just didn't care about The Beatles any more and were happy enough to leave it to those who were pushing behind the scenes. Had things been different, perhaps that last single and album wouldn't have been released.

But this isn't meant to be about the disappointments of their human side; this is meant to be about their greatness. It's easy to say, as we still do to this day around the pubs, that Yoko split up the band. Maybe she did, inasmuch as she was around at that time and she didn't help matters. But the point still is that they *had* to split up. Hey, and you know what? She was around only because her husband *wanted* her around, it's as simple as that.

But the important thing is that The Beatles are bigger than that. And you know what else? If I'd really met George and nearly joined The Beatles, just think of all the millions who would have been deprived of that magic – the magic of their music, the magic we've all enjoyed over the years. No matter what our station in life, no matter how poor or rich we may be, we can all still take the exact same solace and joy from the gift of their music.

Oh, hey and listen, just before you go, there really is a happy ending to all of this; apart from me and Marianne Burgess and Jonathan, that is. Our Kathleen (I have to be careful when I say that, now I've got a daughter called Kathleen, but our Kathleen, as in my sister), well, you'll never guess what she did.

She eventually found her mister right. He'd been there, under her nose, all these years. My friend and songwriting partner, Vincent McKee, eventually came clean about all the wee visits to her flat and asked her out on a date. She accepted and seven months later they were wed. Who'd have figured that? Just like the song says: "It's a long and winding road."

The Do-Not Press
Fiercely Independent Publishing

Keep in touch with what's happening at the cutting edge of independent British publishing.

Simply send your name and address to:
The Do-Not Press (Dept. FTB)
16 The Woodlands, London SE13 6TY (UK)

or email us: **first@thedonotpress.co.uk**

There is no obligation to purchase
(although we'd certainly like you to!)
and no salesman will call.

Visit our regularly-updated web site:

http://www.thedonotpress.co.uk

Mail Order

All our titles are available from good bookshops, or (in case of difficulty) direct from The Do-Not Press at the address above. There is no charge for post and packing for orders to the UK and EU.

(NB: A post-person may call.)